Praise for *Aarial* from Younger Readers

"*Aarial* takes you on a magical journey where you cannot tell what is reality and what is fiction. Entering Dylan's world was an experience I will never forget; I loved it."

CARLIE MINUK, Calgary, Alberta (age 14)

"One of the best books I've ever read…and I've read a lot!"

KALEY JUVONEN, Calgary, Alberta (age 12)

"I thought *Aarial* was a really great book. I spent all my spare time reading it until I was finished. I couldn't stop reading it but at the same time I didn't want it to end. I haven't enjoyed a book as much since I read the *Harry Potter* series. I especially liked how Dylan could do anything in his imaginary world. I wish my own world was more like that."

SIMON PENNY, Clarkes Beach, Newfoundland (age 13)

"I like this book because of its detail in the storyline and the two different realms each with their own stories. It was really interesting seeing a story from two views, the real world and this other realm. This kept the story very interesting and made the book really great to read."

OWEN KASPER, Calgary, Alberta (age 12)

"Thank you, Mr. Paulson, for writing an amazing story. I hope a sequel comes out."

EDUARD ANGHELESCU, Calgary, Alberta (age 12)

"Dylan is a character that everyone can relate to in a way."

PAUL LINEHAM, Calgary, Alberta (age 12)

Praise for *Aarial* from Adult Readers

"A fast-paced tale of magic and reality that, once begun, is impossible to put down."

MICHAEL HARE, Owner of *Owl's Nest Bookstore*, Calgary, Alberta

"This creative, well-crafted book takes you on a fantastic journey. Exciting twists and turns make it a page-turner. The story, the characters, and the plot grab you and hold on as Dylan pursues his quest. A great tale!"

SUE HILL, Owner of *Monkeyshines Bookstore*, Calgary, Alberta

"Suspenseful and filled with both action and magic, *Aarial* manages to be both a dark and uplifting story of change and renewal. It will keep you turning pages."

DEREK DONAIS, Author of *MetalMagic: Talisman* & *MetalMagic: Revelation*, Strathmore, Alberta

"*Aarial* is an adventure filled with opposites and contrasts that take the reader into two unique worlds. Dylan escapes reality by withdrawing into a world where control, power, and acceptance replace the loss in his life. Imagination and symbolism are portrayed in Dylan's alternate world of escape. *Aarial* is a captivating novel that takes you through a journey of descriptive imagery and compassion."

JUDI EKELUND, Teacher, Calgary, Alberta

"Paulson's strengths go beyond creating magic systems; his prescience and inner knowledge of the classroom and the teacher-student relationship make this book shine. *Aarial* is a solid debut and I look forward to reading more from Paulson in the future."

JOSHUA PANTALLERESCO, Author of *Veritas*, Calgary, Alberta

"As a teacher I have met many intriguing, imaginative, and troubled youth, and I found it both familiar and brilliantly refreshing to delve into the world of Dylan and the power of *Aarial*. Although the book is geared towards young teens, I found myself gripped by the plot and lost many hours of sleep so I could finish just one more chapter. Collin Paulson writes with the clarity and understanding of an educator working with youth today and, at the same time, brings the world of Dylan and *Aarial* alive for us to explore."

CINDY WOOLFREY, Middle School Teacher, Calgary, Alberta

"A compelling story for old and young alike."

C. HARPER, Psychologist, Calgary, Alberta

"A perfect novel study for students with behavioural challenges as many of them can truly relate to Dylan's real-life situation."

L. WILSON, Special Education Teacher, Calgary, Alberta

"I've seen that teens can relate to this novel because of the fantasy and imagination that's involved…just like in video games."

CINDY URVALD, Behaviour Support Worker, Calgary, Alberta

AARIAL

It has been such a pleasure teaching you over the past 2 years, Riley.

Published by Black Fly Publishing
E-mail: contact@aarial.ca
Website: www.aarial.ca

Second Paperback Edition – April 2013
17 16 15 14 13 — 1 2 3 4 5 6 7 8 9

Library and Archives Canada Cataloguing in Publication

Paulson, Collin
    Aarial / Collin Paulson. — 2nd pbk. ed.

Issued also in electronic formats
ISBN: 978 – 0 – 9918519 – 0 – 4

    I. Title.

PS8631.A874A27 2013   jc813'.6   C2013 – 902114 – 0

TECHNICAL CREDITS:
Editing: RACHEL SMALL, *Faultless Finish Editing*, Calgary, Alberta
Front and Back Cover Illustration: DAVID WILLICOME, <davidwillicome.com>, Calgary, Alberta
Design & Production: JEREMY DROUGHT, *Last Impression Publishing Service*, Calgary, Alberta
Printed in Canada by *Houghton Boston Printers & Lithographers*, Saskatoon, Saskatchewan

COLLIN PAULSON

BLACK FLY PUBLISHING
Calgary, Alberta

Contents

Aarial is dedicated to Naomi and Elyse,
who kept pestering me to "hurry up and finish."

Acknowledgements

ARIAL SAT ON MY BOOKSHELF FOR several years without an audience. It would still be there if not for the encouragement of an amazing group of ten and eleven year olds. I would like to thank my 2005 – 06 grade five class at Nellie McClung School. Their enthusiasm for the story was the spark I needed to continue.

Thank you Rachel Small for your keen eye and thoughtful questions. I didn't realize how much I needed an editor until you took a look at it.

I would also like to thank two artists. David Willicome took a scene from *Aarial* and brought it to life for the front and back cover. I am in awe. Dawn Heinemeyer is responsible for the medallion and floor plan of the prisoner's-wing. Thank you for taking the picture in my head and transferring it to paper.

Thank you Jeremy Drought, at *Last Impression Publishing Service*, for putting this all together and making it presentable. Your talents are countless and your advice was invaluable.

Finally, I would like to thank every student I have ever taught. You may not know it, but a piece of you is in this story.

All journeys have secret destinations of which the traveler is unaware.
MARTIN BUBER

1

The Medallion

WITH HIS HANDS BEHIND HIS HEAD and eyes unfocused on the ceiling, Mr. Peters teetered on the hind legs of the heavy oak chair. He was oblivious to the mess that surrounded him. Yesterday's art lesson had been a success, even though it looked like a paint store had exploded in the room. Each cluster of desks displayed colorful artwork, which would soon replace the students' charcoal drawings that had decorated the walls for the last month.

A knock at the door startled Mr. Peters out of his daydream. He lost his balance and tumbled backward. The chair slammed onto the floor at the same time as his head hit a wooden bookshelf.

"Ow!" the teacher bellowed.

Wedged between the bookshelf and the seat of his chair, he felt like a helpless turtle.

"I am such a twit."

A lopsided, backward somersault freed him from the predicament. Slowly, he rose to his feet. Mrs. Miller, the school secretary, stood in the doorway, cringing at what she had just witnessed.

"Sorry about that," she said quietly. Her hand covered her smile, and she swayed uncomfortably at the door. "Are you okay?"

Mr. Peters smiled sheepishly and rubbed the back of his head. "What can I do for you, Mrs. Miller?" he inquired as he lifted the chair upright.

She tilted her head in the direction of the hallway and whispered, "Your new student is here, Mr. Peters." Then in a louder voice, "Come on in, Dylan."

Dylan stepped cautiously into the room. The first thing Mr. Peters noticed was his filthy appearance. His dusty blond hair was tangled, and he wore a soiled red jacket that hung down to his knees. Mr. Peters did not know his age, but he guessed that he was older than his other students.

"Good morning, Dylan. How are you?"

Mr. Peters smiled as he walked over to the disheveled boy, whose sloping shoulders lifted slightly and darting, blue eyes connected with his eyes in the form of a greeting. He extended his hand, and Dylan shook it tentatively. An invisible cloud of stale cigarette smoke followed the boy into the room.

"I've heard a lot about you. I'm happy you're joining our class."

Dylan smiled nervously, but his focus quickly shifted from Mr. Peters to the floor, then to the wall, and finally rested upon his new teacher's desk.

"What's that?" Dylan pointed to a plastic figurine.

"I confiscated that from one of my students. I think it's a samurai warrior."

"Why do you have it?"

"Sam was playing with it during math class," Mr. Peters answered.

"Will he get it back?"

"Eventually."

"Why did he bring it to school?"

"Sam said he needs it for protection."

"What protects him now?"

"Uh...nothing. He doesn't need protection." Mr. Peters nodded a thank-you to Mrs. Miller as she turned to leave. "Your desk is over here, Dylan. Would you like me to help you unpack your school supplies?"

"Yeah...I guess," Dylan said softly.

He shoved his hands into his pockets, rounded his shoulders, and followed Mr. Peters. Dylan unzipped his backpack and started pulling out school supplies, toys, and small, unidentifiable objects.

He was cramming everything into the desk when Mr. Peters said, "Can you take some of these things home, Dylan? Your desk is too small to house everything you have in your bag."

"Yeah...I guess."

Mr. Peters continued, "You'll like it here, Dylan. The students in our class are very nice. Would you like to make some new friends?"

"Yeah."

Dylan bent over to pull a binder out of his backpack, and a medallion on a tattered, woven leather cord slipped out of his shirt as he straightened up. Mr. Peters was immediately drawn to it. The dull, brass medallion displayed two rounded blades framing a large, central sword—all three weapons shared the same handle.

"Where did you get that charm, Dylan? It's beautiful…and ominous! I've never seen anything like it."

Dylan straightened up, and his piercing blue eyes connected with Mr. Peters's. "I won it, and it's a medal— not a charm!" he asserted indignantly.

Mr. Peters was taken aback by the boy's sudden display of confidence. Dylan was instantly taller and broader.

"Where would you win something like that?"

Dylan paused. "I defeated the horrible Tracker, and I took it from him when I crushed his skull and cut off his head."

Mr. Peters stared at the boy, uncertain of how to respond. An uncomfortable smile appeared on the teacher's face.

"Oh…well…uh…"

An announcement came over the intercom. "Mr. Peters, you have a call on line one. Mr. Peters, line one."

"Uh…I…uh…I have to take that." Mr. Peters pointed to the door and walked in the direction of his finger. "Make yourself comfortable, Dylan. I'll be back…I'll be back in a minute."

Dylan watched Mr. Peters step nervously out of the room. The samurai warrior caught his attention again, and he walked over to it. Dylan picked it up and studied the grimace on the small man's face. Then he noticed a large picture on the wall beside Mr. Peters's desk and stepped back to get a better view. Enormous trees filled the photograph. They were perfectly straight, reaching for an unseen sky. Only the rough bark of the trees was visible, and behind the trees were the faint outlines of more trees and then complete darkness. Dylan stared into the blackness of the picture and wondered at the depths of the forest.

Suddenly, a small silhouette of a head appeared from behind a tree. Dylan's heart skipped a beat. He gasped and took a step back. As quickly as the silhouette had appeared, it was gone. Dylan leaned in to examine the picture for signs of the mysterious image. He was close enough to distinguish colorful dots making various patterns on the paper, but the figure had disappeared.

The sound of the bell startled Dylan. Seconds later, he heard the din of students pushing their way into the school. Dylan suddenly felt apprehensive as a number of students filed into the classroom. He quickly sat down, pulled out a copy of *The Hobbit*, and pretended to read. He noticed three boys enter the room in a rush.

"Give me back my hat, Jake!"

"Why, Teddy Bear? You gonna catch a cold?" the bigger boy mocked. A toque was pulled tightly over his massive head—dusty blonde curls sprouted out from beneath the brim.

"My grandma made it!"

"Oh, well that's different," teased Jake.

The bully pulled the hat off his head and presented it to Ted, the boy he had called Teddy Bear, as if it were a royal offering.

"Here you go."

Just as the boy reached out for it, Jake flipped it over his head to a third boy, who had been watching the incident and laughing. He quickly threw it back to Jake as Ted spun around helplessly. The smaller boy exhaled defeat and stood still while Jake danced a jig.

Another boy entered the room and warned, "Mr. Peters is coming."

Jake stopped dancing and blurted, "Give me a hug, Teddy Bear" as he dropped the hat into Ted's hands. Ted turned away quickly and bumped into Mr. Peters, who was carrying a cup of coffee.

"Whoa. Slow down, Ted," cried Mr. Peters as he lifted his cup out of the way. A few drops splashed over the rim and landed on the carpet.

"Sorry, Mr. Peters," Ted apologized. "I have to pee. I'll be right back."

Dylan watched Mr. Peters move clumsily across the room toward his desk. His giraffe-like strides made him look as if he were travelling in slow motion. Out of the corner of his eye, Dylan sensed movement in the picture. He turned to the photograph and again observed the silhouette of a head peer around one of the trees. The shadowy figure did not disappear this time. He was mesmerized by it and could not avert his gaze. Time stood still.

"Dylan…Dylan." With the third "Dylan!" a huge black fly bounced off the photograph.

Dylan jumped. The spell was broken. He turned his head in the direction of the call. The students were gathered on the carpet in one corner of the room, and Mr. Peters was sitting on a chair in front of them. All eyes were on the new student.

"Come and join us, please," requested his new teacher.

Dylan stood up and took a step toward the group. He glanced at the picture one last time; the silhouette was gone. As he proceeded toward the corner of the room, he felt his face burn. *Look away!* he wanted to scream at the students. Sheepishly, he bent down and focused on the ground. He sat with one leg folded under his seat and wrapped his arms around the other leg. Dylan stared at the torn threads on the knee of his jeans.

"Class, I'd like to introduce you to Dylan. Dylan, what's your last name?"

Dylan continued to stare at his knee as he mumbled, "Chevalier."

Mr. Peters had not heard what Dylan had said, but he saw his discomfort, so he cut his introduction short. "Dylan just arrived from Edmonton, so let's show him our hospitality and make him feel welcome. Ted, please give Dylan a tour of our school."

Ted smiled. "Yeah, sure."

He stood up and walked toward the door. Dylan remained seated and played with a small pebble that had caught his attention.

"Okay, who brought in a newspaper article for News Hawks today?" asked Mr. Peters as he searched the faces in the group.

Janna's hand shot up immediately.

"All right, Janna! We can always rely on you."

Janna made her way awkwardly to the front of the group, stepping over hands and legs. Mr. Peters noticed Ted swaying nervously at the doorway. He glanced at Dylan, who was batting something back and forth between his hands.

"Ted is waiting for you, Dylan."

Dylan stood without averting his focus from the ground. All eyes were on him again. For the second time since he had arrived, his face reddened. With his hands in his pockets and his shoulders hunched, he dawdled toward the door. Ted greeted him with a nervous smile. His initial excitement of being free to wander the halls disappeared. Ted felt a little uncertain about this unfriendly stranger.

As the two boys left the room, they heard Mr. Peters say, "Okay Janna, what have you got for us today?"

The hallway was quiet and empty. Coats lined the corridor and muffled the sound of the boys' footsteps. Ted stopped and looked to the end of the foyer; then he turned and peered the other way.

He smiled mischievously at Dylan and pointed to one side of the hall. "This...is where we hang our coats." Then he pointed to the other side of corridor. "Don't hang your coat on this side, or the wicked Miss Rodent will shred your jacket with her teeth, tie you up in the sleeves, and shove the rest of it down your throat."

Dylan straightened up. Ted noticed a slight smile appear on his face. Without warning, Ted leapt at the coat rack. He put one of the hoods of the hanging jackets in a headlock. "This is what I...would like...to do... to you, Miss Rodent," he said as if pained by the struggle. The jacket was draped over his back and was putting up a good fight, but Ted appeared to be gaining control. Finally, he threw his opponent over his back to the ground. He rolled around on the floor, grunting and groaning, throwing punches at the hood. Then the jacket rolled him over onto his back, where he struggled for a moment. Finally, he gained control and flipped the jacket over, but he was choking. "I...can't...breathe." Ted tried to loosen the sleeve's tight grip around his neck when a teacher walked out of her room and looked down at Ted.

"What are you doing, Ted?" she asked calmly.

Ted jumped up. "Oh. Hi, Miss Roland." Ted paused to catch his breath. "I was just giving our new jacket...er...um...our new student a tour of the school, and I noticed that someone had knocked this coat off its hook. I was putting it back."

Dylan smiled as he watched Ted try to explain his behavior. Miss Roland had her hands on her hips, and she appeared stern, but Dylan sensed that she was amused.

"Have you met, Dylan, Miss Roland?" Ted inquired as he hung up the jacket.

"No, I haven't." She extended her hand. "I'm pleased to meet you."

Dylan shook her hand and muttered a greeting. Ted forced himself between Dylan and Miss Roland, breaking their grip.

"We have to go," blurted Ted, and the two boys raced down the hall.

They disappeared around the corner into the next hallway and then stopped and burst out laughing.

"Did you see her face?" Ted inquired through his giggles. "Doesn't she look like a rat?"

Dylan smiled into his hand without speaking.

"We better hurry up. We haven't gotten very far, and Mr. Peters won't be happy if we miss math. Mr. Peters will probably hear about my battle with Jane's coat, but he won't care. He doesn't mind if we have fun as long as we get our work done. This is the gym. Do you like gym?"

Ted continued the tour of the school, talking incessantly. He was starting to feel more comfortable with Dylan. Even though Dylan said very little, Ted had a good feeling about him. Dylan laughed at his jokes and put up with his crazy imagination. Finally, they stopped in the library.

Dylan was awestruck. It was the biggest library he had ever seen. He walked away from Ted and stepped through the aisles. He ran his fingers along the shelves and stopped several times to view some of the books. As the pages flipped through his fingers, he took in the smell of paper and ink. He preferred the older books with yellowing pages; they gave off the strongest odor.

Ted followed him and continued talking. He asked questions without receiving answers and commented on anything that popped into his head. Dylan was unaware of Ted's presence. He was alone when he was with a book.

Something caught Dylan's eye. He stopped, crouched down, and pulled out *Where The Wild Things Are*. "Have you read this? I love this book."

"Yeah," Ted mocked, "I read that in grade two." His focus went from the book to Dylan's neck, where he spied a large leather knot. "What's on the rope tied around your neck?"

Dylan's glower forced him back a step, but he couldn't turn away from his penetrating eyes.

"It's a medal."

Ted swallowed hard and whispered, "Can I see it?"

Dylan rose. He pulled the medallion out from under his shirt and held it in the palm of his hand.

"Cool!" Ted reached out. "Where did you get it?"

"I defeated the horrible Tracker, and I took it from him when I crushed his skull and cut off his head."

Ted froze. He searched Dylan's eyes for a sign of make-believe. His blank expression was difficult to interpret. Ted swallowed noisily. He didn't really want to know, but he couldn't stop himself from asking.

"Who's Tracker?" he squeaked.

2

Impending Doom

"TRACKER WAS A TROG WHO WORKED for Nero. He was sent to stop me from fulfilling my mission for Queen Gaia."

"Wait. You're losing me. Who the heck is Nero?" Ted asked. "A trog? What's a trog? You were on a mission for a queen? What are you talking about?"

"Let me start from the beginning."

Dylan slid under the computer table in the corner of the library, and with a wave of his hand, motioned for Ted to join him. Ted's curiosity overpowered his reluctance. He scanned the library to see if anyone was looking.

The light beneath the table was dim, and the sound of Dylan's voice was clear and haunting. At first Ted was apprehensive, but Dylan's words pulled him into the story, and his anxiety disappeared. The boys became oblivious to their surroundings.

"I grew up in a small village called Duffle in the highlands of Milo. The landscape is…was…it *is* rugged and beautiful. For many generations, my people lived off the land. We grew most of our own food, and we needed very little from anyone. We did some trading with other villages, but for the most part, we supported ourselves. Life was hard, but we were happy," Dylan said. He hesitated before speaking again.

"My twin sister, Taya, is small but tough. We don't always agree, but we usually get along. She has a quick temper." Dylan's eyes widened. "Her eyes burn when she's angry. Even my mother backs off when Taya gets that rabid-dog look in her eyes. I never understood how someone could go from looking like a cherub to a wild beast in the blink of an eye." He glanced up at Ted and smiled.

"My mother's black hair reflected sunlight. It looked like she had a halo. Her skin was as white as snow." Dylan pictured his mother's face. "It embarrassed me, the way men looked at her."

"Why did you say *was?*" Ted asked. "Is she dead?"

Dylan did not speak for a moment.

"I don't know," he said quietly. "I haven't seen her for a long time. I don't know if she's alive or dead. I don't even know if Duffle still exists. I don't know anything anymore. I've been away far too long."

Dylan rubbed his forehead and continued slowly. "My father, Macor, was a giant man. He was a leader in the community and an advisor to the king. The people of our village loved and respected him, but they also feared him because he was unpredictable. When wronged, he struck out with the ferocity of a wolverine, and there were times when innocent people were injured due to his wrath. The guilt he felt following his rage tore him apart. He always made amends to the innocent victims whenever possible, but it was often too late.

"The root of the problem was *Aarial*, a special power that was passed on to him from his forefathers. Aarial is believed to be the name of my ancestor who first possessed it. In Duffle, my last name is Aarial. I don't know exactly where this power comes from or how old it is, but it consumed him and threatened to take over his will. He often cursed the power, for he didn't have control over it.

"Our village was prosperous, compared to neighboring towns. We were united, and this brought us great success. Our people did everything for the good of the community. We worked together and helped each other in any way that we could. We paid a large portion of our earnings to King Ramen because he owned the land. There were some who complained about paying the king so much, but my father would quickly hush these people. We all knew the story of the village of Scopus, which had rebelled. With a heavy hand, the king's army had quickly put an end to the people's struggle and left their village in ruins.

"The royal family possesses a power that's stronger than Aarial. I've been told that my blood relatives and the king's ancestors battled for power hundreds of years ago. They destroyed most of my family and gained control. Generations of animosity between my ancestors and the king's forefathers forced my family into hiding. Everyone knew the Aarial name, and they were willing to keep us hidden. But the king's father reached out to my great grandfather in his final years, and our families formed an alliance that benefited both the king and my people.

"King Ramen was a kind man who was fair and honest. As long as he got his share of our earnings, he allowed us to live in peace and harmony. The king had one son—Nero. Nero was cruel and heartless as a child. I was told that he once tore the wings off a bat and taunted it with a stick while it slowly bled to death. He grew up to be a man of great stature, feared by all. He had a scowl on his face that never changed, and it is said that flowers wilted under his joyless glare.

"I overheard my father talking to my mother about Nero on several occasions. My father had never feared anyone or anything, but he was afraid of Nero. He was afraid of what Nero might do as king."

"This is a great story!" Ted interrupted.

"Story?" Dylan retorted.

"Sorry, Dylan. I just thought…"

"You just thought what? You think my story is fantasy?"

Ted looked away from Dylan's scowl. "I just think…your life is exciting. I wish my life was more of an adventure. Please tell me more."

Dylan's anger faded with a sigh.

"King Ramen was getting old, and his health was failing. He was often in bed for days at a time. The sicker King Ramen got, the more worried my father became. Nero had never liked my father. He felt that he had too much influence on his father's decisions. King Ramen tried to convince Nero of the benefits of working with my family. Nero would nod and appear to agree, but Ramen knew he was not convinced that Macor was of any use to his kingdom. I've been told that on his deathbed, the king pleaded with Nero to keep the union between our two families alive. Nero agreed to his father's wishes, but when Ramen died and his power was transferred to Nero, the new king went back on his word. It is rumored that the first words he spoke after his father's death were, 'Bring me his head.'

"My father knew of the impending doom, and he went into hiding while Nero recuperated after the transfer of power. He sent a message to me through Ravelle—a childhood friend of my father's. I was told to meet him by the Gnarled Oak near Gilmore Pond when the sun was at the highest point in the sky. I sensed that my life was never going to be the same."

Dylan took several breaths while Ted waited silently, hoping for the story to continue.

"I got a lot of work done that morning, but I don't remember doing it. My mind was distracted by the sense of doom that hung in the air with the misty shroud that blanketed the crops. At one point, I looked back over the field I had tilled that morning, and I was surprised to see how much I had completed. I brushed the hair away from my eyes and looked to the sky. The sun was a white disk through the fog—directly overhead.

"I dropped my shovel and ran across the field. At full speed, I leapt over grass and rocks, ducked under branches, and jumped through creeks that led into the forest. My heart pounded, and I started to wheeze. I wanted to keep running, but my body wouldn't allow it. I slowed to a quick walk. Beads of sweat rolled down my face. A crow screamed above my head, and I looked up. The bird wasn't visible, but I felt his presence. I spun around and saw a squirrel jump from a rock to a tree.

"The forest had become foreign to me. I didn't recognize it as the place my sister and I loved to explore. For some reason, I felt like a stranger in an alien landscape. I looked around for a familiar tree or rock, but I didn't recognize anything. I needed to rest and think, so I sat down on a boulder. Out of the corner of my eye, I saw something move. Startled, I leapt off the boulder and turned to see a squirrel sitting right next to the spot I had been sitting. He dropped an acorn and jumped to a tree, and I picked up the acorn while he watched me. Quietly, I walked toward him and held out my hand, showing him the acorn. He jumped from the tree to the ground and then leapt to another tree. I followed.

"This went on for a great distance. I wasn't sure if we were playing or if he was leading me somewhere. After a while, the purpose of my trip into the forest had slipped my mind as I was caught up in the cat-

and-mouse game. Suddenly, we came upon the creek and familiar swimming hole. The recognition snapped me out of the game. I knew where I was. I turned to look back at the squirrel, but only his back end was visible. I watched him fly through the trees, and then he was gone.

"I had to get to my father. I sprinted through the trees faster than I had ever moved. I felt unstoppable as I ran alongside the river. I didn't tire. The noise of my pounding feet became a concern, so I slowed my pace and stepped lightly through the underbrush. On my right was Gilmore Pond, and up ahead was the familiar Gnarled Oak. I stopped a short distance from the tree and examined my surroundings. Everything looked the same, but it felt different.

"There was a stillness in the forest. The stillness became a part of me. My breathing slowed, and my heart paused. Everything moved in slow motion. I sensed that there was something amiss, but I didn't know what. My eyes travelled from the roots of the tree to its base and up the trunk. Then my vision locked on an unfamiliar sight. There was a lip or ridge of bark protruding from the tree about halfway up. I hadn't noticed it before.

"Slowly, I circled the tree and observed that the lip of bark wrapped around its circumference. It looked like a giant nest made out of bark. The unusual sight didn't frighten me; instead, I was drawn to it. I wrapped my arms around the tree, and it exerted an energy that sent shivers up my spine. My hands gripped the wrinkled bark, and I wrapped my legs around the trunk. I inched my way up, grabbed hold of the first branch with one hand, and unwrapped my legs. I dangled from the limb by one arm for a moment, and then swung my other hand up. When both of my hands gripped the bough firmly, I walked my feet up the tree and wrapped one of my legs around the branch before pulling myself up. The climbing was easy from that point on because there were so many branches. As I approached the lip of bark, I noticed a light coming from the nest. The underside of the leaves above the nest glowed.

"I held my breath and gripped the ridge with both of my hands. Slowly, I pulled myself up. My eyes rose above my fingers, and I had to squint to protect myself from the blinding light. I gasped for air, and my heart skipped a beat at the sight of a kneeling, hooded figure. I lost all strength and dropped down until I was barely hanging on by my fingertips. As I began to weaken, a powerful grip seized my wrist—"

A firm hand gripped Dylan's shoulder. "Where have you boys been?" Dylan and Ted peered out of their hiding place into Mr. Peters's narrowed eyes. "We've been looking all over the school. Do you realize what time it is? You've been gone most of the morning."

"Oh. Sorry, Mr. Peters," Ted replied shakily as he slid out from under the table. "Dylan was just telling me about…his life."

"Well, you can talk on your own time. Now get back to class."

The two boys sensed Mr. Peters's irritation.

"Come on out, Dylan. I'm not mad at you. I was just concerned. We've been searching the halls for you."

Slowly, Dylan crawled out from under the table. He wouldn't meet Mr. Peters's gaze and stared at his teacher's shoes as he followed him through the library. Just before they reached the classroom, Mr. Peters crouched down to his level.

"Dylan, look at me."

Dylan looked into Mr. Peters's eyes for a split second and then focused on the ground.

"You're not in trouble, Dylan. I was just concerned," he said emphatically. "You need to let me know where you are when you're out of the classroom."

"Okay," Dylan muttered at the ground.

"We're reading until lunch time. Do you have a book?"

"Yeah."

Dylan's face burned as he stepped into the classroom. He sat down at his desk and pulled out *The Hobbit*. The pages slid through his fingers as he searched for the dog-eared corner that marked the spot he had last read. The scent of the yellowed pages put him at ease, and he jumped into the story.

A short time later, he felt someone watching him, and he started to blush. He looked around the room but saw that everyone was reading quietly. A buzzing sound raced by his ear toward Mr. Peters's desk. He followed the noise, and his eyes rested upon the picture. Staring out at him from the photograph was the tiny silhouette. Dylan stopped breathing. A few seconds later, the fly that had been resting unnoticed on the picture frame flew away. Dylan shook his head, covered his eyes, and rested his chin upon his desk.

3
Lost Child

THE BELL RANG, BOOKS SLAMMED SHUT, and everyone jumped up and headed for the door. Sam started talking to Mr. Peters, who was shuffling papers at his desk.

"We went to Calaway Park on the weekend," Sam said excitedly. "My big sister was afraid to go on the roller coaster, but I wasn't. I went on it five times."

Mr. Peters watched Dylan while Sam went on. He tried to show interest in Sam's story, but he was not paying attention. He nodded and asked the odd question, but his thoughts were on the new boy, who remained in his desk with his head down and his ears covered.

"We also went out for pizza, and I ate six pieces by myself. My mom said she didn't understand how such a skinny boy could eat so much. She said that she wished she had my metabolism. What is metabolism? My sister—"

"Excuse me, Ted," Mr. Peters said, interrupting his student.

"It's Sam!"

"Oh, yeah, right. Sorry, Sam. Can you tell me about your weekend later?"

Sam frowned and shuffled out of the classroom. Mr. Peters pulled up a chair beside Dylan.

"Are you okay, Dylan?" Mr. Peters waited for a response. "Dylan."

Dylan turned his head toward Mr. Peters. He quickly straightened up in his chair, stared at his desk, and started picking at a torn label.

"We should have cleaned your desk better before you arrived. This desk was covered with stickers. We couldn't get them all off." Mr. Peters paused and then asked again, "Are you okay, Dylan?"

"Yeah."

"Are you sure? Is something bothering you?"

Dylan continued to pick at the label. He shook his head.

"It must be tough coming to a new city, not knowing anyone. I moved a lot when I was young, and I hated arriving at a new school, feeling unwanted…without a friend."

Dylan stopped picking at the label and stared at his desk. He sniffed away a tear and straightened up.

"Would you like to talk about how you're feeling, Dylan?"

Dylan did not respond.

"Do you miss your friends?"

"I don't have any friends!" he spat.

"What about Ted? I bet the two of you will become friends. Look how well you got along this morning. Ted wouldn't spend that much time with you if he didn't like you. He won't do anything for an hour if he doesn't like it. I can't get him to spend two minutes reading a book."

Dylan glanced at Mr. Peters and grinned.

"Do you like Ted?"

"Yeah. He's kinda weird, though," Dylan said, smiling again.

"He has a very *unique* imagination. What were you two doing for so long?"

"Talking."

"About what?" Mr. Peters asked.

"I was telling him about my past and where I come from."

"You talked about Edmonton for that long?"

"Yeah…I guess."

Mr. Peters stood up and patted Dylan on the back. "Well, it's lunch time. You should go eat."

As the two of them left the classroom, Dylan glanced over his shoulder one last time. He breathed a sigh of relief at the empty forest. "Only trees," he whispered.

Mr. Peters watched Dylan grab his coat, run down the hall, and throw his body at the door. The door slammed against the outside wall. Mr. Peters cringed at the bang.

Determined footsteps echoed behind the teacher. *Click, clack! Click clack! Click, clack!* Mr. Peters turned to see Mrs. Evans, the principal, marching toward him.

"Come with me," she said quickly. "I have to show you something."

Two of Mrs. Evans's strides matched one of Mr. Peters's, and yet he had to quicken his pace from his usual saunter to keep up with her.

"Dylan's file arrived, and you won't believe the size of it." The principal looked over her shoulder and up at Mr. Peters as they proceeded down the hall. "I've never seen a thicker file in my career. They've written an encyclopedia on this kid, and there's still more to come from Edmonton."

Mr. Peters immediately noticed the open file on her well-organized desk as they walked into her office. The edges of it were tattered, and pages stuck out in all directions.

"I've only flipped through it, so I don't know all of the details, but from the little I have read, I can see that he has lived a horrendous life. He's only twelve years old, and he's been in eleven different schools and at least eight homes—ranging from foster care and group homes to treatment centers and stabilization programs. He only lived with his abusive biological mother for two years. There's a court order in place that won't even allow him to visit her. His father is barely mentioned in the report, so he was probably never around."

Mr. Peters sighed and rubbed the back of his neck.

Mrs. Evans continued. "Dylan has two older brothers from different fathers. He rarely sees them. The oldest brother abused him, so his social worker is reviewing that relationship and deciding whether or not they'll be allowed to see each other. He has seen his other brother on rare occasions, and they seem to get along. Apparently, Dylan asks to visit him regularly. This poor little guy has probably never felt loved by anyone. He's been shipped around so much." Mrs. Evans handed the report to Mr. Peters. "Flip through it when you get a chance."

Mr. Peters carried the report to his room and dropped it onto his desk. After opening his lunch bag and grabbing a sandwich, he sat heavily in his chair and sighed. He wanted to see all the different places Dylan had been, so he started by flipping through the assessments and evaluations, only paying attention to the dates and places. After a few had slipped through his fingers, he noticed that Dylan's last name was spelled differently on many of the reports. He went back to the beginning and started flipping again, just looking at the names this time: Chevalier, Chevaliars, Chevaliere, Shevalier, Chivalier. Mr. Peters closed the file and stared out the window.

Ms. Steinwood, the grade 5 teacher, peered into his classroom. "Eating alone today?"

"Yeah. Did you hear about my new student?"

"Wasn't he supposed to arrive a week ago?"

"He was supposed to, but he just got here today."

"What's he like?" Ms. Steinwood could see Mr. Peters's concern.

"He's a quiet, sad little boy. He certainly stands out from the kids in this community. His clothes don't fit him right, and he smells. I don't think he's had a bath in weeks. Look at this file."

"Is that his?" Ms. Steinwood's eyes widened as she adjusted her glasses with both hands. "He's going to need a cabinet drawer to himself. Have you read it?"

"No, I just got it, and I've only just started flipping through it. One thing I noticed is that there are five or six different spellings of his last name. No one has taken the time to find out how to spell his name. He's just another troubled kid not worth getting to know."

"There are many lost children out there." Ms. Steinwood sighed. "We just don't see them in this school very often. Sorry, but I can't talk right now. I have to run. Have a good lunch."

Mr. Peters rested his chin on his hands and his elbows on the desk. He stared at the black-and-white photograph of Dylan, taken several years earlier.

"This kid has no identity," he said softly.

4

A Tearful Transfer

TED WAS PERCHED HIGH ATOP THE monkey bars when he spotted the lone figure walking across the field. The figure's eyes searched the ground as he moved. Every few steps, he would crouch down and examine something in the grass. He stepped across the pebbles beneath the creative playground, and Ted could see that his pockets bulged. They were full of colorful rocks, bottle caps, plastic figurines, and other treasures that had caught his eye.

His winter jacket was open and hung loosely from his shoulders. A chinook wind had warmed the frosty air that preceded the weekend, so most of the students were not even wearing jackets. Almost all of the snow had disappeared, and mud puddles were scattered over the field and playground.

He was only a few feet away when Ted called out, "Hey, Dylan!"

Dylan looked up but could only see Ted's outline, for the sun was directly behind him. He squinted up at the stranger and walked around the monkey bars until he could see who it was.

"Hi," Dylan replied sharply.

"What are you doing?" asked Ted.

"Come here. I'll show you."

Dylan looked around for a sheltered spot while Ted grabbed his coat, which he had draped over one of the bars. Then Ted jumped from the monkey bars and fell forward. His outstretched arms hit Dylan in the chest as he tried to get his balance. Dylan scowled at him.

"Follow me," he commanded.

Dylan led Ted into a clump of small trees and bushes. Pathways led in and out of the trees, going off in all directions.

"This is known as the Hidden Forest," Ted whispered. "It's a great hiding spot in summer. No one can see in when there are leaves on the bushes."

The two boys crouched down.

"Look what I found," Dylan said, pulling out a small, red Swiss Army knife with two blades. Dylan flipped open one of the blades.

"Cool," Ted said excitedly. "You found that?"

"I find lots of cool stuff." Dylan dropped the knife into Ted's hands.

Ted flipped it around and studied it for a moment. "Can you finish telling me about your life in Duffle?"

Dylan grabbed the knife from Ted and shoved it in his pocket. The expression on his face became very serious.

"Before you start, tell me what a trog is. That is such a cool word."

"A trog is a hideous creature. Is it a flying man…or a talking dragon? Is it a he or an it? I don't know which."

Ted's eyes lit up. "So they're a cross between dragons and men?"

"Yeah," Dylan said, hesitating. "Kind of. Anyway, they are the king's spies and soldiers. They fly high above the trees. They watch us and report on what we're doing. When I was young, I saw them a lot, but later on, I didn't see them very often. My father said that King Ramen didn't have enough trog soldiers to keep constant watch over every village, so he sent most of them to communities that were a greater threat to his kingdom. King Ramen trusted my father, and he was pleased with the way my father kept our village under control. The king didn't feel that it was necessary to keep constant watch over us."

"So they can talk?" Ted inquired shakily.

"They can talk, but not very well. Their speech is harsh and raspy. The only trog I've heard speak is Tracker." Dylan shuddered with the utterance of his name. "Their voices are very difficult to listen to. The thought of it gives me chills. When they speak to you, their deep, gruff voices seem to surround you and come at you from all directions."

Ted swallowed. "I don't know if I want to hear any more. They sound scary."

"Okay," Dylan said quickly, and he stood up to leave.

"Wait!" Ted grabbed Dylan's arm and tried to pull him down.

Dylan looked down at him and smirked.

"Tell me about what happened to you at the Gnarled Oak."

"Are you sure you want me to continue?"

"No, I'm not sure, but I can't help myself. I'm too curious."

Dylan crouched down beside Ted and dragged a stick through the mud. "I will continue, but you must promise not to tell anyone."

"I promise."

Dylan reached into his shirt, pulled out the medallion, and slipped the leather cord over his head. With the speed of a frog snatching a fly in midflight, Dylan seized Ted by the wrist. Ted tensed up and tried to pull his hand away. The earnest expression in Dylan's eyes calmed Ted's nerves, however, and he stopped struggling. Dylan placed the medallion in Ted's hand and closed his fingers around it.

Ted opened his hand and studied the medallion. He flipped it over several times, scrutinizing both faces. Until this moment, he had not noticed that the three weapons sharing the same handle protruded on one side but were embedded on the other.

"This is so cool. We learned about this in art. It's called white space." Ted looked up at the sky and shook his head. "No, that's not it…negative space—that's what it's called, negative space."

Dylan shrugged his shoulders, unaware of what he was talking about.

"See, this one side is an image of the weapons, while the other side of the coin…er medal is the opposite. The space around the swords is what's emphasized. Have you ever seen that old *Bugs Bunny* show?"

Dylan nodded.

"You know when Daffy Duck runs through a wall or a door and all that's left is his outline? That's negative space."

Dylan's body language revealed his disinterest in the art lesson.

"Sorry, I just think that it's kinda cool."

Dylan closed Ted's fingers around the medallion a second time. "Repeat after me—*Should I repeat what I've been told.*" Dylan stopped and waited for Ted.

Ted paused. "Should I repeat what I've been told."

"*Tracker's fate will lie before me.*"

Ted swallowed and his voice cracked. "Tracker's fate…will lie before me."

Dylan smiled and released Ted's unsteady hand from the medallion. "Should I continue?"

"Yes, please." Ted was nervous and excited at the same time.

◆ ◆ ◆

mY ARM FELT LIKE IT WAS going to be pulled out of its socket as the giant hand pulled me above the lip of the tree-bark nest. Another hand gripped me under my other arm, and I was dragged inside. The surface of the nest was so smooth that it was slippery. The intense light shooting up from the core of the tree forced me to squint. I faced my savior, or enemy, for I did not know which the person was. All I could see was the outline of the massive, hooded form. Gravity pulled me toward him, but I clung to the edge of the nest and pushed down my heels. Everything slowed as he removed his head covering. The rhythmic drumming of my heart exited my body and filled the night.

"*Father!*" I gasped, finally able to breath again. I slid toward him. "You scared me!"

He placed his hands on my shoulders and looked into my eyes. His scrutinizing gaze touched my soul. I was overwhelmed by the power he emitted and unable to move. Finally, he smiled.

"Welcome," he said. "Thank-you for coming, Son. I can see that you are ready. I was concerned, but the sight of you puts me at ease, for I see that you have the strength. Ravelle was right. He always knew that you would be a powerful Aarial."

"Ready for what?" I cried.

"Son, you need to know about Aarial. We don't have much time, so please listen closely. Aarial has been with us for generations. It's an awesome force that can enhance or destroy. I had difficulty controlling it, and it almost destroyed me. You are more suited for it than I. Your strength will increase tenfold. You will develop the ability to communicate with the earth and learn from her. Your mind will be sharper, and you will have great insight into the workings of man.

Everyone who possesses Aarial adapts it to suit his individuality. You may discover things that were unknown to me. I could do things with the power that my father and grandfather couldn't do, and I couldn't do many of the things they could do. It will become a part of you, just as it became a part of me."

"I don't know what you're talking about. Aarial is just a name to me. I don't understand what you're saying."

"You will, my son. Just remember that you are in charge. Don't allow it to take control as I often did. You will need training. Listen to Ravelle. He's a great teacher. He'll help you to comprehend it."

"Ravelle? The blacksmith?"

"Yes. He has trained all of us, even the original Aarial."

"You're confusing me, Father."

"Don't concern yourself with understanding, Dylan. I didn't understand when my father transferred the power in his final hours."

My father stopped talking. He must have seen the concern in my eyes.

"Are you dying?" I whimpered. "You can't leave me. I need you. We all need you. Please, Father!" I hugged him, and he reassured me that everything would be okay.

"But why? Why are you leaving us, Papa?"

He placed his hands on my shoulders again and looked into my eyes. Through my tears, I perceived his anguish.

"Listen closely. Ramen has died and Nero is king," he said hastily. "I am a threat, and he will not allow me to remain advisor. He wants complete control of the kingdom, and he knows I have great influence on the people of our village. He will not allow me to live. He cannot allow me to live."

"It would be better if you kept the power, Father. Under you, our village can unite and fight Nero. You're the only one who can stop him."

"No." He paused and looked past me, over my shoulder. "I can't stop Nero. His strength is too great. He will destroy Aarial and me. When I die, Aarial dies...unless I pass it on to you. You will continue the Aarial line. Eventually, you will turn it over to Queen Gaia."

"Who is she?"

"Ravelle will explain more later."

"Will Nero come for me?"

"Probably…but I'm his main concern right now. I'm leaving Duffle, and he will pursue me. This will give you time to train and to learn about Aarial."

"You're leaving without Aarial? How will you defend yourself?"

"I've learned many things under Ravelle that will help me. I will not have the power, but I will have much of the knowledge. Nero will capture me—that is certain—but it will take him time, and that's what we are looking for. You need time to develop Aarial."

"Oh, Father. Please don't go!" I pleaded.

"Son, I have to go. We must transfer Aarial now."

My father sat down cross-legged, placed his fingers on my temples, and instructed me to place my fingers on his temples. The light from the core of the tree projected skyward between our knees. My vision fixed on a tear that formed in the corner of his eye. It did not run down his face. It rested upon his lashes as he stared into my eyes. I felt a slight pain in my temples, and then everything faded to darkness.

◆ ◆ ◆

THE SOUND OF THE BELL STARTLED the two boys out of Duffle. They looked at each other for a moment and then stood. Ted glanced down at the muddy ground they had been sitting in. He pulled his pants away from his skin and cringed at the thought of having a wet bum for the entire afternoon. The two of them proceeded slowly toward the door while the other students hurriedly pushed their way into the school.

5

The Silhouette

DYLAN'S MOOD WAS EVIDENT IN HIS slumped shoulders and dragging feet. He collided with Maggie as she was hanging up her jacket.

"Watch it!" he spat.

Maggie turned to see who had bumped into her, and when she saw Dylan's fiery grimace, she backed away and fled into the classroom. Normally she would have confronted the culprit, but she could tell by Dylan's eyes that addressing the issue would only lead to more trouble.

Dylan walked into classroom and sat down at his desk. The other students were gathering at the meeting corner, but Dylan was unaware of them. He glanced at the picture on the wall, and then quickly looked away. He noticed a Ziploc bag full of coins on a shelf beside Mr. Peters's desk. He was on it in a flash.

"Why do you have this?" Dylan asked, holding up the bag of money for Mr. Peters to see.

Mr. Peters looked at Dylan vacantly. "Oh, hi, Dylan. How are you? What was that?"

"What's this money for?"

"I use it in math."

"Do you keep it here all the time?" Dylan responded quickly.

"Uh, yeah. Why?" Mr. Peters turned back to his desk and continued shuffling papers.

"Boy, in my old school, you couldn't leave money lying around. It would disappear in a second. Kids were always stealing stuff. Once, I left a comic book on my desk and then went to the bathroom. When I got back, it was gone. I clobbered Toby. He was always taking my things."

Mr. Peters stopped what he was doing and watched Dylan. The sudden conversation surprised him.

"That doesn't sound like a very safe place," said Mr. Peters.

"Oh, you got that right. There was stealing and fighting, and there were only six kids in my class."

"Oh, by the way, Dylan, I have a question for you. How do you spell your last name?"

Dylan put his hands in his pockets and lowered his head. "It starts with c-h," he mumbled.

"Yes, I know that, but how do you spell the rest of it?"

Dylan shrugged his shoulders.

Mr. Peters raised his eyebrows. "You don't know?"

"I can't remember. I always get it wrong."

"Really? Okay. Well, don't worry about it. We'll make sure you learn it." Mr. Peters smiled and stepped toward the students waiting at the meeting corner. "Come on, Dylan."

Dylan tossed the money into the air, caught it behind his back, and dropped it heavily on the shelf. Then he walked to the edge of the group and crouched down on one knee. He studied the carpet and started collecting little pebbles into a pile. Mr. Peters talked while Dylan gathered rocks. He started explaining the writing assignment that they were going to be doing for the afternoon and then drew a large circle on the board with lines extending outward. Dylan looked up briefly and thought it was a drawing of the sun.

"Let's do one example together," Dylan heard Mr. Peters say. "Who is our character? It could be a person, an animal, whatever you want it to be."

Brenda's hand pointed to the ceiling immediately, and she shouted out, "A cricket!"

Mr. Peters turned to the board and wrote *Cricket* in the circle.

"Okay. Tell me about the cricket. What is he or she like?"

Mr. Peters proceeded to write down the students' responses on the board. Dylan looked up at the board and saw the words—*green, small, hops, fast, jumpy.*

Mr. Peters turned to the class and said, "Okay, we know what he looks like and some of his actions, but I want more depth. I want to know more about his personality. If I were to describe Ted, I might say he's creative, funny, intelligent, sensitive, friendly, etc."

Ted smiled shyly as Mr. Peters described him.

"Crickets are very important to the Chinese, you know," Dylan interrupted. "They are a sign of good luck."

Mr. Peters was startled by Dylan's intelligent response.

"How do you know that, Dylan?"

Dylan shrugged his shoulders. "I just do."

"Well, thank-you for that, Dylan. Please raise your hand next time."

Dylan lowered his head.

"I feed crickets to my pet sssnake," hissed Jake. He turned his head and smiled at Dylan. "That just shows how lucky they are."

A small group of boys giggled.

Dylan clenched his fists. "No," he sneered. "That just shows...how STUPID you are!"

A hush fell over the room. Everyone was shocked by Dylan's response to the bigger boy. Jake opened his mouth to say something, but he stumbled over his thoughts and stared at the ground, red faced and steaming.

Mr. Peters spoke. "Okay boys, that's enough now." The silence in the room was palpable. "Now, think about Dylan's comment."

"About Jake being stupid?" Ted blurted. Peals of laughter broke out.

"Now, now, that's not nice, Ted." Mr. Peters retorted firmly. "I don't want to hear any more comments like that." Mr. Peters paused and scanned the faces. "Dylan said they're a sign of good luck. How can we apply what he said to this particular cricket we're writing about?"

Janna raised her hand, and when Mr. Peters nodded at her, she said, "He's proud. He is loved and respected by the Chinese, so he's proud."

While the character analysis continued, Dylan made shapes with the pebbles he had gathered.

"What are you doing?"

Dylan looked up at the sound of his teacher's voice. Mr. Peters did not hide his annoyance. Dylan noticed that everyone was gone, which made him wonder how much time had passed. He stood up and glanced around the room. Most of the students were in their desks.

"Where are you supposed to be right now?"

"In my desk?" Dylan answered sheepishly.

"Do you know what you're supposed to be doing, Dylan?" Mr. Peters's voice was firm, and deeper than usual.

"Uh, no."

"Please pay attention to what's going on. I shouldn't have to repeat my instructions." Mr. Peters sighed. "Go back to your seat."

Mr. Peters stepped away and asked Ted to explain the assignment to Dylan. Ted tiptoed over to his new classmate and tapped him on the shoulder. Dylan spun around, grabbed Ted's fingers, and bent them backward. Ted exhaled a feeble yelp and stepped back. The color drained from Ted's face at the sight of Dylan's burning eyes.

"Oh. Hi," Dylan said quickly, embarrassed by his reaction. He turned around and lowered himself back in his chair.

Dylan felt his teacher's eyes on him, but he avoided eye contact. He turned in his seat, and Ted sat down beside him and quickly explained the assignment. Then he noticed the outline of Dylan's medallion through his shirt.

"When can you finish your story?" he asked.

Dylan stared directly into his eyes. "Story?" he said angrily.

Ted's head snapped back at the suddenness of Dylan's response. He paused for a moment before he spoke again. "When can you tell me more about your life in Duffle?"

Dylan turned his head away from Ted. "Whenever."

"Can you tell me about it today? After school?" Ted looked up and noticed Mr. Peters approaching. "Meet me under the computer table after school," he said quickly. Ted rose and pulled his wet pants away from his bum. He smiled at Mr. Peters as he passed by.

"Do you understand what you're supposed to do?" Mr. Peters asked quietly.

"Yeah, but I can't write," Dylan responded flatly.

Mr. Peters brainstormed some ideas with Dylan, and when he seemed satisfied that Dylan could do it on his own, he stood up. "Please listen next time."

Dylan winced at the minor scolding and turned his head toward the window. Out of the corner of his eye, he saw something move. A fly bounced off the glass of the mysterious photograph. His gaze moved along the wall toward the picture and rested upon a red thumbtack. He knew the silhouette was there, but he resisted looking. Finally, he could not endure any longer. He stared at the photograph. The silhouette was clearer than it had been earlier in the day, revealing strands of hair that protruded from the head of the creature.

His heart stopped and then beat at light speed when he noticed a hand waving at him, beckoning him to follow. Dylan was drawn to the figure. Something pulled at him. He was losing his will to resist and was about to stand when a student passed between him and the poster. He quickly looked away and put his head down on his desk.

"Are you okay, Dylan?" Mr. Peters asked on his way to help a student beside him.

Dylan nodded and quickly pulled out a pencil and notebook. "I can't write," he said to himself. "I'm too stupid." He reached into his desk and pulled out *The Hobbit*. "Maybe this will help."

A short time later, Dylan looked up and saw Sam at Mr. Peters's desk. He was talking about something he had done on the weekend.

Dylan's ears perked up when he heard, "Where's my samurai warrior?"

Dylan watched Mr. Peters shuffle papers around on his desk. He opened all of his drawers and looked under his chair. Then he searched the shelf beside his desk.

"I don't know, Sam. I must have misplaced him. He'll turn up. Don't worry." Mr. Peters smiled and said, "Perhaps he ventured off to do battle. He is a warrior after all."

Sam smiled and walked away. Dylan reached down and touched the outside of his pocket. He could feel the outline of the samurai through his jeans.

Mr. Peters got up from his desk and walked around the classroom. He crouched down beside several students and talked to them about their work. When he walked by Dylan's desk, Dylan put his hands over his work and blushed.

"How are you doing, Dylan? Let me see what you've done. I want to know what kind of a student you are."

Dylan moved his hands away.

"What is this? You're just copying from *The Hobbit*."

"Have you read this book?" Dylan asked quickly. "It's a very good book."

"It's a great book, Dylan, but that's not what I asked you to do." Mr. Peters's spoke sharply.

Dylan's head drooped, and he spoke into his shirt. "I can't write," he said sadly, "and it's too loud. I'm not used to so much noise."

"It's okay, Dylan. I understand. This school is very different from what you're used to. It's going to take time for you to adjust." Mr. Peters patted Dylan's shoulder and walked away.

Dylan continued copying *The Hobbit*.

A few minutes later, Mr. Peters returned.

"I like to keep track of my students' birthdays, so I can embarrass them by singing 'Happy Birthday.' When is your birthday, Dylan?"

Dylan looked down at his desk. "I can't remember."

"You don't know when your birthday is? Have you never had a birthday party?"

"No," he responded sadly.

"Have you ever had a cake or received presents?"

"Yeah...sometimes, but I don't know when."

"Is it in summer or winter?"

"Winter, I think. I remember playing outside in the snow with a toy truck. It was cool. Is it Friday?"

"Uh, no," said Mr. Peters, surprised by the sudden change in the conversation. "No, it's Wednesday. Why?"

"Just askin'." Dylan smiled and looked down at his book.

The bell rang and everyone slammed their books closed and sped out of the room.

Ted leapt over to Dylan's desk. "Don't forget to meet me in the library."

Dylan shuffled to the door, and he turned at the sound of Mr. Peters's voice. "See you tomorrow. Have a good night."

"Bye," Dylan responded, and he stepped into the hall.

6
I'll Cut You Up

DYLAN GRABBED HIS COAT AND HURRIED into the library. He slid under the computer table, out of breath. Ted was already there. He had made a cushion out of his jacket for the two of them to sit on.

"I can't stay long," Ted stated. "I have piano lessons after school."

"You're lucky."

"Why do you say that? I hate playing the piano."

"I don't get to do things like that."

"How come?"

"I don't know. I move around a lot. I was in soccer once, but I got kicked out. The coach didn't like me."

"I would trade my piano lessons, art lessons, and hockey for a week in Duffle. It's such a cool place."

"It used to be cool…before Nero took over. He's evil." Dylan stared out into the library.

Ted waited in silence for a moment. "What happened after you passed out?"

Dylan began slowly. "The transfer of power is hard on the human body…"

● ● ●

I PASSED OUT FROM THE PAIN. WHILE I slept, I had strange but wonderful dreams. I saw things in the forest I had never seen before. It was unlike any dream I'd ever had. I travelled through passageways that led into fairy tales.

I communicated with the earth as my father had said I would. I can't explain it. You have to experience it to understand it. I learned about the history of our land and my people. I learned about our connection to the earth. I learned…that the earth is alive. It's a living organism.

When I awoke, it was dark. I lifted my head and saw that the light coming from the center of the tree had dimmed to the brightness of a night-light. My father was gone. With each heartbeat, I felt a sharp, throbbing pain in my skull. I couldn't move. I was still for a long time, thinking about what had taken place. The whole conversation with my father seemed distant. My dreams were clearer than the real world. I was overcome by exhaustion, and I fell asleep again.

I awoke again to the chirping of a squirrel. He stood just above my foot on a branch above the nest and was turning an acorn in his paws. He would spin it, take a bite, look at me, and then repeat the whole procedure. He did this over and over. I lay there for a minute trying to get my bearings. I didn't know what was real anymore.

The air was cool, and I shivered as I stood up. I reached for the sky and yawned. My hand brushed against a branch, and the dew rolled down my arm and into my sleeve.

The squirrel dropped the acorn onto the platform where I had slept. I picked it up and looked into his tiny eyes. "Thank-you, but I don't eat acorns."

My stomach grumbled as the squirrel dropped another acorn into the nest and watched my reaction. Again, I picked it up. I smiled at him. I couldn't tell if it was the same squirrel as the one who had led me to the Gnarled Oak, but I thought that it probably was. As I leaned toward him with the acorn in my hand, he froze and watched my every move, but he didn't run. The squirrel was completely still when I gently placed the acorn between his paws. He spun the acorn around, took a bite, and dropped it.

I got the feeling he was trying to tell me something. I repeated my actions and so did he. This went on for several minutes. I figured he was telling me to taste it—just like a mother will do when she's trying to coax a baby to eat.

I took a small bite. The flavor was almond, and the texture was crunchy but chewable. This was no ordinary acorn. I took second bite. The squirrel jumped to another branch and dropped another acorn. I reached for it and sat down to eat. Suddenly, the squirrel was leaping from branch to branch, dropping acorns and chattering away.

After my third handful, I started getting a little sick of them. The hunger pang in my stomach had disappeared, but I didn't feel fully satisfied by the light snack. The squirrel noticed that I had stopped eating, and he hopped down and sat across from me.

"Thank-you for sharing your breakfast with me, but it's not quite enough. Your acorns are better than I thought they would be, but I need something a little more filling."

I felt a little silly talking to the squirrel, but he appeared to be listening. He approached me slowly, and I reached out to pet him. He backed off when I moved my hand. A minute later, he approached me again. I could see that he was tentative, but he slowly closed the gap between us. I reached for him again. Slowly, he turned, as if showing me his tail, but he wouldn't let me touch him.

"What shall I call you, little fella?" I didn't feel quite as silly talking to him anymore because he really seemed to be paying attention. "What's your name?"

He hopped away from my hand and spun around to look at me. He was eating an acorn as he watched me.

"Acorn! How about that? That's a good name for you. Acorn. Come here, Acorn."

Suddenly, he leapt up onto a branch and chirped at me. I watched him fly from tree to tree, getting lower and lower to the earth. Then he was on the ground looking up at me. Without hesitation, I felt myself leap for a branch on another tree. I barely got my grip on that bough and then was flying through the air, heading for another limb. I hung from this branch and rested my feet on a lower one. Before I could catch my breath, I sailed through the air again, swinging from branch to branch. Finally, I leapt for a limb too close to the ground. As I swung, my toes hit the earth, and I fell face first into the cold dirt.

I cried out in pain just before the wind was knocked out of me and I could no longer make a sound. I rolled around on the ground for a few minutes, writhing in pain, uncertain of what hurt most. I grabbed for my toes, which felt broken, and then I rubbed my ribs and tried to ease the sharp pain. I felt my knees burn, so I reached down with one hand to soothe them. Then I grabbed my head, and when I pulled my finger away, I spotted a dot of blood on it.

Acorn's shrill chirping sounded like laughter. I suppose I did look kind of funny, rolling around on the ground trying to suck in air, reaching for different parts of my body. When I could breath again, I rolled onto my back and stared up through the trees at the blue sky.

Slowly, I pushed myself up onto my elbows, dragged myself backward, and leaned up against a tree. My pants were torn and I could see dirt, pine needles, and leaves stuck to my bloodstained knees. I lifted up my shirt—my chest was scraped but the skin wasn't broken. My hands didn't have a mark on them. I must have fallen so fast that I didn't have time to break my fall with them. I tasted blood in my mouth, and when I touched my lip, I discovered it was cut. I felt a warm trickle on my forehead. It was also bleeding.

Acorn hopped over to me. He was now silent and appeared sympathetic, if that's possible. I looked at him and started to laugh when I thought about what he was seeing. It must have been quite the sight.

"I bet you've never seen anything like that before," I giggled. "What was I doing? I can't believe I did that. It was kind of fun though."

I looked up and tried to map out the path I had taken through the trees. To my surprise, the ridge of bark around the Gnarled Oak was gone. I stood and approached the tree. As I circled it, I tripped over a root and stumbled. There was no sign of the place I had slept the previous night.

I sat down and thought about where I had been the day before. Had it all been a dream? No. I could remember everything so clearly.

Acorn chattered and began running through the trees, so I got up to follow him. He led me to the pond, and I stripped down and dove in. The cold water felt good on my body. I swam until I heard a scream come from the shore—Acorn. The noise he was making was so loud and intense that it startled me. I watched him jump frantically from tree to tree. He was trying to tell me something.

I swam to shore as fast as I could, gathered my clothes, and followed him through the underbrush to a very dense part of the forest. He ran into a hole under the roots of an uprooted tree, and I squeezed through the narrow opening after him.

When my eyes adjusted to the light, I could see that we were in a very large cave. The walls were a tangle of dirt and roots. Water seeped down the walls, but the ground was surprisingly dry. I noticed a small beam of light shining through a spot on the ceiling of the shelter. I had to watch my step, for the ground was uneven and there were rocks and roots blocking my path. My muscles tensed as I peered through the opening. Dozens of trogs flew overhead in pack formation.

We remained in the cavern for what seemed like hours. I didn't want to leave until Acorn felt it was safe. I knew at this point that Acorn was going to be important to me. I wondered if this was part of Aarial.

I explored the cave while waiting for a sign from my new friend. Passageways extended in several directions from the main cavern. I followed a few of them but didn't allow myself to get too far away from the main entrance. Each room was well lit by small holes in the ceiling. I walked along the corridors and noticed that just as each tunnel darkened, a light in the distance appeared. I didn't know where the passageways led. Was I going deeper into the earth, or was I following trails just below the surface of the ground? I didn't go far enough to find out.

At the sound of Acorn's chirping, I made my way back to the entrance. He let me know it was safe to leave, and I followed him out of the opening into the light. It felt good to breathe the fresh air. I didn't realize how damp and musty the air in the cave was until I was out.

It was a warm day, so all of the dew had evaporated. I heard birds singing, and I felt the warm wind dry the moisture on my skin. After I had stretched and sucked in as much air as I could, I turned to look back at the cave entrance, but it was gone. It had become a tangled mess of roots and soil. I looked back at Acorn, who had been watching me. I rolled my eyes and sighed as he started shouting at me again.

By now, I was starving. I didn't know where we were going, and I didn't care. All I could think of was my stomach. I started to feel weak, and I didn't know if I could go any further when I spotted a patch of strawberry bushes. Immediately, I started gathering berries and popping them into my mouth. I ate voraciously until my hunger disappeared.

Acorn then led me into a dense part of the forest, and I sat down at the base of a tree. An intense feeling of sadness came over me. I was getting tired of our travels—I desperately wanted a place to stop and rest for a while. I started to think of my family and the home I had left. I knew I couldn't go back to them yet, for I would attract Nero, who was probably looking for me already.

I dozed off into a fitful, dream-filled sleep. I remember dreaming of running through the grass over a treeless landscape with trogs in close pursuit. I tripped over a stone and fell to the ground. Lying on my back, I watched the gathering trogs, hoping they hadn't seen my resting place. I noticed them circling above me when Acorn bounced off my chest, awakening me.

He led me to an old tree that appeared to have been struck by lightning. It was charred and broken, and the top was decaying on the ground. Acorn climbed the stump and I followed. Climbing it was difficult because there were no branches to grab onto, and it was so huge that I had trouble wrapping my arms around it. I inched my way up, and as I pulled myself to the top, a silver blade blinded me for a moment. The knife's tip was embedded into the wood, and multi-colored jewels in the handle sparkled in the sun's light.

I climbed into the hollow at the top of the tree and pulled the knife out of its bark sheath. My new friend sat silently on the edge of the tree, watching my excitement. A shockwave went up my arm when I wrapped my fingers around the handle. I felt powerful. With one swing, I sliced off a piece of bark with very little effort. I stood at the top of the tree, swinging the knife around my head, fending off imaginary villains.

I was about to climb down when I noticed something else sticking out of the decaying pulp. I brushed away the wood chips and uncovered a leather pouch. I couldn't tie it around my waist because the bindings were too short, so I tied it to my ankle and slid the knife into the sheath. Then I scurried down the tree, confident that nothing could harm me with my weapon.

For the rest of the day, I leapt through the forest attacking innocent trees, cutting off their branches. I stabbed and jabbed at invisible creatures until the brightness of day began to wane. The sun passing behind Mount Niko worried me. I was hungry again, but I was more concerned about where I was going to sleep than what I was going to eat. The forest can get very cold, and I was worried about the trogs finding me in the night.

Acorn had disappeared. I hadn't seen him for hours. "Just when I need your help, you disappear," I complained. "What kind of friend are you?"

I wandered through the forest for a while, looking for a place to sleep. I found a spot within a cluster of trees where the ground was soft and hidden from view. As I lay down on my temporary bed, I heard a twig snap.

"Who's there?" I shrieked.

I was on my knees, peering out of the trees, when I heard another *snap*. My heart pounded against my rib cage. Slowly, I reached down to my ankle for my knife. The power of the knife electrified my body again. My confidence rose as my fear ebbed. I crawled out of my hiding spot with my knife in hand and there—standing right in front of me—was Acorn.

"Thank goodness," I croaked.

Then, *crack!* I heard another branch snap.

We both froze. I leaned into the dreary, dense forest, all senses alert. A hollow *thud* made me spin around, and I leapt up with my knife a-blazin'.

"Who's there?" I hollered in a powerful voice I didn't recognize. "I'll cut you up! Identify yourself, or prepare to die."

Roaring laughter filled the air and was quickly muffled by a rough layer of burlap, which was being pulled over my face. A sack restrained my limbs, and I was flipped upside down. The next thing I knew, I was folded in half, bouncing up and down over my captor's shoulder. I heard the creature's booming voice echo in the forest.

"I'll cut you up," he mocked. "I'll cut you up."

• • •

Bang!
The two boys jumped and stared up at the underside of the tabletop.

"What are you guys doing under there? It's 4:30." A bloated, red face peered under the table. "You should have been home an hour ago."

Ted spoke quickly. "Sorry, Mr. Grant. I didn't know it was so late. My mom is going to kill me. Bye." He quickly gathered his things and disappeared in a flash.

Dylan remained under the table, afraid to move.

"Come on, kid." Mr. Grant paused for a moment, waiting for a response. He peered under the table. "Are you okay?"

"Yeah."

"Well, get outta here! I have work to do."

Dylan gathered his bag and jacket and crawled out from under the table without making eye contact. He put his head down, stepped over a vacuum cleaner, and sped out of the school.

7
Too Many Questions

"MORNING, MR. GRANT."

"Hi, Mr. Peters. How are you?"

"Pretty good. How 'bout you?"

"Fine. Oh, I met your new student yesterday," Mr. Grant called out as Mr. Peters walked away. He looks like he's been through the ringer."

Mr. Peters stopped and turned to face him. "Yeah, he's had a rough life."

"I had to kick him out of the school at about 4:30 yesterday afternoon."

"Really? What was he doing here that late?"

"He and another kid were hiding under a table in the library." Mr. Grant twirled his moustache and looked up at the ceiling. "Who was that other kid?" he said to himself, just loud enough for Mr. Peters to hear. "Uh…Sam," he said. "No, that other kid that looks like Sam."

"Ted?" asked Mr. Peters.

"Yeah, that's him. Ted and…"

"Dylan."

"Yeah, Ted and Dylan."

"What were they doing?" Mr. Peters inquired as he walked toward the caretaker.

"Oh, I don't know…talking. Who knows? I don't think they were doing anything wrong, but I let them know that I wasn't pleased. They looked pretty scared when I chased them out. I don't think they'll do it again."

"We have to give this kid a break, Mr. Grant. This is his first experience in a regular classroom. He's spent his entire life in special programs—both in and out of school. We need to make him feel welcome and wanted."

"That's good to know, Mr. Peters. Let me know if there's anything I can do."

"Thanks, Mr. Grant. I think I'm going to need all the help I can get."

Mr. Peters's footsteps echoed eerily off the walls as he proceeded down the darkened hallway. At the door to his classroom, he fumbled with his keys and dropped his briefcase. A memory of a panting boy sprinting up the basement stairs in a panic flashed before him. The silence and darkness sent a shiver up his spine. "Come on, come on, come on," he repeated frantically as he tried one key then another. Turning the third key, he fell into the room and flicked on the lights. A gasp of relief accompanied the buzz of the fluorescent lights.

The first thing he noticed upon entering the room was Dylan's file on the edge of his desk. Mr. Peters draped his jacket over his chair, set his briefcase on the floor, and then walked across the hall to the dimly lit library. The teacher stood a short distance from the boys' hiding spot. When his eyes adjusted to the dark, he spotted a small object. He could not tell what it was until it was in his hands. He studied it curiously and wondered how Sam's samurai had ended up beneath the computer table.

"How do I deal with this?" he whispered to himself. "I hope this isn't a sign of things to come."

Back in the classroom, he read through Dylan's file. Page after page, the same words were repeated over and over—*disruptive, dishonest, stealing, fighting, manipulative, lying.* He had been moved so many times from one home to another that Mr. Peters wondered how he had any good qualities at all. He gazed at the black-and-white photograph of Dylan on the report. *From this picture, you would think he was a normal kid,* Mr. Peters thought. *Behind that face is one messed up little boy.*

Knock, knock!

Mr. Peters jumped and looked over at Ms. Steinwood, who was standing at the door. "Whoa! You scared me."

"Sorry. You sleep here last night?"

"No, but it sure seems like it sometimes," he said with a yawn.

"Is that the same file you were reading yesterday?"

Mr. Peters nodded. "This young man has never had a home. He's never been loved by anyone. He doesn't stand a chance in this world."

"Perhaps you're being a little overly dramatic," she stated. "Do you really think you can predict his future?"

Mr. Peters smiled. "You're right. I shouldn't make such grand statements. Many functioning adults have had terrible childhoods."

"The question is, does he stand a chance in your classroom?" asked Ms. Steinwood bluntly.

"I don't know. He hasn't displayed any of the behaviors they describe in these reports."

"Not yet."

"Yeah, he's only been here one day. Hopefully we can build on the positives instead of focusing on the negatives. Enough about him. How are you, Ms. Steinwood?"

"Good…things are good. Our wedding plans are coming along. I'm not feeling as overwhelmed as I was two weeks ago. Everything seems to be falling into place."

"That's good."

"Sorry to change the subject, but how is our little friend Albert?" asked Ms. Steinwood.

"He's a nut. God, that kid makes me laugh. Some days I want to strangle him, and other days, I just have to laugh. You know about his farting problem, right?"

Ms Steinwood nodded and laughed.

"He has got the worst gas. The students spread like ripples from a pebble in a pond when he lets one rip. Well, the other day I had had enough and decided to talk to him privately about his little vapor problem. I looked at him directly and said, 'You have a gas problem.' His expression froze, and he stared into my eyes. 'That's okay. Everyone has gas. I would like you to leave the room when you feel one coming on. Do you understand?'

"The next day, I saw Albert teetering back and forth from one foot to the other. He looked at me and smiled and then tore out of the classroom. I remember thinking how strange this was, since, as you know, he usually moves like a sloth. Then I remembered our fart conversation. That's the latest on Albert."

A voice came over the intercom. "Mr. Peters, you have a call on line two. Mr. Peters, line two."

Mr. Peters stood up and walked toward the door. "I wish they'd fix my classroom phone."

Ms. Steinwood nodded in agreement.

"I get more exercise answering the phone than I do at the gym."

"It never ends, does it, Mr. Peters?" Then in a singsong voice, she said, "'Mr. Peters, my child has a toothache. If he's in too much pain, could you make sure he lies down? My child has a sore toe. Could you carry him to my car? I want little Johnny to be a brain surgeon. Could you give him a little extra attention?'"

Mr. Peters laughed out loud and walked to the phone in the library.

"Mr. Peters here."

"Hi, Mr. Peters. This is Elaine Truss—Dylan's foster mother."

"Oh, hello."

"I have a huge favor…" She coughed into the phone. "I have a huge favor to ask you."

"Okay?"

"I have an appointment at noon, so I won't be home for Dylan at lunch. Can he eat at school today?"

"Uh…yeah…sure. He can eat with me in the classroom." Mr. Peters paused. "Just so you know, this can't be a regular occurrence unless something is arranged with the lunchroom staff."

"Yes, I know, Mr. Peters. It won't happen again. Thank-you."

As Mr. Peters walked back to his classroom, Miss Roland called out cheerily, "Good morning, Mr. Peters."

"Hi, Miss Roland. How are you?"

"Good, thanks. How are you?"

"Fine."

"I ran into Ted wrestling a coat in the hallway yesterday."

Mr. Peters smirked. "Yeah, that sounds like Ted."

"My students aren't allowed to roam the halls freely. It must be nice being in your classroom. Please try to keep them…"

Mr. Peters pretended not to hear her, and as he entered his classroom, he muttered, "Shut up, you old bag. Your students aren't allowed to breathe without…Oh! Dylan!" Mr. Peters froze at the sight of Dylan sitting at his desk. "You startled me!" The teacher walked toward him. "You're here early. What can I do for you?"

"Oh, nothing. I just didn't want to hang around on the playground. Sometimes I get into trouble when I hang out."

"That's the only way to make friends, Dylan. Please go outside until the bell rings. It'll only be ten minutes."

Dylan stood up and walked toward Mr. Peters, ignoring what he had just said.

"Did you know that snakes don't have eyelids?"

The teacher shook his head, which encouraged Dylan to continue.

"Some snakes only eat once or twice per year. Boa constrictors can live for twenty-five years and grow to be thirty feet." Dylan pointed at the wall. "That's like from here to that wall."

"Boy, you sure know a lot about snakes, Dylan. How do you know so much?"

"From books and TV. Did you know that snakes' jaws dislocate when they swallow their prey?"

"Wow! That's very interesting."

"Yup. That is interesting."

Dylan stopped talking and stared at a picture of a wolf on the wall.

"Dylan?" Mr. Peters paused. "Do you know anything about this?" Mr. Peters pulled the plastic warrior out of his pocket.

Dylan lowered his head. "What about it?"

"I found it in the library," Mr. Peters said calmly, "and I was wondering if you know how it got there. Mr. Grant said he found you in the library yesterday after school." He paused again and watched Dylan's face redden. "You're not in trouble, Dylan. I'm just curious as to how it got there."

"I didn't steal it."

"Oh, I know that. I wouldn't be holding it if you stole it. Do you know how it got into the library?"

"Yeah."

He stood still for a moment. Mr. Peters could tell that he was wrestling with himself over what to say.

"I put it in my pocket yesterday," he said slowly, then quickly added, "I wasn't stealing it. I put it in my pocket when all the other kids came into the classroom. I didn't want to put it back on your desk because I thought someone might see and accuse me of stealing. I was going to return it later. Kids always blame me. I wasn't stealing it. I have a million soldiers like that of my own. I don't need yours."

"Thank-you for being honest with me, Dylan. I really appreciate it. If you ever want to borrow anything from me, just let me know. I don't mind lending things out."

Dylan nodded.

"Now run along. Go outside and play for a few minutes."

Just as Dylan started walking toward the door, the bell rang. Dylan looked back at Mr. Peters and smiled.

Mr. Peters rolled his eyes. "Go hang your jacket up."

Dylan walked into the hall, and just as he was about to hang up his coat, Janna placed her jacket over the hook he was reaching for.

"Excuse me!" he spat angrily, putting his hands on his hips. His lower jaw protruded, and his furrowing brow resembled that of a wild animal. Janna leaned away from his glare.

"Excuse me, but that's my hook."

Janna swallowed and responded, "Nobody has a hook. We use different hooks all the time."

He picked up her jacket, threw it to the ground, and hung up his coat. Janna glanced at her jacket then snorted like a wild bull and threw his coat to the ground. The hallway was now silent, except for the clicking of heels. Just as Dylan was about to push her, the principal stepped between the two students. Dylan backed off immediately and lowered his head.

"Come with me, young man," commanded Mrs. Evans, and she strode away from the scene.

Dylan scowled at Janna, picked up his coat, and followed the principal.

Tears welled up in Janna's eyes, and she ran into the washroom followed by three of her friends. A rush of students flowed into the classroom and told Mr. Peters what had happened. The teacher asked his students to read quietly when Janna returned. He walked over to her desk.

"It's not your fault, Janna," Mr. Peters said soothingly. "Dylan has a temper."

Janna sobbed, "Yeah, but why did he get so mad about something so stupid? I don't get it."

"I'm not sure, Janna. We'll try to find out. In the meantime, try to forget about it. It won't happen again."

A short time later, while the students were working on math problems, Mrs. Evans brought Dylan back to class. An immediate silence filled the room as he entered. All eyes were on him, and he knew it. He stared at the ground as he moved toward his seat. Mr. Peters stood up and told the student he was helping to go on to the next question.

"I'll be back in a minute," he whispered.

Mr. Peters followed the principal into the hallway. The students heard their voices but could not make out what they were saying. Dylan sensed his classmates' curiosity. He pulled out his book and was immediately oblivious to the chattering and giggling that went on around him.

Dylan kept to himself for the rest of the morning. He ignored the other students' glances but found it difficult to concentrate with all the talking going on. When the bell rang, Dylan jumped up to leave the classroom. He stopped at the sound of Mr. Peters's voice.

"We're going to eat in the classroom today."

"Oh, yeah. I forgot," Dylan answered.

Dylan returned to the classroom with his lunch. He sat down at his desk and carefully unwrapped a sandwich while Mr. Peters shuffled papers on his desk. A few minutes later, Mr. Peters came over and sat across from Dylan with his lunch. Dylan grinned at the sight of his teacher crammed into the little desk.

"What's for lunch?" asked Mr. Peters.

"Tuna…celery…uh…cookies…and an apple."

"That's a pretty healthy lunch."

"Yup," Dylan responded with his mouth full of food. "I am a good eater."

"What's your favorite kind of food?" asked the teacher.

"Uh…pizza."

"So, how do you like our school?"

"It's okay."

"Do you like Calgary, Dylan?"

"Yeah, but it's too big."

"Calgary and Edmonton are not that different in size." Mr. Peters bit into his apple. "Why did you come to Calgary?"

"I came with my grandma."

"I didn't know you lived with your grandma, Dylan."

"Well, I just call her that. She's not my real grandma." Dylan rubbed his eyes and spoke into his hands. "She's a *foster* mom."

"How long have you lived with her, Dylan?"

"A long time. Maybe two years."

"That's nice."

"No, it's not," Dylan responded without hesitation.

"I don't want to pry too deeply, but why do you say that?"

"She's mean. She follows me everywhere. And she yells all the time. I hate living with her."

"There must be some good things about her," said Mr. Peters.

"Well, I don't know any. You ask a lot of questions."

"Sorry, Dylan. I'm just trying to get to know you."

They sat in uncomfortable silence for a few minutes. The sound of the students getting out of the lunchroom program echoed in the hall. Ted peered into the classroom as he dropped his lunch bag into the basket at the front of the room.

"Hi," he said from the doorway. He entered the room and hesitated at the first desk he reached. "Can I stay in?"

"No!" Mr. Peters hollered, pretending to be angry. "What is it with you guys always wanting to stay in? Go get some fresh air."

Ted growled like a tiger and displayed his teeth. He dropped to the ground and crawled toward the door. Dylan chuckled.

"Hey, Ted!" called Mr. Peters.

Ted stood up on his hind legs and turned. "Yeah?" he snarled. Then he licked his paw and pretended to clean behind his ears.

"Perhaps you *can* stay in. Would you like to keep Dylan company? I have a few phone calls to make. Is that okay with you, Dylan?"

Dylan smiled at Ted. "Sure."

Mr. Peters looked from Dylan to Ted and back at Dylan again. They were beaming.

"The two of you are conspiring," Mr. Peters said. "What's going on?"

"Nothing, Sir." Ted raced over to the other side of the room. "Can we sit under your desk, Mr. P.?"

"The two of you won't fit under there."

"Sure we will."

Ted pulled Mr. Peters's chair out of the way and crawled under the desk.

"See. There's loads of room, Mr. Peters."

"What are you going to do under there, Ted?"

"Uh…we're going…" He looked around the room. "We're going to play cards. Grab a deck, Dylan."

Dylan walked over to the shelf Ted had pointed to and picked up the cards. He glanced at his teacher and quickly joined Ted under the desk.

"No gambling, boys!" barked Mr. Peters as he strode away, shaking his head. "They have the whole room to themselves and they choose to squeeze under my desk."

Mr. Peters heard Ted explaining the rules of crazy eights as he left the room.

Ted peered out from under the desk. "Okay, the coast is clear," he whispered. "Who kidnapped you? How did you get out of the sack?"

Dylan closed his eyes and breathed in.

Collin Paulson

8
The Earth is an Artist

IREACHED FOR MY KNIFE AND TRIED to cut my way out. I became frantic. My blade cut through the bag in several places, but the material wouldn't open up. I stopped fighting when I felt cold metal on my cheek. The sack was enclosed in a bag of steel chain mail. The air in the sack had a horrible stench to it, and the thought of previous cargo in the bag made me gag.

The material that separated me from the forest muffled the sounds of the outside world, but I could hear the beast that was carrying me. He grunted and panted as we bounced through the forest. I don't know for how long we travelled like this—I was in and out of consciousness.

When I awoke, I was facing a small fire and wrapped in animal fur. A pot hung above the coals. Shadows flickered in the dark. There was an aroma like I had never experienced. It made my mouth water. I assumed the scent was coming from the pot—some type of stew. I hoped it was not going to become Dylan-stew.

My eyes travelled around the room in front of me. The walls of the cave appeared to be solid rock. Shelves had been carved out of the rock, and I noticed pots and pans and fruits and vegetables stored on them. Hanging from a hook above a table was a rabbit and a large bird. Against another wall was a bed raised up off the ground on logs. I wasn't certain if this was real or if I was dreaming. Exhaustion overcame awareness, and I fell asleep again.

When I awoke the second time, I heard footsteps shuffling about the room. A huge shadow appeared on the far wall. I closed my eyes and listened. An overwhelming sense of doom came over me. I wondered if this was the end. As I lay there waiting for my life to be taken from me, I heard a rather pleasant-sounding, raspy voice. It had a familiar ring to it. It was not the voice of the person who had captured me. I opened my eyes and watched. The man paced back and forth, talking to himself. He had a cloak similar to my father's, but I knew it was not my father, for the person I was watching was thin and hunched. I heard him talking to himself.

"I'm getting too old for this. How am I to find the strength?" He sighed.

Then in a much more confident, powerful voice, he said, "Don't be a fool! You have the strength. It is he who needs the strength."

"But it takes so much out of me. I don't know if I have the ability… or the confidence."

"You have the experience, old man. The confidence will come. You can do this in your sleep. You felt this way last time."

"Yes, and look what happened to Macor."

I perked up at the sound of my father's name. The hooded man spun around.

"Finally. You rise." He moved toward me. "Welcome to Agora."

I did not move. I stared into the dark hood and could hear my heart pounding as the figure pulled the hood back.

"Ravelle!" I cried. I was on my feet and across the room instantly. "It feels like days since I've seen a familiar face."

The old man's hypnotic gaze took me in. The wrinkles around his face did not seem to match his haunting and intense gray eyes. I loosened my grip on him.

"Where am I? Why am I here? Who brought me?"

"Whoa. One question at a time." Ravelle smiled and led me to an odd-looking seat carved into the rock. He dragged over another chair as I sat down. "You are in Agora, beneath the earth's surface. Agora is an extension of the cave you were in yesterday. You are here to learn the powers of Aarial. Tiko, my apprentice, brought you here." Ravelle rubbed his chin. "Are you afraid?"

"I was…until I saw your face," Dylan answered.

"My face should only give you more reason for concern."

His eyes narrowed as he looked straight into my eyes. The seriousness of his expression made me look away.

"I'm going to cause you great distress. You are also going to experience great joy."

I did not know whether to laugh or cry. The sound of Ravelle's voice was comforting, but his words were unnerving.

"I knew from the day you were born that you possessed a quality unlike any of your forefathers. I saw in you the power, strength, and wisdom of Aarial—the original. He was a great man. You will also be great, if you are dedicated. The county of Milo and the entire world depends on you. Nero needs to be stopped. He has evil ambitions and will stop at nothing to get what he wants."

"I'm just a boy! I have no powers. How can I take on such responsibility?"

"You'd be surprised at the powers you possess deep within you." Ravelle's voice was clear and calm. "Yes, you are a boy. And yes, the responsibility is too much for you at this time, but you will learn. Don't be afraid. There will be plenty of time for that. Even if you didn't want the responsibility of Aarial, you'd have no choice. The stirrings would be too strong. I'm here to train you and guide you, but in the end, it is you who will determine the limitations of your abilities. You are the youngest ever to possess Aarial. In time, you will gain the confidence and wisdom to take on your task."

"My task?"

"Your mission is to defeat Nero and transfer power to the rightful heir—Queen Gaia."

"Defeat Nero? What are you talking about? Have you seen him?" I raged. "I am a boy, and he is a KING!" I leaned forward, resting my elbows upon my knees. "Not only am I to kill a heavily guarded king, but I'm to meet up with some queen and transfer a power I don't understand. Do you know how ridiculous this sounds? Who do you think I am?"

"There are things in this world you cannot understand. Give it time. Everything will become clear."

Suddenly, I felt very alone. I pictured my mother and was suddenly overcome with despair.

"I miss my home, Ravelle."

"Your home will never be the same, Dylan. Agora is your home now and will remain so for an indefinite period of time—at least until your training is complete."

Ravelle paused and watched tears well up in my eyes.

"Everything is different. The peaceful life you once knew no longer exists. There has been a change in our world, and it's up to you to restore harmony. I see the fear and sadness in your eyes, Dylan. You will not do this alone. Many allies will assist you. Some will surprise you with their support. You need to be extremely cautious, but at the same time, trust your instincts—you will know who is an ally and who is a foe. The earth is with Aarial, and she will be your greatest ally."

"I want to go home," I pleaded.

"You can't, my son. It's not safe. Nero will be looking for you."

"Please. I just want to see my village one more time."

Ravelle shook his head and scanned the ground. We shared the same pain. It was obvious that he also wanted to return to the comfort of the village he had known for so many years.

"We have to start training immediately," Ravelle said. "The more time we have, the better."

"Can I see my mother and sister one more time?" I saw the doubt in his eyes. "Please Ravelle! I need to see them! I'll go crazy if I can't let them know where I am and that I'm okay."

"Your mother knows, Dylan. She knows about Aarial and the transfer between you and your father."

"Please. I just want to say good-bye."

Ravelle understood my angst, but he was concerned about my safety. He sat in silence for a long time.

Finally, he said, "I don't think it's a good idea, but let me ponder it awhile."

"Okay. Thank-you, Ravelle."

"Before you can understand Aarial, you need to understand yourself, your heritage, and our world."

Ravelle stood and reached for my hand. Studying my palm, he said, "You have a greater understanding of Aarial than you think. The fluid that runs through your veins has a memory. Aarial is in your blood."

He motioned for me to follow him. We proceeded out of Agora and walked through a narrow passageway. Beams of light guided our walk, indicating that it was daytime. I had lost all sense of time since being captured.

"Where is Tiko?" I asked.

"He's taking care of some business for me. He's a very important part of your training. You will get to know and respect him. I have great ambitions for him. He possesses great determination, and he's very loyal."

The passageway led into a room that opened up into a great cathedral of rock formations. Ravelle called them stalactites and stalagmites. Light shone in from several holes in the ceiling and spotlighted the beautiful formations. The beams of light crisscrossed over each other and bounced off the walls. I was awestruck. I stood still and gazed up at the alluring spectacle. Water seeped down the walls and gathered in small pools. In the distance, I heard the sound of a babbling brook. I felt Ravelle's eyes upon me.

"Sometimes, I forget the beauty." Ravelle's voice echoed off the wall behind me. "I need new eyes to remind me of its splendor."

He stopped talking and surveyed the room. I watched the serious expression leave his face and all his troubles wash away as he took in the sights and the sounds.

"I remember my first visit to Stellar Hall. I was just as impressed then as you are now."

He led me to a creek within the hall and asked me to sit in a hollow that had been cut into the rock. The seat was very comfortable and seemed to conform to my body. The creek on my right emitted beautiful music, and the magnificent sights of the cave lay before me.

"There is nothing like the sound of water to let your mind wander— the sound of the pounding waves on a beach, the roar of a rushing river, or the babble of a quiet brook. Even the drip of a leaking roof causes one to turn inward. This is your first task—turn inward."

"What do you mean?"

"You'll understand soon enough," he said, and he walked away.

I rested my head upon the rock and closed my eyes. I could not remember a more comfortable place in my life. Then it started. My mind began to wander. I thought about my home, my family, and the stories I had been told as a young boy about my ancestors. I envisioned the entire county of Milo. I felt the connection between all of the people and the importance of every individual to the community—from the tiniest baby to the oldest woman. Everyone relied upon one another in some way.

The strange thing was that I didn't see it with my eyes. I was an outsider viewing it from above and from below. It was more than seeing; it was beyond sensing—my mind and the earth were one.

I saw the leaves taking in the sunlight and water. Ants marching in a line carried food toward their homes. A hawk swooped down and snatched a mouse in its claws. I travelled through the earth, passing rock, dirt, worms, clay, and water.

Suddenly, a story began to unfold. A large bearded man was running through a dark passageway. He looked frightened. I sensed that he felt trapped and was looking for an exit. I watched him trip over a root and stumble into a room of light. He was in Stellar Hall. He wandered around the room and gazed up and down. The initial panic vanished from his face. He was at ease. Finally, he sat down on the rocks. I recognized the spot he rested upon. It was the very same spot I was resting upon. He scooped a handful of water from the creek and drank. Then he poured it over his head and reclined.

As he rested, I could see that he felt great peace within himself and his environment. Suddenly, a light from the ceiling shone into his eyes. He appeared to be getting instructions from the light. I watched his expression change from one of curiosity and uncertainty to one of great understanding. A smile appeared on his face and the light disappeared. Again, he went to the river and drank. When he sat back down, I sensed a change in him. He was no longer the same person. The man sitting there did not have a beard. I watched his face change again and again. Each man sat in the same position with the same expression. With every new face, I could see each new body sink deeper and deeper into the rock. The rock was starting to change shape to suit the men. I don't know how many faces passed before my eyes, but I felt a connection with each one of them.

Finally, I saw my grandfather. He was much younger than I had ever seen him, but I was certain it was him. He didn't have wrinkles or gray hair, but he had the same massive head. I recognized his giant nose and jaw. He also didn't have the scar across his chin that I remember caressing as a youngster. Then I saw my father as a young man. He was broad and handsome.

My eyes shot open at the final image—it was *my* face! I hadn't noticed the light until that moment. It wasn't blinding; I didn't have to squint. I felt great comfort in it. Then the beam of light showered a message upon me. I don't know how the message was transmitted, but this is what I received: *The earth is an artist and you are her masterpiece. Respect your creator, and you will succeed.*

The light dimmed and then disappeared. I leaned over the creek and gulped the water greedily. An energy flowed into my body. Then I got up and started walking around Stellar Hall, thinking about what had just happened. I thought about the hidden power in the earth. I thought about my ancestors. And finally, I thought about my home and family. I now understood my importance and the need to carry on Aarial, but I couldn't help but feel a great sadness and sense of loss.

Nightfall was approaching, as revealed by the dimming beams of light coming through the ceiling. I walked toward the door and froze at the sight of Ravelle watching me. We didn't exchange words as we walked back toward Agora.

A wonderful scent met us in the passageway, and I felt my stomach grumble. The tunnel opened into Agora, and I saw the warm light of the fire and a man standing over a pot, stirring it. My pace slowed when he looked up, for I knew who it was.

"This is Tiko," Ravelle said with a smile.

I gave a quick hello, and Tiko grunted something. Ravelle and I sat down at the table that had been set with bowls, spoons, and cups. Tiko picked up the pot from the fire and walked over to us. He dipped a spoon into the pot, tasted the stew, mixed it again, and then plopped a spoonful into each of the three bowls. Tiko took another spoonful and tasted it again. As he walked back to the fire, I heard him growl, "I'll cut you up." He laughed and set the pot onto the fire.

"Don't mind him, Dylan," Ravelle reassured me. "His mind is a little foggy at times, but he's very loyal and quite bright in many ways. He knows the ways of the earth like no other."

Tiko smiled and repeated "I'll cut you up" quietly to himself when he came back to the table and sat down beside me. I watched him gulp down his food like a great hunting dog. The stew was very good, and all three of us ate in silence for a period of time. Tiko reached behind him and grabbed a basket filled with flat, round bread. He tore one piece in half and handed me the other half.

I looked at the man smiling at me. Stew dripped down his chin and several teeth were missing from his happy grin. I couldn't help but smile back. He reminded me of a big happy dog whose only goal in life is to please you. I thanked him for the bread and ripped it into pieces.

Ravelle dragged bread across his empty plate as he spoke. "We go to Duffle tonight. It's risky, but we'll go. Finish up your dinner and then we're off."

"Where's my knife, Ravelle?"

As I spoke, my knife appeared in Tiko's palm. It looked like a toy in his giant hand, and I understood why he had giggled at the thought of me harming him with such a tiny instrument.

The three of us sat down near the fire, and Tiko and Ravelle drew a rough map in the dirt. We discussed the plan for several minutes. The seriousness in their voices frightened me. I didn't understand. Finally, Tiko said, "Let's roll."

Tiko led the way down a new passageway while Ravelle brought up the rear. I was comforted by the thought of being in the middle. We travelled for what seemed like hours. We were moving at a great pace, and I had difficulty keeping up to Tiko. Ravelle told me that this was a good way to start my training. I had to be in shape. The tunnel was fairly flat at the beginning, and then we started a steep climb. I watched Tiko's torch get further and further away. Finally, his torch stopped moving, and then it was no longer visible. I continued to travel up the tunnel as fast as I could and bumped into him in the darkness.

A blue light shone upon his face, and when I looked to the source of the light, I saw the moon over Duffle. We were standing inside Mount Niko, looking out over the landscape through a jagged opening in the mountain. I saw smoke rising from the village and thought of my cozy home. I pictured my mother baking bread and my sister placing wood into the hearth.

My heart stopped at the realization that the smoke was not rising from the chimneys but from houses that appeared to be burned to the ground.

"I need to go see!"

"It's not safe, Dylan," Ravelle responded. "There may be spies watching."

"Please, Ravelle. I have to know what's happened to my people...to our people."

Ravelle and Tiko exchanged glances, and then we were off again. I had no trouble keeping up because we started going down. I don't remember anything about the downward trip. When the tunnel flattened out, we lay down on our bellies and slipped out into the cool, moonlit air. We got to the edge of my village very quickly. The devastation was heartbreaking. Cautiously, we walked down Main Street to find homes burned to the ground on either side. The coals were still warm, and I wondered if we could have done anything if we had arrived earlier. There was no sign of life.

When we reached the spot where my home had been, I stood on the street and stared. The stone fireplace stood like a monument above the rubble. My home was now a smoking pile of ash and burning embers. Tears rolled down my face as I sifted through the debris.

The light of the moon reflected off an object in the ashes. I reached down and picked up a gold chain. As I placed it on my chest, I looked up at the stars. It was the necklace my father had given my mother years before. She had always worn it with such pride and loved to look at it in the firelight. I examined it and wondered how the clasp had been broken.

● ● ●

BEEEEEEEEEEEP!

Ted stiffened at the sound of the bell. When he looked up at Dylan, he saw that a single tear had moistened his cheek.

9

Anger Comes Easy

THE CLAMOR OF STUDENTS ENTERING THE school reverberated in the hallway. Dylan wiped his face and jumped out from under the desk. Ted followed and slid Mr. Peters's chair back. Mr. Peters entered the room and greeted the two boys as they flew from their hideout.

Dylan was in his desk with his head down when Tony tapped him on the shoulder. Dylan spun around. "WHAT!"

"We're…we're meeting…we're meeting…we're meeting on the carpet," Tony stammered.

Dylan's outburst startled Mr. Peters, who turned to see what was going on. "Oh," Dylan said quickly, and he put his head back down. A few minutes later, Dylan stood up, walked over to the group, and took his usual seat at the back. Several students glanced up as he approached the meeting area. They exchanged glances, whispers, and giggles. Dylan felt their ridicule as he sat down heavily and bumped a student with his knees.

Wendy turned to see who had bumped into her, and he glared at her. "You got a staring problem?"

Wendy straightened up and turned back to Mr. Peters at the front of the group. Mr. Peters gave the class instructions for the afternoon while Dylan played with something in his hands.

"Put that away!" Mr. Peters said firmly.

Dylan jumped and then furrowed his brow. The class was given final instructions before being asked to move to their work areas.

"Come with me, please!" Mr. Peters demanded as he walked by Dylan.

The teacher sat down at the back of the room on the choir risers. Dylan shuffled over to him with his head down.

"Have a seat, Dylan. We have to talk."

Dylan lowered himself onto a step on the same level as the one Mr. Peters was sitting on. "What are these for?" Dylan asked, patting the plastic bench.

"These are risers. You stand on them during choir performances in the gym, so everyone can be seen. Now…you've been raising your voice a lot, for what appears to be no reason."

"When?"

"Many times. Just now, you yelled at Wendy when she looked at you."

"They bug me."

"Who bugs you, Dylan?"

"All of them."

"You think the whole class is bugging you?"

"I don't like people staring at me."

"Of course they stare. Your outbursts attract attention. They're not used to kids shouting out."

"Kids in my other schools used to shout all the time and no one cared."

"Well, we're not at your other school, Dylan. You're in a school where that's unacceptable. Please try to ignore the other students. You're only going to get yourself into trouble."

"Sometimes…I just get so angry." Dylan raised his head and looked at Mr. Peters. "I don't know why."

"The greatest remedy for anger is delay." Mr. Peters paused. "A roman philosopher once said that."

"The anger comes easy," Dylan responded. "It's the delay that's hard."

Mr. Peters smiled. "Try counting to ten."

"I've tried that. It doesn't work."

"How about a poem or a saying that you repeat to yourself?" Mr. Peters rotated his body and pointed to a quotation on a poster of a path winding through green, rolling meadows. "How about that?"

It's not the road ahead that wears you out,
it's the grain of sand in your shoe.

ARABIAN PROVERB

"Memorize that, or any quote, and repeat it over and over until you cool down. What do you think?"

Dylan shrugged. "Maybe."

"You have to make a real effort to stop shouting out in class, Dylan. That's the best way to stop all of the unwanted attention."

Dylan stared at his hands. "I'll try."

"One more thing, Dylan. I want you to sit at the front of the meeting area for a while. You're not paying attention, and I can't continue to repeat the instructions for you."

Dylan nodded.

"I know this school is very different from the other schools you've attended. I know that this is a big change for you, but you're going to have to make an effort to fit in." Mr. Peters paused. "You seem to like it here."

Dylan lifted his shoulders in indifference. "Yeah, I guess. I don't get yelled at all the time."

"Well then, prove that you belong."

Mr. Peters explained the assignment then looked around the room for a partner for Dylan. He noticed that Albert was alone.

"Albert!" Mr. Peters yelled across the room. "Come over here, please."

Albert stood up and waddled to the back of the classroom. His sloping shoulders and little potbelly that pushed his overalls away from the rest of his body made him look like a little old man. He was looking at the ground when he got to the back of the room.

"Albert, this is Dylan. You're going to be working with him on your animal research."

Albert lifted his shoulders and tilted his head to one side as if to say, "I don't care," which is something he often said.

"Where would you two like to work?" asked Mr. Peters. Neither one of them responded. "Gather your things, Albert, and you can work at Dylan's desk."

"But I vant to vork at my disk," Albert whined.

Dylan raised an eyebrow at the sound of Albert's accent.

"Well, why didn't you say that?"

"I don't know."

"Is that okay with you, Dylan?"

Dylan shrugged his shoulders.

The two boys walked away from Mr. Peters. Dylan grabbed his pencil box and a notebook from his desk. Out of the corner of his eye, he noticed the poster, but he forced himself to look away and proceeded toward Albert's desk. Albert was beside it, punching at imaginary enemies that appeared to be attacking him from all sides. Every so often he would do a karate kick and would almost land on his bum.

Dylan paused and watched Albert for a moment. He also saw Mr. Peters observing the whole scene. When Albert noticed his teacher glaring at him, he sat down and started going through his cluttered desk drawer. He pulled out a variety of curious objects and toys. All of a sudden, Albert closed his desk drawer with one hand while the other was still inside.

"Uhh! Ya got me," he cried out in mock pain.

Albert held the drawer shut while he tried to free his other hand.

"Help!" he shrieked in agony. "Dis is it. Dis is de end! I am going to be sucked into my disk and never return. Help!"

Dylan's nostrils flared, and he exhaled angrily through his nose. Then he slammed his hand against the drawer. Albert let out a yelp, slid his hand out, and stared up at Dylan in fright. Dylan leaned over his desk and stared into Albert's cowering eyes. Glancing over his shoulder, he saw Mr. Peters walking toward them, so he backed off and pulled up a chair beside Albert's desk. Albert slowly straightened up in his chair, afraid to look at Dylan. He opened his notebook and picked up his pencil.

"Remember, all you should be doing right now is brainstorming a number of animals that interest you!" Mr. Peters hollered over the buzz of the classroom. "You don't have to agree on one particular animal yet. Just come up with a list."

Mr. Peters leaned on Albert's desk and asked, "How are we doing?"

Dylan, who was still visibly annoyed at Albert, focused on Mr. Peters's hand. Albert studied his blank page nervously. Mr. Peters looked at Albert's empty page.

"What animals interest you?"

"Dragons!" Albert cried excitedly.

"Well, dragons are very interesting, Albert, but I'd like you to research real animals," Mr. Peters responded. "Perhaps you can study dragons another time."

"Snakes," Dylan hissed.

"Good. Write that down, Albert. Don't worry about your spelling. We're just brainstorming."

Albert wrote down *snks* then stared off into space, thinking of other animals.

"Sharks," said Dylan.

Albert wrote down *shks*, and Mr. Peters walked away. Albert's eyes shifted nervously.

"You can't even spell," Dylan mocked angrily. "I can barely tell the difference between your *sharks* and *snakes*. You're a moron."

Albert looked away and pretended to think of other animals, trying to hide his hurt feelings. Suddenly, he straightened up with excitement and wrote down the word *dnke*. He covered it with his hand and started chewing the end of his pencil.

Dylan pushed his hand away. "What's that?" he asked curtly. "Dinkee? What's a dinkee, you moron?"

"Donkey!" Albert yelled back.

Mr. Peters heard the yell and looked up. Dylan felt Mr. Peters's eyes. Through clenched teeth, he spoke quietly but forcefully. "Donkeys are boring. Donkeys just eat grass. Donkeys don't kill anything."

"Dragons!" Albert blurted. "I vant to research dragons,"

Dylan's brow furrowed as he spat out, "We can't! Mr. Peters said!"

He grabbed Albert's pencil just as he wrote down a *d*. Albert reached for it but missed, so he stood up and grabbed it out of Dylan's hand, bumping Dylan's pencil box to the ground. Dylan slammed Albert in the chest and knocked him off his feet. Then he kicked him in the chest. Albert was on the ground trying to get his breath back when Mr. Peters stormed over.

"GET OUT!" Mr. Peters screamed, more loudly than he ever had. "This is not acceptable! I don't care what you were allowed to do at other schools! This will not be tolerated here! Go to the office!"

The room was silent. Students shifted uncomfortably in their desks, uncertain of where to look.

"You're no different than my other teachers!" Dylan stormed out of the room with his head down and his arms flailing.

Mr. Peters crouched down and put his hand on Albert's back as he got his breath back.

"Are you okay, Albert?"

"Ya," he croaked. Mr. Peters helped him into his desk.

"Tony, can you please ask the librarian to call the office and tell them Dylan is on his way down." Then more loudly, he said, "Sorry for the interruption, class." His voice cracked. "Please continue with what you were doing."

A short time later, the principal came to the room and asked for Albert to come to the office to explain his side of the story. Albert walked nervously out of the room, several steps behind Mrs. Evans.

The class continued working and developing strategies for their research projects while Mr. Peters circled the room and offered advice and assistance to those who needed it. Then the assistant principal, Mr. Bowman, came into the room and told Mr. Peters that Mrs. Evans wanted to talk to him in the office.

"I'll watch the class," Mr. Bowman said.

Mr. Peters noticed that Ted was in a group of three, so he asked if he would mind working with Dylan. He was surprised by Ted's excitement. The teacher led Ted to the nurse's room, where Dylan was sitting with his head down at a table.

"Dylan, you and Ted will be working together on the animal research project."

Dylan did not respond.

Mr. Peters proceeded through the nurse's office into Mrs. Evans's office, where she was waiting for him.

"He's an angry young man," stated Mrs. Evans as Mr. Peters closed the door.

"Yes, he is. I feel for him, I really do, but I don't know how to handle his outbursts."

"I hate to come down too hard on him," responded Mrs. Evans. "He's been dealt with so severely in the past and it hasn't worked. We need to try to correct his behavior by demonstrating compassion. I'll call the area office that oversees all of the schools in the south to see if they can send someone out to help us with this young man. I'd like to hire an assistant who can work with him one-on-one." She paused for a moment. "I've never met such a damaged child."

"I want to help him," Mr. Peters exclaimed, "but I'm concerned for the safety of the other children in the class. Albert was being his usual self—nothing bad—just goofy."

"Oh, I know what Albert can be like. We're going to have to keep an eye on Dylan and keep him away from Albert. He doesn't like Albert." Mrs. Evans breathed heavily and sat back in her chair. "I talked to Dylan for a long time about his history. He's very perceptive and knows that he's different from the other kids. He hates being so different. He wants to fit in, but he says his anger chases other kids away."

"I realize that, Mrs. Evans, but how are we going to deal with these behaviors?"

Mrs. Evans thought for a moment. "I don't know. I told him that he'll be doing community service in the school over the next two weeks. I think part of the problem is that he feels isolated and abandoned. Perhaps if he feels connected with the school and the community, his behavior will improve.

Mr. Peters walked quietly through the nurse's room. The two boys were so deep in conversation that he decided not to disturb them from their work. He walked around them and back to the classroom.

Collin Paulson

10
Life or Death

DYLAN SAT MOTIONLESS AND STARED AT his hands. Ted slid a chair across the floor and sat down. He shifted uncomfortably and looked away from Dylan. When he looked back, Dylan was watching him. The boy focused on his hands again and began slowly.

● ● ●

I FELT SO ALONE. I'D NEVER FELT so alone…all of my family and all of my friends—gone. The worst thing was that I didn't know what had happened to any of them. I took comfort in not seeing any bodies. Had they all been captured and taken to the castle, or had they escaped into the forest? I didn't know what to do. I had forgotten about Ravelle and Tiko. I was lost in my own thoughts.

"Come!" I heard Tiko's voice. "Look." He was kneeling down in the middle of the road, examining the ground.

There were a great number of footprints—horses, humans, dogs, and, most certainly, trogs. Trogs rarely landed in our village, so the sight of footprints meant something terrible. In the past, the people of my village had shuddered when they flew above us. I can't imagine how they reacted when the trogs landed.

"Where is everybody?" I asked quietly.

Tiko and Ravelle shook their heads without looking up. The silence was frightening. I could feel a gentle breeze in the warm night air. The breeze carried smoke and the smell of charred remains. I felt uneasy standing in the ashes of my once-thriving village.

The silence was broken by a muffled thump. We were all startled out of our thoughts, and we turned to face Acorn. He was standing on a charred fencepost.

"Acorn!" I yelled.

I ran toward him, and he hopped onto the remains of a cart. Suddenly, I felt a little embarrassed to be chasing after a squirrel so excitedly in the midst of all the devastation. Tiko and Ravelle were looking at each other inquisitively, probably wondering what had gotten into me.

"I know this sounds ridiculous," I said, "but Acorn is a friend of mine. He's helped me several times."

"That's not ridiculous, Dylan," whispered Ravelle. "You are learning the ways of the earth. You have started to connect with her. I'm glad. Can you communicate with the squirrel?"

"Well," I said, uncertain of how to explain myself, "kind of. We don't speak to each other, but I feel like he can read my thoughts and lead me to whatever it is I'm looking for."

"Be aware, Dylan, for spies can take odd forms," replied Ravelle. "You cannot always be certain who is friend and who is foe."

We watched Acorn leap from one object to the next, getting further away from us.

"Come on!" I called over my shoulder. "He wants us to follow him."

Ravelle looked at Tiko and spoke cautiously as they started walking. "I don't like this—being led through the woods by a squirrel."

Every time we got within reach, Acorn fled deeper into the forest. I got the feeling that he enjoyed watching us stumble through the bush as he flittered about, chattering to himself. It sounded like he was laughing at us. Then he was gone, and the three of us stopped and stared at each other. We were standing just below the Gnarled Oak.

While Ravelle and Tiko searched the area for signs of danger, I studied the tree to see what condition it was in. The nest where my father and I had transferred power was no longer there. I smiled as I stared at the spot that Taya and I had used as our hiding place from imaginary evils. Two branches ran parallel to each other, making a large platform where we often planned how to defeat our imaginary enemies.

Suddenly, a chill went through my body. I thought I saw something move in the tree. I backed away and pretended to study the ground for tracks. Hiding behind a leafy bush, I stared up at the tree. For several minutes, I crouched behind the bush without moving. I decided that my eyes were playing tricks on me, and just as I was about to reveal myself, I heard Ravelle call "Dylan!" At that moment, a head appeared from behind the bough. Without even thinking, I ran for the tree and scurried up the trunk. I didn't feel any fear. I climbed like I had never climbed before.

"What are you doing?" Ravelle yelled.

While standing on the first branch, I reached down and pulled out my knife. The jolt of power went through my arm and into the rest of my body. I felt invincible. Slowly, I kept climbing, keeping my eyes on the spot where I had seen movement. Standing below the platform, I stopped and listened for a moment. The stranger was breathing faintly, but quickly. I sensed that the hidden form was afraid. I didn't understand how I could sense such a thing, but I did. I decided that it was too dangerous to look over the bough, for I might get my face slashed. I scurried further up the tree, past the platform, and looked down.

"Taya!" I cried.

She jumped as I called out her name. I put my knife away and leapt down to her.

"Oh, Taya. What's happened?" I asked as I pulled her into my arms.

She pushed me away until she could see my face clearly. Her eyes were filled with fear, and she cried out in pain and joy. Tears rolled down her face as she struggled to speak. "Are you real? Is it really you, Dylan?"

She was in great agony, and I could feel her pain. I rested her head gently upon the bough and then hurried down the tree to inform the others that I had found my sister. Tiko leapt up the tree with great agility and carried her down as gently as a kitten.

The three of us hurried back to Agora through an entrance I had not seen before. All of my thoughts revolved around my sister as we travelled through the dark passageways. Tiko placed her on a bed of blankets and then stood above her while Ravelle examined her. She didn't appear to have any external injuries except for a blow to the head—the blood on the wound had coagulated in a mass of hair and dirt. Her usually muscular, square stature was rounded and broken. Taya's face was black from dirt, except for a line below each eye where a stream of tears had carried the dirt away from her face. Ravelle looked up at me and shook his head.

"It doesn't look good. She's very weak."

I knelt down beside Taya and put her hand in mine. Something struck me in the forehead. I cried out and pulled my hand away.

"What was that?" I searched for the object that had hit me.

"What was what?" Ravelle asked.

"What hit me?"

Ravelle looked at me curiously. "Nothing hit you."

"It felt like something struck me," I responded. "I felt a sharp pain in my head."

He looked at Taya. "Was it on the left side of your forehead?"

"Yes, it was. Why?"

Ravelle put his hand on my shoulder and spoke solemnly. "You're feeling your twin's pain."

"What do you mean?"

"It is Aarial."

"Well, can I use it to help her?"

"Perhaps, Dylan, but it's dangerous to do so. You've only just received Aarial, and you have not yet developed its healing powers. There has only been one other who had the power to heal, and it almost destroyed him, several times."

"I want to try, Ravelle."

"It's risky, Dylan. If she's close to death, it will most certainly kill you and her. If she still has life left in her, she may pull through and you may die. Or…both of you may pull through. I emphasize 'may.' It's very risky."

"I'll take that chance."

Before Ravelle could utter another word, I placed both of my hands on Taya's head. A sharp pain shot into my skull and spread throughout my body.

The room was dark when I came to. I tried to sit up, but I didn't have the strength. I lay completely still, trying to think of what had happened. The memory of my home came into my mind, and I felt a sense of loss. I remembered walking around my village in horror. I was thinking of my family when I thought of Taya. My head throbbed, and the pain got worse as I strained to look around the room. Taya was completely still on the other side of the fire. She shimmered in the dimly lit room. I couldn't tell if she was alive or dead. I tried to call out, but I had no voice.

"Welcome back, my friend." The sound of Ravelle's voice was comforting. "We thought we'd lost you. Do you have any idea how long you've been out for? It's been two days since I saw you move."

I tried to ask about Taya, but I couldn't speak.

"I think she's going to be okay," he said, as if reading my mind. "She's had a rough time, but she seems to be healing. She called out for your mother two days ago, but that was the last thing she said."

I was relieved by the news of my sister. My head was pounding and my body ached. I drifted off again. I saw my father eating and drinking with Nero in a palatial room. They were laughing and enjoying themselves while my mother served them. Ravelle and I charged into the room with our swords blazing, and at the sight of my father, we stopped in astonishment. Nero and my father burst out laughing. Then we dropped our swords and joined my mother in her serving duties.

The next thing I knew, Nero and my father were arguing. My father knocked Nero's goblet to the floor and leapt through the window. I watched him turn into a hawk and fly away. My mother and I looked at each other in horror, and Nero smiled at us menacingly. He pulled two chairs away from the table and invited us to sit. We sat down nervously, and Ravelle picked up the serving dish and started filling our plates. Nero sat down at the other end of the table. He lowered his head as if to say grace, then he lunged at me and struck me in the forehead with a spoon.

I awoke to the sight of Taya leaning over me. Her sad eyes made me want to get up and hug her. I tried to sit up but couldn't. She wiped the tears from her face and dabbed my forehead with a wet cloth. I smiled up at her. Her brown eyes sparkled in the light of the fire, and I felt her strength as she held on to my hand.

"How are you?" I asked slowly. My throat was dry and sore.

"I'm fine," she responded. "You're the one we're concerned about. You need your rest. Don't talk. We'll have plenty of time for conversation."

Taya lifted my head and placed a firm pillow under it. Ravelle smiled at me as he carried a bowl of soup to my sister. She spoon-fed me just as I remember my mother feeding her as a child. The warm broth soothed my throat.

Over the next few days, my sister and Ravelle nursed me back to health. Slowly, I regained my strength, and I started to move about the cave. I slept a lot during that time, but when I was awake, I spoke to my sister about the good times. She said she would tell me everything when I was strong enough.

Through Taya, I eventually learned what had happened to my village. Two or three days after my father and I had disappeared, Nero pronounced that all of the leaders of the surrounding area were to meet with him to celebrate his crowning. According to rumors, most of these men were decapitated at the ceremony; their heads were stuck on poles and paraded around his courtyard. Apparently, Nero was furious that my father hadn't shown up for the meeting. Trogs came to my village and turned the place upside down looking for him. Finally, Nero himself came to the town and said that if Macor's whereabouts were not revealed, every home in Duffle would be destroyed by the next sunrise.

The people gathered and decided that they had to leave, for they didn't know where my father was, and they wouldn't tell even if they did. Three quarters of them fled to the forest before Nero returned with the trogs. He was enraged to see that almost everyone was gone, and his anger led to the destruction of our homes. He gathered up the remaining residents, including my mother, piled them into a wagon, and took them back to his palace. Taya didn't know what their fate would be at the time. She believed it was death.

She said that my mother hadn't wanted to leave because she thought that my father might return to the village and would need to be warned. When the trogs entered our house, they caught my mother pushing Taya up into the rafters and out of sight. One of the trogs grabbed my mother by the neck and threw her to the ground. Taya leapt down and bit the trog on the arm—so hard that he let go of our mother. With his other hand, he knocked Taya to the ground and then kicked her several times. She was left, bleeding and unconscious. They probably thought she was dead. The trog grabbed my mother and took her away. As Nero and his troops left the village, they burned everything to the ground. Acorn, at least I think it was Acorn, awakened Taya, just as our house was about to collapse. She escaped through the back window and hid inside the cold storage room. She lay there for a day before fleeing to the forest.

* * *

"OKAY BOYS, GO BACK TO CLASS now," said Mrs. Evans.

Ted looked over his shoulder at the principal and smiled. Dylan closed his eyes and pushed his chair away from the desk.

Collin Paulson

11

Rejection

(four weeks later)

"**H**ELLO. MR. PETERS?"

"Yes, this is he," the teacher answered into the phone.

"This is Mr. Kruger, Dylan's social worker."

"Oh, hi. I'm glad to finally talk to you."

"Yes, I'm sorry I haven't had a chance to speak with you earlier," Mr. Kruger apologized. "How long has he been at your school now? Almost a month?"

"Just over a month," Mr. Peters answered. "Time has flown by since he arrived."

"How's he doing, Mr. Peters?"

"Not great. He's constantly in trouble for swearing, threatening and pushing other students, throwing rocks—you name it, he's done it. The principal and I have spoken to him countless times about controlling his anger. We've tried to teach him some anger management strategies, and he tries to learn them, but all is forgotten in real-life situations."

"Yes, this sounds very familiar, Mr. Peters. A lot of people have tried, but he's a challenge. Does he have any friends?"

"Well, there is one boy who likes him, but even he seems to be avoiding him lately. He's too unpredictable, and he pushes kids away with his outbursts."

"What about you? How are you doing, Mr. Peters? Many teachers have given up on him."

"I'm okay, but I get frustrated with the amount of time I have to spend with him. I feel like I'm neglecting my other students because he requires so much of my time."

"Do you think he should be back in a behavior class?" asked the social worker.

"Hmm…well, that would make things easier for me," answered Mr. Peters, "but I don't think it's the best place for him. In my classroom, he gets to interact with average kids who may not be perfect but who rarely strike out or really hurt each other. This kind of positive role modeling is good for him."

"I agree," Mr. Kruger stated, "but you're responsible for all of your students, not just Dylan. You can't allow one child to take up all of your time."

Mr. Peters sat down on the library desk. "You're right. The other students are missing out."

"Don't get me wrong, Mr. Peters. I'd love to see him in a regular classroom, but maybe he's not ready."

"I don't want to give up yet. Oh, by the way, I'm getting an aide next week. The principal has been trying to find one for a while, but most of them don't want the stress of working with someone like Dylan. It's going to be her responsibility to deal with him on a regular basis, so I can spend time with the rest of my class."

A rapid fire of words blasted into the library. Mr. Peters held the phone away from his ear and looked into the hallway.

"I just wanted to play. I didn't do anything. Just go away! Leave me alone! Can't anyone leave me alone?"

"I have to go, Mr. Kruger. Please keep in touch."

"Okay, I will. Let me know—"

Mr. Peters hung up the phone before the other man could finish his sentence.

Dylan stormed into the classroom and flopped down on the risers with his hood pulled over his head and face. Mr. Peters left the library and was about to enter the classroom when he ran into Mr. Bowman in the hallway.

"He got into a fight with a number of boys on the playground," he said quietly. "I only saw the end of it, but they appeared to be teasing him. Miss Roland told me that she saw him smiling and trying to join them in their game, but they ran off. He continued to follow them and tagged them as they ran. Then they circled him and started making fun of him. This is when I saw him pull Lyle's jacket over his head and throw him to the ground. Then he lunged at Sam's neck and pushed him. The other kids played a part, and we need to deal with all of them, but I wanted to remove Dylan from the situation. I'm going to gather up the other students, and we're going to have a meeting in the office."

"Can it wait, Mr. Bowman? I want to have a class meeting first."

"Yeah, sure. That's fine."

"I'll send them to you when we're finished, Mr. Bowman."

Mr. Peters walked over to Dylan and sat down on the riser across from him.

"Are you okay, Dylan?"

"What? You're always blaming me!" he wailed.

"I'm not blaming you for anything, Dylan. I don't think you're listening to me. I asked if you are all right," he said calmly.

"What do you care? Nobody cares. Nobody wants me."

"Whoa. Slow down, Dylan. We are—"

"You don't care. Nobody does."

"What's bugging you, Dylan? There seems to be more to this than the fight you had on the playground."

Dylan's eyes welled up. "Grandma doesn't want me anymore. She said I'm too much trouble. I have to go to a respite home."

"For how long?"

"It's supposed to be for two or three days, but usually it's longer."

"So a respite home is just short term."

Dylan nodded.

"Well, maybe it will be good for both of you to get away from each other. Sometimes we need a break from the people we love, Dylan."

The warning bell rang.

"I want to talk to you about this in more detail, Dylan, but right now I need to get ready for class. Now, you had a problem on the playground, and—"

"But they started it."

"I don't know what happened, Dylan, and I want to get to the bottom of it. I know the other kids played a part and that you aren't the only guilty party. We're going to talk to all of you, but right now, you need to go to the office and wait until we have time to deal with it."

"What about them?" he spat angrily.

"They will be dealt with. Don't worry about them right now. I'd like you to go to the office and cool down."

Mr. Peters walked away. He knew from past experience that hovering over Dylan while asking him to leave did not work. It was best to give the instructions and walk away. He was at his desk shuffling papers when Dylan got up and walked out of the room.

Thirty seconds later the bell rang. Several students rushed to Mr. Peters and tried to give their versions of what had happened on the playground, but Mr. Peters stopped them.

"Hold your tongues. We're going to deal with this as a class. "

Mr. Peters waited until all of the students were at the meeting corner before joining them. He walked sternly to the front of the room without smiling at anyone. Everyone stayed silent while he took attendance.

Then he said firmly, "Okay. What happened?"

Nobody spoke.

"I want to discuss this with the entire class because this isn't the first time we've had to deal with a problem like this, and it won't be the last."

Slowly, Lyle raised his hand. "Me, Sam, Tony, Jake, and Alex were sitting on the rock when Dylan came running up and asked to play. We said we weren't playing, and we walked away, but he kept following us. So we ran, and then he started tagging us, saying, 'you're it,' but we weren't playing tag. Then he grabbed me and threw me to the ground. Sam came to help me, and he threw him to the ground. Then Mr. Bowman took Dylan away."

"Why do you think he wanted to play?" asked Mr. Peters. No one raised a hand. "Who does he usually play with?"

Janna said, "No one. He usually plays alone."

"So why did he want to play with you guys?" Mr. Peters asked again. "Alex?"

Alex spoke into his hand. "Because he has no one else to play with."

"Think about how it would feel to come to school every day knowing you don't have any friends, knowing that the other kids will laugh at you and tease you," said Mr. Peters. "I heard that some of you were calling him names. Is that true, Tony?"

"Well...yeah, I guess," answered Tony. "We didn't want to play with him, so we told him to get lost."

Lyle said, "He plays too rough. He's scary, sometimes."

Mr. Peters thought about this for a moment. "I understand. He does play very rough, and he gets carried away."

"And sometimes he punches and kicks," Sam added.

Mr. Peters sighed and scanned the faces before him. "I have to tell you about Dylan's background. I can't go into a lot of detail, but I think all of you need to know a little about Dylan." The teacher scanned their silent faces.

"Dylan stands out. His life is unlike any of yours. He's lived in many different homes and has attended many different schools. This is his first experience in a regular classroom. Most of his schooling has taken place in very small classrooms with other students who have trouble in regular classrooms. How many of you have moved?" A few hands went up. "Moving can be very difficult. Am I right?" Several students nodded.

"Dylan doesn't have two parents who move with him and comfort him when he's upset. Usually when he moves, he lives with adults who are strangers to him. He's never had the same parents for more than a year or two. Put yourself in his shoes. What if you didn't have parents and you were shipped around from home to home every couple of years?"

He paused and looked at the ground. "Dylan has a temper. We all know that, and it can be scary at times. I understand that. But as a group, we have to try to make Dylan's year a positive one. He needs to know we care about him. Who are Dylan's friends?"

Lyle responded, "He doesn't have any friends. Sometimes Ted talks to him."

Ted's head went down, and he stared at the ground.

"You're right, Lyle," agreed Mr. Peters. "The only student who spends any time with him is Ted." Mr. Peters paused for a moment. "I would like all of you to try to include Dylan in some of your games. I'm not telling you that you have to play with him. I would just like you to try. You don't have to be his best friend—just try to make him feel welcome."

Carol's hand went up, and then she spoke. "But…what if he gets angry at us and yells. What should we do?"

"I don't have all of the answers," responded Mr. Peters. "If possible, try to include him in your games and activities, and if he gets too carried away, just walk away. Perhaps tell him that if he's not interested in following the rules of the game, then he can't play. Tell him that when he's ready to follow the rules, he can join the group again. He needs to be given a chance to play with you.

"If he blows up, stop the game immediately and let him know that you won't put up with that kind of behavior. He'll listen to you better than he'll listen to me or any of the other teachers. Again, you don't have to be his best friend—just include him. I think he needs to feel a sense of belonging. We all need that."

Then Mr. Peters sent Lyle, Tony, Alex, Jake, and Sam down to the office to meet with Dylan and Mrs. Evans. They retold their version of the story.

"Do you understand what they just said, Dylan?" Mrs. Evans turned toward him. "You just wanted to play, but they were afraid. If you want to play, you need to be less rough. And you boys," Mrs. Evans said, glaring at the five, "you need to try to be a little more understanding. How long have you boys gone to this school?"

"Since kindergarten," Lyle responded.

"Me too," agreed Tony.

Alex nodded in agreement.

"Jake and I have been here since grade 1," Sam stated.

"So you guys have always gone to this school. You've been friends for a while. Dylan just arrived. Think about how you'd feel if you had to leave all of your friends and try to make new ones."

Dylan leaned forward in his chair. He did not make eye contact with any of the boys, but he looked in their direction and focused just above their heads. His jaw protruded as he spoke forcefully. "How would you feel if you were always blamed for everything and got in trouble all the time. Ever since I was this high," he said, motioning with his hand, "I've been blamed for everything. Other kids always pick on me and tease me."

The boys stared at Dylan as he went on. He talked about his life and some of the things he had experienced. Mrs. Evans was surprised by Dylan's speech. She observed that the boys listened intently and even responded with gasps at some of the things he said.

When Dylan finished speaking, Mrs. Evans said, "Okay boys, how do you feel about this? Do you have a better understanding of what Dylan has been going through in this school?" They all nodded. "What are you going to do in the future?"

Alex spoke up. "We'll try to include him." All of the other boys agreed.

"I'm pleased with our meeting," said the principal. "Thank-you. I feel like we came to an understanding. I'm going to ask you to do community service for the time you've spent away from the classroom. Now, I'd like you to all shake hands and go back to class."

"Yuck!" Jake blurted.

Mrs. Evans straightened up and stared at him. "What did you say?"

Jake turned red and stared at the ground. He looked up, and when he saw Mrs. Evans's angry glare, he looked away again.

"Repeat what you said," Mrs. Evans said firmly.

"I said 'yuck.' I don't want to touch him. He's dirty."

Mrs. Evans raised her voice. "Did you get nothing out of this meeting?"

Then she looked at the other boys and tried to speak calmly. "I want to thank all of you for coming today. You can go back to class…everyone except for Jake. We need to continue our conversation."

As Lyle left the office, he met Jake's tearful eyes with a sympathetic shrug of his shoulders. The door slammed shut.

The rest of the day went smoothly. Mr. Peters noticed that the students tried to include Dylan in their activities, and he seemed to enjoy the positive attention. At the end of the day, Mr. Peters called Ted over to his desk.

"I've noticed that you and Dylan aren't hanging out together anymore. Is it just my imagination or have you been ignoring him? You seemed to have such a good friendship."

Ted was silent for a moment. "It's my parents. I want to be friends with Dylan. I like him, but my parents are worried. They've heard stories about him, and they told me not to hang out with him."

"I see," said Mr. Peters. "How do you feel about this? Do you want to be friends with him, Ted?"

"I do, but I'm worried about what my parents might do. Sometimes they ground me."

"Well, thank-you for telling me that, Ted. You're in a difficult situation. You can go now." Mr. Peters turned back to his work.

Ted left the room and froze at the sight of Dylan sorting books in the library. He tiptoed softly down the hall after quietly gathering his things. Then he stopped, exhaled, dropped his backpack, and walked into the library.

"Hi, Dylan," he sang brightly.

Dylan mumbled a greeting back and continued filing books.

"I haven't talked to you for a couple of weeks," Ted continued. "I know you're probably mad at me because you think I've been ignoring you…sorry about that. It's just that I've been so busy lately. My parents have put me in all these after-school clubs, so I have to rush home every day." Ted felt ashamed to be lying.

Dylan spoke into the books. "What about recess and lunch time? You haven't been talking to me during those times either."

Ted stumbled over his words and tried to come up with an explanation, but Dylan cut in. "I don't care. I don't need friends. You don't have to be my friend," he said emphatically. "I just have one request," Dylan stated, "and then you can go your own way. I need to finish telling you about my training and my battle with Tracker. I have to do this before I go back. I don't know why; I just do."

"I want to hear it, Dylan," he replied. "I really do. I can stay for a while, but then I have to go."

"Go then!" Dylan spat. "I'm not gonna beg."

Ted remained silent for a minute and watched Dylan continue to file books. "I want to hear it. Please finish. I can stay as long as you want me to."

Dylan spun around and studied Ted's face.

"You really do want to hear it, don't you?"

Ted nodded. The boys glanced around the library and then ducked into their secret cave under the computer table.

12
Sword in the Stone

"**W**HERE WAS I?"

"You told me about Nero and the trogs and how they destroyed Duffle," Ted answered.

"Right." Dylan hesitated for a minute. "Taya escaped into the forest and climbed the Gnarled Oak. She lay there for a couple of days, expecting to die, since she had a concussion and internal injuries. She was terrified of being caught by Nero and his troops, and she wanted to die in peace. She didn't want to be taken prisoner and tortured by them, so you can understand her fear when she heard us. She thought that we were Nero's men. Anyway…you know the rest of that part."

"Tell me about Tracker," Ted interrupted.

"We're getting there. You need more information before I get to him."

● ● ●

RAVELLE AND TIKO SPENT MONTHS TRAINING Taya and me. Ravelle hadn't wanted to train both of us because he had never trained more than one person at a time and said that training one person took so much of his energy.

"We're inseparable," I had told him. "I will never leave her, so you need to train us both. Then we can help each other."

He eventually agreed that having both of us trained would be beneficial. He was just concerned that he wouldn't be able to give me the necessary attention. He said that Taya could learn a lot but she would never understand or connect with Aarial.

During our training, Ravelle would often sit and give instructions while Tiko demonstrated proper fighting techniques. At times, Tiko's demonstration would frustrate Ravelle, and he would decide to show us himself. We spent hours repeating the same moves over and over; it was exhausting. We started our training by learning a form of wrestling without weapons. Then we moved to using clubs as a form of defense. Ravelle didn't want to risk either one of us getting injured, so we weren't allowed to use swords until he felt we were ready. Then, Tiko, Taya, and I took turns sparring with each other.

I would sit with Ravelle for long periods of time while Taya and Tiko fought. He would explain some of the mistakes and demonstrate better ways of defending and attacking. He would do the same with Taya when I was battling Tiko.

Even though Tiko appeared clumsy, he was extremely agile. At first, I could tell that he was holding back. I was certain that he could defeat me quite easily. As our training progressed, Tiko started to fight harder and harder, until I felt that he was fighting with all his might.

Most of my evenings were spent in Stellar Hall, where I learned the ways of the earth. Through the light, I studied landscapes and learned ways of communicating with our planet. I can't explain what I was learning because it's so foreign to anyone who doesn't possess Aarial. The earth and I seemed...connected. I saw things from different perspectives and angles. My vision was 360 degrees, and I could sense my environment with my whole body. I didn't understand it, but Aarial became a part of me that I didn't question.

I slept well at night, but I was haunted by a recurring dream. I pictured my father running for his life with trogs in close pursuit. With each dream, they got closer to capturing him. I told Ravelle about this and asked him if the dreams were real. He said that they could be. He didn't know if my father was still alive, but he thought that he was, because he hadn't seen any trogs for a long time. He believed Nero had sent out most of them to kill my father and that they would return once Macor was dead. I kept my dreams from Taya.

Most of our training took place underground. Ravelle didn't want to risk being caught. On rare occasions, we left our nocturnal world and trained under the sun. This was a great pleasure for Taya and me. I didn't realize how damp it was and how claustrophobic I felt underground until I was allowed to train in the open air and feel the sun and wind on my skin.

Part of our training was physical conditioning for the purpose of travelling. Ravelle said we were going to need to be able to travel for long periods of time without tiring. Acorn often appeared when we were aboveground, and he trained me to travel in the trees. Taya tried to learn how to travel as Acorn and I could, but I realized that this was a part of Aarial, so she would never master it. In a short time, I was almost as agile and quick as Acorn. We often made games out of training, which annoyed Ravelle. He was always very serious and didn't believe in making the training fun.

Then it happened…

One frosty morning while we were training aboveground, I sensed danger. I alerted the others, and we went underground. Silently, from beneath the earth's surface, we watched a huge form block out the sun. We all froze at the terrifying sight. It was a trog, but unlike any of the ones we had seen. Ravelle told us that this was Tracker—the head trog. He explained that Nero had complete trust in Tracker's leadership and allowed the trog to rule any way he chose. Ravelle said that he thought Tracker might be looking for me. He knew that Tracker had other duties as well, but he believed Nero would be looking for me to destroy my bloodline completely. He thought that Nero would probably use my mother as a hostage to get me to turn myself in.

That night, Ravelle took me aside. "You must realize that no matter what happens, you cannot give yourself up for someone else's life. This may sound selfish, but if you're killed, there's no chance for Duffle…or any other communities. You're the only one who can save our world. Do not give in to your sense of duty to your family. You will most certainly be killed if you're captured. You may save one life in return for your own, but your life is worth that of a thousand men, for only you possess the power to defeat Nero."

With my training came a sense of confidence in my abilities. Ravelle didn't say much, but I knew that he was impressed by what I was able to do. One day he told me I was ready, and he took me into a secret room connected to Stellar Hall. I hadn't seen it before because the doorway was invisible. Ravelle placed his hands on the wall and chanted an ancient hymn that I remembered hearing my father hum. He tapped the rock in three places, and it opened up. In the center of the room was a spectacular sword. Its blade was encased in stone. Ravelle and I circled it while he spoke.

"You now have the internal ability to handle the sword. I didn't want you to use it until you were ready. If you had trained with it all along, you would have relied on its powers rather than developing your own abilities."

We continued to circle it, and he went on.

"The sword is Olam. It hasn't been used for many years, since we have known peace for generations. It is only unsheathed in times of strife. Every Aarial has trained with it, but few have had to wield it in combat. You will be the first to carry it for an indefinite period of time."

Rays of light from the ceiling illuminated the magnificent jewels in its handle. The blade gleamed, throwing shards of light off the walls. We stopped circling and Ravelle nodded. I knew what I was to do next. I walked over to Olam and grasped the handle. An electric shock went through my body and propelled my hand away. The feeling was similar to the one the knife I carried on my ankle gave me, but the power was tenfold. I reached for it again and felt the surge of energy, but this time I was ready for it, and I pulled it out of its stone sheath. As I held it above my head, a beam of light blasted out from the place where the sword had been.

The sword felt so natural in my hands. I circled it around my head and passed it from hand to hand. It weighed no more than the small knife I carried, but the power in its grip was unbelievable. After several minutes of battling imaginary villains, I felt a bead of sweat run down my face, and I began to tire. Ravelle had been watching me intently the whole time. He walked over to me as I embedded Olam's point in the soil at my feet and leaned against its handle. Ravelle tied a sheath around my waist, and I slid Olam into it. I was overcome with exhaustion. The sword had drained all of my energy. My knees buckled, and I looked up at Ravelle. I was confused—I barely had enough strength to stand.

"It's okay," he said as he pulled me up and wrapped my arm around his neck. "Olam will drain you of your energy until you learn to harness its energy."

Ravelle laid me down on my bed beside the fire. He undid my belt that held the sheath, but he couldn't lift the sword. He asked for help, and he, Tiko, and Taya used all of their strength to remove it from my bed. I slept soundly for the rest of the night.

Over the next few weeks, Olam became a part of my training. Ravelle reminded me that I had to build up my strength before I would have the ability to use the sword all the time. Most of my training was with the club, and then the last few minutes of each day I trained with Olam. Every day, the amount of time I trained with Olam was extended, and each day I felt great exhaustion afterward.

My sister also trained with a sword, as did Tiko. I loved the sound of metal on metal and the shower of sparks each time our weapons connected. I don't know when it happened—I guess it was a gradual process—but eventually, I could train with Olam all the time and not feel complete exhaustion.

Ravelle thought it was important to begin training outside more because most of my battles would take place aboveground, so we spent little time inside Agora for the rest of my training. On one particular day—the most terrifying and exciting day of my life—we were working very hard. I was so involved in my battle with Tiko that I neglected my senses. My heart dropped when I saw Tracker perched high up in a tree, observing the whole scene. His ominous, massive wings framed his muscular body, and his giant brow shaded his face in darkness.

I backed away slowly while screaming at the others to take cover. As I turned to run, Tracker leapt off of his perch and began pursuing me. I felt the wind from his wings as I dove into Agora's entrance. It closed up behind me, and I huddled with the others as we listened to Tracker pound at the entrance. When the pounding stopped, we got up and peered out through the numerous spy holes in the cave. I saw him fly above us, searching for an opening. Then we heard a bang at the entrance again. I knew that this was going to be my first battle.

For the first time in my life, I understood fear, real fear—the kind that immobilizes you. I had secretly hoped that I would not have to use my skills and Aarial. Taya told me that she would not allow me to go alone. She said that she was going aboveground and that I couldn't stop her. She was right. I knew that when she got an idea into her head there was no stopping her. She was the one who came up with the plan that would help me get into position and prepare myself for battle.

Taya left the cave through an entrance behind Tracker and ran to a nearby tree. Tracker heard her footsteps and turned to see her running through the forest with great precision. The giant trog swooped through the air and was above her in seconds. I was out of the cave by this time, and I watched him glide over to her. Taya scurried up the tree and hid. I saw Tracker frantically trying to get at her, but he was too big to fit through the branches. He circled the tree several times and knocked branches away with his great wings. Taya stood motionless in a crook of the tree in a shower of leaves and twigs.

I climbed a knoll and pulled out my sword. The power surged through my body, and I could sense everything that was going on. I knew how Taya was feeling, and I could see Tracker from all angles. I seemed to have eyes in the ground and the trees. I struck a rock with my sword and sparks flew in every direction. I prepared myself for battle.

Tracker stopped flailing his wings and peered over at me. As he did, the tip of Taya's sword pierced Tracker in the chest. With a horrifying howl, he spun around and grabbed her arm with his foot. He pulled her out of her hiding spot. I watched him hang motionless in the air for a split second with my sister in his claws. Her sword fell to the ground. He seemed dazed by the gash that was dripping purple blood. Then all of a sudden, he flew at me with a vengeance. He screeched a horrible cry as he passed over my head, and Taya struggled to free herself from his clutches.

Tracker was now high above me, looking down. His usually graceful flying was labored, and he tilted to one side. I didn't know if he was having trouble flying because my sister was in his claws or because he had a huge wound in his chest. He came at me again. I raised my sword above my head and readied myself for battle.

As he neared, I realized that I couldn't strike him with my sword, for I might hit Taya. Instead, I turned and ducked. A heavy blow to my back knocked me off the knoll. Tracker had struck me with Taya's body. I looked up and saw my sister's immobile body rising above the trees.

I sheathed Olam and rushed back to the top of the knoll. Tracker came at me again. I was going to try to grab Taya as he passed, but I was struck a second time by Taya's motionless form. Again I stood up and faced Tracker as he circled and came at me. This time, I grabbed on to my unconscious twin, and Tracker carried the two of us away. He had difficulty flying but was able to lift us both off the ground. I reached down to my ankle, pulled out my knife, and stabbed him in the thigh. He let out a great cry and dropped us into a tree. The two of us bounced off several branches before landing upon the ground. We were battered and bruised. As quickly as I could, I pulled Taya into one of the passageways that opened up, where Ravelle and Tiko were waiting to tend to her.

I gathered up all of my strength, and Ravelle tossed me my training club as I ran out of Agora. I climbed to the top of the hill again and pulled out Olam. Tracker was perched high up in a tree. I could see him licking his wounds, watching me carefully. He drew his sword and flew at me.

I took a deep breath and waited. I had confidence in myself, and I knew the power of Olam, so I stood firm. His first pass was easy to fend off. Our blades connected and threw a few sparks, but that was all. The next time he came at me, he hovered just above the ground and circled me as our swords made contact. Time stood still as the battle raged on. Sometimes he was on the ground, standing on his feet; other times, he fluttered just above me. I was able to strike him in the head with my club several times, but I couldn't get at him with my sword.

Tracker backed himself up against a tree at one point, and I stabbed at him. For a second, my blade stuck into the tree, and I couldn't defend myself. I felt his blade slice open my shoulder, and warm blood trickled through my skin. Angered, I pulled my sword out of the tree and struck back. Sparks flew each time our weapons clashed. Tracker jumped up and kicked me in the chest, and I fell to the ground. As he tried to pounce on me, I was able to strike a blow, and I pierced him in the shoulder. The two of us backed away.

He flew up into a tree, and I hid beneath a protruding rock. As I lay there, gathering my strength, I felt a tremor throughout my body. I pictured my father. He was being attacked by trogs. There were dozens of them. They were flying at him from all angles, pulling at his clothes and skin. Two of them grabbed him by the arms and carried him over a ravine. I had never before witnessed such terror in his eyes.

"*NOOOO!*" I bellowed as I watched the two trogs release him over the ravine. Full of rage, I ran from my hiding place, howling obscenities. Tracker leapt off his perch and hurtled toward me.

"En garde, you Fais du Braire!" I howled.

My voice echoed throughout the forest. Every muscle in my body contracted. I was a madman. I didn't care what happened to me now: I wanted revenge. Tracker had to die. My rage gave me power.

As Tracker neared, I lowered my sword to lure him in closer. When I felt his wind and inhaled his fowl stench, I swung my sword, knocking his weapon to the ground. Then I stabbed him in the breast, and he fell into the dirt. I stabbed at him again, but he rolled away and tore at my back with his claws. I felt no pain.

I held my club in my left hand and Olam in my right. Olam blazed as it entered his back. Tracker tried to crawl away, but he couldn't. I stabbed him again, but instead of removing my blade, I twisted it, enlarging the hole and grinding his bones. As I pulled my blood-dripping sword out of his body, he collapsed.

I walked up behind him and raised my club above my head. I placed all of my strength behind the blow and felt his skull collapse beneath my club. Then grasping his medallion, I pulled it tight and swung Olam at his neck with my eyes closed. The medallion came free and I fell back. I lay on the ground, staring at the lifeless form. As a black, silent cloud enshrouded me in a cloak of darkness, all I could picture was my father.

13

From the Carpet to the Forest

DYLAN FINISHED SPEAKING, AND HIS HEAD dropped forward until his chin rested upon his chest. Ted sat quietly, thinking about what he had just heard. The silence struck him, and the change in Dylan stopped his heart. Sitting beside him was a small, shrunken, and defeated boy.

"You killed Tracker!" Ted said excitedly, trying to coax him out of his silence.

Dylan did not speak. His eyes were open but vacant.

"What's wrong, Dylan? Are you okay?"

Dylan continued to stare at the ground, his body unmoving. He would not or could not respond. "You're a great fighter," Ted said shakily, full of anxiety. "How did you do it? I would have peed myself at the sight of Tracker."

Ted poked Dylan on the arm. When he did not respond, he poked him again. Finally, he grabbed his shoulders and shook him. Dylan's hands dropped from his lap to the floor. Letting go of Dylan's shoulders, Ted frantically looked around the darkened library for help. They were alone. When he turned back, Dylan was lying on the floor. Ted panicked and shook him violently.

"Wake up!"

The outline of the medallion under Dylan's shirt caught his eye, and he pulled at the leather cord. The density of the object surprised him. He squeezed it with all his might and pulled it tight. Ted leaned into him; their noses almost touched.

Ted whispered, "You killed, Tracker." Dylan's arm moved slightly. "You saved your sister." His eyes shifted. Ted pulled the medallion and lifted Dylan's shoulders off the ground. He leaned in and shouted, "You avenged your father's death!"

Dylan snapped out of the trance. He shook his head, glanced up at Ted, and smirked. "You gonna kiss me?"

"No!" Ted spat, letting go of the medallion and straightening up. "You were all weird. You weren't answering me."

"Your breath stinks, Ted." Dylan pushed himself up to a sitting position and winced as if in pain. "Did a skunk die in your throat?"

Ted smiled. "Are you okay?" he asked quietly.

Dylan looked around the library and slid his hands through his hair. "You killed Tracker. That's awesome."

"Yeah."

"What happened next?"

Dylan sat quietly. Finally, he turned to Ted, who was waiting for an answer, and muttered, "Nothing."

"What do you mean nothing? How could nothing have happened?"

Without emotion, Dylan answered, "That's it. Nothing else happened because…it hasn't happened yet."

"Huh?" Ted's eyes narrowed. "What do you mean it hasn't happened yet?" Ted thought for a minute and then said, "Do you mean—"

Dylan interrupted. "I have to return to Duffle to complete my mission."

"I thought all of this happened a long time ago. Do you mean to say that it's going on right now?" Ted was excited but confused.

"I have to return to Milo and the land of my people. Nero has destroyed Duffle, and he'll continue to destroy the world if I don't stop him. I'm the only one who can stop him, for I possess Aarial."

"When are you going?" Ted asked.

"I don't know…soon. I'll be called back. It's already started." Dylan thought about the poster beside Mr. Peters's desk. "I've been called back several times, but I've resisted. I want to gather my strength."

Dylan crawled out from under the table and stretched. He looked down at Ted, who was staring up at him, then he turned and walked away. Ted followed Dylan out of the library and watched him pass through the darkened hallway. His silhouette disappeared around the corner while his footsteps hung in the air, reverberating off the walls.

Ted sighed. "Good luck, Dylan."

"Do you know what time it is, Dylan?" Mr. Peters asked curtly. "Why do you continually come into the school half an hour before the bell rings? I've asked you so many times to wait outside, but you continue to come in. I have a lot of work to do, so please leave the school so I can get ready for class."

Dylan left the room and stood in the hall. Mr. Peters listened for the sound of the door opening and closing, and when he didn't hear it, he walked into the hall and saw Dylan staring up at the artwork.

"Grandma doesn't want me anymore," he stated flatly.

"You said you were going to a respite home for a couple days."

"No, this is different. She said she's tired of me and that she can't handle me anymore. She said I'm out of control. She doesn't like me."

"What is she going to do? Where are—"

"She's giving me up—forever. She's not my real grandmother, you know?"

"Yes, I know that, Dylan."

"I just called her that."

"Where will you go?"

"I don't know. They're looking for a place."

"How do you feel about leaving her?"

Dylan shrugged his answer and walked toward the exit.

"Dylan!" Mr. Peters called out.

Dylan stopped and faced his teacher.

"Come back. I want to talk to you." Dylan proceeded into the classroom and followed Mr. Peters to the risers.

"What you're going through is awful." Dylan could feel his teacher's penetrating eyes. He bounced a pebble around in his cupped hands and watched it roll about freely. "No one should have to experience what you're going through, Dylan. The challenges you face in your life are too great for any child. I don't want to make light of what you're dealing with, but you will grow from these difficulties." Mr. Peters paused.

"Life is a book, Dylan. Everything that happens in your life is recorded in this book. Every chapter, every sentence, every word and punctuation mark affects the story. Sometimes we have control and at other times it seems we are guided by outside forces. Some chapters are boring and seem irrelevant, and they are soon forgotten; others are exciting and fun. The challenging ones, the ones that make you want to look away and pretend they aren't happening, are the ones that shape us and make us who we are. These are the ones that make you think and analyze the story more deeply. These are the chapters we remember. They change our lives, for better or worse—we are the ones who decide which it will be. We can grow or self-destruct. Again, I don't want to belittle what you're going through, but try to think of these negative experiences as the beginning chapters of a very exciting book that will change the world."

Dylan glanced over at Mr. Peters. Their eyes locked. Mr. Peters smiled at Dylan, trying to read his emotions.

Dylan exhaled. "When do the good parts come?"

Mr. Peters smiled again. "They will come. I promise you. Your book is just beginning." They sat in silence for a moment. "Would you like to stay in until the bell?"

Dylan shook his head and walked out of the room. Mr. Peters followed him into the hall and watched him throw his body into the door. It swung open and slammed into the outside wall.

"Was that Dylan leaving the school?"

Mr. Peters turned to see Ms. Steinwood walking down the hall carrying an armful of books.

"How could you tell? Was it the sound of the crumbling wall?"

"You sure know when he's around. How's he doing these day?"

"Not much has changed. He's continually getting into fights. If he isn't punching, he's yelling. The other kids have tried to be his friend, but I can't blame them for not including him. If I were a kid, I wouldn't play with him either."

Ms. Steinwood nodded. "There are many adults I don't want to spend time with. No one can force me to hang out with people I don't like. Why do we keep forcing the students to do what we wouldn't do?"

Mr. Peters stepped toward her. "I have such mixed feelings about him. He is a really neat kid and very likable, but I get so angry with him sometimes. Rarely is it one big incident. Usually, it's the dozen little things that build up. Then someone comes to me with some minor complaint about him and I blow up."

"I know what you mean," Ms. Steinwood said.

"I try to be fair, but it's very difficult. I'm on edge whenever he's around. Actually, that's not always true. When I'm alone with him, we have some great conversations. He's very bright in so many ways."

"Yes, I've noticed that too," responded Ms. Steinwood. "I've spent some of my recess supervisions talking to him. He must have spent a lot of time reading and interacting with adults over the years because his verbal skills are really advanced. He is very worldly for such a young boy. How's his schoolwork?"

"Horrible, but I guess that's to be expected. School isn't important when basic survival needs aren't being met." Mr. Peters lowered his voice. "He just told me that his foster mother is giving him up."

"Oh no! That poor boy," Ms. Steinwood said, shaking her head.

"He is an unloved, unwanted, and forgotten child."

"How do you think this is going to affect your class?" asked Mrs. Steinwood.

"I'm worried. Whenever something negative happens to him at home, we see it in class. I'm going to try to be sensitive to what he's going through, but if his behavior harms the students in my class, I'll... well, I don't know what I'll do. I'm really at a loss with this kid. I don't know how to deal with him."

"If I were you, I would be asking for a special placement for him."

"So that he can be rejected again?"

"You can only do so much."

"I met Mrs. Giles yesterday. She's Dylan's new aide. Her sole responsibility is Dylan. I'm hoping that she can deal with him so I'm free to spend time with the rest of the class."

"Does she know what she's in for?" Ms. Steinwood asked.

"I don't think so. She's worked in a lunchroom program and one-on-one with certain students, but she's never worked with someone with serious behavioral problems. She has a very nice manner and is soft-spoken. Dylan may respond well to her."

Ms. Steinwood shook her head. "Do you really believe that?"

"No, not really." Mr. Peters paused. "He's going to chew her up and spit out the bones."

Ms. Steinwood laughed softly. She jumped at the sound of the bell and rushed away as if pushed by the wave of children flooding the school. Mr. Peters entered his room. Within seconds, his students were pushing their way into class and gathering at the meeting area. Dylan went to his desk and rested his head upon his folded arms. He watched the students stream into the classroom. They talked, laughed, and shouted as they entered. Dylan felt an invisible force pull at him. With his eyes closed, he turned and faced the picture. The image was burned onto his retina, so he didn't need to look at the photograph. He sensed movement in the image just as he heard his name.

"Are you joining us, Dylan?" Mr. Peters called out.

Dylan could almost feel something tugging at his shirt as he approached the meeting area. He pushed his classmates aside as he slid down the wall into a spot that was not big enough for him. Tony and Alex grumbled and separated as Dylan settled between them. From his position, he could see the photograph, but the details were faint.

Mr. Peters took attendance and let the students know what they were going to be doing for the day. Then Mrs. Giles walked into the room and sat down at one of the desks behind the students. Mr. Peters smiled at her. The students turned to see who their teacher was smiling at.

"I would like to introduce all of you to Mrs. Giles," Mr. Peters announced. "She is going to be helping us out. Some of you will be getting to know her very well."

"I already know her," Lyle interrupted. "She's my next-door neighbor."

"Well, that's good. Then you can make her feel welcome." Mr. Peters reached for his guitar. "Okay, what should we sing today?"

Someone shouted, "That Beatles song."

"Oh, I hate that song," whined Dylan. "We just sang that the other day."

"Then sit in the hall if you don't like it," Mr. Peters responded angrily.

Dylan's eyebrows narrowed and his lower lip protruded as his body wilted.

Mr. Peters strummed and sang out, "What would you do if I sang out a tune."

The students responded, "Would you stand up and walk out on me?"

"Lend me your ears and I'll sing you a song," sang Mr. Peters.

"And I'll try not to sing out of key."

In unison the whole class and Mr. Peters sang, "Oh, I get by with a little help from my friends."

The students swayed and smiled as they sang. Some of them had their arms around each other and belted out the tune. Others sang quietly or hummed to themselves. Everyone was involved—except for Dylan. With his medallion in his hands, he stared at the faraway picture of green. Suddenly, a fly caught his eye. It landed on Mr. Peters's guitar. No one seemed to notice but him. Then it took off. It buzzed through his teacher's hair, bounced off two walls, and flew into the picture.

Dylan sat upright, looking for the fly. It was gone. As he continued to search for it, the far wall quivered—all color faded and then evaporated. He stood and observed a wall of trees in a lush forest.

Mr. Peters looked down at Dylan, who was leaning on Alex. His head rested upon the other boy's shoulder, and his eyes were closed. Alex scowled at him and moved out of the way. Dylan slid down the wall and rested on the ground, unmoving.

"Dylan!" The music stopped instantly. "Sit up!" Mr. Peters commanded angrily.

Dylan did not move.

Again Mr. Peters yelled, "Sit up!"

For a moment, there was stillness—stillness unlike anyone in that room had ever experienced. Everything stopped. They stared at their immobile classmate, and Mr. Peters rushed over to him. He lifted his head and called, "Dylan! Dylan!! Can you hear me?"

Dylan walked toward the other side of the room. As he stepped over the students, he heard his name. He looked back and saw his classmates standing over a body in the meeting area. Everything was happening in slow motion. From behind one of the trees, he observed a tiny figure, no taller than a yardstick, staring out at him. The creature waved. He drifted toward it as it disappeared into the woods.

Each one of his footsteps pounded in his head. From some distant place he heard his name being called again and a jumble of noises that faded as he walked. The muted sounds became more distant with each stride. Just as he stepped from the carpet onto the forest floor, he turned to see a shimmering crowd of students standing over the prostrate figure.

"Dylan, can you hear me?" The teacher checked his pulse and glanced around the room at the frightened faces. "Everyone go back to your seats and read." He looked up at Ted, who was kneeling beside him. "Go tell the librarian to call Mrs. Evans, Ted." Ted did not respond.

"TED! MOVE!"

Ted remained frozen. Mr. Peters heard one of his students yell into the library, "Get Mrs. Evans! Dylan is dead!"

14

Trust in Aarial

THE DENSE, DARK FOREST EXHALED A dampness that Dylan could taste. In a trance, he stepped cautiously, pushing branches out of his way. He froze at the sound of a bird, then lowered himself and hid behind an uprooted tree. The moss and plants growing out of its roots indicated that it had fallen years before. He slid into the shelter of the roots, which formed a cave. It was a shallow hideout, but a good spot to rest.

He awoke with a start, and it took him a moment to realize where he was. He looked down at his shoulder, where blood had coagulated. His whole body ached. Something in his hand caught his attention, and he glanced into his palm. He could not make out the details of the metal disc, but he knew what he was holding. There was a rustling outside his hiding spot, and he held his breath. A face appeared in the dark, and he gasped at the sight.

"Taya!"

"He's here!" she shrieked. "Are you okay?"

Dylan nodded.

"We've been looking for you for hours. I saw you fall after you defeated Tracker but then you disappeared."

Tiko and Ravelle arrived and shot Dylan a quick greeting. "We have to move. We're going to be swarmed by trogs."

Taya and Tiko wrapped Dylan's arms around their shoulders and lifted him up. Dylan tried to walk with them but the pain was too great. His feet dragged along the forest floor. The medallion fell out of his hands, and they all stopped and stared at it for a moment. Then Taya reached down to pick it up.

"No!" Ravelle cried. The three of them studied Ravelle's pained expression. "Is that Tracker's?"

Dylan nodded.

"Let Dylan pick it up." Ravelle's face revealed that it was important that only Dylan touch it. "I don't know why, but I don't think any of us should put a hand on it."

Taya and Tiko helped Dylan bend over, so he could pick it up. He put it around his neck. The four of them continued on in silence. Just before the ground opened up to Agora, Ravelle checked the sky one last time. Then Tiko and Taya set Dylan down beside the fire and fed him a flavorful, medicinal liquid.

"You have proven to be a very worthy recipient," Ravelle said. "We saw most of the battle, and you were impressive. You're ready to go out on your own. There is little that I can teach you now. Our world is closing in, and Nero needs to be stopped. You must fulfill your mission."

"What is my mission, exactly?"

Ravelle stopped for a moment and stared into the fire. Without changing his focus, he spoke. "To be honest, I'm not certain. I'm aging, and my mind is foggy." He paused. "Your mission may become clearer over time. There are two things you need to do, and I don't know in which order you should do them. Number one...or two: you need to find Queen Gaia. She'll be able to help you, and us. Number two...or one: you need to destroy Nero. That's all I can tell you."

"How do I do those things?"

"You'll learn as your journey progresses. I'll send word when I know more, and you'll meet people along the way who may be able to help you. You may also meet those who will cause you harm. Be mindful. Trust in Aarial."

"It isn't comforting to know that you, my mentor, who trained me, don't know exactly what I'm supposed to do or how I'm to do it."

Ravelle did not respond. He continued to gaze into the fire.

Dylan was suddenly aware of the weight around his neck. "You looked terrified when I dropped Tracker's medallion. Why? Should I get rid of it?"

Ravelle was quick to respond. "No! It may be of some use to you. Soon, everyone will know that you killed Tracker. Take what you can from the medallion, and use it to defeat your opponents. I suspect there is a power within it." Ravelle handed him a flask. "Drink this."

Dylan gulped it down.

"Rest now, and in the morning, you must be on your way."

"But…I need more rest, Ravelle. My entire body aches."

"The elixir you just drank will give you your strength back and heal your injuries. Rest now."

The night was filled with countless dreams, but all Dylan remembered was wandering aimlessly with no direction in mind. He was enjoying the sights, smells, and sounds of the forest when a loud crack knocked him down and woke him. Slowly, he got to his feet, expecting to experience pain but feeling none. Ravelle smiled at him.

"I feel good," Dylan said. He exhaled and stretched his arms above his head.

Ravelle smiled and poured him a bowl of brown, steaming stew.

"Everything is ready. I packed for you. There is a flask of the elixir in your bag—use it sparingly. I want you to leave before Taya gets up. She wants to go with you, but it's too dangerous. You must go on your own."

"She won't like that," Dylan protested. "Taya is a good fighter. She can help me."

Ravelle shook his head and spoke calmly and with conviction. "You'll be tempted to look after her. Yes, she's a good fighter, but she doesn't have the strength, or Aarial. Nero will use her as a pawn if she's captured, and you'll risk everything to save her. It's better if you go on your own."

Dylan knew Ravelle would not be swayed. They ate breakfast in silence. Each was lost in his own thoughts, which were very similar. Dylan was afraid to venture out on his own, and Ravelle was afraid for him, but both knew he had to leave. There was sadness in the air. They wondered if this was the last time they would see each other.

Dylan left Agora and headed east. Ravelle had suggested that he head toward Nero's castle. He had been walking for about an hour when he noticed the sky beginning to lighten. All of a sudden, he stopped. Something in the air told him that he was being watched. After a moment, he continued, but slowly. Movement caught his eye, and he spun around. Standing on a rock was a familiar rodent.

"Acorn?"

The squirrel chirped and ran off into the forest. He set off in a slightly different direction than Dylan had been travelling, but Dylan followed him anyway.

"What have I got to lose?" he asked himself. "I haven't been given any directions."

Soon after he had started walking, he stopped again, sensing danger. The wind carried it like a foul stench, but there were no visible signs of trouble. Dylan continued to move. The forest ahead of him was getting lighter and seemed to be thinning. The trees ended before a large, grassy field. On the other side of the field was another thick forest. Acorn flew past him and ran into the grass.

"How did he get behind me?" Dylan wondered.

Dylan watched him disappear and hesitated. The idea of running across an open field did not appeal to him.

"Well, he hasn't misguided me before," Dylan thought. "I'll follow."

He studied the heavens and then ran into the grass. His backpack bounced as he moved. Halfway across the field, a great screech echoed throughout the sky, and he was knocked to the ground. Within seconds, his sword was drawn, and he was ready for battle.

"En garde, you Fais du Braire!"

The trog came back for more, and just as Dylan swung at him with his sword, he swooped out of the way. Dylan continued to run to the shelter of the forest. He felt the trog's presence and quickly turned for another swipe. Catching the trog off guard, he nicked him in the chest. The wound triggered something in the creature, for it went crazy and started attacking blindly. Dylan stood his ground and used all of his skills to fend off the crazed trog. The wound did not appear to be slowing him down. Then Dylan stabbed at the beast with all his might, but he missed and fell to the earth.

Tracker's medallion slipped out of his shirt and rested upon his chest. He stood and faced the trog again. The medallion caught the trog's eye, and he let down his guard for a split second. Dylan saw fear in the eyes that gazed upon his medallion as he drove his sword through the creature's chest. The trog lay on the ground, gasping for air. Slowly, it crumbled, and the last breath of air left its convulsing body.

Dylan ran across the rest of the field and into the woods. The battle had drained his energy, but he continued to move. As he stumbled through the forest, he looked for a place to hide. A steep cliff rose out of the ground. He followed the rock face for almost an hour and knew that he could not continue for much longer. He stopped to catch his breath and leaned against the rock. Just in front of him, he spotted a thick, knotted mess of trees and shrubs.

Dylan tried to squeeze himself between the cliff and the trees, but he could not, so he followed the cluster of trees away from the wall. After walking a brief distance, he tripped on a root, and as he lay there, drained and in need of rest, he noticed an opening under the thicket. On his belly, he slithered into the den of trees. The cave opened up so that he could stand on his knees without hitting his head. Dylan removed his backpack and collapsed.

Collin Paulson

15
Heroes and Villains

MRS. EVANS RUSHED INTO THE ROOM and flew over to Mr. Peters, who was leaning over Dylan, trying to rouse him.

"His pulse is fine, and he's breathing," Mr. Peters blurted out without looking up.

Most of the students were in or near their desks. None of them were reading. They were either standing up or sitting tall in their chairs. All of them were watching. The room was silent, and the students passed questioning looks to one another. No one was quite certain how to react. Several of them wondered if he was actually dead. Mrs. Evans leaned over Dylan, and Mr. Peters moved out of the way while she examined him.

"Should we call an ambulance?" he asked.

"I don't know what to do," she replied shakily. "I suppose we should."

Mr. Peters whispered in Dylan's ear. "If you can hear me, move your fingers." Dylan remained limp. Mr. Peters checked his pulse again. Then without warning, Dylan sat up. He stretched his arms above his head and smiled.

"Can't a guy get some sleep around here?" he said with a yawn.

Mr. Peters turned red. "Who in the hell do you think you are?"

"You just swore," Dylan responded quickly. "Teachers aren't supposed to say *hell* in front of the kids."

"Get out! That was the last straw. You are not welcome back in this class until I see some real changes."

Some of the students smiled uncomfortably while others stood motionless with eyes wide open. Everyone was relieved that he was not dead. Dylan left the room with Mrs. Evans, who did not ask for an explanation. She ordered him to sit in a chair in the office and called his foster mother to explain what had happened. She asked her to come pick Dylan up and instructed her to not return with him until Monday.

Ms. Truss's anger was evident in her expression when she arrived. She yelled at Dylan and told him to get into the cab that was waiting for them. Dylan did not speak or look at her. He ran ahead and jumped into the vehicle, leaving the door open for her.

ARLY MONDAY MORNING, MRS. EVANS, MR. Peters, Dylan, and Ms. Truss gathered in the principal's office. Dylan did not make eye contact with any of them.

Mr. Peters started. "Tell me why I'm upset about what you did last week."

Dylan stared at the ground and responded, "Because you thought I was dead."

"Your little performance was frightening to me and everyone in the classroom."

"I was just playin' around."

"We didn't know what was happening. I want you to promise that you will never do anything like that again."

"I promise."

Mrs. Evans spoke. "What do you promise, Dylan?"

"I promise to never scare Mr. Peters again, and I promise to be good."

They discussed the incident for several minutes, and then Mrs. Evans asked Dylan and his foster mother to wait outside the office.

"I'm not worried about him doing *that* again," said Mr. Peters. "It was a silly stunt, but no one was hurt by it. I'm still concerned that he's going to injure someone though. He's so volatile. What can we do about that? My students' safety has to be the priority."

Mrs. Evans said, "I've spoken to Mrs. Jules, a behavioral specialist who advises teachers with students like Dylan. She's going to try to come this week or next."

"Why hasn't she come before this?"

"I think it's because he came from Edmonton. The follow-up should have been in place, but he fell through the cracks."

"What kind of a punishment should we give him?"

Mrs. Evans thought for a moment. "He's been severely punished in the past and that hasn't worked. I'd like to give him more community service. I still believe in it. What do you think?"

Mr. Peters did not speak for a moment. "I agree with you, but I must admit, I'm very skeptical that it will improve his behavior. Nothing seems to work with him."

Dylan was called back into the office.

"In all stories," Mr. Peters began, "there are heroes and villains. How do you want to be viewed?"

"What?" Dylan squinted at his teacher. He thought it was an odd question under the circumstances and had been expecting another lecture about bad behavior. "I don't want to be either. I want to be ordinary."

"You want to blend in?"

Dylan nodded.

"Then why do you behave in such outlandish ways?"

Dylan shrugged.

"What you did last week makes you stand out. Your regular outbursts put you in the limelight." Mr. Peters hesitated for a moment. "I don't think you want to be anonymous. Deep down, you want to be noticed. Again, I ask the question—do you want to be viewed as the hero or the villain? You decide."

"Sometimes the hero is the villain," Dylan mumbled.

Mrs. Evans leaned forward. "Dylan, you will be performing community service for your misbehavior."

"Okay." Dylan said nervously.

"You will be working in the library a few hours a week."

"Really?" Dylan was surprised. "That's it?"

"You seem excited," Mrs. Evans responded.

"I thought I was going to have to clean out toilets or something gross."

"No," Mr. Peters smiled. "Not this time anyway."

To Mr. Peters's surprise, Dylan was much calmer than usual for the rest of the week. His tantrums lessened and he kept to himself. Mr. Peters introduced Dylan to Mrs. Giles and tried to get the two of them to work together, but he was not receptive to her. Instead of forcing the issue, Mr. Peters asked Mrs. Giles to work with Brandon, Peter, and Charlie—three boys who also needed extra attention.

Whenever the recess bell rang, Dylan ran into the library and received instructions from the librarian. Dylan felt privileged to work in the library. He loved to be surrounded by shelves of books. Hiding in the dark aisles with hundreds of stories was an adventure to him. He wondered why anyone thought it was a punishment.

EARLY FRIDAY MORNING, HE WALKED UP to one of the walls in the classroom and looked at a dark, mysterious picture one of the students had painted. Mr. Peters did not address him. He could tell that there was something on Dylan's mind, so he waited for him to speak.

"I've been there," he said.

Mr. Peters looked over at him curiously. "Where have you been, Dylan?"

"There." He pointed to the painting. "That dark, shadowy forest."

"That's a painting, Dylan."

"Yeah. I've been there."

Mr. Peters did not know how to respond. He just watched Dylan walk around the room and look at pictures on the wall.

"Grandma says I'm too much trouble and am ruining her life," he said without emotion. Dylan turned around and looked at Mr. Peters. "She follows me everywhere, you know. I'm not even allowed to be alone in my room. She doesn't trust me."

"What does she think you're going to do?"

"I don't know...burn the house down or something."

"Have you ever started a fire?"

"Yeah, but that was a long time ago, when I was younger. I think she's afraid of me." He shoved his hands into his pockets and changed the topic. "I'm meeting a family this weekend and spending one night with them."

"What do you know about them, Dylan?"

"They have a horse."

"Wow! That's exciting. So, they live in the country?"

"Yeah…I guess." He continued to study the artwork without expression.

"How do you feel about this, Dylan?"

"Mmm…I don't know."

"It sounds like the kind of place you would like."

"Yeah…I guess."

"What else do you know about them?"

"They have two little kids." He scrunched up his face.

"Well, that's okay. You like younger children. I'm amazed at how well you work with Jacob in Miss Kelly's class."

"He's funny for a little kid."

"Well, this might be okay. Are you going to give it a chance?"

"Yeah, I guess. They might adopt me."

"I hope it works out for you, but try not to get your hopes too high. When do you leave?"

"At lunchtime."

"Oh, I don't think we can allow that," Mr. Peters teased. "Friday afternoon is a busy time. You can't miss such an important day."

"We don't do any work on Fridays," Dylan said. "It's like a day off."

"Shhh," Mr. Peters whispered. "We don't want this getting around the school."

Dylan smiled and walked into the hall. Mr. Peters felt the door smash into the wall as Dylan exited the school.

"I have to get Mr. Grant to fix that door," the teacher told himself.

Mr. Peters stood at the window and observed Dylan walk across the compound. When he stepped onto the grass, he crouched down and picked something up. He examined the object for a moment and then dropped it into his pocket. Then a sheltered corner between the outside gym wall and an adjacent classroom caught Dylan's attention.

As he approached the secluded spot, Dylan noticed a black fly dive into his shirt. He grabbed the material and tugged at it frantically, trying to free the trapped insect. Then he pulled the shirt away from his skin and peered in. He quickly lost interest in the fleeing insect at the sight of his medallion; it was glowing. As he pulled at the cord, he scanned the area for onlookers. He was alone.

Dylan held the medallion in one of his palms and examined it. Then he placed his other hand overtop and slid down the wall into a crouching position. A dull glow emanated from between his fingers. He raised his hands toward his face, as if praying for forgiveness. He closed his eyes and squeezed his palms together, releasing an intense heat and the faint scent of burning flesh.

16

The Familiar Stranger

DYLAN SLEPT SOUNDLY FOR A SHORT period of time in the shelter of the trees. He dreamed of happier times in Duffle. His entire family was sitting around the dinner table, laughing and eating breakfast. They cleared the table, cleaned their dishes, and got ready for the day. Taya punched her brother on the arm, and he chased her out the door and into the yard. Turning back toward his house, Dylan saw his father step through the door. Just before his foot touched the ground, he turned into a hawk and flew away. Dylan watched the bird circle above his head. He called out to him, but it was too late. The bird seemed to evaporate and then condense into a cloud.

Dylan ran toward the house to alert his mother, but before he could get to her, she stepped out and turned into a dove. She also evaporated before his eyes. He heard his sister scream, so he ran in her direction. He froze when he saw a trog rise out of the trees with his sister in his talons. His own screaming woke him, and he was face-to-face with a small, wrinkled, charcoal-skinned creature. The whites of his eyes almost glowed due to the contrast between his skin and eye color.

"Who…who…who are you?" Dylan stuttered as he pushed back against the wall, his heart pounding against his rib cage.

"Relax, Screaming Boy," the creature mocked in a high, squeaky voice. "I have come to take you to your people."

"How do I know I can trust you?" Dylan asked, knife in hand.

"You don't, but I'm all you've got, so you can stay here and cry or you can come with me, Nervous Boy." The creature spoke quickly and haltingly—at times, without spaces between words.

Dylan fumed. "I'm not crying, little man!"

"Well, you're pouting."

"No, I'm not."

"Yes, you are."

"No, I'm not."

Dylan stood angrily and bumped his head on a branch. He was knocked back to the ground. The creature laughed.

"Be careful, Clumsy Boy. You don't want to hurt yourself."

Dylan scanned the enclosure. It was dimly lit, but his eyes adjusted quickly. The creature jumped to an entrance. Dylan watched the little man peek out of the hiding spot. He flew from one side of the shelter to the other so quickly that Dylan did not see him move.

Dylan wrestled with his thoughts. *Here's a stranger, the very same stranger who peered out at me from the poster, telling me that he's going to take me to my people. Do I go with him or go off on my own? I don't know where I'm going or what I should be doing, but if I go with this…thing, he may lead me into danger.*

"Eat this." A small bundle flew into Dylan's hands. "Then we're off."

Dylan unwrapped the package. It was a dense piece of bread filled with fruit and nuts. The wonderful flavor and freshness surprised him.

"Who are you?" Dylan asked.

"Why does that matter?"

"Well, I'd like to know your name if we're going to be spending time together. I'm Dylan."

"I know who you are, Stupid Boy. I've been watching you for a long time. I have orders to take you to your people."

"Who are you referring to, when you say 'your people'?"

"The people of Duffle, Question Boy. Now stop the interrogation and eat."

"Duffle was destroyed. Where are you *really* taking me?"

The little man did not respond. Dylan continued to eat, and just when he was getting thirsty, a skin of water landed in his lap. The creature was now sitting across from him, and the two of them scrutinized each other for a few minutes. Dylan no longer felt threatened by the unusual character.

"Let's go!" The creature suddenly jumped to the entrance and surveyed the landscape.

Dylan moved toward the opening, but before he got there, the little man was gone. He looked out and saw him standing behind a tree. A split second later, he disappeared again and popped back out from behind another tree. Dylan watched him flit from tree to tree. Then he was back and standing beside Dylan.

"It's safe. Follow me, Slow Boy. Try to keep up."

Dylan knew he was in for a challenge. He had prided himself on his ability to travel quickly, but he had never seen anyone move like this. Before Dylan could ask a question, the creature was up ahead, standing behind a boulder. Dylan peered out and ran to the rock, but just as he got there, the little man vanished. Dylan spied him up ahead, and again, just when Dylan moved within reach, he disappeared.

They proceeded like this for hours. Dylan was beginning to tire. He wanted to let the little man know that he needed to stop for a moment, but he could not catch up to him. Yelling out was not an option—he did not want to attract unwanted attention. Just as Dylan was about to collapse, the little man led him into another cave, very similar to the last one. It was a dugout with branches overhead. The shelter of the leaves muted the sounds of the forest. Dim beams of light shone into the shelter and bounced off his companion's iridescent black hair, revealing a prism of colors.

Someone had prepared them a meal of fresh bread and warm soup, but no one was around. Dylan nestled himself into a rounded spot in the ground, and the little man served him.

"Who gave you orders to take me to my people, Little Man?"

"Again with the questions. I hate questions."

The two of them ate quietly, and then the little man finally broke the silence. "I take my orders from the earth. Don't ask what I mean, for you would never understand."

"I think I do understand," Dylan responded. He paused before he spoke again. "I've been in touch with the earth, and I've learned things that I cannot explain. Tell me about the earth."

The little man was silent for a moment and then he started. "The earth is everything. It provides life; it takes life; the earth is life. Every part of the earth is vital for every living creature. We are connected to her." He scooped the dusty floor into one of his palms.

"This soil is alive. You are a part of it as it is a part of you. Your body is made up of particles that have lived in other life forms, and the components of your body will continue to shape other lives. You never really die—you just transform." He stopped speaking for a moment and let the dirt slip through the fingers of one hand into the palm of the other.

"Your origins are dust…and your end is dust. You have no choice in that." The little man let the dirt slip though his hands like sand in an hourglass. Then he blew the remaining dust into the air. The tiny particles filled the shelter and danced in the light.

"Your choice lies in what you do between the dust you were and the dust you will become. You can change the world, or you can float—aimlessly and without purpose. The choice is yours. You are the earth and the earth is you." He paused for a moment. "I take orders from the earth…as do you. You just don't know it yet."

The two of them sat in silence for a moment. Dylan contemplated what he had just heard. Parts of it made sense while much of it confused him.

"You have been given special powers, Baffled Boy, and you are to use them to make things right—to rejuvenate the earth."

"Now you've lost me. I don't understand how my powers will rejuvenate the earth."

"You will see, Worry Boy. Don't concern yourself with details. You have a mission, and I'm here to assist you."

"But I don't understand my mission."

"You will as time passes. You have much to learn."

"Why are we going to visit the people of Duffle?"

"I don't know. Perhaps you have something to learn. Every experience is a teacher. The purpose of the lesson is not always obvious at the time it's taught. Enough talk. Eat."

When they had finished eating, the two of them rested for a while. Dylan sat back and thought about all the things that had happened to him since the last time he had seen his father, at the Gnarled Oak. The power he had gained was very exciting, and his abilities often surprised him, but a great sadness and sense of loss weighed down on him. He missed the warmth and sense of community Duffle had provided.

Suddenly, the little man jumped up and startled Dylan back to reality.

"Let's go, Sleepy Boy. No more time wasted."

They continued on as before. As the light dimmed, a musty, sweet scent rose up from the forest floor. Dylan began to worry that he would not be able to see his new companion in the dark. He decided that he had to tell him to either slow down or walk with him. Just as Dylan was about to speak his mind, the little man was off again, and Dylan collapsed.

"I'm going to sit here and make him come back to me," Dylan said with an exasperated breath. "I'll never catch up to him long enough to tell him what I'm thinking."

Dylan waited. After several minutes of silence, he thought he'd better get moving. The little man was nowhere to be seen. Dylan listened but all was quiet, which was more terrifying than noise. His heart started to pound. Dylan walked slowly through the trees. He was alone and terrified. With his sword drawn, he looked for shelter. He could sense that he was being observed, so he turned in the direction of the watchful eyes. A silhouette stood in the final minutes of the setting sun. Dylan's heart dropped, and he prepared himself for battle. The figure walked toward him. Dylan stood his ground and prepared to strike.

The silhouette spoke calmly. "Hello, Dylan."

Dylan recognized the voice but could not make out who it was. He stood still and waited.

"You have forgotten your relatives so quickly?"

"Uncle Tanu!" Dylan yelled, and he ran toward him.

They embraced in silence. Then Tanu put his arm around Dylan, turned him around, and guided him through the forest.

"Did you see that little dark guy?" Dylan asked.

"You mean Micro?"

Dylan looked at him curiously.

"At least that's what we call him," Tanu added.

"Where did he go?"

"Who knows? He started appearing a short time ago. He comes and goes. No one knows where he comes from or where he goes."

The night was upon them before Dylan was aware of it. He did not know for how long they had walked together, but it was getting late. The moon shone down on them as they walked into an opening in the forest. A tangle of shrubs, very similar to the one Micro and Dylan had found shelter in previously, came into view.

Tanu put pressure on his shoulder. "Bend down and crawl on your hands and knees."

They entered a warm little dwelling. The moon shone through the branches, and he could see that it was a very comfortable home. Dylan observed many of the same household items that had been in his aunt and uncle's home in Duffle. There was a scattering of objects on the ground, including toys, pots, and pans. Dylan was about to ask about his aunt and cousins when he heard voices. They were coming from a small cave dug into the ground. Dylan looked in, but it was black. He stood still and waited. The appearance of a face startled him.

"Oh, Dylan!" Aunt Vena shouted as she hugged him. "We have missed you so much."

His two cousins appeared and smiled at him shyly. Their faces were streaked with dirt.

"Are you alone here?" Dylan asked.

"No, there are about forty of us," Tanu replied. "When the trogs destroyed our village, some of our people were killed; some were captured and taken away; the rest of us fled. Everyone with children left the night before the trogs came. We were concerned about our families."

"Where's everybody else?"

"I've heard rumors of others living in distant lands, but we don't travel far away from this place. We are comfortable but always in fear. Most of our movement takes place at night. There are eyes out there." Tanu paused. "Enough about us, tell us about you and what you've been doing."

Dylan talked at length about his training and some of his adventures.

"What do you know about Nero and his plans?" Dylan finally asked.

"I've heard that he's looking for complete control over everything," his uncle replied. "He kills anyone who questions his authority. I've even heard that he plans to kill all of the men in Milo, but I don't believe this. There are many rumors, and it's difficult to know what the truth is."

The conversation stopped with the sound of voices. Several men and women crawled into Tanu and Vena's home. Dylan knew all of them. Each one of them hugged him upon entry and then sat down, forming a circle. This was the sense of home he had been missing. It did not matter that they were not in Duffle. Several of the people were his parents' closest friends, and he remembered their regular visits to his home in Duffle. The conversation started with a discussion of old times. They laughed and enjoyed themselves like days of old. Then the conversation gradually turned to what was happening in the present.

"There are rumors about you, Dylan," Pectus said cautiously. "We don't know what to believe anymore. What is your role in the world?"

Dylan did not speak for a moment. He was trying to understand the question, and he wondered about the rumors.

"I'm not certain what my role is, but Ravelle believes I have a part to play. I have much to learn."

"Do you possess Aarial?" asked Vena.

Dylan was uncertain of how to respond. He looked to Tanu, who nodded.

"Yes, I do. My father transferred it to me before he fled."

"I'm pleased that it is you who possesses Aarial," Pectus said. "We've always known that you are different than most, and you will serve the power well. Your father was a great man, and he did his best, but he had difficulty with it."

"I have control of Aarial, and I'll use it to the best of my ability."

"You're all we've got. No one is willing to stand up to Nero. A small number of people have tried and perished in the attempt. He's too powerful. Are you heading toward the castle?"

"I'm not sure. Ravelle gave me two tasks. He told me to destroy Nero and find Queen Gaia, but I don't know which is the priority. He said that Queen Gaia would help me, so I think I should find her first, but I've never heard of her. Do any of you know anything about Queen Gaia?"

Dylan scanned their faces, but they averted their eyes from his gaze. No one spoke for a few moments. Then Tanu spoke up. "I've only heard about her. She is supposed to have great powers—powers beyond all comprehension. I heard your father curse her many times, but he would never tell me who she was. I'm sorry, but I cannot help you. I don't know anything about her."

Vena interrupted. "It's getting late. Dylan has had a long day, and he needs his rest before he leaves."

"What?" he blurted. "You're making me go?" An uncomfortable silence filled the room. "For so long, I've yearned for the comforts of home. This is the closest I've come in a long time. I want to stay."

"This is not comfort," Tanu said. "This is survival. It's temporary and won't last. I'm not asking you to leave, Dylan, but I want you to consider a few things. Our future depends on you. You're the only one who can make things right." Then he stopped for a moment, choosing his words carefully. "You're welcome to stay for as long as you like. Our fear is that Nero will be drawn to our homes in search of you. We're fairly safe at the moment, but we're concerned about our families."

"I understand." Dylan's feeling of rejection blanketed his words.

One by one, his friends left the shelter. On their way out, they embraced Dylan and spoke words of encouragement. His heart sank with the last farewell.

Tanu and Dylan spoke quietly while preparing his bed. "Do you understand, Dylan?"

"Yes, I do, but that doesn't make it any easier. I'm constantly leaving the ones I love."

"We'll all be together one day, Dylan. Comfort is a wonderful thing, but you must continue your quest. Your role is bigger than this. You have a heavy burden, and I'm sorry for that, but you are our future. Our thoughts and hopes are with you." His eyes expressed an awareness of the fact that they may never see each other again. "Good-night, Dylan."

Dylan lay down and stared up at the ceiling. His mind raced as he went over the events of the day. He thought about his travels with Micro and all the things that had been said, but one phrase kept repeating itself—*Your origins are dust, and your end is dust. You have no choice in that.*

Just as he was drifting into sleep, the uncertainty of tomorrow snapped him wide awake again. He felt his stomach tighten at the idea of leaving. Exhaustion finally caught up with him, and he dozed off with the comfort of a silent whisper: *You can change the world, or you can float—aimlessly and without purpose…change the world or float…change the world or float…change the world or…aimlessly and without purpose… aimlessly and without purpose…aimlessly…aim…less…ly.*

Collin Paulson

17
Fear of the Unknown

DYLAN WALKED INTO THE CLASSROOM LOOKING bedraggled and disheveled.

"How was your weekend, Dylan?" Mr. Peters asked from his desk.

"Okay, I guess."

"I was thinking of you this weekend. How was your visit with the family in the country?"

"Mmm…not so good."

"Why? What happened?"

"They didn't like me."

"Why do you say that?"

Dylan did not answer. He stared at the ground and shifted his weight from one foot to the other.

"What happened, Dylan?"

"They think…I'm dangerous, and they're worried about me being around their kids."

"What happened, Dylan?"

"I started a fire." He quickly added, "But it was a small one."

"Oh, Dylan! Why did you do that?"

"I don't know."

Mr. Peters shook his head. "So you chose to be the villain—again."

Dylan's brow furrowed and he lowered his head.

"Remember the other option."

Dylan spun around and sprinted out of the classroom. Mr. Peters leaned back in his chair and stared up at the ceiling. He inhaled deeply and let out a heavy sigh before he shook his head and went back to his work.

Mrs. Carter, the resource teacher, stepped into the room. "Do you want me to take Dylan for the first period this morning and work on some math with him? I really enjoyed working with him last week."

"That would be good. Thank-you so much."

"I should be able to take him for an hour, three out of five days, if that works for you."

"That sounds great. It will be such a relief. Oh, I'll warn you that he may be a little off this morning—more than usual. He didn't have a very good weekend."

"Why? What happened?"

"His social worker is trying to find another placement for him, and he met the family considering it. It sounded like a great place and a nice match for him."

"What happened?"

"He started a fire."

"Oh my God!" Mrs. Carter blurted out.

"Why do you think he would jeopardize his placement like that?" Mr. Peters asked. "It's got to be better than where he is now."

"Fear of the unknown," Mrs. Carter said bluntly. "He may not have it great where he is, but it's what he knows."

"Yeah, I guess. His foster mother doesn't give him any privacy. The poor kid is followed from room to room. He's not even allowed to go to the bathroom in privacy. He has to leave the door open."

Mrs. Carter nodded with a look of understanding. "It's not as easy as you think, Mr. Peters. I took in a foster child a few years ago, and I did things that I thought I'd never do. I also followed him everywhere. He wasn't as difficult as Dylan, but many of his behaviors were very similar."

"How old was he?" Mr. Peters asked.

"Uh…nine or ten. He used to do such strange things. I caught him playing with matches many times. I became very neurotic. It got to the point where I didn't allow him out of my sight. I once caught him putting turpentine in a shampoo bottle. I wanted to help him, but my kids were small at the time, and I was worried about them. I know Dylan's foster mother isn't an ideal caregiver, but I can relate."

Mr. Peters did not say anything for a moment. "Wow, you've really opened my eyes. I can't imagine what it's like to deal with him all day. I only have him five hours a day."

The bell rang, and the students started streaming into the classroom. Mrs. Carter waited for Dylan by his desk. When he saw her, he cringed and ran straight over to the meeting area. He could feel her watching him, but he resisted looking directly at her. Out of the corner of his eye, he saw her finger move. She was smiling at him and beckoning for him to follow her.

"Aah, I hate math," he whined as he stood up and proceeded over to the door.

He was leaving the room when Mrs. Carter said, "You'll need your math scribbler, Dylan."

"Oh!" he moaned. He stomped over to his desk, lifted up the desktop, and searched for his book.

"Your desk is out of control," Mrs. Carter said with a smile.

"I just cleaned it," he said angrily. "I can't find it. Someone must have stolen it."

"Here, take this one." Mrs. Carter reached into his desk.

"I can do it!" he screamed. "You're ruining my day, you know!"

Mrs. Carter did not say anything. She walked out of the room, and Dylan followed her with his head down.

Mr. Peters greeted his students and got them started on their math. Brandon, Peter, Charlie, and Albert went to the library to work with Mrs. Giles. The students had been working quietly for forty-five minutes when Dylan flew into the classroom. His papers ruffled as he ran, and he was out of breath when he collapsed into his seat. He looked over at Mr. Peters, who was smiling at the flurry of activity.

"When's gym?" Dylan asked between gasps.

"It looks like you had your exercise for the day."

"I want to play badminton."

Mr. Peters walked over to him and leaned on his desk.

"Please, Dylan," he said quietly. "Look around you. Your classmates are trying to get their work done. You need—"

"Yeah, but when's gym?"

Mr. Peters smiled and gave up. "Soon," he said.

"I know what *soon* means," Dylan said, "but teachers don't."

Again, Mr. Peters smiled. "We'll be in the gym by 10:30."

"Are we playing badminton today?"

"Yes, we are."

"Can I play you?"

"We'll see."

"Oh, that's another one I hate. *We'll see* always means no."

"I have to supervise the class, so I won't be able to play with you the whole time. I will try to fit in a game once everyone gets going. There are twenty-eight badminton players in this class who'd like to play you."

"They all suck."

"That's not true, Dylan. There are some very good players in this class."

Before Dylan could say another word, Mr. Peters called out, "Put your books away and sit quietly at your desks."

Within seconds, the room was silent. All the students had their arms on their desks and their heads rested upon their forearms. A few students could be heard hushing others.

"Why is it that everyone can be ready for gym instantly but it takes you ten minutes for other subjects?" Mr. Peters asked.

"Because gym is fun!" someone shouted out.

Mr. Peters turned. "Oh, and math isn't?"

Several students shouted, "Noooo!"

"I like math, Mr. Peters," Michelle blurted out cheerfully.

"You would!" laughed a student on the other side of the room.

Jennifer hit Michelle over the head with a teen magazine. Michelle stuck out her tongue and crinkled her nose at Jennifer.

"Okay, Albert's group line up."

Albert stood up. As he walked over to the door, he swung his hips and stuck out his tongue at his classmates.

"Okay, Albert's group, sit down."

Everyone not in Albert's group laughed, and Albert ran back to his seat with a red face. "Thanks a lot, Albert," someone hissed through clenched teeth. "Now we're going to get the crummy racquets."

Mr. Peters called one group at a time to line up. The students were very well behaved after seeing what had happened to the first group. No one wanted a racquet with missing strings. Then Mr. Peters walked to the front of the line and waited for the students to be still.

"Okay, when we get to the gym, grab a racquet and a partner and start hitting the birdie back and forth."

Mr. Peters proceeded down the hall with his students in close pursuit. As each student passed through the gym doors, he or she raced to the badminton racquets, which were in buckets along one wall. Jennifer grabbed a racquet an instant before Dylan, but he ripped it out of her hands. He smiled and ran off. She was about to say something but realized that she didn't have time to complain because all of the best racquets were being scooped up.

It took a few minutes but finally everyone had a partner—except for Dylan and Albert. Albert was hitting his birdie as high as he could, trying to get it stuck in the rafters. For every hit, he missed three or four times. Mr. Peters laughed quietly to himself.

Dylan started running all over the gym screaming, "WATCH OUT!" Even though he appeared out of control, he never missed the birdie. Mr. Peters was just about to warn him to stop running when he ran into Janna.

"Hey!" Janna screamed. "Watch where you're going."

Dylan screamed back, "Stay out of my way!"

He was about to scream an obscenity but noticed his teacher observing him. Dylan sped to another part of the gym and continued like nothing had happened.

The only two without partners could not play together; Mr. Peters knew it would be unsafe for Albert. The teacher walked over to Dylan, and Dylan knocked the birdie in his direction. Mr. Peters picked it up.

"Why don't you have a partner, Dylan?"

"Because everyone is lousy."

"I'll play with you for a few minutes, and then I'll find you a partner."

The two of them hit the birdie back and forth. Dylan never missed a shot. Mr. Peters started to challenge him with more difficult shots, and he was able to retrieve all of them.

While they rallied, Jake disrupted his classmates' games by hitting their birdies across the gym. Mr. Peters heard the complaints, so he caught the next wayward birdie and glared in Jake's direction. Jake stopped immediately and went back to playing with his partner.

Without taking his eyes off Jake, Mr. Peters spoke to Dylan. "You're very good, Dylan. Where did you learn to play like that?"

"I don't know," Dylan responded. "Serve, Mr. P."

"I have to get around to everyone. I'll find you a partner though."

Dylan continued playing by himself while Mr. Peters circled the gym, praising the students. Every once in a while, he would stop a game to give a tip or demonstrate a skill to a pair of students.

When he got to Sam and Tony, Mr. Peters jumped in and caught Sam's serve behind his back. "Hey, Tony! I want you to play Dylan."

"Oh…he's mean," Tony replied.

"You're a very good player, and he needs someone who can challenge him."

"What am I? Chopped liver?" Sam whined.

"No. You're also very good, Sam," Mr. Peters responded.

"Yeah, right," Sam said sarcastically. "Who am I going to play?"

"You can play Albert."

"He can't even hit the birdie."

"So teach him."

Sam started complaining again but stopped when he saw Mr. Peters's expression.

While Mr. Peters talked to Tony and Sam, Jake began interrupting others' games again. He was about to hit Dylan's birdie when Dylan spun around and faced him with fire in his eyes. His sudden movement caught Jake off guard. Jake's head snapped back, and the birdie bounced off his head and fell to the ground.

"Touch my birdie," Dylan seethed, "and *you*. Will bathe. In a pool of blood."

Jake froze, eyes wide open. He laughed uncomfortably and smiled without joy. Slowly, he turned and went back to join his partner, who was also speechless.

Mr. Peters led Tony over to his new partner. He put his hand on Dylan's shoulder, unaware of what had just happened. "I have a partner for you. I want you to be nice and play fairly."

"Who is it?" Dylan looked in the direction Mr. Peters was looking. "That kid? He's a geek."

"I will not have this, Dylan. If you're going to insult the other students, you won't be playing at all."

"Okay. I'll play him," he said grudgingly. "What's the kid's name?"

"You don't know his name?" Mr. Peters asked. "After all this time, you haven't learned his name?"

Dylan did not respond. He looked at the ground.

"His name is Tony. Now have fun."

Dylan hit the birdie to Tony, and he returned it. Mr. Peters watched them for several minutes. Then he continued circling the gym.

Sam and Albert attracted his attention. Sam stood straight up and hit the birdie to Albert, without enthusiasm. Albert swung at it two, three, four times and looked to the direction it should have gone. He was surprised to see it lying on the ground by his feet. He picked it up and swung; it fell to the ground. Again, he picked it up and swung; it fell to the ground. After the fourth attempt, the birdie flew over to Sam who hit it, again without enthusiasm. It was a perfect shot for Albert, but he missed it, and it fell to the ground. Again, Albert picked it up and swung. He missed, and continued to try to hit it. Mr. Peters was about to help Albert when he heard Dylan.

"You no good bum—you'll never amount to anything!" Dylan screamed at Tony. "You'll always be a bum!"

"Go to the office!" Mr. Peters yelled.

Dylan bounced his racquet off the floor. He stamped his feet violently as he marched toward the door. Just before he exited the gym, he turned; his face was bright red.

"YOU ALL SUCK!" he screamed.

Some of the students stopped and laughed, but most of them just continued playing. Dylan stormed back to the hallway outside his classroom. He knocked several jackets to the ground as he grabbed his coat. Then he lunged at the door and left the building.

In the upper tower of the creative playground, Dylan curled up into a tight ball. The flimsy tin walls helped shield him from the frigid wind, but a mighty blast whistled through the cracks. A black fly successfully challenged the powerful gust by gripping onto a red, metal bar just above his head. Its wings vibrated rapidly.

Dylan felt the heat of the medallion and reached into his shirt. He placed the object into one of his palms and pressed his other hand over it. A dull glow emanated from between his fingers and warmed his hands. He brought his hands toward his face until one knuckle touched his nose. He closed his eyes and squeezed his palms together. A delicate burning smell wafted into the air.

18
Ancient Enemies

WHILE DYLAN SLEPT, NERO FUMED. HE paced back and forth, cursing and yelling profanities at the stone walls. In the corner of the room, two trog guards cowered, awaiting instructions.

"I can't believe he killed Tracker! He was the only bloody trog with any sense. Without him, you're lost. I keep telling you to work as a team, but then you go off on your own and get killed. This used to happen before Tracker rose to the top of your smelly pack. Somehow, he could get you to work together."

Nero paused to catch his breath. "He's just a boy—he's a pip-squeak! How could he have killed two of my trogs? And now I hear that he has Tracker's medallion. Who knows what kind of advantage that will give him? I want him captured and brought to me!"

As Nero spewed the last few words, he flew over to the two guards and picked them off the floor—one in each hand. He glared into the eyes of one of them and then into the eyes of the other. "Assemble all of the trogs and soldiers," he hissed with great intensity. Then he dropped them to the floor. "DO IT NOW!"

• • •

"**P**SSST. PSSST. PSSST!"

Dylan jumped to his feet and looked around the shelter. He heard giggling from a dark corner.

"Good morning, Startle Boy."

"Micro!" Dylan cried in a low voice. "What are you trying to do to me?"

"I'm trying to wake you, Frightened Boy. Get your things together. We have to go."

"What's the hurry? It's still dark out."

"You can't stay in one place for too long. There are people looking for you, and you will bring danger to anyone associated with you. Let's go."

Dylan grabbed his bag and threw it over his shoulder. Micro was out of the shelter before Dylan was ready. He looked around the room and thought of the previous night and how much he had enjoyed the time with his people. He closed his eyes tightly and then opened them and walked toward the entrance.

It was still dark outside, but the moon was bright, and stars filled the sky. He scanned the forest and saw Micro, who allowed him to catch up.

"You have to keep up, Slow Boy," Micro said as he looked around the forest.

"I'm trying, Micro, but you're too fast. Where are you taking me?"

"I don't know. All I know is that I am supposed to guide you there."

"That doesn't make any sense. How can you guide me there if you don't know where I'm going?"

"You ask too many questions. All you need to know is that I will never be too far away."

Dylan's sigh expressed his frustration. He said nothing more and followed Micro through the forest. Micro moved more slowly than he had the previous day, and the gap between them was only a few paces. When Dylan sped up, Micro sped up. When Dylan slowed, Micro slowed.

When daylight replaced darkness, they had travelled a fair distance. Just as Dylan was tiring and losing his stride, Micro sat down on a stone.

"Rest," he uttered.

Dylan collapsed at the command and stared up at the bright blue sky. He lay there for several minutes before realizing that he was hungry. He reached into his bag, which Aunt Vena had filled with food. The first thing he grabbed was a flat piece of bread covered with some kind of brown, chunky paste. He wondered what it was but decided that it didn't really matter.

After several mouthfuls, he looked around for Micro, wanting to offer him some food. Dylan peered over the fallen tree he was leaning against and shivered at the sight of Micro dabbing at small bugs with his moistened finger and placing them on his tongue. The little man looked up at Dylan and smiled, revealing black bug specks on his tawny teeth. Dylan felt like gagging, so he turned around before he lost his appetite.

Following his fill of bread, he ate some dried fruit and stared up at the heavens. A bird circled high above his head, and the warmth of the sun and comfort of the mossy ground put him at ease. He drifted in and out of dreams.

"WAKE UP!" echoed throughout the forest.

He knew Micro had woken him, but he was nowhere to be seen. Dylan grabbed his bag and scurried up a massive tree. His vision was sharp, and he sensed everything around him. Danger filled the air. He could smell it—the pungent scent of trog filth. Dylan waited silently, looking for his enemy. Branches rustled, and out of the dense brush, a trog came into view. Dylan held his breath.

The trog was sniffing like a bloodhound and walking toward Dylan's tree. Dylan climbed around to the other side so that he would be out of sight. He heard each step and sensed that it was getting closer. Then… silence.

Dylan knew that the trog was directly below him—one of his wings came into view— so he gripped the handle of his sword and got ready to pounce. The trog circled the tree and then stood right below Dylan again. Slowly, he tilted his head skyward. Just as the creature's focus locked on his enemy, Dylan leapt out of the tree, pulling his sword out of its sheath on the way down. Before the trog knew what had hit him, Dylan's sword went right through his chest. With one final gasp, the trog vomited blood and let out a horrible cry. Dylan withdrew his sword and stepped away from the dying creature.

"You are a *stupid* bunch!" he hollered. "I curse you for forcing me to kill you!"

Dylan collapsed on the ground, gazing sideways at his latest victim. His ability to kill gave him no satisfaction. He pondered his next move and looked around for Micro. He was nowhere to be seen.

"I can't wait for him," Dylan whispered despondently.

Dylan dragged his sword through the grass, discoloring it with purple trog blood. After sheathing the blade, he threw his bag over his shoulder and ran off in the direction they had been travelling before they had stopped to rest. The sun was directly overhead. He didn't know where he was going, but he knew that he had to keep moving. The light breeze felt good on his damp forehead. It was the hottest part of the day, and Dylan was starting to tire. He decided to look for a place to rest.

From the top of a rocky knoll, Dylan spotted a deep, green pond. He was hot, and the water looked so refreshing. When he got to the water's edge, he looked around and sniffed the air. He was alone. Within minutes, he was naked and swimming in the cool mountain water. The lake was calm, but Dylan could feel a slight current pulling him away from the shore. Sunlight reflected off a jewel on the hilt of his sword and blinded him for a second.

Where would I be without my sword? Dylan thought.

He swam to shore with his head out of the water, never taking his sight off his weapon.

At the water's edge, he grabbed his things, and then he ran naked through the woods. He stopped when he reached the cover of the trees. He felt safe there, so he decided to wait out the heat of the day aboveground. Dylan put his clothes on, climbed a misshapen tree, and rested on a large branch, high above the ground. Some time later, he awoke to the sound of a distant jingle. The sky was beginning to darken.

How long have I slept? he wondered.

Dampness had risen from the forest floor. He remained completely still, trying to make out the source of the sound. His tension rose with the sound of the bells getting louder and louder. He got into a comfortable position on his branch and kept an eye on the spot where he thought the sound was coming from.

The outline of a man appeared. With every step, the jingle of bells rang out. Someone followed behind the man. Then another person behind the second. A string of people was approaching.

Dylan did not move. As the people neared, details came into view. The person in front was a man, and he carried a large pole covered in feathers. Every few feet, he pounded the shaft on the ground. The impact produced a hollow sound. Dylan could see that they all had bells wrapped around their ankles, and with every step, they jingled.

The line of people was passing directly under his tree. Dylan lay on his branch and watched silently. He was fascinated by the display and wondered who they were and what they were doing. His vision followed the seemingly endless line of people into the forest.

Something in the line glowed. As the light got closer, he saw that it was actually several lights on a circular holder being carried on someone's head. A beautiful girl came into focus beneath a heavenly crown of candles. Wavy, black hair framed her perfect complexion. He had never seen a more beautiful human being. Just as she was about to pass under his tree, she glanced up without tilting her head.

Dylan was certain that they had made eye contact, and he felt his heart pound. He wondered if it was her beauty or the fear of being caught that had quickened his heart. He continued to gaze upon her until she was out of sight.

Then he focused back on the spot where the line of people was coming from. Another glowing crown appeared from out of the forest. The person carrying this light was much slower, and shaky, for the lights flickered. When the bearer of light came into view, Dylan could see that it was an old woman; two younger women assisted her. Dylan watched them intently. The old woman was dressed in the same white gown as the young woman and had the same crown of candles upon her head. Dylan saw that the procession ended just beyond her.

Behind her were six children—three girls and three boys. As the end of the procession passed under the tree, Dylan sighed, relieved that he had not been discovered. He was also very curious. The ceremony that he had observed was beautiful, and he wondered what they were doing.

Just as the last boy was about to step out of sight, he turned and looked directly up at Dylan. Dylan did not move. The boy waved and motioned for him to follow them. Then he was gone. Dylan wondered if they had all seen him. His curiosity got the best of him. He knew he had to follow the group to find out what they were doing.

Watching the light bob up and down, he stepped quietly through the forest. The intensity of the crown guided him through the night. Then the light stopped, and he heard chanting. From behind a tree, he could see the procession gathered at the shore and the moon's reflection on the water. He found the chanting and the calm lapping of the waves hypnotic and soothing. His mind wandered at the sound of their voices.

A long silence startled him, and he focused on one man, who took the old woman in his arms and embraced her. The crowd was solemn, but no one was crying. Four men walked into the water and pulled a raft, which was being pushed by another man who had just appeared, to shore. The men rested one side upon the shore and steadied the other in the water. The man who had hugged the old woman led her onto the raft. She sat crossed-legged and looked out to the middle of the water. Then the men who were in the water pushed her away from shore, and she floated away.

Dylan thought that she must have been pulled with the undertow he had felt earlier in the day.

The crowd continued their somber song and watched her silhouette fade into the night. In unison, they lowered their heads and chanted. This was followed by several minutes of silence.

The silence was broken by a man's voice, but Dylan could not tell who was speaking. "You are welcome to join us." Everyone turned, and one by one, the people formed a procession and walked back the way they had come.

Dylan froze against the tree. His mind raced. *Who is welcome to join them? Me?* He did not move, just listened. *Should I join them? Maybe they know of Queen Gaia.*

Dylan sat alone with his thoughts for a few moments.

The touch of a soft hand alarmed him. He jumped to his feet and saw a small child smiling up at him. Dylan smiled back. Then the child put his hand in Dylan's and led him toward the procession. They walked hand in hand at the end of the line. Dylan sensed he could trust these people.

They walked through the forest for several minutes before coming upon a great arch of rock. A light shone inside the cave. Dylan walked into the shelter and observed everyone standing around a large fire that reached toward the top of the cave, which opened to the sky. The small child led Dylan toward the wall, and they walked up a steep rock to a dusty platform where they could watch the proceedings.

Several children were already there, and they greeted Dylan with smiles. A large man stood over the beautiful girl and chanted. Then he removed the crown of lights and held it above his head. He spoke a few words while looking through the crown toward the sky. Then he tossed it into the fire, and a joyous shout erupted from the crowd. Everyone began singing and dancing wildly for a minute and then stopped. Dylan felt all eyes upon him. He looked down at the faces staring up at him.

"We have been awaiting your arrival; it has been prophesied. You are the one who will set things straight."

There was silence for a few moments, and then Dylan spoke. "Thank-you for your hospitality. All I want is a warm meal, your company, and the warmth of your shelter."

With these words, the group started moving, and before Dylan's eyes, a great feast materialized. Dylan and the child climbed down and walked among the people, who spread as they passed. Dylan stood face-to-face with the man who had greeted him.

"Welcome, from the people of Tipple. I am Sheil."

Dylan gasped, and his voice cracked when he said, "I am Dylan, and I come from…I come from…far away."

"You come from Duffle," the man stated. A great outcry echoed off the walls of the cave, and the mood changed instantly. Dylan suddenly felt afraid. "You come from Duffle, and you need not fear. The trouble between our people is ancient history. No one even remembers why we're supposed to hate each other anymore." The man paused and spoke to the crowd. "Eat, be merry, and show Dylan the hospitality of

Tipple." Then he spoke directly to Dylan. "When you've had your fill, we will talk."

Again, the mood changed instantly. The warmth and hospitality that had initially greeted him returned. Dylan walked among the crowd of smiling faces. The people shook his hand and spoke kind words to him. He thought back to the stories he had heard about Tipple. *Greedy, violent, cannibals* were just a few words that came to mind. *These cannot be the same people I've been told about,* Dylan thought. *They seem kind and generous. Why am I supposed to be a sworn enemy of a people I don't even know?*

Dylan consumed a large amount of food and drink, and when he was so full that his belly ached, he asked to see Sheil. He was led down a short corridor to a private room in the cave wall. Sheil was seated on the floor, and when he saw Dylan, he stood up and put his arm around him.

"Come in, my friend."

The two of them sat crossed-legged on a floor of blankets. Dylan studied the walls of the cave while Sheil studied him. Colorful drawings, revealing stories of struggles and triumphs, surrounded them.

"Tell me of your travels," Sheil requested.

"I have travelled far and learned much, but one of the most important things I have discovered is how kind and generous your people are. In my mind, you were closer to trogs than humans."

"You have heard ghastly things about our people."

At this, Dylan nodded.

"In the distant past, the people of Duffle and Tipple had their battles, but there has been no conflict in my lifetime or my father's lifetime. That is ancient history, and yet rumors still exist. My people know very little about you, and until today, you knew very little about us; finding out the truth is the only path. We are more similar than we are different." Sheil paused and gazed into Dylan's eyes. "The human being is a complex creature, and we often do things that don't make sense. We need the *other* to define the *us.*"

Dylan's puzzled expression put a smile on Sheil's face. He paused for a moment.

"We elevate ourselves by denigrating others—the more superior a group feels, the more cohesive it becomes. We convince ourselves that we are better and that you are greedy savages who drink the blood of your enemies or drown your babies in oil. I can see by your expression that these things have been said about us.

"A group creates an enemy in order to remain strong. We designated you as our enemy. If Duffle didn't exist, we would have found someone else to hate. We're all human, and we all belong to the human race. It doesn't matter that I'm from Tipple and that you're from Duffle. We're all distant relatives, but that doesn't seem to matter to most people."

The two of them sat quietly for several minutes, and Dylan thought about what he had just heard.

"I'm pleased that I have met you and your people," Dylan finally said. "You are no different than my community. If I complete my quest and get back to Duffle, I'll let them know what I have learned. Our leaders will get together and straighten things out. There's no reason why we cannot be friends and work together."

"Those are nice sentiments, and I hope that what you say is true, but there will be people who will resist such a union. Some people will always feel the need to create divisions. Nothing unites a group like a common enemy."

After a few moments of silence, Dylan asked, "How have you been affected by Nero?"

"He slaughtered many of my people, and some were captured and taken to his castle. They killed Tikva, our leader. He is sorely missed." He paused for a moment. "We are a strong people, and we are well trained, but we could not defeat the trogs and Nero's men. There were too many of them. Our village was burned to the ground, and we have been forced into hiding. We have made our new home as comfortable as possible, but we're tired of hiding." Sheil leaned back on one arm. Tell me about your quest."

"I'm still unclear about what my quest is. All I know is that I am to seek Queen Gaia," he paused, "and destroy Nero."

"You've been given an ominous task, for Nero is a very powerful man with the support of many. How do you intend to get to him?"

"I don't know. I was hoping to find Queen Gaia first. She'll be able to help me. Do you know anything of Queen Gaia?"

"She's a rumor," Sheil said with certainty. "She doesn't exist."

Dylan felt his heart pound and his face redden.

"No! She's not a rumor! My quest revolves around finding her. She cannot be a rumor."

Sheil did not speak for a moment, for he saw the impact of his statement.

"My people have searched for her for generations to no avail. We believe she is a myth. I don't want to destroy your spirit, but I think you should look elsewhere for assistance. I can see that you have superior powers. Your eyes reveal great wisdom, understanding, and strength for such a young man. You need to find the strength within yourself. Turn inward and don't rely upon a myth."

Dylan wanted to scream. He did not know what to say or do next. *Is half of my mission a myth?* He wondered. *How do I deal with this news?* Dylan rounded his shoulders, leaned forward, and stared at the ground. The powerful warrior had become a frail child.

"Turn inward," Sheil repeated, and he got up from the floor and left Dylan alone.

Dylan's mind wandered for several minutes. Then, in a flash, his body shook, and he was completely focused. He saw himself in Stellar Hall, in the seat by the river. Everything he had learned came back to him. All the wonders of the world passed before his eyes and shot electrical impulses throughout his nervous system. His convulsing body shook violently—faster, faster, faster.

CRACK! echoed in his skull. With the last image his body stiffened, and as it faded his body softened. Slowly, he became aware of his surroundings. He felt rejuvenated and ready to continue the journey. It did not matter if Queen Gaia did not exist. There was a Nero, and as long as he lived, there would be evil. He decided that he would not give up on the queen but that his main focus at this moment would be the king.

I will find and destroy him. Tomorrow, I head for the castle.

Sheil entered the room and observed that the warrior had returned. He smiled.

"You have turned inward."

Dylan opened his eyes.

"That is where your strength lies."

The noise from the celebration was dying down, as was the light.

"Rest now." Sheil pulled a blanket over his shoulders and lay down. Dylan did the same. The two of them stared into the fire until their eyelids closed over their tired eyes.

Collin Paulson

19

The Knife

THE COMMOTION OF STUDENTS BOUNDING OUT of the school startled Dylan. He rubbed his eyes and peered through the cracks of the playground tower. Sam scampered clumsily across the field with Jake in close pursuit. He tripped over the playground perimeter, and Jake landed on top of him.

"I gotcha!" Jake rolled Sam over and pinned his arms to the ground with his knees while sitting on his chest.

"Get off, Jake!" Sam exhaled, trying to catch his breath. "I was just joking."

"Well, so am I," Jake giggled.

He dangled a spit snake over Sam's face.

"Oh, gross!" Sam howled. He could barely breathe, but he was able to force out his words. "You're disgusting!"

Jake chuckled. The spit snake went up and down, each time getting a little closer to Sam's nose. Finally, Jake sucked it in, and Sam stopped struggling for a moment—believing it was over.

Then Jake snorted and gagged, gathering the saliva mixture of spit and nasal mucous.

"No, no, no!" Sam pleaded. "Please don't."

Sam shook his head frantically and closed his eyes while Jake sloshed it around in his mouth. He opened his eyes only to see the biggest spit snake *ever* appear between Jake's lips. Sam froze, fearing any movement might detach it from his lips. Closer…closer…closer. Just as Jake was about to suck it in, Dylan stood up on the creative playground and startled the bully, who glanced up at him. The snake dropped into Sam's eye and drained into his hair.

"You pig!" Sam sputtered, wiping his face with his jacket sleeve. "You disgusting pig!"

Jake loosened his hold on Sam, who twisted out from under him.

"I'm sorry," Jake apologized. "I didn't mean it. I wasn't gonna *really* do it."

Sam shoved Jake in the chest and walked away, tears streaming down his face. Jake looked up at Dylan, who glared down at him with a frightening expression that Jake could not interpret.

"It was just a joke," Jake said guiltily. "I was just playin' around." Jake kicked the ground and walked away.

When the bigger boy was out of sight, Dylan jumped off the creative playground and ran across the field.

After lunch, Mrs. Evans walked to Mr. Peters's room and stood in the doorway. She watched the students for several minutes before Mr. Peters noticed her.

"Your little friend didn't show up to class this afternoon?" Mrs. Evans spoke quietly, so the students wouldn't hear her.

"No, he didn't. I feel guilty saying this, but I've really enjoyed my class without him. My stress level is way down."

"Don't be concerned, but I thought you might want to know that he isn't at home." She stepped into the room and smiled at the students who noticed her.

Mr. Peters raised his eyebrows. "Where is he?"

"I don't know. His foster mother isn't concerned. She said that he often disappears when he's mad. He'll turn up."

"I hope so. I feel even guiltier now. I've enjoyed this afternoon so much. I forgot what a neat group of kids these are. I haven't been allowed to enjoy them since Dylan arrived. He takes all of my time."

"I'm sure your students feel the difference when he isn't here."

"They do. Everyone is very nice to each other. No one is rude or disruptive."

"Someone would step into his place if he weren't here though."

"What do you mean?"

"I've seen it many times. One child becomes the bad kid, the focus of all the problems in the classroom—the scapegoat. When that child leaves, someone else replaces him."

"Really!"

"It's true. I've experienced it. No one in this class would compare to Dylan, but someone would take his place. Remember the problems you had with Jake."

Mr. Peters thought for a moment. "Yeah, he was a bit of a challenge... and still is at times. He often picks on the others, but he's usually more playful than mean. I think his size is part of the reason he takes on the tough-guy persona. He definitely seeks attention, but he's more of a show-off or class clown than a bully."

"How are things going with Mrs. Giles?" Mrs. Evans asked. "Does Dylan like working with her?"

"She's very nice, and the kids like her, but she can't work with Dylan. She's tried, but he won't listen or respond to her. He doesn't like her. I don't think he likes women. Mrs. Giles works with some of my other students who need extra help, so I'm freed up to work with Dylan and the rest of the class."

"She was hired to work with him."

"I know that, but what can I do? He refuses to work with her."

Just then, Albert walked up to Mrs. Evans and showed her his work, which she complimented.

When Albert walked away, she asked, "How's Albert doing?"

"Oh, fine. He's way behind, and he has very few friends, but he seems happy. He can be such a nut, but I think it's just because he's so immature. I hope he grows out of it. Did I tell you what he did yesterday?"

Mrs. Evans shook her head. "What now?"

"I was teaching a math lesson and writing on the whiteboard. When I turned around, he had his nose taped to his forehead. I don't know how he did it, but it was the funniest thing I've ever seen. He looked like a little pig. It took all my power to show him I was angry, when really, I just wanted to laugh."

"Well," Mrs. Evans responded with a chuckle, "at least you've got some good stories to tell.

EARLY THE NEXT MORNING, DYLAN SAUNTERED into the classroom.
"Where were you yesterday afternoon, Dylan?"

"I was abducted," he said casually while studying the new artwork. "These are cool. When did you do these?"

"Yesterday."

"Oh, no fair. Why didn't you wait for me?"

"We can't sit around waiting for you to show up. Who abducted you?"

Dylan turned excitedly and walked over to Mr. Peters's desk. "Teenagers! Teenagers abducted me and beat me up."

"Are you okay?"

"Yeah...I guess."

"I don't see any bruises, Dylan. What did they do?"

Dylan shuffled from side to side. "They took me to their clubhouse and made me do awful things."

"Why would they abduct you?"

"They don't like me," Dylan responded quickly.

"Who doesn't like you? All teenagers?"

"That's right."

"Why is that? What do they have against you?"

"I don't know. All I know is that teenagers don't like me."

"Do you *honestly* believe that every teenager is out to get you?"

"Well, maybe not the teenagers in China...but they haven't met me. If they met me, they wouldn't like me, and they would try to get me. I need to protect myself."

"Protect yourself? What do you mean?"

"Just what I said." He threw two punches at an imaginary enemy, then he kicked him and stepped over top of him.

Mr. Peters smiled. "You better go burn off some of that energy outside."

Dylan turned and ran out of the room.

The bell rang several minutes later, and students began filing into the classroom. Mr. Peters was at his desk when Mr. Bowman walked in.

He spoke quietly. "A student just told me that Dylan showed him a knife."

"Again?" Mr. Peters shook his head. "Who said it? Remember the last time this happened? Brian accused him of having a knife, but we came to the conclusion that he was just trying to get him into trouble."

"No, one of the younger students told me. He doesn't have a history of lying. He's certainly more credible than Brian."

Mr. Peters did not say anything for a moment. Then something occurred to him.

"I think Dylan may be a little paranoid. He told me that he was abducted and abused by teenagers. He said he needs to protect himself. That's why he missed yesterday afternoon."

"Well, that's funny, because one of our parents said she saw him wandering aimlessly through the streets yesterday afternoon."

"The last time I asked him about the knife, he denied it. What do you suggest, Mr. Bowman?"

"I don't know. We need to see the knife before we can do anything though."

"Well, I'm not going to search him. I'm going to be direct. No more beating around the bush and asking nicely. Can you watch my class for a few minutes?"

Mr. Bowman nodded and walked toward the front of the meeting area.

"Come with me," Mr. Peters said sternly as he passed Dylan's desk and left the room.

With his hands on his hips and his eyes narrowed, Mr. Peters waited at the coat rack.

"Give me the knife!" Mr. Peters commanded.

"But…"

"Don't even start trying to deny it. I know you have a knife, and I want you to give it to me. Now!"

Dylan knew there was no way of talking himself out of this one. He didn't say anything for several seconds, and he swayed and frowned up at the ceiling.

"No more delays. Give it to me now."

Dylan walked over to his jacket and slowly reached into his pocket. He pulled out his red Swiss Army knife.

Mr. Peters took it without looking at it. He glared into Dylan's eyes. "Why do you have this?"

"I told you! I need protection!"

"From who? That little kid you showed it to?"

"No, from the teenagers."

"You don't need protection from the teenagers."

"Oh, you don't believe me?"

"No, I don't."

"No one ever believes me!" Dylan screamed, and he turned to run away.

"Don't you move!"

Dylan stopped, but he didn't turn around. He stared at the ground.

"Do you know what this knife means?" Mr. Peters walked up to Dylan and held the knife in his face. "You can be kicked out for this. If parents feel that their children are in danger, they'll have you removed from here. Is that what you want?"

Dylan remained silent.

"Talk to me, Dylan." Mr. Peters paused. Then he spoke more gently. "Do you want to be here?"

"I don't care."

"Okay, well that's fine. I want you to think about this. I know you like it here. We want you here, but we won't be able to keep you if this continues. The safety of the students is our priority."

"What about my safety?"

Mr. Peters shook his head. "You just don't get it. Why am I wasting my breath? Think about where you want to be and decide what you are going to do to get what you want."

Dylan tried to jump in, but Mr. Peters put up his hand. "I don't want to hear any more excuses. We are through talking. You are going to the office until…" Mr. Peters shook his head without completing his sentence. "Wait here. Mr. Bowman will escort you down to the office."

Dylan slid down the wall and sat on the floor while Mr. Peters walked into the classroom. Everyone was sitting in a circle. Mr. Bowman was telling the story of the Minotaur while several of his students stood in the middle of the group calling out the dialogue. Mr. Peters held up the knife for the assistant principal to see. He nodded his approval and continued the story.

A black fly soared over Mr. Peters's shoulder and into the library. Dylan followed it into a dimly lit corner. It landed on an encyclopedia and proceeded to clean itself under Dylan's scrutinizing gaze. A moment later, a waft of warm air drifted out of his T-shirt. The tension from his tightly wound body evaporated as he raised his warming hands toward his face.

Collin Paulson

20

Tikewa

ATHUNDEROUS CANNON ECHOED OFF THE WALLS. Instantly, Dylan was on his feet, weapon in hand. He scanned the room for the source, ready to attack. With the second blast, he lowered his sword and exhaled deeply.

"Whoa! That is some snoring," he said, looking at the resting Sheil. Dylan giggled to himself and rubbed the sleep out of his eyes. He looked around the darkened room and swept his hand across the floor to locate his belongings. The brief sleep had refreshed him, and he was ready to go. Sheil grumbled, and Dylan stopped moving for fear of waking him.

"Head back to the lake and down the river."

"What? Why?" Dylan bent over Sheil.

Sheil rolled onto his stomach and continued snoring. Dylan grabbed his bag, which he had used as a pillow, and crept out toward the dim, orange light coming through the doorway.

The floor of the celebration room was littered with sleeping bodies in several clusters. Dylan thought that they were probably gathered in family groupings. The fire was tended to by a frail old man, who smiled up at Dylan as he stepped around and over the bodies. Dylan nodded and walked past him. Two young men stood outside the cave, guarding the entrance.

"Good luck," whispered one of them. "We're counting on you."

"Wait!" said the other, and he ran into the cave. He returned with a bag and handed it to Dylan.

"What's this?"

"Food. You'll need to keep your strength up."

"Thank-you so much. The people of Tipple are very kind and hospitable."

The two men smiled and nodded.

Dylan continued walking in the direction he had come from the night before. It was still dark, but he could tell that the sun would be up soon. By the time Dylan got to the spot where he had watched the ceremony the previous night, the sky was beginning to brighten. He stopped and looked out across the lake. It was calm and peaceful. Dylan shuddered at the thought of jumping into it. It looked so much colder this morning in the damp, cold air.

He pulled his hood over his head and continued on. The shoreline was flat and smooth, which made for easy travel. Soon, the lake became a wide and fast-moving river. The forest became thicker and more tangled, and there were spots where the path became impassable. To get around the trees and thickets that pressed up against the river, he headed away from the bank several times but did not venture too far. He always returned to the river that was guiding him to where he did not know.

A delicate spider web caught Dylan's eye. Light splintered through hanging water droplets and filled the web with color. A large, black spider rested comfortably in the centre. Then, without warning, a yellow spotted insect struck the web and fought to get away. The spider raced over and cut most of the threads that connected the fly to the web. With two remaining threads that acted as an axle, the spider spun the immobile fly and wrapped it in a tight, silk package. Then the spider returned to its resting spot.

Whap!

Dylan was suddenly knocked off his feet. While falling, he sensed a trog land on the ground in front of him. Startled, Dylan jumped up and ran into the forest. The trog began chasing after him, but his wings got caught between a cluster of trees. When Dylan saw that the creature was restrained, he rushed back to attack. Just as Dylan reached him, the trog freed himself and fell forward. Dylan swiped at his wing with Olam and sliced off the tip. As the trog cried out in pain, Dylan took off sprinting through the forest in the direction he had been heading.

Angered, the trog launched itself into the air and over the river, where he noticed Dylan running through the heavy foliage. Dylan stopped. The trog flew past him and then circled back, looking for an opening in the trees. Dylan sensed anger in the creature's menacing, bloodshot eyes.

After a few moments of indecision, he continued on down the river. Dylan travelled quickly and paid attention to his senses; an hour passed. *No sign of the trog. I think I lost him*, he thought, relieved. His throat was dry, so he stopped along a muddy riverbank and cupped his hands. He drank heavily, and just as he started to relax, a noise startled him. He spun around, lost his balance, and slipped into the river.

The rushing current carried him away from the riverbank, and soon, he was travelling at great speed. He desperately grabbed at branches and roots that had been bent by the current, but he could not grip the slippery vines. His hands burned from the friction, but he did not pay attention to the pain.

Thump!

Dylan was instantly dazed. A large branch that hung over the river had knocked him beneath the water's surface. He gasped for air as the force of the river pressed him against a tree, knocking the wind out of him. He reached blindly for a branch above his head and managed to pull himself out of the water.

Out of the corner of his eye, he saw movement. The trog flew at him feet first with his wings extended behind him—like an eagle diving for fish. Dylan drew his sword in a flash and stabbed the trog through the heart. Holding onto Olam with all his might, Dylan slid it out of the trog as the creature fell over top of him and into the river. He watched the trog float away from him on his back. His wings spread out across the surface of the water. Then he was gone, over the edge of a giant waterfall.

The branch Dylan held bent with his weight, and he prayed for strength—for himself and the branch. He managed to get on top of the bough, and he hugged it tightly. Then he inched his way toward the tree. The branch swayed as he moved, but as he got closer to the base, it became more stable. Finally, he was aboveground, and he dropped to the forest floor. He lay back and looked up at the sky, trying to catch his breath.

The crash of the waterfall was so loud that it overpowered all other sounds. The air was filled with mist that came down like rain. Dylan was soaked and bruised. His arms and chest were bleeding from hanging onto the branch so tightly. He managed to get up, and he stumbled downstream a few more feet. From the edge of a rock precipice, he looked over the falls. He could not see to the bottom, but he heard the crashing of the water on the rocks below.

Like a strike of lightning, his senses kicked in and he spun around. His heart stopped. The arrowhead pointing at his skull dripped a cloudy, poisonous liquid. A quick scan of the area revealed a dozen small, dark men with unusual markings on their faces. Several of them had taut bows with arrows in them pointing directly at him. Those without bows had spears above their heads, ready to be launched. Slowly, Dylan turned back to the waterfall and looked into the bottomless hole. Then he turned to face his attackers and collapsed. He sat cross-legged and stared up at them—helpless.

For several minutes, Dylan studied the men as they did him. Finally, he relaxed. He did not have the energy to resist, and he no longer sensed that he was in danger. His father had told him about the forest dwellers, and he believed that these were them. They were called Tikewa. His father had spent time with them as a young man, so he knew something about their culture. He remembered his father telling him that one of them had even come to live with him in Duffle for a time. According to Macor, the Tikewa were a peaceful people who were closely connected with the earth.

Dylan stood and the natives tensed up. "Tikewa?" Dylan asked.

Quick glances passed among them, and Dylan smiled at their surprised expressions. One of the natives spoke directly to Dylan. He could not understand the words, but he understood the message. With his spear, the man pointed to where he wanted Dylan to go. They parted and made a path for him to travel through. Even though these men were his captors, Dylan felt safe and protected. He knew that if any trouble arose, they would not allow him to be harmed.

He was led into a very dense part of the forest. The sky was barely visible even though it was the middle of the day. For most of the journey, his eyes focused on the uneven forest floor. Movement caught his attention, and he looked up. Another forest native stood in the middle of a clearing. He looked directly into Dylan's eyes. Instantly, hundreds of Tikewa appeared, and they all stared at him. Dylan did not know where they had come from, for they had appeared without warning. There were women and children and men of all ages.

"Welcome," said the man who had first appeared in the opening. "We waiting for you."

The sound of English shocked him.

"You speak my language?"

"Yes, I learn from you father, Macor."

"How do you know who I am and who my father is?"

The man paused and spread his arms away from his chest. "Wind tells all." Then he paused again. "My English no good. I not speak it for long time."

Dylan smiled. "I understand you very well."

"I am Icka." Then he waved his hand around his head and said, "These are Tikewa."

"I am Dylan."

"Come, Dylan. Eat."

Dylan followed Icka while everyone else stood motionless. As he passed, they stared at him shyly or nervously; Dylan could not tell which. He glanced at a small child who was holding onto his mother's leg. He stared up at Dylan and timidly hid behind the woman. A tender smile caught Dylan's eye, and he smiled back. The child's mother also smiled.

A spongy, green moss cushioned each footstep as they proceeded toward a lovely bubbling brook. Icka led him to a large boulder with two seats carved into it. They sat down while the Tikewa prepared a special feast in Dylan's honor.

Dylan turned to Icka, who was patting a gecko and watching it run from hand to hand. "Are you in charge here?" Dylan asked.

"In charge?" Icka asked. "What is *in charge?*"

Dylan thought about his words. "Are you the leader?"

At this, Icka turned red. "No," he said quietly. "Tikewa have no leader."

"But you appear to be the leader."

"Only because I speaks English. Tikewa have no leader. No leader needed. Long time ago, one man try to lead. He did much trouble. We are a group. All need all. Everyone has a part. We works together. I speaks English, so I get respect for that. Someone else—good hunter. All know who is goodest hunter, but we never speak it."

"What is that?" Dylan pointed to the gecko on Icka's arm.

"It is Kado—very important animal. All life good. Kado as important as you. Some people kill without respect. This make us sad. We only kill what is need and we thank the animal for its life. All the world is one. When one life end, we all hurt."

Dylan turned to face Icka and said, "Do you know Queen Gaia?"

Icka looked up and thought for a moment. "No, I not know Queen Gaia."

Dylan looked away, disappointed. *Why did Ravelle tell me to find her?*

"You mean Maia?"

Dylan looked at him. "I was told Queen Gaia. Who is Maia?"

"Maia is every place; in all things, everywhere. She is Kado." Icka stopped for a moment and watched the gecko run up his shoulder. "She is this rock." He patted their seats with his hand. "She is all," he said, spreading his arms and reaching for the sky.

"Where do I find her?"

"You have find her already. You sitting on her, and you breathe her."

Dylan put his head in his hands and breathed a heavy sigh. He spoke quietly to himself while Icka continued speaking. "Why can't anyone give me a straight answer? No one knows her. How am I supposed to find her? The people of Tipple are probably right. There is no Queen Gaia, and if there is, she'll have to find me because I'm not going to waste any more time chasing after a myth."

Icka continued. "Maia is all that we are and all that the world is. The waters flow—"

"When are we eating?" Dylan interrupted. "I don't..." He stopped, wishing he could suck his comments back into his mouth. He looked at Icka, who stared at him in silence.

"I'm sorry, Icka," Dylan whimpered. "I'm tired and hungry. It was rude of me to interrupt you. I have not—"

"Lunch time!" Icka screamed. Then he laughed and screamed it even louder. "Lunch time!!"

Then the whole forest screamed "Lunch time!" in a single chorus. The sound of those two words in this foreign place sounded very funny to Dylan. He looked up and saw that everyone was laughing.

"Come." Icka grabbed his arm and pulled him off his seat. They stood slightly above the group.

Dylan scanned the feast laid out before him. It was a potpourri of colors and smells. A variety of food had been placed in large wooden bowls and giant, heavy leaves. There was fruit he had never seen, vegetables of unusual shapes and textures, and a number of different types of nuts.

Before they ate, the Tikewa stared up at the sky and then down at the ground. They swayed and spoke in unison. Then they dropped to the ground and placed their noses in the dirt. Dylan tried to follow, but he was too busy observing. Then with a clap and a shout, they all jumped up. Dylan scooped his food onto a leaf, mimicking the others' actions. Then they sat down to eat. There was little conversation while they ate.

Dylan observed his surroundings and wondered if the Tikewa were aware of the goings-on around them. *They keep to themselves, so they probably don't know about Nero.* Then he thought about what Icka had said about the connection of all living things. They would be affected, Dylan decided, but he did not know how or when.

As they were finishing their meal, the forest began to darken. Suddenly there was dampness in the air, and Dylan felt a drop of rain on his nose. He looked up and saw that the sky had clouded over. Another drop fell into his eye. Everyone got up immediately and cleared the feast away as the rain started to come down on them.

Icka appeared behind Dylan and said, "Come."

Dylan followed Icka a few hundred feet to a shelter made out of bent branches and the very same leaves that had held their food. The den was warm and dark. Dylan felt chilled in his damp clothes.

"Here," Icka said, and handed him a fur blanket. "Take off wet clothes."

By the time Dylan had his clothes off, a fire had been lit and Icka was warming himself. Dylan heard voices approaching and he looked out the entrance. A number of people made their way into the den. There were two women, another man, and six children. Then another man came in carrying a small child. Dylan tried to determine who belonged to whom. At first, he thought that one of the women was Icka's wife, for they seemed to be very fond of each other. Then he thought that the other woman was Icka's wife. He gave up and thought about more important things, like where he should go next.

Icka broke the silence. "Where you go now?"

Can you read my mind? Dylan thought. He shrugged his shoulders and stared into the fire. No one spoke for a long time. Everyone seemed to be deep in his or her own thoughts.

Again, Icka broke the silence, "Go to Ahava."

"Where is Ahava?" Dylan asked.

"Never-ending water." As he said this, he waved his hand around the room. "Water with no end to see."

"Do you mean the sea?" Dylan asked.

Icka nodded.

"I have heard of the sea, but I've never been there."

Dylan stopped speaking and tried to picture it. He could not imagine a body of water that went on forever.

"Why should I go to the sea?"

Icka shrugged his shoulders. "I not know." He thought for a moment and then said, "Because you have never been."

"How do I get there?" Dylan asked.

"Follow the river. It go to Ahava."

"How far is it?"

"Two days." At this, Icka wrapped a blanket around himself and lay down. The others did the same.

For someone who claims not to be a leader, he certainly has a lot of followers, Dylan thought.

He watched a drop of water build on his shirt, which was hanging near the fire. It fell. Another drop grew slowly and fell. His mind started to drift to the rhythmic sound of his dripping clothes.

● ● ●

"WHERE IS THAT PIP-SQUEAK?" NERO SCREAMED at the two trogs standing in front of him. "You boobs are useless. There's a small boy out there killing trogs, and you can't do anything about it."

He paced up and down the hall while the trogs stood at attention. They shifted uncomfortably, trying to appear straight and tall. Nero kicked the floor and then the wall.

"I want him HERE! Now, what is the problem?"

One of the trogs spoke. "If you wanted him dead, there would be no problem."

Nero rushed at the trog and spat, "Well, I want him alive, you smelly piece of crap. Bring him here—alive!"

"We've underestimated his abilities."

"Have you been working together?"

The trogs shifted uncomfortably.

"No? You haven't been, have you?"

At this, they shook their heads.

"You're a bunch of insolent imbeciles! You need to work together if you want to capture him."

The same trog spoke cautiously. "Trogs don't like each other. We don't work well together."

"Well, you better learn QUICKLY," he shouted, and before the final word exited his mouth, Nero spun around with his sword and lopped off the trog's head. The second trog winced at the sight and waited for his punishment as his partner's head rolled across the floor and rested against his foot. The headless body remained upright for a moment before the weight of its sheathed sword pulled it to the ground.

"Feed this corpse to the dogs!" Nero commanded. "Then put the head on a pole and parade it around your quarters. Let it be an example to you all."

The trog remained motionless.

"Get out of my face before I make mincemeat out of you!"

As the trog walked out of the room with his partner's head under his arm, he heard Nero scream, "If I don't see that delinquent in two days, more heads will roll!"

21

In Need of Protection

MRS. EVANS WAS AT HER DESK when Mr. Peters peered into her office.

"Come in, Mr. Peters. How are you?" she asked.

"Not good."

Mrs. Evans put her pen down and looked up at him. "What's wrong?"

"This whole Dylan thing is getting to me. I waver back and forth on where he should be. I'm worried about the other students in the school, and I'm worried about Dylan. He's been moved around so much, and I know that if we fail him, it could really hurt the little progress he's made." He paused for a moment. "This knife issue worries me. I'm concerned that someone is going to get injured."

"I understand where you're coming from. We can have him removed over this, you know. This is a very serious issue."

"Where would he go?"

"I don't know...a special placement...a behavior class. It's hard to say. We have the behavioral specialist coming. Do you want to wait for her?"

"I guess we should." Mr. Peters hesitated. "He's going to need constant supervision."

"Mrs. Giles can do that, Mr. Peters."

"He doesn't like her."

"Well, that's too bad. He's shown us that he cannot be trusted. I'll let him know that we're concerned about the safety of the other students."

The secretary knocked on Mrs. Evans's door. "Dylan is here."

"Send him in, please," Mrs. Evans requested.

Dylan walked into the room without saying a word.

"Good morning, Dylan," Mrs. Evans said. "Sit down, please." She pointed to the chair across from her.

165

"Do you know what this meeting is about, Dylan?" Mr. Peters asked.

"Yes," Dylan said to the ground.

"Tell me what it's about," said Mrs. Evans.

"It's about the knife."

"That's right. Why do you think we're concerned about you carrying a knife?"

Dylan shrugged his shoulders. "I don't know."

"We're concerned that someone might get injured. I know you wouldn't intentionally harm someone, but you could by accident."

Dylan shifted in his chair. "That knife couldn't hurt a fly. It's so small."

"It doesn't matter how big it is, Dylan. A knife is a knife."

"Yes, it does matter. A machete or a sword is dangerous, not a pocketknife."

Mrs. Evans sat up in her seat and spoke firmly. "We are *not* going to argue about the size of the knife. It does *not* matter how big it is. A sharp implement of any sort can be dangerous. What were you intending to do with it?"

Without speaking, he slouched further down in his seat. Then he pulled the hood of his inside jacket over his head and lifted the lapels of his jean jacket up around his jaw to hide his face.

"Sit up straight!" Mrs. Evans demanded angrily. "Pull your hood down and look at me."

"Why do you have to stare at me?"

"Sit up, now!"

At this command, Dylan sat up straight and uncovered his face.

"Answer my question."

"What was it?"

"What were you going to do with the knife?"

"Nothing. I need it for protection. Without it, I'm defenseless."

Mr. Peters spoke. "Defenseless? Against what?"

"I told you already. There are people out to get me. I need to protect myself."

"Who is out to get you?" Mrs. Evans asked.

"Everyone—especially junior high kids. They don't like me."

"How do they even know you?"

"They just do. I don't know how they know me. They threaten me when I walk home from school."

"You know what I heard the other day, Dylan?" Mr. Peters asked, leaning forward. Dylan looked at him. "One of the students in our class said you followed her and her friends home and called them names as they walked. They said you were swearing at them for no reason."

Dylan slumped into his chair and proceeded to cover his face again.

"Sit up straight and let me see your face!" Mr. Peters said.

He sat up again. His blushing face revealed his guilt.

"Could it be you who is intimidating others, rather than others intimidating you?"

"NO, the big kids are imitating…inti…mat…ing… bugging me."

"Well, I don't know what to believe anymore, Dylan," Mr. Peters stated flatly. "You used to be honest with me, and now all I seem to get are lies. You told me that the other kids were setting you up, and then I learned that you follow kids home and call them names. You said you didn't have a knife, but now I find out that you had one all along. What are we supposed to do next?"

"Spank me."

"DON'T get smart with me! You need to think about where you want to be. If you want to be here, then you need to change your behavior."

Mrs. Evans leaned forward and looked straight into Dylan's eyes. He looked away. "This is very serious, Dylan. We want you at this school, but weapons are unacceptable. At this point, I'm not sure what's going to happen."

"Am I going to be kicked out?"

"Well, that has a lot to do with you. What do you want?"

He looked at the ground and said quietly, "I wanna stay."

"Good. Now what are you going to do to ensure that you're allowed to stay?"

"I'll be good."

"What does that mean, Dylan?"

"I won't carry knives."

"There has to be a lot more than that."

"I won't carry knives. I won't yell. I'll do my work."

"I'm happy to hear that you want to be here, Dylan," said Mr. Peters, "but we need a real commitment. I know that we're not going to see a huge improvement immediately. Making a change in your life takes time. I'm not going to expect miracles. What I do expect is that the students in this school feel safe. You've got to promise that you won't threaten anyone or harm anyone in any way. Can you do that?"

"I think so."

"We're going to help you, Dylan. We don't expect you to do it on your own. Mrs. Giles is going to accompany you everywhere you go when you're on the school grounds—in the morning, at recess, and at lunch."

"Oh! I hate her. She follows me around like Grandma."

"Well, your actions have brought this on. We need to supervise you to make sure that the students in this school are safe. Prove to us that she doesn't need to follow you."

"For how long?"

"She's going to accompany you until you've shown us that you can be on the grounds without supervision. Do you understand?"

"Yes," he grumbled.

"Where did you get the knife, Dylan?"

"I found it. I found it in the alley."

"It looks pretty new."

"When do I get it back?"

"You don't."

"But it's my property. You can't steal it from me. I need to protect myself."

"You are not getting it back."

"Can I take it home and leave it there?"

"No."

"Oh, great. How am I going to be able to defend myself now?"

"Dylan, you don't need to protect yourself," assured Mr. Peters. "If you're afraid, we'll protect you. Is there any way you can find out the names of the students who are bothering you? We can visit their school and get to the bottom of it."

"I don't know their names, and I wouldn't tell you if I did. They would hurt me more if they found out I was a snitch."

"Perhaps we could get a cab to take you from school to home and back again," Mrs. Evans interjected. "We don't want you feeling threatened. We want every child in this school to feel safe. Would you like us to get you a taxi?"

Dylan thought about it for a moment.

"Would you like that?" she repeated.

"I guess."

"Well, I'll look into it."

The bell rang just as the teacher and student left the office. Several students were already sitting at their desks when the two of them walked into the room. Mr. Peters proceeded to the front of the class and wrote on the whiteboard.

There is nothing in a caterpillar that tells you it's going to be a butterfly.

BUCKMINSTER FULLER

Then he turned around and faced the students, who were contemplating the quote. After several quiet moments, he spoke. "So… what will you become?" He gazed into the eyes of each and every one of his students.

Finally, he broke the silence. "We have the library for thirty minutes. Return your old book, find a new book, and sign it out. Then come back to the classroom and read quietly."

Dylan jumped up excitedly.

In the library, Mr. Peters leaned on a bookshelf and watched the students mill about. Albert was dancing on the risers in the story corner. Mr. Peters did not say anything. He knew that Albert would eventually look at him. Sure enough, a few seconds into his dance, he looked over at Mr. Peters shyly. Mr. Peters glared back, and Albert stopped immediately. Under Mr. Peters's scowl, he wandered around picking up books and putting them down. He tried to appear like he was reading, but Mr. Peters knew that he wasn't.

"Look what I got, Mr. Peters." Janna held up a drawing book.

Mr. Peters smiled and watched her walk back into the room. It wasn't long before half of the class was in the library and the other half was in the classroom. Mr. Peters walked into the classroom and stood in the doorway. He could see into the library from where he stood. Some of the students were playing around in the classroom, so Mr. Peters hushed them and asked them to read. Soon, everyone was back except for Albert. Mr. Peters hurried him along by choosing a book for him.

Alexandra ran up to the teacher with a line of three girls following her. "Can we read in the hallway under the jackets, Mr. P.?"

"Are you going to read?" Mr. Peters asked.

"Yes, yes, yes!" she responded quickly.

He smiled at her enthusiasm. "Okay. No warnings though. If I catch you gabbing, you're back in here."

Before Mr. Peters finished his sentence, they were out the door.

The only movement the teacher noticed from Dylan was the turning of pages. Reading was one activity he could focus on for hours. Mr. Peters walked over to his desk and doodled while the class read. He was unaware of Dylan's presence until the boy cleared his throat. Mr. Peters looked up from his drawing to see Dylan standing beside him and looking over his shoulder.

"You're having a good morning, Dylan."

"Yeah, I guess. Did you draw that?" Dylan asked.

"Yes, I did."

"Wow! You're an artist.

"Well thank-you, Dylan. I'm not an artist, but I like drawing."

Dylan pointed at one of the figures in the drawing. "Who is that?"

"Oh my God, Dylan!" Mr. Peters grabbed Dylan's hand and turned his palm up. "What's wrong with your hand?"

Dylan quickly pulled his arm away and shoved both of his hands into his pockets.

"It looks like you've been branded."

"What's that mean?"

"You know, what farmers do to cows."

Dylan swayed uncomfortably.

"Has someone hurt you, Dylan?"

"No, I did it to myself. I like to make indents in my skin with my medal."

"It looks like more than just an indent, Dylan. Your hand looks like it's been burned."

"No, it's okay," Dylan said with a laugh. "It's not burned. Can I go to the washroom?" he added quickly.

"You're just trying to change the topic, aren't you?"

Dylan shrugged his shoulders.

"All right, but go quietly."

Dylan tiptoed through the classroom, exaggerating each step. He looked back at Mr. Peters, who was smiling at him.

The girls in the hall were looking at an anatomy book and giggling at pictures of naked women. Just as Dylan stepped through the doorway, they flipped to a drawing of a naked man, and they all burst out laughing. Dylan's blood boiled, and his face reddened at what he thought were their taunts.

He clenched his fists and screamed, "What's so funny, you Gollums?"

The girls' laughter stopped, and they looked up at Dylan, who was shaking with anger. No one said anything for a moment until Alexandra asked, "What's a Gollum?"

Mr. Peters had heard Dylan yell, so he got up and walked toward the door.

"A Gollum is a pasty creature who lives underground, eats raw fish, and says 'my preciousss.' You are a Gollum, my preciousss," Dylan said in a foul voice with a scrunched-up face.

The four girls were speechless for a moment. Then one girl giggled, and at that moment, they all burst out laughing. The veins in Dylan's neck popped, and he shook with rage. At the sight of Mr. Peters, he fled down the hall and into the washroom. Mr. Peters looked down at the girls, who covered their faces with their books. They were shaking and trying to hold their laughter in. Janna was the first to break, and as soon as she laughed, they all erupted.

"Okay, ladies, that's enough. Were you teasing Dylan?"

"No. Honest, Mr. Peters. We were laughing at…at …Alexandra told a joke. Honest. We weren't teasing him."

"All right. Well, come back into the classroom."

They stood up and stumbled into the room, giggling as they proceeded to their desks. Mr. Peters watched them for several minutes and noticed conspiratorial looks pass among them. Every so often, he would hear a burst of laughter come from one area of the room.

"I can see that some of us need to burn off some energy," Mr. Peters said sharply. "Janna's desk group—please line up at the door quietly."

Within seconds, all of the students in Janna's group were lined up at the door. Soon, everyone was in line and waiting for instructions. Dylan returned from the bathroom to see his classmates getting ready for gym.

"Oh, thanks for waiting," he said sarcastically.

He pushed his way in front of Albert, who was about to push him back until he noticed Mr. Peters glaring at them. Dylan tried not to look at Mr. Peters, but he felt the daggers.

"As soon as everyone is in line, we'll get started."

Mr. Peters stared at Dylan and waited. Dylan did not move for what seemed like minutes. Grumblings came from the other students, but no one said anything directly to him. Finally, he turned away from the line and kicked the ground.

"Now I'm going to get a broken racquet. Thanks a lot!" he yelled at the whiteboard.

Mr. Peters spoke up. "When you get to the gym, grab a racquet and a partner and hit the birdie back and forth to each other. See how many times you can hit the birdie without it touching the ground. Dylan, sit on a bench and wait for me."

Mr. Peters turned and the group followed him. The students at the front of the line were on his heels. Mr. Peters had to walk quickly to avoid being run over. The line slowed behind Albert, who was doing a little dance as he walked. He would run ahead a few steps, do a twirl, and stop. This continued for most of the walk to the gym. He stopped every time Mr. Peters turned around.

When they reached the gym, the students ran through the doorway, and Mr. Peters smiled at the determined looks on their faces. He waited for all of the students to pass and looked for Dylan after the last student had run into the gym. He went to the door and looked down the hall—Dylan was nowhere to be seen. Walking out into the hall, he saw movement out of the corner of his eye.

"What do you want?" Dylan mumbled.

Mr. Peters smiled at Dylan, who was crouching in the corner. "Come in, please."

Mr. Peters walked into the gym, sat on a bench, and watched his class practicing. He was impressed by how much they had improved. Then he saw Albert. Again, he was alone and trying to hit the birdie as hard as he could. He jumped with every swing so that his feet left the ground. Every few swings he would actually hit the birdie, and it would fly into someone's space. Albert was constantly spinning around looking for it, whether he had hit it or not. The birdie spent most of the time on the ground.

"Take your time, Albert. Take your time, and hit it lightly. You don't have to kill it."

Albert nodded. This time he moved in slow motion, and of course, the birdie travelled at regular speed. It hit the gym floor before he had even swung at it. Dylan entered the gym and sat down beside his teacher.

As Mr. Peters spoke, he continued to watch the group. "You've had a pretty good morning, Dylan. Let's keep it up. What happened in the classroom?"

"Nothing."

"You yelled. Why did you yell?"

"Because you made me come in last. Now all the good racquets are gone."

"I made you? How did I do that?"

"You made me go to the end of the line."

"Why did I do that?"

"I don't know."

"So you think that you should be allowed to go into the line anywhere you choose."

Dylan tried to interrupt.

"Listen to me," Mr. Peters said forcefully. "What would happen if everyone could join a line wherever they chose? What would happen?"

Dylan thought for a moment. "You wouldn't have a line."

Mr. Peters turned and faced Dylan. "That's right. You wouldn't have a line. You would have chaos."

"Well, you shouldn't have lined up before I got back in the room."

"I apologize for that, Dylan, but I can't make the entire class wait for you."

"Can I go play now?"

"In a minute, Dylan. How are you going to play if I let you get a racquet?"

"What do you mean?"

"I'm talking about how you're going to treat your partner."

"I don't want a partner. I'll play you."

"No, Dylan. You are going to play someone else. Watch the other students for a moment and tell me what you see."

"They're lousy."

"No, Dylan, they're not lousy. They're just learning, and they're improving. Very few of them are as good as you, but they're trying. What I want you to watch is how they interact with each other. Watch what happens when someone makes a mistake."

The two of them sat, and Dylan watched intently.

"There." Mr. Peters pointed to Janna and Mickey. "Watch how they interact."

"But they're girls. Boys don't play like girls."

"Just watch." After a few moments, Mr. Peters asked, "What did you see happen when Mickey made a mistake?"

"Nothing. They laughed and continued playing."

"Did you see anyone get angry?"

"No."

"Why is that?"

"Because they're girls."

"Okay, let's watch Jeff and Tyler. What do they do when they make mistakes?"

"Nothing. They just continue playing."

"Yes. What would happen if Jeff called Tyler a name every time he missed the birdie?"

"They would get into a fight."

"And would they play together?"

"No."

"Tyler wouldn't put up with that, would he?"

Dylan shook his head.

"Jeff would never have a partner. Why do you think you have so much trouble finding a partner?"

"Because I don't want one."

"That could be part of it, but the main reason is the way you treat them. Are you nice to them?"

"No."

"You yell at them. Would you like a partner who yells at you?"

"No."

Mr. Peters pointed to his head. "So up here, you know what is and is not appropriate behavior."

Dylan nodded.

"You're a good badminton player, and I can see why you get frustrated with people who aren't as good as you, but that's no excuse for abusing them.

"I want you to play with Jeff. The two of you are the best players in the class. You're not competing with each other—just start off hitting the birdie back and forth. Are you going to be able to play with him and stay calm?"

"Yes."

"I'm holding you to that. I also want to know that you're going to come to me if there's a problem. Don't blow your top. I can help you work out any problems that arise."

Dylan nodded.

"And one more thing. I don't want you to leave the gym or the classroom without permission. I worry about you when you just run away. If you're angry, I want you to find a seat and cool off or to just tell me you need to take a walk. Okay?" Mr. Peters paused. "Okay?"

"Okay. I get it! Can I play now?"

"Yes, go get a racquet and come back here."

Mr. Peters yelled out across the gym. "Jeff! Jeff!"

Jeff stopped and turned to Mr. Peters. He had seen Dylan with his teacher a few minutes earlier, so he knew what he was going to be asked. His shoulders dropped as he walked across the gym. Mr. Peters watched Dylan walk from bucket to bucket, looking for a good racquet. He swung several of them and then dropped them into the buckets angrily.

"Yes, Mr. Peters?"

"I want you to play Dylan."

Mr. Peters could tell that Jeff was not happy about this.

"You're one of the best players in the class, and I want you to play with him. He's a very good player."

Jeff didn't say anything.

"Are you okay with this?"

"He *is* a good player, but he's mean," Jeff answered.

"I've talked to him, and he's going to try to be nice. Please give it a try. Just this once."

On the other side of the gym, Jake walked up to Ted and put his arm around the smaller boy.

"Hey, Ted?" Jake said affectionately.

"Yeah," Ted responded nervously, looking at him sideways.

"Who married Salty Sally?"

Ted glanced toward Mr. Peters, who was deep in conversation.

Jake read his thoughts. "Don't worry. I'm not going to do anything. It's just a joke." Then he repeated, "Who married Salty Sally?"

"Who?" Ted squeaked.

Jake slobbered all over his index finger, stuck it in Ted's ear, and rotated it. "Wet Willy!" He howled with laughter.

Ted pulled his shirtsleeve over his hand and rubbed his ear frantically. "That's gross!"

Jake ran back to his partner, who had fallen to the ground in peals of laughter. Ted scowled at them and went back to his game. Inside he boiled with rage. His anger was directed more at himself than Jake. He felt helpless and weak, not being able to defend himself against the bigger boy's derision.

"Are you sure you're okay with this, Jeff?"

Jeff nodded his head, knowing that it didn't really matter if he was okay with it or not. Dylan returned to the bench.

"All the good racquets are gone," he whined.

"That one looks fine. Okay, Dylan, Jeff has agreed to play with you. I want to see how well you can cooperate."

"C'mon," Dylan said, and he ran out into the middle of Lyle and Sam.

"Hey, get out of our court," Sam yelled.

Dylan glanced over at Mr. Peters. Then he moved to an open spot in the gym. Mr. Peters nodded his approval. Jeff followed him and hit the birdie into the air without enthusiasm. Dylan hit it back. Jeff batted at it, but it was out of reach, and he didn't run for it. Dylan did not say anything. He hit Jeff's serve back, and Jeff ran for this one and hit it back. Mr. Peters stopped watching when they started hitting the birdie back and forth consistently.

Mr. Peters circled the gym, observing and giving tips to the students as he passed them. Then he heard yelling, and he turned to see Dylan hit Sam on the bum with his racquet.

"Sit down, Dylan!"

Dylan stomped angrily over to the bench and sat down. Mr. Peters could see that he was still fuming when he arrived.

"First, I want to thank-you for following through and sitting down when I asked you to. This is the second time you didn't run away when you were angry."

Dylan broke in, yelling, "That kid stepped in front of me and got in the way of my birdie."

"Well, I'm sure it was an accident."

"Yeah, but we were just about to break the world record."

"That does not excuse you from hitting him. I want you to apologize."

"No way. He should apologize to me."

"You hit him. He didn't touch you. Go apologize."

Dylan screamed "NO!" and threw his racquet at the wall. It bounced and struck Lyle on the back. Dylan ran out of the gym and down the hall. Mr. Peters looked through the doorway and saw Dylan slip and fall as he rounded the next corner. Then he was out of sight.

A sharp pain in the knee that had hit the floor forced Dylan to sit and examine the quickly forming bruise. A black fly caught his eye. He sprang up and followed it around the corner into the next hallway. It bounced off the wall several times and then dropped into the hanging coats. Dylan spread the jackets apart and saw the fly fall to the ground and land on its back. He scooped it up gently in his palms and watched it struggle.

A final buzz seemed to echo off the walls and then the fly was silent—lifeless. Dylan cupped his hands and slid down the wall between the jackets. He picked up a piece of torn lined paper and folded it into an envelope. After carefully placing the insect into the envelope, he folded it over and slid it into the front pocket of his shirt.

Once again, Dylan felt the warmth of Tracker's medallion on his skin. A blanket of tranquility surrounded him as he pulled at the leather cord to reveal his prize. Dylan placed the medallion between his palms. The familiar dull glow emanated from his hands as he raised them toward his face and closed his eyes. The intense heat and faint smell of burning flesh filled his nostrils as he squeezed his palms together.

22

A Piercing Cry

DYLAN SAT BOLT UPRIGHT. SWEAT POURED down his face, and he was shaking. Something terrifying had awakened him, but he could not remember what. He thought for a moment, trying to recall his dream, but it was gone. With the back of his hand, he wiped the sweat from his face while glancing around the room. He could see very little, but he heard the sleeping sounds of his hosts. He reached for his belongings and left the shelter without a sound.

The air was crisp and moist, and the trees dripped from the previous night's rain. Dylan breathed heavily and watched his breath dissipate into the air. The sound of rushing water grew louder as Dylan bounced along on the spongy, wet ground. At the river's edge, he glanced upstream and saw that he was at the bottom of a giant waterfall. The power of the crashing water fascinated him and sent a chill up his spine.

Dylan turned and began walking with the river. He moved at a great pace and travelled a good distance before daylight chased away the dark.

At a calm inlet that formed a swirling pond, Dylan dipped his hands into the icy water and splashed it on his face. The numbing water refreshed his spirit. He gazed into the reflection that appeared before him; it was foreign. His hair had grown into a knotted mass. Even his features had changed. He thought he looked older, more mature—more like his father. Then he slapped the water and watched his reflection splinter. Seconds later, his face reappeared, just as before. He stood and smiled at the warmth of the sun.

The beautiful surroundings and wonderful aroma put him at ease. He wished that he could sit for a moment and relax, but he knew he had to keep moving. Dylan travelled quickly and took many short breaks, usually to get a fill of the luscious berries that seemed to be ripening before his eyes. He tried to stay close to the river, but this was not always possible. Sometimes he rested aboveground in the trees, which offered some safety and good aerial views.

Following the river provided some comfort; it gave him direction. Icka's suggestion to go to the ocean had given him a destination. He did not know why he was going there, but the reason was not important. At this moment, a destination was more important than a reason. The thought of seeing the "never-ending water," as Icka had described the sea, kept him going. He could not imagine such a sight.

The day was coming to an end, and he had travelled far without any problems. He wondered why he had not encountered any trogs. As the sky darkened, he started to look for a place to spend the night. He stopped and listened. The forest was coming to life with the creatures of the night. The full moon provided enough light for him to keep moving, but he moved slowly and cautiously. His sword was drawn, and every one of his senses tingled. Danger was afoot.

A piercing cry echoed throughout the forest. Dylan froze. A burst of several short, high-pitched squeals was followed by one last shriek that filled the night, and then...silence. Dylan sprinted in the direction of the noise. Grunting, slurping, and ripping noises led him to the edge of an opening in the trees. The moonlight revealed the massive wings of a giant trog devouring a black-haired corpse over a boulder. Dylan watched for a moment and contemplated his next move—fight or flight? He knew he could get away unnoticed because the trog was so preoccupied.

Then it struck him—the iridescent black hair, the high-pitched squeal. His heart raced and his anger flared. Dylan's feet barely touched the ground as he flew at the winged soldier.

Before the trog was even aware of his presence, Dylan had hacked off one of his wings. The stunned creature reared up with blood and flesh dripping from his fangs and reached for his rusty weapon, which was leaning against the boulder. But before the trog could even lift his sword, Dylan sliced off his arm. The trog cried out and backed away, but Dylan lunged forward, and Olam sliced open the trog's neck. The creature fell back, gripping his throat with his remaining hand. Coughing up blood, the trog collapsed—wheezing and gurgling.

Micro's lifeless eyes gazed up at the stars; his shredded body dangled over the stone. Dylan looked away and closed his eyes.

"No, no, no," he cried quietly.

He dragged his fingers through Micro's coarse, black hair. Except for a nick on his face, his head was untouched. Dylan tried not to look at his mangled body, but it was impossible not to see. Suddenly, he felt sick. He turned and vomited in the grass.

Then he started running. He had to get away. Tears streaming down his face, eyes blurred, he dodged the trees and trampled the undergrowth beneath his feet. He lost his balance and fell into a hollow in the ground that was hidden by the branches of a misshapen tree. He slipped further into the large, well-hidden hole. Here, he dropped his bag and broke down in heaving sobs. As he lay there whimpering, he started to shake. The chill of the evening was upon him. He grabbed the blanket from his backpack and pulled it over his head.

Collin Paulson

23

Chandelier Ballroom

mORNING SOUNDS AWAKENED DYLAN FROM A fitful sleep. Tears had hardened in the corners of his eyes and sealed them partially shut. Slowly, he forced them open and stared up at the branches overhead. An immense sadness weighed down on him and pinned him to the ground. His excitement to see the ocean had disappeared, as had his desire to continue the journey. An hour passed. He did not move.

A whisper stopped his breathing. *Your origins are dust, and your end is dust.* Micro's voice penetrated his mind. *You never really die—you just transform.* The words felt like a warm blanket.

Finally, with great effort, he forced himself to sit up. "I have to get going," he said quietly. A hunger pang rumbled in his belly. "I'll travel for a while before I eat. I need to preserve my rations."

The trail he walked was flat and smooth. With every step, the river widened and appeared to slow down. Dylan wondered how many others had passed this way before him. Again, he felt a pang in his stomach, so he sat down and leaned up against a tree. The last of his provisions were stale and dry.

Dylan stared out over the river despondently. He thought about everything he had lost since he had begun his journey. Tears rolled down his face at the thought of giving up.

"This is too much for me," he whispered. "What's left to fight for anyway? My father is dead. My friends and family are gone. I'm alone. This entire mission is hopeless…pointless."

Suddenly, a man appeared. Dylan gasped, and his tears stopped instantly. The tall, hairless man stood on a slow-moving raft on the river. His expressionless eyes locked on Dylan, who felt his very soul was being scrutinized, judged, by the disturbing, unmoving stranger.

Slowly, the raft carried him away. Then he was gone. A chill ran down Dylan's spine.

Dylan stood up, gripped a branch with one hand, and leaned out over the river. He spotted the boatman pushing himself away from the riverbank with a long pole. Then he saw it.

"The ocean! I've made it." In the distance, a vast body of water displayed the curvature of the earth. Dylan exhaled the tension and sadness he had been feeling. "Never-ending water. Water with no end to see."

He quickly gathered his things and headed downstream. The trees along the river began to thin and were replaced by flattened grass. Staying hidden in the shelter of the trees was no longer possible if he wanted to get near the shore. The lure of the ocean drew him nearer.

While standing on a low cliff, he swayed with the wind and looked across the great expanse. The powerful wind tossed his hair and coated his lips with salt. The churning surface of the water was mesmerizing. A shiver brought him out of his reverie. Scanning the shoreline, he spied what looked like a path down to the water's edge. He jumped into a dugout that led to the path, and the wind stopped as soon as he landed in the hollow. Even though he was several hundred feet from the water, he felt the ocean spray on his skin. He sat in the protected shelter and continued to stare out to sea. Listening to the rhythm of the waves, he fell into a trance. His mind wandered.

He was soon overcome by an urge to touch the water, and just as he was about to proceed down the steep path, the boatman appeared near the shore. Dylan's heart dropped, and he drew his sword. The tall, hairless man did not move or speak. Dylan saw that he was unarmed, so he let his guard down. The man slid down the path to the water's edge and looked back up at Dylan from the beach. Dylan sensed that he was supposed to follow. He kept his sword drawn but carried it by his side as he followed several steps behind the boatman.

The sand ended at a red rock wall that reached to the sky. A small boat was tied to a wooden stake embedded in the sand. The man untied the boat and Dylan stepped in carefully. He made his way to the back, or the front—he wasn't sure which—and the man pushed off the shore and jumped in.

As his new companion began paddling along the rock face, Dylan gazed out to sea and then up at the jagged, red rock. As they glided away from shore, Dylan noticed that the rock face no longer touched the water. The ocean was now under the cliff. As they proceeded, the gap between the water and the rock widened, and it wasn't long before they moved beneath the cliff into a giant cave.

Water droplets formed on the sharp points of the rock above their heads. Dylan fell into a trance listening to the quiet dipping of the man's oar and the plop of water droplets echoing off an unseen distant wall. As they moved through the water, the light began to dim, and for a moment, Dylan was blind. He searched the distance for light as the fear of being transported into a black void rose up in him.

A dim light in the distance calmed his fears but only slightly. The further they travelled, the more he could see. Then the ceiling that was previously within reach opened up and disappeared into the darkness. Giant stalactites hung above their heads. Some of the formations touched the water, and the boatman had to steer around them.

They continued rowing for what seemed like hours. Dylan twisted and turned, trying to take in all of the sights. They approached one stalactite that looked like a giant black shadow, and as they passed by, the light they were rowing toward reflected off the magnificent structure and revealed its brilliance. Dylan wondered how such beauty could be so well hidden. The man continued rowing, expressionless, silent.

Dylan was taken back to Stellar Hall for a moment. The structures, the colors, the air—it was all very similar here. He knew he should be afraid, sailing into the dark, foreign place, but he felt more relaxed and at ease than he had in a long time.

The light continued to grow as they travelled into the void. Hanging torches flickered and danced on a distant wall. Then Dylan spotted a shadow running along the rock face. The shadow's source was slightly hunched but moved quickly. It soon disappeared over a ridge. A short time later, Dylan felt the boat come to a stop, and he was thrown off balance. The boat rested upon the sand. He glanced back at the hairless man, who lifted his head and looked to the direction the hunchback had run. Dylan understood the silent message and got out of the boat.

It felt good to be on solid ground again. He approached the wall and traced his fingertips over primitive drawings of stories that meant nothing to him. A scraping noise broke the silence, and he turned to see the hairless man digging his paddle into the sand and pushing away from the shore. The boat backed into the water and then turned and headed back the way it had come. Slowly, the boatman disappeared between the noble, graceful stalactites that sparkled in the torchlight.

Suddenly, Dylan sensed an observer, so he drew his sword and turned quickly. The hunched man cringed at the sight.

"You…you w-won't need that, S-s-sir," the man stuttered. "F-follow me." He ran off.

Dylan followed him up a small hill of sand that led to a large tunnel. Torches lit the tunnel and brightened small rooms that extended from the passageway. Decrepit-looking people dressed in rags occupied many of the rooms. Some of them laughed hysterically as he passed while others squinted up at him without a sound.

The tunnel led to a large room, where several people were gathered about the feet of an ancient man. Dylan had difficulty looking at him, for he was a hideous sight. Flaking, wrinkled skin hung from his shriveled and misshapen body. He was folded up in a chair, and his head tilted back and to one side. Everyone stared at Dylan as he entered the room.

The old man spoke in a clear voice. "Welcome."

Dylan remained silent and bowed low. The old man waved his hand, and everyone scattered. They were alone.

"You fear me. Why?"

"I fear no one." Dylan's voice cracked as he spoke.

"You fear no one?" The old man's laugh echoed off the walls. "You don't have to impress me, young man. We are all afraid. I know all about you. Come closer."

Dylan approached, but he could not look at him directly. The old man sensed Dylan's discomfort.

"I was as you are, and I am as you will be. Do not fear the future." The old man stopped speaking and closed his eyes. "Growing old is a wonderful part of life. You and I are not so different. Before my eyes is beauty, and before your eyes is a beast, but we are more similar than we are different. We see, hear, feel, taste, and smell. This is your future; do not fear it—just as you should not fear your past."

Dylan forced himself to look at the man without averting his gaze.

"Ah, now you look at me. Am I really so ugly?"

Dylan did not know how to respond. He quickly said no, and the old man laughed again.

"I am Xander, and this is my home. Welcome." Then he paused to catch his breath. "I have been waiting for you."

"You have?"

"Ah, your journey is well known to those who need it."

Dylan could not hide his confusion. "Hmm. Well, thank-you for your hospitality." Xander laughed at Dylan's expression. Dylan continued. "I sense that you have great wisdom, Sir."

"How do you sense wisdom, my boy?"

"I can't explain it. I just do." Dylan paused. "May I ask you a question?"

Xander smiled and nodded. "You may ask me anything you like. I cannot promise to know the answer, but I'll try my best. And if I don't know the answer, I'll fake it. Sometimes being wise means more than having the correct answer."

"Who is Queen Gaia and where do I find her?"

Xander did not speak for a moment. He looked up at the ceiling. "I cannot say that I really know who she is, for I've never met her. I do know where to find her, though."

"Please tell me! Where?"

"She is everywhere. She can be found in the sky and in the sea."

Dylan put his head in his hands and grunted. "Not long ago I was told that she was in running animals and in the stones that litter the earth." He paused for a moment. "These vague answers frustrate me." Then he looked up at the ceiling and spoke to no one in particular. "Can no one give me a clear answer?"

Xander howled with laughter.

"You show your age, my son. Real questions only lead to more questions; there are no solutions. Fools convince themselves of 'truths' so that they can sleep at night. I rarely sleep."

Dylan did not pay attention to Xander. He was deep in thought. Again he spoke, but more to himself than Xander. "I wish I had paid more attention to my father. He would have given me answers." He stared at the ground.

Xander replied, "Fathers come in many forms. You are fortunate to have met many on your journey."

Dylan looked up. "How do you know who I've met?"

"I no longer travel, Dylan, but I see beyond these walls." Xander paused and examined his fingernails. "You do not need to inherit someone's genes to consider him a father."

Dylan moved closer to Xander and spoke to him directly. "What do I do now? I am on an aimless mission. Where should I go?"

"We aren't always aware of where we're heading. Sometimes we need to get there before we understand the path. Look inside and follow the path that's in your heart."

Dylan turned away from him. Tears of anger poured over his cheeks. He clenched his teeth. "Again, you respond to my question without an answer!"

"I cannot give you the answer. It needs to come from you."

Dylan stood up but then he realized that he had nowhere to go.

"Enter the room behind me."

Dylan furrowed his brow at the solid wall of rock. Xander laughed at his puzzled expression.

"Come," Xander said with a giggle.

Dylan walked behind the old man, who lifted his cane and touched the wall. An entrance appeared. Dylan bent forward and looked inside. He took a step back out and was about to speak when Xander asked, "Does it look familiar?"

"It's just like Stellar Hall, but without color."

"Yes it is. This room and Stellar Hall are connected, even though they are very far apart. Welcome to the Chandelier Ballroom."

Dylan stepped into the spectacular gallery. The beauty took his breath away. Delicate fingers of clear, frosted crystal extended from tall, white pillars. Beams of light shone through tiny holes in the ceiling and lit up the impressive white stalactites and stalagmites. Chandelier Ballroom was as white as Stellar Hall was colorful.

Dylan circled the room and took it all in. He wasn't sure if the tinkling melody that filled his head was imaginary or real. He was in the moment and at ease. All of his troubles vanished.

Around a corner, he spotted a reservoir. He peered into the deep, crystal-clear pool. The water in his cupped hands seemed to magnify the medallion impressions on his palms. At this moment, he did not want to be reminded of his battles, so he closed his eyes and drank. The water was more refreshing than any he had had since leaving Stellar Hall.

He removed his clothes and dove into the pool. The water invigorated his spirit. Suddenly, a powerful light blinded him. His ancestors passed before his eyes, and he was pulled deep into the pool, which led to subterranean rivers that flowed into the ocean. Then his body shot to the surface and into the sky, and he flew above the earth at great speed. With each new terrain, people with various skin colors and unique features flashed before his eyes. It was at this moment that he realized just how small his world was.

He was now above Duffle, and he followed the path from Stellar Hall to Xander. Then he flew along the shore, crossed the mouth of the river that emptied into the ocean, and glided up the riverbank to a castle. Dylan was not sure whose castle it was, but he felt an evil spirit as he glided above it.

It must be Nero's.

Dylan did not know if he was seeing the past, the present, or the future and wondered if time had any bearing on the vision. He hovered above the castle for a moment and then flew back over the land to Duffle.

He carried on past Duffle and over Gilmore Pond. The dim light of the Gnarled Oak caught his eye. Suddenly, his mind and body were connected again. The light that shone into his head slowly faded until it was gone. He floated for a moment and thought about what he had just seen. He was at ease. All tension had washed away. For some reason, his mission made sense. He was not certain why he felt better about it, but he was glad he did. He dressed quickly and left the ballroom, finding Xander in the exact same position.

"Thank-you, Xander."

"Don't thank me. This is your destiny."

"What is?" Dylan tilted his head.

"Everything you have done since you left your home. What has felt like an aimless journey has been very purposeful. The path you have followed is the one you were supposed to take." Xander smiled. "Continue to trust in Aarial."

A man peered into the room. Xander nodded a silent message. A moment later, the man returned with two others, who brought trays of food.

"Let everything go, and eat. You have much to think about, but for now, enjoy your food and get a good night's rest."

An unappetizing aroma filled the room. The hunchback ladled a milky soup into a bowl. Unrecognizable objects floated in the liquid. Dylan did not want to know what they were, so he did not ask. The bread that went with it was stale and salty, but that did not matter to him. He was too hungry, and it filled a space in his stomach. As Dylan finished the meal, he started to drift.

"Now you may rest," Xander whispered.

Dylan leaned back against the wall and shut his eyes. When he opened them a few minutes later, he saw someone leaving the room. On the ground, just in front of him, was a thin mattress with a pillow and blankets. He looked up at Xander, who smiled at him. Dylan lay down immediately. It felt good to lie on a bed. He could not remember the last time he had reclined on something soft.

"Sleep now, and in the morning, my boatman will take you where you want to go."

Instantly, Dylan fell into a deep sleep.

24

Stand Up For Yourself

"LEAVE ME ALONE!" DYLAN SCREAMED AS he ran into the classroom and dropped into his seat.

Mr. Peters shot up from his desk and walked over to Mrs. Giles, who had just entered the room.

"What's going on?" Mr. Peters asked.

"Dylan knocked a little boy down," Mrs. Giles answered.

"We were just playing!"

"Do you think they were playing?" Mr. Peters asked his aide.

"They might have been, but I couldn't tell from where I was. The other child got up and chased after him. It was hard to tell if he was angry or happy."

"Now, you tell me what happened, Dylan. We've only got a minute before the other students start coming in."

"Nothing. We were just playing."

"Who's *we*?"

"That kid that I read with."

"Jacob?"

"Yes!" Dylan spat angrily.

"Okay, well that may be so, but Mrs. Giles didn't know that. You should have explained it to her instead of running away."

"Why does she have to follow me all the time? I'm tired of it."

"You tell me why she has to follow you, Dylan."

Dylan did not answer. He focused on his desk and picked at a sticker.

"Tell me why she has to follow you, Dylan," Mr. Peters repeated.

He glanced up to see the two adults looking at him.

"Quit staring at me. I know why."

Mr. Peters turned to Mrs. Giles. "I'll take care of this. You go get a cup of coffee."

As she walked away, Mr. Peters went back to his desk. He spoke to Dylan from his seat.

"You left the gym again yesterday."

Dylan glanced over at him.

"It worries me when you leave the school."

"It does not. No one cares about me."

"I am *very* concerned about you, Dylan. There are many of us in this building who want to see you succeed, but you just keep pushing us away."

Dylan shook his head and continued to pick at the label on his desk. "I'm going to a group home," Dylan whispered.

"I thought you were supposed to be leaving Grandma a long time ago."

"She keeps changing her mind. She just keeps me because she gets money from the government for taking care of me." Dylan dropped his head. "I hate group homes."

"I'm sorry to hear that, Dylan. I truly am, but try not to worry about it until you know for sure. You've been told so many things that haven't come true. Let's just wait and see."

Mrs. Evans and another woman appeared at the door.

As Mr. Peters stood, he said, "Get out a book and read until the bell rings, Dylan."

In the hallway, Mrs. Evans introduced Mr. Peters to Mrs. Jules, the behavioral specialist. Mrs. Evans left them alone to talk about Dylan.

"I'm really just here to observe today," Mrs. Jules blurted without pauses between her words. "I've overbooked myself, so I'm in a bit of a rush."

"Okay." Mr. Peters couldn't help but smile at the pace of her speech. "Well, how can I assist you?"

"I'd like to meet him and talk to him, but for the most part, I want to observe his interactions. I've heard bits and pieces about Dylan, but I don't know a lot. Fill me in on what I should be looking for."

"Oh, boy." Mr. Peters paused. "There are too many things."

"Okay, that's fine. I will just observe *everything*. Do you have time to talk during lunch?"

Mr. Peters nodded. "Let me introduce him to you."

Just as he finished speaking, the bell rang and students started filing in.

"I can introduce myself. You get yourself ready for class."

The two of them walked into the room together, and Mr. Peters went to his desk and picked up a few things before proceeding to the meeting area. Mrs. Jules looked up at some of the art decorating the walls.

Dylan was watching the students drift into the room and run to the meeting area when Mrs. Jules caught his eye. He glanced at Mr. Peters to see if the stranger wandering around the classroom surprised him.

Everyone was in the meeting area when Mrs. Jules walked over to Dylan. He immediately stood and was about to join the rest of the group when she spoke.

"Hello, Dylan. I'm Mrs. Jules."

He glanced up at her suspiciously and breathed a greeting.

"Did you do any of the artwork on the wall?"

"Yeah, I did the mountains over there." He pointed.

"It's very good."

Dylan felt the students' eyes upon him, and he quickly got up and ran to the meeting area. As he slid in behind the group, his knees hit Sam, who turned around angrily.

"Watch it," he hissed through clenched teeth.

"Sor-ry," Dylan said, exaggerating the word.

Sam scowled, but Dylan ignored him and looked intently at Mr. Peters. When Sam turned to face Mr. Peters again, Dylan snarled, baring his teeth. Then he stuck up his middle finger and shook it. The students who saw the incident giggled uncomfortably. Dylan turned tentatively and saw Mrs. Jules watching him. His eyebrows narrowed and his face reddened. A small pebble caught his sight, and he batted it into the crowd of students. Then he looked up at the numbers written on the board.

0, 1, 1, 2, 3, 5, 8, 13, 21

"So, from yesterday's investigation, can we conclude that this is the correct sequence of numbers?" Mr. Peters asked the class.

They all nodded.

"Good. Now, we could continue our investigation to find the next few numbers, but I'm wondering if we need to. Can you determine the next numbers by looking at these?" He pointed at the board.

They stared at the numbers for a few moments before Ted shouted, "No!"

"Why not, Ted?"

"Because there's no pattern."

"Really?"

"Well, I thought there was a pattern yesterday," Ted added. "That's why I got it wrong when I wrote 1, 1, 2, 2, 3, 3."

Suddenly, it hit Dylan. "I know!" he shouted. "The next number is 34!"

"Shhhh." Mr. Peters put his finger to his mouth. He smiled at Dylan. "Maybe, maybe not." Then he spoke to the class. "If you think you know, keep it to yourself for right now."

Mr. Peters explained the next part of the lesson and handed out chart paper. Some of the more advanced students who could explain their answers to Mr. Peters worked on a more challenging problem. The others continued to try to find the pattern by continuing yesterday's investigation.

When the recess bell rang, everyone ran outside to play in the snow that had fallen the night before. Mrs. Giles followed Dylan out the door. He was ahead of her and continued moving until he thought he was far enough away. She watched him from a distance.

"How did this morning compare to other days?" Mrs. Jules asked Mr. Peters when she returned to the classroom.

"It was better than usual. He was fairly calm."

"Mrs. Evans told me about the knife incident. That's very disconcerting."

"Yes, it concerns me as well," Mr. Peters responded.

"We can deal with that later. I'd like to talk about what I saw today."

"Okay."

"You spend too much of your time with him. You have an aide—she should be working with him."

"I agree, but they don't have a very good relationship. He usually listens to me, but he won't listen to her."

"Well, I'm sorry, but that's her job. If she can't do her job, you need to get someone who can."

"She's very good with Albert and some of my other students who need some one-on-one attention. She spends a lot of time working with them, so I can work with Dylan."

"But she's here to work with Dylan to free up your time."

"I agree. I could use some relief. She's so nice though…and she tries to be so helpful."

"You can't keep her because she's nice. For her to be helpful, she needs to supervise him directly."

"You're right." Mr. Peters paused for a moment. "I need a coffee. Let's talk on the way down to the staff room."

TED AND SAM FOUND A CLEAR patch of snow without footprints. Their shuffling feet traced out a large circle, and Dylan watched as the snow maze took shape. Jake stood on the tower of the playground and yelled down at Ted.

"Hey, Ted. You wanna Hurt's Donut?"

Sam glanced over at Ted, who pretended not to hear Jake and continued with his project.

"Hey, Ted!" Jake repeated. "You wanna Hurt's Donut?"

Ted looked up at the bigger boy and shook his head. Jake jumped down and walked through the maze, ruining the intricate design. Sam and Ted pretended not to be bothered by this.

"I asked you a question, Ted. Do you want a Hurt's Donut?"

Without looking up, Ted spoke quietly into his jacket. "No thanks, Jake."

"Oh, come on. How often does someone offer you a donut?"

"Have a Hurt's DONUT!" And with that, he slugged Ted on the arm. "Hurts! Don't it?" Jake held his stomach and laughed. "Do you get it? Hurt's Donut? Hurts, don't it?"

Ted cringed at the pain and rubbed his shoulder. "Ha, ha. Very funny, Jake."

Even though Sam did not see much humor in the incident, he roared with laughter. To vent his anger, Ted ignored Jake and chased after Sam.

"You jerk," he yelled at Sam. "How would you like it? Do you want a Kill's Donut?"

Ted stopped chasing him and stomped away to find a new spot to create his maze. Sheepishly, Sam shuffled over to the new maze and started helping Ted. No words passed between them. When Jake was out of sight, Dylan strode over to the two boys, careful not to step on the design.

"Stand up for yourself!" Dylan said harshly. "Where's your self-respect?"

"He's too big, Dylan."

"Have you seen him bug me?"

Ted shook his head.

"That's because I stand up for myself."

"He's just thinks you're crazy." Ted smirked. "He's scared of your craziness."

Dylan smiled. "Well, it works." Then he turned to Sam. "And you," he said, pointing, "you are a coward. I saw him drop a booger in your face the other day. And now you're his buddy? Laughing at his jokes? What's wrong with you?"

Sam responded with a red face and a kick in the snow. The two boys froze, and the blood drained from Ted's face with Dylan's next words. It was not the words so much as the way they sounded.

"Join forces and defeat your opponent as one!" The words came at them from above and echoed all around them, as if they were standing within the walls of a canyon.

At the sound of the bell, Dylan turned and walked away.

25
Outside Help

"**H**EY, WHAT'S WITH ALL THE SNOW all over the carpet?" Mr. Peters asked. "And look at your hair! You guys are soaked!"

"We made snow angels at recess," Janna blurted out.

"Well, that's great, but next time, brush it off before you come into the classroom." He frowned and shook his head.

"Ted and I shared a donut," Jake snickered.

"That's nice, Jake."

Mr. Peters glanced at Ted as he entered the room and dropped heavily onto the carpet. His folded arms, clenched teeth, and shallow breathing did not correspond with Jake's remark.

"What's wrong, Ted?"

"Nothing," he spat curtly.

"Are you sure?"

Ted nodded his head and straightened up. The anger did not leave his face.

"All right, well come and talk to me if you need to."

"Okay."

"Okay class, we're continuing on with the author's workshop. Those of you who are working with Mrs. Giles, get your writing folders and meet in the library."

Brandon, Peter, Charlie, and Albert stood up and left the meeting area. Dylan looked up at his teacher, whose expression said *get moving.* He stood slowly and walked toward the door.

"Don't forget your folder, Dylan."

"Ooh," he groaned, and stomped back to his desk.

Mrs. Jules seated herself at a table in the library and Dylan joined the writing group at a nearby table. Mrs. Giles spoke to them for a minute before asking them to start writing. She sensed Dylan's anger.

"Are you okay, Dylan?" she asked. "You seem a little off."

Dylan scowled and glanced up at Mrs. Jules, who was watching him. "You're freaking me out!" he spat. "Stop looking at me."

"Dylan, go back to class," Mrs. Giles said forcefully. "This isn't working today."

Dylan bounced out of his chair, and it flew into a bookshelf. He stomped angrily back to class. Mrs. Jules waited for a moment before following him into the room.

"Why are you in here?" Mr. Peters asked angrily.

Dylan did not answer. He stared at his desk.

"I am in the middle of a lesson right now, and these students need me just as much as you. Get out a book and read. I do NOT want to hear from you until I'm done."

Dylan continued to stare at his desk.

"Get out your book. Now!"

Dylan felt Mrs. Jules's eyes on him, but he tried to ignore her. He lifted the top of his desk and pulled out *The Hobbit*. The yellowing pages slid through his fingers as he inhaled deeply.

Albert returned to the classroom to sharpen his pencil. On the way, he leaned over Dylan's desk and whispered something.

"You're the GOOF!" Dylan leapt out of his seat and stepped toward Albert.

Mr. Peters stormed across the room. "Get out!"

"What about him?" Dylan hollered.

Mr. Peters eyeballed Albert. "I'll deal with him. Right now, you're going to the office."

"Screw off," Dylan yelled, and he raced out of the room.

Dylan stormed down the hallway. He spotted an open door and stepped into the boiler room cautiously.

"Hello?" he called out.

In his head, he worked out an excuse to use if he got caught. *My teacher needs a broom.*

No one answered, so he took a few more steps. Huge, colorful pipes wound their way around the confined space. As he leaned forward and peeked around the corner, the envelope slipped out of his pocket and onto the floor. He dove at it and picked it up gently. The soft hum of the boiler slowed his pounding heart as he crouched down between two large boxes. Carefully, he opened the envelope and slid the fly onto his palm. Dylan studied it intensely for a few moments and nudged it gently with his pinky finger.

The warming beneath his shirt drew his attention, and he returned the fly to the envelope. Dylan placed the medallion between his palms. The familiar dull glow emanated between his fingers. He brought his hands toward his face and closed his eyes. The intense heat and subtle scent of burning flesh filled the air as he squeezed his palms together.

"**D**ID YOU CALL HIM A GOOF?" Mr. Peters asked.

"No," Albert answered tentatively.

"Yes, you did," Carley interrupted. "I heard you."

"Why are you trying to get him into trouble, Albert?"

Albert shrugged his shoulders and stared at the ground.

"Go to the office and explain this to Mrs. Evans."

Mr. Peters glanced at Mrs. Jules nervously. An uncomfortable smile appeared on his face as he raised his eyebrows and threw up his hands in dismay. He wondered if her stone-cold stare was criticism of the way he had handled the situation or just her usual demeanor.

After the bell had rung and the students had been dismissed for lunch, Mrs. Jules walked up to Mr. Peters and said, "I have to be at another school in thirty minutes, so I can give you fifteen."

"That's fine. Have a seat," he said, pointing to a chair at the round table in the corner of the room.

"Now, I don't know Dylan as well as you do, but I'll give you my opinion anyway."

"Okay."

"As I've already mentioned, Mrs. Giles needs to be doing more. Dylan should not have come back to the classroom when he had a problem in the library. If she can't handle him, he should be going to the office, not coming back here for you to deal with. He is her responsibility." She paused for a moment and then continued. "Take all academic pressures off him. He has more important things to work on."

Mr. Peters nodded. "Yeah, that's a good idea. That would be one less struggle."

"And what's the deal between Albert and Dylan? There's a history that I don't know about, isn't there?"

"Albert is a little goofy. He's very immature and likes to tease Dylan. I don't understand why, because Dylan is so much bigger than him, and he's punched him before. I don't know why he eggs him on like that."

"Dylan has punched him?" Mrs. Jules's nostrils flared.

"Yes."

"You should keep them completely separated. They should not be working together or interacting in any way."

"Okay."

"He should be separated from any student he doesn't get along with."

"That accounts for almost everyone."

"Well, at least separate him from the students he could be violent with. He has trouble focusing, so get him to sit right at your feet when you're meeting with the class. Also, you need to be consistent and firm with him. I noticed that people seem to tiptoe around him so as not to upset him. I understand that, but you must not let him get away with anything. If he gets away with some things, he'll get away with everything. He is in control of the situation. You want him to be in control of his behavior, not the behavior of everyone around him." She paused and took in a deep breath.

"I'm very concerned about the knife incident. I can seen how volatile he is, and I'm afraid he's going to seriously harm someone."

Mr. Peters squinted. "I don't honestly think that he would hurt anyone."

"Not intentionally, but he might by accident."

"I agree." The teacher nodded. "He said he needs it for protection. Dylan seems to have a real fear of teenagers, and I think his fear may be justified. Apparently, the other foster child he lives with is a teen, and he threatens him and calls him names."

"Well, we have little control over what happens at home. We have to deal with him while he's here. Have you set up a behavior contract with him?"

"No, I've been looking into it, but I haven't had a chance."

"Try it. They don't always work, but it doesn't hurt to try. What does he like to do? What would be a reward for him?"

"He likes playing Minecraft on the computer."

"Okay, so that can be his reward. Keep the contract simple. He can earn points for things that you'd like to see him working on. Every time he does something that you've outlined in the contract, he gets a point. When he gets to ten or fifteen points, he gets extra computer time. A contract can help a student think ahead and try to do good things in order to get something."

Mrs. Jules stood and extended her hand. "Please keep me informed. I don't envy you. You certainly have your hands full."

"Well, we'll get through it." Mr. Peters shook her hand. "Thank-you for coming, Mrs. Jules."

Collin Paulson

26

Sacred Ground

"FORM...STRUCTURE...BALANCE!"

"What?" Dylan automatically grabbed for his sword. It took a moment for him to realize where he was. He moved toward Xander and waved his hands over his host's open eyes—no response.

"What did you say, Xander? Are you awake?"

"All...living things," he gurgled. "All living things...in a spiritual dance." The boy stared into his vacant eyes. ". . . form...structure... balance..." His voice trailed off. Dylan glanced down at Xander's gnarled hands, which gripped a tattered blanket. "You cannot... dance alone."

"Who?" Dylan asked. "Who can't dance alone?"

Xander gasped, like a drowning man coming up for air.

"What?"

"Who can't dance alone, Xander?"

Xander cleared his throat and twisted his crippled back. "I observed a great dance. All creatures moved as one. Then one animal pulled away and tried to form another dance. The once-beautiful rhythmic movement became erratic and awkward. Both dances collapsed upon themselves."

"What does that mean?"

"Humans cannot dance alone."

Dylan stared at the ground and chewed on his thumbnail.

Xander smiled. "I hope you slept well, my boy."

Dylan looked up. "I feel good, and much more focused. Thank-you for letting me into the Chandelier Ballroom."

"I'm glad it was helpful. Now eat."

The breakfast was just as unappetizing as the previous night's meal. Dylan choked it down without enthusiasm. As he finished up, the hunchback handed him a leather pouch filled with food. Dylan nodded his thank-you.

"It's time for you to be on your way, Dylan. May Queen Gaia grace you with good fortune."

Dylan gripped one of Xander's hands in his and stared straight into his face. "You have given me the strength to continue. Thank-you."

Xander shook his head. "It's all you, my boy."

The hunchback led Dylan back to the beach he had arrived at the day before. The boatman sat on the sand staring out over the water, and as Dylan approached, he stood and walked over to the boat. He steadied it while Dylan got in and then pushed off. Dylan was surprised at how quickly they were out of the cave and on the open water. Time had moved so much more slowly the day before.

There was a dampness in the air that chilled Dylan to the bone. He lifted his collar and tucked his face into his shirt. What began as gentle rocking became violent crashing as they neared the beach.

"Please take me across the mouth of the river and drop me off on the other side," Dylan hollered above the crashing waves and swirling wind.

The hairless man did not acknowledge his request. Dylan was about to repeat himself when he noticed the change in direction. He could see and feel the river that flowed into the ocean slowly pushing the boat out to sea. The boatman appeared to be struggling slightly, but he paddled against the current without complaint.

As they neared the shore on the other side of the river, Dylan noticed a speck hovering high above them. He could not tell what it was, but he hoped that it was a bird. The boatman also noticed the flying object, and Dylan could have sworn that the boat sped up.

Dylan shivered as he looked out at the treeless landscape beyond the sandy beach. The permanently bent grass would not provide any shelter or protection from an air attack.

As they neared the beach, Dylan crouched down in the bow of the boat and held on to the gunnels. The boat hit the sand and he leapt out. Without hesitation, he turned and pushed the boat back out to sea. The boatman studied the sky before dipping his paddle back into the water. Dylan watched him for a moment and then turned away from the churning waters.

The wind pushed Dylan across the sand toward a rocky overhang. At the top, he glanced out to sea and wondered if this would be his last view of the never-ending water. Then he turned to face the direction he would be travelling. Dylan's heart dropped at the sight of endless prairie. There was nowhere to hide. He looked up at the drab, overcast sky one last time before setting off.

A powerful wind behind him attempted to set the pace, but his feet could not keep up because of the deep grass and inclined landscape. Each step through the tangled mess took so much energy. Dylan carried on for several hours before the landscape leveled off and started going downhill. A sharp drop surprised Dylan, and he tumbled forward and landed on his back, gasping for air. He lay there for a few moments.

"Oh my God," he exhaled. *This is so frustrating,* he thought. *I'm exhausted and I haven't even gotten anywhere. This is going to take me forever!"*

He sat up and surveyed his surroundings while gnawing on a piece of dried meat.

The grass seems to be thinning. I should be able to move more quickly.

A quick glance at the sky revealed another hovering speck.

I better get going. I don't want to be caught in the middle of…nowhere.

He continued on at a much quicker pace. As he proceeded, frequent glances skyward revealed that the flying object was getting larger, but he could not tell what it was. It was either a trog or a very large bird. Something told him to pick up the pace, so he started jogging.

The landscape before him began changing. The flat grassland was now rolling hills with a few clumps of trees. He stopped for a moment to rest and looked up at the hovering creature.

Oh crap! he thought. *It is a trog.*

It was high above the ground, so Dylan had time to prepare for battle. He leapt up and sprinted away. The ground fell away sharply and forced him off balance as he scrambled downhill. In the distance, he could see a uniform pattern of structures within some sort of fence.

He could not tell what they were. With every step, the trog got closer to the ground.

There was a faint odor in the air that intensified as he moved forward. It seemed to wrap itself around his legs and slither up his body like a snake. Soon it was so strong that it brought tears to his eyes.

"What is that?" Dylan spat. He covered his mouth with his arm and breathed through his sleeve, which seemed to have absorbed the scent like a sponge absorbs water.

Dylan sensed that the trog was within striking distance, but he kept running. Just as the beast was on top of him, he dove into the grass and the trog flew past him. His enemy returned and swiped at him feebly but missed. Dylan was out of breath, and he decided that he'd better save his energy for the fight, so he stopped and breathed deeply. The trog landed just in front of him.

Dylan screamed at him, "En garde, you Fais du Braire!"

The trog came at him quickly and furiously. Dylan stood his ground and waited for the attack. The trog put all of his weight into the blow that Dylan ducked under, and Dylan's elbow hit him in the back as he passed by. The trog lunged at him again, and this time, he aimed at Dylan's waist instead of his head. Dylan leaped over the trog's sword and stabbed him in the shoulder on his way down. The trog screamed and fell into the dirt.

"You are a STUPID bunch!" Dylan screamed. "You have no skill. All you have is power, and power is nothing—without skill!"

The trog snorted angrily and gripped his sword with the opposite hand.

Dylan pulled out Tracker's medallion and held it up. "Look what I can do! You are nothing to me!"

The trog's eyes widened at the sight of his master's medal. He backed away and hesitated. Then he breathed deeply and exhaled a shower of phlegm. A powerful screech exited his body, and he ran at the boy.

For Dylan, the moment slowed as the trog approached. He leapt out of the way of his enemy's sword and gracefully stabbed the creature in the back. The trog fell to the ground. His final gasp echoed in Dylan's skull as he pulled out his sword and looked to the sky; several specks hovered high above him now. There was no time to rest. Everything returned to normal speed.

He took off running, and as the ground leveled off, the stench became unbearable.

"I can't stop," he gagged into his shirt.

A quick glance up revealed five trogs in all. Up ahead, he noticed that what he had thought was a fence was actually a giant hedge. A trog flew just above his head. It turned sharply, just before the hedge, and came back at him. Dylan continued to run, for he knew that he was outnumbered.

If I can get to the shelter of the hedge, I can rest before my next battle.

Another trog swooped over him. They seemed hesitant to get too close. Dylan wondered if they were afraid or if they had a plan. Three trogs landed, almost simultaneously, between him and his destination. He stopped for a moment and waited for them to make the first move. No one stirred.

In a flash, Dylan felt a great pain in his head, and he became disoriented and unable to see. The talons dug into his face as he was lifted off the ground. He cried out as the trog lifted him over the others. As the beast neared the hedge, he turned away. Sensing the trog's hesitation, Dylan struck him in the breast, and he faltered and crashed into the hedge, releasing Dylan from his talons. Dylan slid down the branches inside the thicket and bounced from branch to branch before resting upon the damp ground.

His face, neck, and shoulders bled profusely.

"Ooh," he moaned. "Ooh."

Dylan did not move. The pain was too great. He drank the elixir Ravelle had given him and lay there for several hours, watching the trogs. They paced back and forth and appeared to be looking for a way into the hedge, but they stopped short of it. Dylan wondered why they did not just tear the branches apart and come after him. They appeared to be afraid of something bigger than his sword.

Eventually, Dylan felt his strength come back to him. He pulled himself into a seated position. Every part of his body ached but nothing was broken. The blood had coagulated on his skin, which cracked as he moved. A small amount of blood trickled through the scabs and coagulated again.

From where he sat, he was able to see through to the other side of the hedge. He noticed one of the structures he had observed from a distance. It was a pyramid of logs with a platform on top. On top of the platform rested the remains of something. The skeleton was huge—too big to be a human's. It was wrapped in a uniform that hung loosely and blew in the wind. Dylan turned his gaze to the waiting trogs, and it hit him like a flash.

"Holy crap!" Dylan exhaled. *They're wearing the same uniform. This is a trog cemetery! No wonder they're afraid. This place is disgusting!*

Dylan looked back at the death monument. He could now see one of the wings, and a sword that hung loosely from a belt.

Which way do I go? He looked from the cemetery to the trogs and back again. *I can't go back. There are too many of them…and I sure don't want to go in there.*

He sat for a moment and thought about his next move. Then he stood. The pain didn't stop him from pacing slowly and stretching his limbs. Several wooden cairns rose up ominously while others disappeared into the thick fog. He turned back at the drooling trogs, who studied him intently.

I have no choice.

He peered into the cemetery and inhaled the dense, moist air. The smell was now a part of him, and as a result, less offensive. It was impossible to tell how big the graveyard was, as the fog was so thick. With a deep breath, he stepped over a branch into the burial ground. He looked back, but the barricade obscured the trogs. Their cries reverberated in his skull.

Dylan walked cautiously past the first pyramid. While studying the decaying corpse, he tripped over a stone and fell to the ground. He gazed up at the dead trog against the white sky. As he backed away, he saw the faint outline of the trogs flying along the hedge, but they still would not enter the area. He stood up slowly and proceeded on.

The still air was cool and calm. The wind that had been blowing all day long had died down. He did not feel that the live trogs were a threat, but the dead trogs terrified him. Death had always terrified him. He had never been able to attend funerals or look at dead animals without shuddering.

Most of the cairns supported fully decomposed skeletons, which were not as offensive as the corpses being torn apart by birds. The wooden pyramids came out of the fog and greeted him every few steps. There was nothing to distract him. The landscape was littered with death. As he proceeded, the horrible smell he had become accustomed to returned.

Dylan stared at the ground to avoid the nightmarish sights. Then one caught his attention. Something pulled him toward it. A fresh corpse. The sight startled Dylan. He tried to look at the ground but could not stop himself from staring up at the gray, decomposing body. Dylan felt like he was going to vomit, but he carried on, trying not to look up. He pulled his jacket up over his mouth in an attempt to block the horrible smell from getting into his lungs.

BOOM! echoed throughout the cemetery.

"What was that?" Dylan spun around several times.

He put his head down and started to run.

"Oomph!"

The wind was knocked out of him, and he fell to the ground. He had run into the funeral pyre supporting the massive fresh corpse. The trog's detached head rolled away from the body and rested upon two supports a few inches from the rest of the creature.

"Oh my God!" he screamed.

Instantly, he was up and running. Another loud *BOOM* shook the ground and knocked him off his feet. He lay on the ground and shook.

"What was that?"

Slowly, he got up again, and just as he was upright, *BOOM!*

Dylan collapsed. With his face in the dirt and hands clenched behind his head, he whimpered, "Oh my God, what have I gotten myself into?"

He looked around but could see very little, for the fog had gotten thicker.

The banging continued in a steady pattern. *BOOM, BOOM, BOOM!* And with every sound, the ground shook. Then there was a pause followed by another *BOOM, BOOM, BOOM!* Dylan clapped his hands over his ears.

A deep voice filled the air and surrounded him. "You have disturbed this sacred ground. You have no respect for the dead. Tracker died by your hand, and now you disturb his remains."

Dylan remained silent. He could not move or respond in any way.

"You have stolen from Tracker, and now you must return what is not yours."

Dylan pressed his hand against his chest and felt the outline of the medallion.

"Return what does not belong to you, and you shall pass."

Dylan knew that he had no choice, so he stood up slowly and walked back to the pyre he had disturbed. He looked up at Tracker's prostrate body and winced. Then he grabbed hold of a brace just above his head. Slowly, he climbed the pyre. It shook slightly, and Tracker's head rocked away from the body, then back to the body, as if it were nodding its approval. Dylan stared at the head as he climbed.

He talked quietly to himself. "Careful…careful…careful." The head rocked with every one of his movements. "Please don't roll off, please don't roll off," he repeated.

At the top of the platform, he pulled the medallion off his neck and placed it on Tracker's chest. Then he steadied himself and jumped from the pyre. He stumbled through the low grass as fast as he could. He passed several more bodies but averted his gaze. He did not want to know how many of the deaths were his doing.

The white sky was darkening as the sun dropped toward the horizon. Dylan travelled on.

The sight of the hedge that bordered the other side of the cemetery quickened his step. Reaching it, he stopped and gazed left, then right.

"This is impassable!" he exclaimed.

He pulled at the thorny branches but could not get through. The hedge was much thicker and more tangled on this side of the burial grounds. He looked back in the direction he had come. Then he ran along the hedge, looking for a more accessible spot.

"There! There's an opening!"

He tugged at it frantically, pulling branches away with his bleeding hands. Then he drew Olam, and with all his strength, he sliced open a hole and climbed in.

The quiet of the hedge slowed his heart and calmed his nerves. He lay there for a time until a grumbling in his stomach brought him out of his trance. The fowl air did not mix well with Xander's almost inedible food, so Dylan only took a few bites before tossing it back into his bag. He wrapped his blanket around his body and collapsed, completely exhausted.

27

The Birthday

THE CARETAKER HAD JUST UNLOCKED THE doors when Mr. Peters arrived.

"How's that kid of yours doing?" Mr. Grant asked.

Mr. Peters slowed his pace to let him catch up. He knew whom he meant but did not like the way he called Dylan *that kid*.

"Who are you referring to?" Mr. Peters asked.

"You know, that new kid."

"I don't have any new kids," Mr. Peters responded.

Mr. Grant looked down the hall and thought for a moment.

"Derek...no, Dylan. How's Dylan doing?"

"He's okay."

"Boy, he's quite the sight. His hair's a mess, his clothes smell, and it doesn't look like he ever bathes."

"Yeah, well, he doesn't have the ideal life."

Mr. Peters did not want to talk anymore, so he walked into his room, pretending not to hear the next question.

Mr. Grant followed him and repeated his question. "Did you need a broom yesterday?"

"Uh...no...why?"

"Well, I caught Dylan running out of the boiler room at light speed."

Mr. Peters tilted his head and stared over the caretaker's shoulder. "Really?"

"Yeah, he said that he was looking for a broom, but he looked pretty guilty if you ask me."

"Hmm...I'll talk to him. You might want to keep that door locked, Mr. Grant."

"Yeah, I usually do." Mr. Grant bit his lip and gazed at the ground. "That's the strange part. I remember locking it yesterday."

Mr. Peters was at his desk working when Mrs. Evans entered the room.

"Good morning, Mr. Peters."

"Good morning." Mr. Peters stopped what he was doing and looked up. "Oh, thank-you for taking care of my star pupils yesterday. What was the end result anyway? I didn't get a chance to talk to you."

"Albert is so strange. I couldn't get a rational thought out of him. He doesn't know why he provokes Dylan. He said he's afraid of him, and when I asked him why he teases him, you know what he said?"

Mr. Peters shook his head.

"'Birds gotta fly.' That's what he said."

"What does that mean?" Mr. Peters chuckled.

"That's what I asked him. He said, 'Birds fly to get food. If they don't fly, they get eaten by rodents. If rodents don't get food, they die. If they die, the birds eat the rodents, so they can fly. If I could fly, I wouldn't eat rodents.'"

Mr. Peters shook his head in disbelief. "That doesn't even make any sense."

"Oh, that's only the part I remember. He went on and on and on. I tell you, that kid's got verbal diarrhea. I don't think he can control the thoughts that come out of his mouth. He says things before he's even aware of it. I had him write about why he teases Dylan and what he'll do next time he gets the urge to provoke him. It took him two hours to write an illegible paragraph. Half the time he was dancing and doing strange movements with his arms. The secretary and I stared him down a few times, and then he'd quickly put his face back into his work."

"What about Dylan?" Mr. Peters asked.

"He didn't show up."

"Oh, well isn't that a surprise," he said sarcastically.

"What about the behavioral lady?" Mrs. Evans inquired. "What's her name?"

"Mrs. Jules."

"Was she helpful?"

"A little. She's going to come back, but for now she wants us to set up specific consequences for specific behaviors. She sent some suggestions to me in a email."

Mr. Peters counted on his fingers. "One, if he's disruptive or noncompliant in class, he goes to the office. Two, if he's violent, shows aggression, or swears at someone, he's to be sent home for the day—an informal suspension. Three, if he uses or displays weapons of any sort, he will suspended, and a meeting will be held at area office to discuss his future placement."

"That sounds fair. I take it he doesn't know this yet."

"No, I'm going to tell him today. I came up with this behavior contract for him," he said, handing it to Mrs. Evans.

"Did Mrs. Jules suggest this?" Mrs. Evans asked.

"Yeah, she thinks working toward something achievable will help him. These are all things he can do without too much difficulty. He doesn't lose any points; he only gains points. This is one way for him to earn something, instead of always having things taken away from him.

"I think it's worth a try, but I don't have a lot of faith in behavior contracts. I've used them in the past, and they rarely help—especially for someone like Dylan. He has so many problems. This piece of paper isn't going to change his life."

"I don't have much confidence in it either, but I thought I should give it a try."

"Well, good luck."

Mrs. Evans left the room, and just as she rounded the corner, Dylan stepped into the classroom.

"Today is my birthday!" he shouted.

"I thought you didn't know when your birthday was," Mr. Peters said.

"It's today."

"Remember I asked you when you arrived? You told me you didn't know. I thought you were just being stubborn."

"It's today," he repeated.

"What is the date today, Dylan?"

"My birthday."

"So if I go look at the calendar," Mr. Peters said with a smile, "it will say 'Dylan's birthday.'"

"No, probably not," Dylan said flatly.

Dylan's mood surprised Mr. Peters. He did not display any remorse for or even an awareness of the previous day's events.

"What are you going to do for your birthday?"

"Nothing."

"You're not going to celebrate?"

"We might have cake. Grandma told me I had to have a good day to get a birthday cake."

Mr. Peters thought for a moment and tapped his forefinger on the desk. "Hmm. Here's a thought—can I take you out for a birthday lunch?"

Dylan's eyes widened, and he straightened up in his chair. "Where?"

"Wherever you want."

His smile quickly disappeared. "Grandma won't let me."

"I'll talk to her. Is she at home right now?"

"Yeah, she's always home."

"Before I call her, I'd like to go over some things. Have a seat."

Dylan sat down on the chair his teacher had dragged across the floor, and Mr. Peters began explaining the potential consequences of his behaviors. Dylan didn't say much but appeared to understand. He liked to idea of earning computer gaming time for good behavior.

"Can we shake on it?"

Dylan nodded and extended his hand.

"So you agree to everything we've discussed?"

"Yes." Dylan nodded again.

"Okay, I'm holding you to this. Now, go outside and play."

Dylan ran out of the classroom and slammed his body into the outside door. Mr. Peters walked into the library and dialed the familiar number.

"Ms. Truss?"

"Yes." She coughed into the phone.

"Hello, this is Mr. Peters."

"Who?"

"Mr. Peters, Dylan's teacher."

"Oh, right."

"I just found out that today is Dylan's birthday, and I'd like to take him out for a special lunch. Are you okay with this?"

"Uh…yeah…sure. Why?"

"I don't normally do this kind of thing, but I thought it would be good for both of us to interact outside of the classroom."

"Boy, you're a sucker for punishment. Make sure you tell him your expectations before you leave because he can be a real…he can be such a jerk. You tell him I said that."

"Uh…no, I won't tell him that. That's not the way I talk to kids."

"Well, maybe you should."

"Well, maybe you…" Mr. Peters stopped himself. "Uh, I have to go. Thank-you, Ms. Truss." He slammed the phone down angrily and walked back to his room.

The news of their lunch date put a smile on Dylan's face. He was in a happy, playful mood all morning, which was almost as disruptive as his defiant behavior. Mr. Peters had to remind him to calm down several times because he was starting to disrupt the class. The teacher did not come down on him too hard though, as his jovial mood was such an improvement over his usual one.

When the lunch bell rang, and most of the students had left the room, Mr. Peters asked Dylan where he wanted to go for lunch.

"Super Burger!"

Mr. Peters wrinkled up his face. "Are you sure?"

"Yup."

"Oh, all right. It's your birthday. Grab your coat and wait for me at the front entrance. I'll be there in a minute."

When all of the students had left the classroom, he grabbed his coat and closed the door behind him.

"Going out for lunch today?" Miss Roland called.

"Yeah, I've got a lunch date with Dylan."

She shot him a look of horror. "Aren't you worried about reinforcing his bad behavior?"

Mr. Peters spoke through clenched teeth. "No! I don't have that concern, Miss Roland."

He sped away from her toward the office.

"And where are you going, Mr. Chevalier?" Mrs. Evans asked Dylan.

He put his hand to his mouth as if to cover up his voice and whispered, "Mr. Peters is taking me out for lunch."

"Well, aren't you special."

He smiled. "It's my birthday."

"Well, happy birthday. I didn't know it was your birthday."

Mr. Peters went into the office to check his mailbox and came out the other door.

"Is the birthday boy ready?"

Dylan smiled at him.

"Well, let's go then."

"Which car is yours?" Dylan asked as they entered the parking lot.

"The green one."

"That's a piece of junk."

Mr. Peters chuckled. "Excuse, me young man, but that happens to be the best car in the parking lot."

"Yeah, right," Dylan said with a laugh.

"The '75 Dodge Dart is the best car ever made."

"Then why are there rust holes on the side?"

"Those are ventilation holes. They're supposed to be there. You realize that you're insulting my baby, don't you?"

"Well, your baby is very ugly. I wouldn't want to meet its mother."

"Don't push your luck, boy."

Mr. Peters opened the door for Dylan and helped him with the seat belt. He had to yank on it to get it to release.

"Is this thing safe?"

Mr. Peters glared at him as he slammed the passenger door shut. The entire car shook from the force. Mr. Peters jumped in.

"Okay, let's go."

As they stepped through the doors of the restaurant, Mr. Peters asked, "Are you okay with this?" He sensed Dylan's discomfort at the sight of dozens of teenagers. "I don't mind going somewhere else."

Dylan moved closer to Mr. Peters. "No, I'm okay," he said quietly.

The two of them looked up at the menu board and then ordered. Dylan didn't say anything while they waited for their lunches. With his tray in hand, Dylan led the way to the furthest corner of the restaurant, where no one was sitting.

"Let's sit by the window?"

"I like it here," Dylan responded.

"But it's so dark."

Dylan collapsed into his chair and started eating french fries. Mr. Peters shrugged his shoulders and sat down.

He held up his glass. "Happy birthday, Dylan."

Dylan held up his glass, and as their cups touched, Mr. Peters said, "L'chaim."

"La what?" Dylan asked

"L'chaim. It's a Hebrew toast which means 'to life.'"

Dylan nodded. "Cool."

Then Dylan began talking, and chewing, without stopping. There was never a lull in their conversation, as Dylan was knowledgeable in so many different areas. Little bits of food sprayed out of his mouth, forcing the teacher to shield his lunch with his hand.

"How do you know so much, Dylan?" Mr. Peters finally asked.

"I don't know. I watch nature shows sometimes. I like the History Channel too."

"You like history?"

Dylan nodded.

"Wow, I'm impressed. I don't know many kids who like history."

"I do. I wish I lived in a different time."

"Why is that?"

"I don't know. I just do."

"Which time period would you like?"

"The past."

"Yes, but which time period—the medieval ages, the dark ages, during the times of the Romans or the Vikings? Which period?"

"I don't know…when they used swords."

Mr. Peters told him about the castles he had seen in Europe and the ruins in Greece and Turkey. Dylan had many questions about the places he had seen and told Mr. Peters that he would like to visit them someday. As they finished off the last of their lunches, Dylan got very quiet.

He glanced around the room and whispered, "I'm going to see my brother."

"Really!" Mr. Peters said excitedly. "You must be looking forward to that."

"Yeah…I guess."

"Tell me about him."

"He's older than me."

"Where does he live?"

"In Edmonton."

"When was the last time you saw him?"

"I don't know. A long time ago."

Dylan's enthusiasm did not match his teacher's.

"Are you okay with this?"

"Yeah, I guess."

"You don't seem very excited."

Dylan shrugged. Then he gazed around the restaurant at the teenagers eating their lunches.

"Can we go now?" Dylan asked.

"Are you finished?"

"Can I drink my milkshake in your car?"

Mr. Peters nodded and stood up.

The two of them drove back to the school in silence. Mr. Peters could tell that Dylan did not want to talk, so he allowed him the private time. They got back to the school twenty minutes before the afternoon bell.

"Why don't you go to the playground until the bell rings, Dylan?"

"Okay." A sad look of gratitude met Mr. Peters's eyes. "Thank-you," he mumbled.

"You're welcome, Dylan. It was my pleasure."

Dylan jumped out of the car and secretly wiped his eyes with his sleeve. Then he sprinted around the front corner of the school.

Mr. Peters sat quietly in his car. Dylan's expression had impacted him like he had never thought possible.

The wind at the back of the school took Dylan's breath away as he rounded the corner. He pulled up the collar of his jacket, folded his arms, and breathed into his chest. Just outside of the Hidden Forest, Jake was approaching Ted and Sam. Dylan walked toward them slowly.

"Hey, Ted!" Jake called. "Do you want another Hurt's Donut?"

Ted shook his head and backed away. Sam was suddenly interested in a thorny branch and studied it intently.

"Oh, come on. Mr. Peters likes it when we share."

Over Jake's shoulder, Ted's and Dylan's eyes connected, and Dylan sent him a silent message. Ted straightened up and squinted at the bigger boy.

"Take another step, Jake…and…and I'll wipe my bum with your shaggy head!"

Jake paused at Ted's tone. Then he burst out laughing. Ted's and Dylan's eyes connected a second time. Dylan slapped his forehead with his palm and shook his head in disbelief. Ted realized how ridiculous his threat sounded, but his body language remained forceful.

"What kind of threat is that?" Jake laughed.

Ted's violent expression stopped Jake's laughter.

"Whoa, Teddy Bear. Relax, man. I'm just joking. Let's be friends. Come on. Shake my hand." Jake extended his hand.

"My hand," Ted spat, grabbing Jake's hand, "may be the last hand… you EVER shake!"

The force of his message pushed Jake back a step, but Ted kept his grip on his palm. He squeezed with all his might, and as Jake tried to pull his arm away, Ted squeezed harder. Dylan nodded his approval, and as he slipped into the Hidden Forest, he saw Sam kneel down behind Jake. With one last violent yank, Ted released Jake's hand, and he tumbled over Sam's back and landed on his neck and head. Sam leapt up and stood beside his friend. The now-growing group of students watching the interaction burst out laughing.

"Did you see that?" someone shouted. "They got Jake!"

Jake jumped up quickly. His reddened face shook, and he wagged his sausage finger at Ted. "You wait, Teddy Bear. I'm gonna get you."

This was Ted's proudest moment, and he wanted to shout out with glee, but he remained firm in his expression and stance. As Jake stomped away, Ted and Sam faced each other. Ted started to shake.

"You were great, Ted," Sam said. "Now *that* is standing up for yourself."

Ted smiled nervously. "I'm a dead man."

"Yeah," Sam agreed. "You are a dead man."

Dylan sat down in the shelter of the Hidden Forest and leaned up against a tree. He pulled out the envelope and shook it gently by his ear, awaiting the familiar sensation beneath his shirt. It didn't come. He patted his shirt, searching for the outline of the medallion. Panic set in. He pounded his chest violently with both hands. The realization that the medallion was gone struck him like a lightning bolt.

"Oh no!" he exhaled. "What am I going to do now?"

He closed his eyes and rubbed his forehead with the rough skin of his branded palm. Slowly, he lowered his hands and studied the indentations. The two impressions stood out like woodcarvings. He placed the bases of his palms together and noticed that the sword on one hand was raised while the impression of the sword on the other hand was indented.

"What did Ted call this?" he asked himself. "White space? No, negative space."

He rolled one palm over the other and adjusted the placement of each impression until they lined up perfectly. The two opposing designs fit together like a magical key and locked his warming hands in place. Dylan closed his eyes and raised his glowing hands toward his face.

28

Unexpected Teamwork

DYLAN AWOKE TO THE SOUND OF birds. While stretching his arms above his head, he peered through the branches of his hiding spot. Beyond the hedge was a lush forest, and the sight brightened Dylan's spirits. He did not want to travel in the open like he had on the previous day. He ate a small breakfast and watched for any indication of danger in the forest.

Just as Dylan was about to leave the safety of the hedge, he spotted a wounded trog outside of the cemetery. Silently, he snuck up behind the great beast. It looked like a bird with a broken wing trying to fly. The trog took a few steps and lifted its wings for takeoff, but just as it got off the ground, it glided back to earth. Dylan watched the trog for a short time. A sensation of sympathy for the injured creature welled up in him.

Suddenly, the trog turned and spotted him. It snarled and hissed, opening its mouth to display its razor-sharp teeth. Dylan stepped out from behind a tree and drew his sword. The power of Olam electrified his body, and he stepped toward the trog, which had drawn its sword.

"En garde, you Fais du Braire!"

In a flash, the trog was upon him, wild and out of control. Dylan stepped aside and sliced open his uninjured wing. The trog screamed and fell into the dirt face-first. Dylan raced over to where the creature lay, and as Olam entered its back, the trog's cry rang out in the forest. Dylan then looked up and spotted a trog circling above him. The dying trog flipped over for one final kick to Dylan's chest. The powerful blow knocked Dylan off his feet and onto his back. As he lay there, struggling to get his breath, he saw two more trogs circling above his head.

His mind raced. *What do I do now?* Two more trogs came into view. *Five? How am I going to defeat so many?* He surveyed his surroundings,

223

looking for a place to hide. *I've got to get out of here. There's no way I can defeat them all.*

Dylan placed one foot onto his opponent's chest and grasped Olam with two hands. As the sword came free, the trog's left shoulder and rib cage collapsed. Suddenly, talons pierced Dylan's chest and back, and he was lifted off the ground. Dylan swung his sword wildly. The first few strikes missed the trog, but the final jab put a hole in his breast, and he dropped Dylan into a tree. Dylan bounced off several branches before resting upon a platform of two large branches. He was restrained by the excruciating pain.

Then it hit him. "Where's my sword?" Dylan cried in a panic.

He rolled onto his stomach and searched the ground. Suddenly, Taya appeared. She ran over to a pile of rocks and started tugging at something. It wasn't until she turned her body that he saw the object she was pulling at—it was Olam, encased in stone.

"Run away!" Dylan hollered. "Hide!"

Taya looked up. Time slowed, and a silence filled the air. He could not see what she was looking at, but he knew from the silent terror on her face. The massive wings produced a wind that shook the branches of the trees. The trog grabbed Taya with his talons, and she stabbed his leg. The creature released one foot but held on to her with the other. The clang of her knife hitting the rocks below broke the silence. Dylan dropped his battered body to the ground and ran out into the clearing, screaming as loud as he could.

"Come get me, Dirt Bags! I'm the one you want!"

The trog continued to soar higher and higher. His flying was awkward and erratic. Then he faltered and started to descend, and Taya stopped struggling for fear of being let go. Dylan's heart stopped when he saw his sister's body drop. Her arms and legs flailed as she plummeted through the air. Just as she was level with the tops of the trees, another trog grabbed her by the shoulders. The momentum of her fall pulled the trog to the ground, and just when it looked like Taya was going to hit the earth, they started to rise. Higher and higher he lifted her off the ground.

Time stood still while Dylan and the other trogs watched Taya disappear in the distance. When she was out of sight, Dylan looked up and saw several trogs diving toward him. He raced to his sword and grasped the handle. The surge of energy electrified his body, and a flash of everything he had been taught and learned about Aarial went through his mind in an instant. The sword glided out of the stone easily, and he ran into the trees.

The first trog to reach him was out of control, and Dylan killed him easily. The creature fell to the ground screaming. As Dylan stabbed him, he heard all of the trogs shriek as if they had also been stabbed. Then there were two upon him, hovering overhead with their swords a-blazing. They kept just out of reach of Dylan's powerful sword, for they knew of the danger if they got too close to his ominous weapon.

Now there were three trogs looming over him, swinging their swords and grabbing at him with their claws. Branches showered down upon them in the flurry of the fight. Dylan internalized the entire scene. He sensed exactly where each trog was and what each one was going to do. As he swiped at one, another would dive at him from behind. His great speed allowed him to spin and stab before any of them got close enough to harm him.

One trog dove at him, and Dylan sliced off his foot, causing him to drop his sword. Then Dylan lunged and stabbed the trog through the stomach. As he pulled out his sword, he was knocked to the ground. The trog who had kicked him pursued and came at him feet first. Still on the ground, Dylan pulled out his knife, rolled out of the way, and stabbed the trog between his legs. He jumped to his feet to face three new trogs, and the battle continued.

The fighting went on for what seemed like hours. Everyone was tiring. Dylan was losing his strength, and so were the trogs. Simultaneously, they all landed upon the ground in a circle around Dylan. The trogs rested while Dylan stood in a ready position. He knew that he could not defeat so many all at once.

Ravelle's words rang out. *They are stupid and arrogant. They want the glory of carrying out a mission alone. Their desire for personal glory will*

intensify because Nero is looking for a replacement for Tracker. They will try to impress him.

Nero must have organized this, Dylan thought. *They are too stupid to plan something like this.*

Dylan felt something in the air, something ominous and frightening. He looked up through the trees and spied countless trogs circling above him.

I have to get out of here. This battle will soon be over, and I won't walk away the victor. The only escape is underground.

Dylan sensed a tunnel nearby. He felt the pull of the underground, and he looked in the direction of the lure. There was a treeless field between him and the opening.

It's too far. I'll be too exposed if I go that way, but what choice do I have?

With his blade swinging, he dashed toward the meadow. The trog in his way was taken off guard and didn't know what hit him when Dylan sliced open his neck and stepped over top of him. Dylan kept his sight on the grove of trees on the other side of the meadow as he sprinted.

Halfway across the field, he was knocked to the ground by a trog's feet. Splayed on his back, he saw several trogs carrying a large net. He got up and continued running. Again he was knocked to the ground, but this time something metal bashed him on the head; blood trickled over his forehead.

Lying on the ground, between him and the forest, was a huge metal net. Dylan jumped up, stumbled over the trap, and looked back at the trogs who were lifting it in their claws. The trees were close. In a few seconds, he would be sheltered by the forest and could then slip into the underground.

The metal web struck him one more time and covered his battered body. He attempted to lift his face out of the dirt, but he was dazed and confused. With great effort, he lifted his head and looked straight into the eyes of a trog who was gripping one corner of the trap. On the other side of the net was another trog. Behind him he saw two trogs grabbing onto the corners with their talons.

Then they started flying along the ground. The ground vibrated with the scraping of metal on earth. In an instant, Dylan was flipped around so that his knees pressed up against his face. He felt himself being lifted off the ground, inside the lattice trap.

A memory of his previous abduction, in Tiko's bag, flashed before him and then disappeared. This time, he was high above the earth, being carried by four trogs to his final destination—and his destiny.

Collin Paulson

29

Family Visit

Mr. Peters walked into the office and checked his mail slot.

"How was your lunch?" Mrs. Evans inquired.

"It was good. One-on-one, he's a neat kid. He's bright and very sociable. I wish he could be like that more often."

"Well, I'm glad you had fun."

"Yeah, it was good. He got a little quiet at the end though. He clammed up when we started talking about his brother. You told me his older brother abused him, correct?"

Mrs. Evans sighed. "Yes, I'm going to have to revisit his file to refresh my memory and find out more."

"Yeah, me too," Mr. Peters said.

The bell rang, and Mr. Peters left the office. He walked quietly behind Albert, who was tiptoeing down the hall, unaware of his teacher. At a corner, Albert splayed his fingers and placed both of his hands on the wall. His eyes widened and his tongue darted in and out. He tilted his head and peered into the next hall. Carefully, he walked his hands around the corner and then hand over hand proceeded down the wall, his tongue darting in and out with each step.

"Iguana?" Mr. Peters asked, breaking Albert's concentration.

Albert straightened up and slapped his hands on his thighs like a soldier at attention.

"Uh…gecko," he responded quickly.

"That makes sense." The teacher smiled. "Well, get off the wall and hurry to class."

Albert grinned.

Most of the students were at the meeting area when he stepped into the classroom. Mr. Peters took attendance.

"Has anyone seen, Dylan?" Mr. Peters asked. "He was here twenty minutes ago."

The students turned their heads from side to side to confirm that he was missing.

"I saw him," Ted exclaimed. "He was on the playground a few minutes ago."

"Hmm. I wonder what happened to him." Mr. Peters paused and glanced at Mrs. Giles.

"I'll take a peek outside," she said quietly.

"Okay, class." The teacher slapped his hands together. "Here's what we're going to do. One of you wanted to know the height of the light pole over the skating rink."

"That was me!" Janna blurted.

"Who cares?" Jake said, exasperated. He turned to Janna. "Don't you know that when you ask a silly question like that Mr. Peters comes up with a stupid problem and makes us do more work?"

Mr. Peters smiled at Jake. "That's a matter of perspective. What one person views as work, someone else sees as fun."

"Yeah." Janna stuck her tongue out at Jake.

"This is a very old problem. There was an ancient Greek philosopher and mathematician by the name of Thales who was hired by the Egyptians to find out the height of the pyramids. Now, this is more difficult than you think. How do you figure out the height of something without actually measuring it from top to bottom? We're going to come up with our own strategies, and I bet one of you will use the same method Thales used."

Mr. Peters surveyed his students intently. "Let's see which one of you thinks like one of our greatest early mathematicians. Okay. I want you to come up with a plan on paper before we actually go outside and test our theories. When you have a group of three, come and get a piece of chart paper and start planning."

A few minutes later, Albert walked up to his teacher. "I don't have a group."

"Why do you always have so much trouble finding a group?"

Albert shrugged.

"I'll find you one." Mr. Peters put his hand on his shoulder and led him around the room. "Albert is going to be working with your group, Ted."

Ted glanced at his partners, Sam and Lyle, who rolled their eyes.

"Okay," Ted moaned. "Sit down, Albert."

EARLY THE NEXT MORNING, MR. PETERS was at his desk working when Dylan suddenly appeared.

"Whoa, Dylan! You startled me," Mr. Peters said quickly.

Dylan did not respond. He stood motionless in the middle of the room staring at his teacher in a trancelike state.

"Are you okay, Dylan?"

Dylan turned and left the room. Mr. Peters chased after him and found him standing in the hallway staring up at a blank wall.

"Dylan? Are you okay?"

Dylan looked up at him blankly.

"What's wrong?"

Dylan shook his head violently and coughed. "Nothing. I'm okay."

"Are you sure?"

Dylan nodded.

"Come into the classroom. I want to talk to you."

The two of them sat down on the risers.

"Where were you yesterday afternoon, Dylan?"

"I was thinking."

"In the future, please let me know when you're going to miss class."

"If I let you know, you'll try to stop me."

"True." Mr. Peters smiled. "Well, I get very worried when you don't show up. You were with me just moments before the bell rang. Where did you go?"

"I can't tell you."

"What were you thinking about?"

"Stuff."

"Are you okay, Dylan?" Mr. Peters studied his eyes. "You don't quite seem yourself today."

"Then who am I?"

"I don't know. You seem a little lost."

"Aren't we all a little lost?"

Mr. Peters jerked his head in disbelief. "That's a very philosophical thing to say, Dylan."

"Can I go now?"

"Yeah, go ahead." Then he added, "What kind of a day are we going to have, Dylan?"

Dylan stood and, before he turned to leave, said, "A good day."

To Mr. Peters's delight, Dylan had a good morning. He had no academic pressures—he still had to do most of the same work as the other students, but Mr. Peters accepted everything he did without question. He no longer asked Dylan to redo his writing, as writing was a challenge for Dylan. As a result, Dylan's behavior improved noticeably.

Just before lunch, Mr. Peters announced, "If everyone finishes up in the next ten minutes, we'll go outside for some free time."

Several students cheered.

THE CHINOOK WINDS HAD MELTED THE snow and left pools of water and mud throughout the playground and field. Some of the students played grounders on the creative playground while others grabbed a ball and played soccer. Mr. Peters helped the soccer players organize into teams while Mrs. Giles watched the children on the playground. Dylan played soccer for a few minutes but quickly lost interest. He walked over to Mr. Peters.

"I have to go home early today, so I can see my brother."

"Yes, I know you're not going to be here this afternoon."

"But I have to leave even earlier than that."

"At what time?"

"Before lunch."

"No one told me that, Dylan. The note said you wouldn't be here this afternoon. I'm sorry, but you're going to have to wait for the bell."

"Oooh," Dylan grunted. He kicked the ground. "Grandma is going to kill me if I don't get home on time."

"You'll have plenty of time."

Dylan turned and stomped away.

"Dylan! Wait! Come here for a minute."

Dylan stopped and turned around.

"Okay, here's the deal. I can't let you leave before the bell rings, but I can let you leave as soon as the bell rings. Go get your bag and bring it out onto the playground, and when the bell rings, you don't have to go into the classroom. You can just leave. Are you okay with that?"

"I guess."

"Have a wonderful weekend."

Dylan ran across the muddy field and into the school. A few minutes later, he came running out of the school with his bag and jacket. Mr. Peters watched him set his things down beside a tree and then walk onto the gravel-filled playground. Dylan studied the ground and continually stopped to look at things that caught his eye and put them in his pockets.

He crouched down and started digging beside a low platform that was being used as the time out-zone for grounders. Then Mr. Peters saw Dylan look up at one of the students and scream, "You...you...you dirt-pig cesspool!" Then Dylan grabbed the student, put him in a headlock, and dragged him through the gravel.

"Stop!" Mr. Peters yelled as he ran toward them.

Ms. Giles was by his side instantly. "Come with me!"

Dylan screamed at her, "Oh yeah, that's fair! Did you hear what he said?"

He stomped away.

"Get over here, Dylan!" Mr. Peters shouted.

"No!" Dylan stormed over to his bag and jacket.

Mr. Peters followed him. "Dylan. You are not going home. We're going to deal with this right now!"

The bell rang and all of the students started running toward the school. Dylan began walking across the field—away from the school.

Mr. Peters shook his head. "I guess it'll have to wait until Monday."

Ms. Giles consoled Shane, who was rubbing his neck.

"Are you okay, Shane?" Mr. Peters asked when he caught up to them.

"Yeah."

"What happened?"

"I asked Dylan to move out of the way so I could swing on the flying squirrel." Shane trembled. "That's all I said."

"Can you take him into the nurse's room, Ms. Giles?"

Ms. Giles nodded as they entered the school.

When the students had gone off for lunch, Mr. Peters dropped into his chair. He let out a sigh and stared up at the ceiling. Closing his eyes, he let out another sigh. "One step forward, two steps back."

Dylan turned at the end of the field and made his way back to the Hidden Forest. The shelter of the trees put him at ease. Once again, he pulled out the envelope and shook the fly into his palm. Other than a torn wing, it looked exactly as it had on the day it died. Dylan wondered why it didn't decompose like other animals.

After placing the fly and envelope back in his pocket, he rolled one palm over the other and adjusted the placement of each impression until they lined up perfectly. The two opposing designs sucked into place. Dylan closed his eyes and raised his glowing hands toward his face.

30

The Truth

DYLAN AWOKE TO A LOUD *clang*. He opened his eyes and searched the dark; nothing was visible. His entire body ached. His mind was foggy, and it took him a minute to gather his thoughts. He remembered the battle and being carried away by the trogs. He did not know where he was now, but he could guess. He tried to sit up but couldn't. Every muscle felt strained. The floor was ice cold. His hand rested upon a blanket, and he pulled it up to his chin. There was an odor in the room—something was rotting. He did not care to guess what it was. An animal scurried across the floor, and he shivered at the thought of living with rats—or something worse.

In the distance, he heard heavy footsteps and the jingle of keys. A door was opened and shut, and the footsteps grew louder. Another jingle of keys, and another heavy metal door was shut. The footsteps were only a few feet away. Keys fell to the floor and someone groaned.

The door to his cell opened, and he felt a cold breeze enter the room. Dylan forced himself up onto his bum and leaned against the wall with the blanket wrapped around his shoulders. A massive figure glided into the room. There were bars between him and the stranger. Light shone from behind the silhouette, and wind blew his cape. The door was shut, and the breeze stopped.

"Finally, we meet," the figure announced. "How about a little light into your lovely abode?" The deep voice reverberated around him.

The silhouette turned around and knocked a flat piece of wood to the ground to reveal a small window. Bright light streamed into the room, and Dylan had to shield his eyes. Slowly, his eyes adjusted to the light, and he looked up. The figure was lit up on one side of his body. He wore a black cape that draped over his shoulders. Long black hair flowed down his back. His face was covered in hair, and his eyes were deeply sunk into his skull. He almost looked like he had no eyeballs at all.

"Are you comfortable?" The voice resonated off the walls. "I try to make all of my guests feel like royalty."

The man took a step toward Dylan and clasped the bars. He rested his head upon the cold metal and smirked. The freezing bars seemed to calm him. He sighed and stepped back.

"You don't want to talk to me? Are you angry with me?"

The man walked over to the window and looked out. Then he pounded his fists against the wall and turned back to Dylan.

"Well, you have no *right* to be angry with me!" he screamed at a volume that shook the walls. "I am angry with you—you've been getting in my way. Who do you think you are?"

He waited for an answer, but Dylan remained silent.

"You've killed my faithful servants." He paused and then howled, "You killed Tracker!" Again he paused and then spoke quietly. "You have no manners."

Dylan sat in the corner of his cell, listening and watching, while the stranger ranted and raved. He started to shiver, and he wrapped the blanket around himself more tightly.

"Do you know who I am?"

"Of course," Dylan muttered.

"Oh, the little man can talk," he said mockingly. "Well, isn't that convenient? I am Nero. I am your nemesis. You are going to die here. You will bathe in a pool of blood."

Dylan spoke up. "Why am I still alive?"

"Because you may be of some use to me, and when I do kill you, it will be slow and painful." He paused and paced the room. Then he walked to the bars and crouched down to Dylan's level. "You probably think you are a pretty good fighter," he said quietly, "but you're not. The trogs were ordered to bring you back alive. They could have destroyed you at any time."

"What do you want?" Dylan said, seething.

"POWER!" snapped Nero. "Power is what I want. I'm going to rule the world."

"Soon there will be no one left to rule. A king cannot rule without subjects."

Nero's laugh echoed around the room. "I only kill the people who get in my way. There will be plenty of peons left to work in my kingdom."

"There will always be resistance from somewhere. People will not allow you to rule."

"They'll have no choice. I'll give them just enough to survive and no more. With your help, I will rule over everything," Nero hissed ominously.

"I will never help you. My power will never be used to control others."

Nero laughed and disappeared into the dark corner. Dylan heard something being dragged across the floor, and the next thing he knew, Nero was sitting on a stool right in front of the bars.

Nero laughed again. "You are naive, my little friend. You think your power is 'good power' and my power is 'bad power'?"

"Of course. My power has never been and never will be used the way you use it."

"Our power is one and the same, you fool. I also possess Aarial."

Dylan gasped. "You lie! You do *not* possess Aarial. It belongs to my family, and it's only used for good."

"Aarial is neither good nor bad. The person who possesses it decides how it should be used. You were raised as a farmer. What do you know about power? I was raised to rule, and rule I will."

"Even if what you say is true, I'll never use Aarial for evil. I choose to be a hero, not a villain."

"I am a hero and a villain." Nero chuckled. "They are one and the same. You are a worker bee, and I am a king. Evil is a perception. The things I do are not evil. Everything I do is for the good of my kingdom. I don't care if a few peasants die along the way. The whole of my kingdom is what matters, not a few revolutionary peasants."

"How can we share the same power? Aarial is only passed on to those who have the capacity to use it. You do not have the capacity."

Nero smiled menacingly. "I can see that some information has been kept from you." Nero leaned forward. "You and I come from the same ancestry." He paused and took great pleasure in Dylan's reaction.

"Many generations ago, there was a king who ruled the land and used Aarial to maintain control. He had two sons. The eldest was to receive the kingdom and the younger was to be his partner, but the eldest would have the final say in all decisions. The younger brother was jealous, and he left. He planned to kill his brother and rule the kingdom, but the younger brother became a farmer and gave up on his plan to rule. The two brothers never spoke again, and they left each other alone. Both possessed Aarial, but they did not rely upon it, for there was peace throughout the land. The younger brother eventually married and fathered many children. Many generations passed, and resentment between my family and your family grew until they were enemies. Many battles were fought. Finally, an agreement was signed and our ancestors lived in peace. For generations, our families went about their business and left each other alone. My father was weak. He should have destroyed your family long ago, but he felt obligated to keep things peaceful. When my father died, I received Aarial, and now, I will rule the world."

"I don't believe you. We are NOT related."

Nero laughed. "We don't just share the same ancestry. We. Are. Brothers."

Nero stopped speaking and smiled on one side of his face. Dylan flew over to the bars and spat in Nero's face.

"We are NOT brothers!" Dylan raged.

Nero grinned and gently wiped his face. "My father often gave in to many of your father's demands. Why do you think he did that?"

"Because they were friends."

"No. It's because my father felt obligated to your father for what your father had given him twenty-five years ago. He gave him a son. His first-born son."

"I'm my father's first-born son," Dylan spat. "I...am his only son!"

Dylan paced the cell, shaking his head and mumbling to himself. Nero watched silently.

"Why would my father give up his son?"

Nero answered, "The king needed an heir, and he could not produce one. Your father could not support a family, for he was poor and unstable. His inability to control Aarial was his downfall. My father convinced your father that his child would be better off with him. Your father told his people that his son died at birth, and they secretly transported me to the castle. Only our parents knew about this."

Dylan's head was spinning. He thought back over his childhood and tried to piece this information into his life.

Suddenly, he stopped and stared into Nero's eyes. "If this is true, then you killed your own father."

Nero smiled. "His blood runs through my veins, but he's not my father."

Dylan jumped at the bars and screamed, "I'll kill you for the lies you tell, or the truth you reveal."

Nero snapped his head back at the sudden outburst. "You are very emotional...brother," Nero mocked.

"I'm not your brother. Don't call me your brother."

Dylan walked to the corner of his cell and slid down the wall. "What do you want from me?" Dylan was physically and emotionally drained. "You can rule without me. I'm not going to help you."

"I don't trust you. I want to know just where you are. And...I want your power."

"You'll never get it. I'll never transfer it to you, and you cannot force me to. When I die, it dies with me,"

"You have much to learn," Nero said quietly. "When you die, Aarial comes to me. If you were to die among lesser men, Aarial would be lost. When I kill you, the transfer will automatically take place. I will have twice the power."

Dylan sat in the corner of the room, pondering what to do next. Suddenly, he stood up. "Where's my mother, and where's Taya?"

"Don't you worry about them. They're fine. I'm showing them a good time."

"What good are they to you? Let them go."

"You're very close to them. They may be of more use than I had ever thought. I assumed you were harder."

Nero turned to walk out of the room.

"What are you going to do with my mother? Your mother?"

Nero stopped for a moment. Then he turned slowly and said, "I've put her to work. She's my servant." He laughed. "Isn't that what a mother is?"

The door opened, and he was gone. Dylan lay back on the blanket that he had rolled into a pillow and looked up at the ceiling. He could hear Nero's footsteps getting fainter. Once again, he became aware of the pain in every part of his body. He tried to ignore it and think about what he had just been told.

31

One Story

"MR. PETERS?"

"Yes?" the teacher answered into the phone.

"Oh good, I'm glad I caught you before school starts. This is Mrs. Peverly, Dylan's social worker."

"Oh…hello…uh…I thought Mr. Kruger was Dylan's social worker."

"Yes, he was for a short period of time. There was a mix-up when Dylan moved to Calgary, so it's taken a while for us to get things straightened out. Can you hold on for a minute?"

Mr. Peters heard the phone drop and then the shuffling of papers.

"Thanks for holding. Anyway, the reason I'm calling is that I thought I should touch base with you and find out how he's doing."

"He's up and down. Some days are good and other days are terrible." Mr. Peters paused. "Overall, I think I've seen some improvement, but he's very unpredictable. His mood changes without warning."

"That seems to correspond with what others have told me about him. There are a lot of disruptions in his world, and you'll likely continue to see the effects of his unstable home life." The social worker took a deep breath before continuing. "I want to inform you about Dylan's weekend."

"Oh yeah, how was his visit with his brother?"

"Not good," she said quickly.

"What is it?" Mr. Peters asked. "Is he okay?"

"Yes, he's okay." She paused for a moment. "As you know, Dylan has been abused by his mother…and others. Well, his brothers, Blake and Sean, fit into the category of *others*. It may be hard to believe, but they have more problems than Dylan. They were still around when Dylan's father was in the picture, and he was a violent man. Dylan's father left just after he was born, which was a good thing. I'm sorry to say that the brothers picked up some of his behaviors. Now, client confidentiality

won't allow me to tell you exactly what happened, but I will tell you that this weekend was a very negative experience for Dylan."

"Oh, no." Mr. Peters sighed. "Was there no supervision?"

"They were being supervised but were left alone for a brief period."

"How was this allowed? You must have known he was in danger."

"We believe it's important for our clients to stay connected with their families."

"At what cost?"

Mrs. Peverly remained silent and then exhaled. "We made a huge mistake. I firmly believe in keeping families connected, but we should have monitored the visit more closely."

Mr. Peters shook his head. "How is Dylan?"

"He's okay. I'm meeting with him today, as is his art therapist. He won't be in school until tomorrow."

"How should we deal with him at school?"

"Just treat him like normal. Don't even ask him about his weekend. If he brings it up, talk about it, but I wouldn't broach the subject if I were you. He may not want to talk about it."

"Okay, thank-you for keeping me informed," he said bluntly. "If anything comes up that I should know about, please phone me."

"Thank-you for your time, Mr. Peters. I'll be in touch."

Mr. Peters hung up the phone and leaned on the desk. He stared blankly at the floor and wondered what Dylan was going through.

THE NEXT MORNING, DYLAN, JAKE, AND Ted flew into the classroom in a flurry of name-calling and yelling.

"Okay! What now, Dylan?" Mr. Peters asked angrily.

"It wasn't him," Ted interrupted. "Miss Rodent sent Jake and me in because Jake's a butthead."

"Who sent you in?"

"Uhh…Miss Roland."

"He pulled down my pants!" spat Jake.

"It was an accident."

Mr. Peters glared at Ted with an expression of disbelief.

"Okay…well…it wasn't exactly an accident," Ted stammered. "But… but he hit me."

"Yeah, well, you pushed me."

"Yeah, and you crushed my fort."

"Enough!" Mr. Peters clapped his hands over his ears. "I don't have time for this. Here's what you're going to do! I want one story. I'm going to leave you two alone for ten minutes, and you're going to come up with one version that you can both agree upon. Do you understand?"

Jake and Ted nodded.

Mr. Peters looked at Dylan. "Why are you here?"

"I'm a witness," Dylan said excitedly. "I saw the whole thing, and Miss Rodent thought I could help."

"First of all, *that* is not her name," Mr. Peters said abruptly. "It is Roland, Miss Roland. Second, does this have anything to do with you?"

"I'm a witness," Dylan responded.

"I realize that, but do you need to be here?"

"Yes! I'm a witness!" he exclaimed loudly.

The teacher's expression revealed his frustration. Then he looked at Ted and Jake.

"Is there any need for Dylan to be here?"

The two boys shrugged.

"Would you like him to stay or go?"

"He can stay," Ted responded quickly.

Mr. Peters glanced at Jake, who nodded in agreement.

"You get ten minutes to deliver one story," Mr. Peters said curtly.

Mr. Peters went back to his desk and tried to read student journals. He couldn't hear every word, but it appeared that the conversation was going well. All three boys spoke calmly, and each of them seemed to listen when one of the others talked. Even Dylan was involved. He nodded and appeared to contribute to what was being said.

Ten minutes later, Mr. Peters put down his pen and walked over to the three boys. "Okay. One story."

Ted began slowly. "I was building a fort in the playground pebbles— for ants. Jake walked over and STOMPED on it." Jake sat upright and was about to say something when Ted added, "He said he was just raising his foot and pretending to stomp on my fort but lost his balance and stepped into it."

"Yeah, he tripped," Dylan agreed.

Mr. Peters surveyed the three faces. "Is everyone in agreement so far?" They all nodded.

Ted continued. "I got so mad that I pushed him to the ground. He said he was embarrassed by being pushed down, so he got up and punched me in the shoulder."

Ted stopped and looked at the ground. His face reddened. Mr. Peters waited for a moment. All three boys appeared embarrassed.

Mr. Peters broke the silence. "And then what happened?"

Jake and Ted stared at the ground.

Dylan jumped in. "That's when Ted pulled down Jake's pants!" he said, pointing at Jake.

"Is this true, Ted?" Mr. Peters asked.

"Yes." Ted spoke into his hand.

A slight smile appeared on the teacher's face, which he covered with his hand, and he breathed in deeply. He was glad all three boys were staring at the ground.

"I can tell that you feel bad about what you've done, and I don't think you'll do it again."

Ted shook his head.

Mr. Peters turned to Jake. "I can see why you're upset. That must have been very embarrassing for you, but you need to take some responsibility in this. Even if you were joking and didn't mean to ruin his fort, you can see the consequences of your actions. This isn't the first time you've picked on Ted. It needs to stop. How do you think Ted feels when he sees you coming?"

"Bad," Jake responded.

"I was bullied by an older boy when I was a kid," Mr. Peters said, "and I was always scared. Now. You both know each other's perspectives on the event. Am I correct?"

Both boys nodded.

"If you can't get along, stay away from each other. I don't want this to happen again. I'll be watching you two. Now run along."

As the boys got up to leave, Mr. Peters asked Dylan to remain seated. He knelt down and looked into Dylan's face.

"I apologize for blaming you. That was wrong of me. I should have asked questions before immediately jumping to conclusions."

Dylan raised his shoulders. "That's okay," he said quietly.

"How does it feel being on the other side of a problem?"

"I like it," Dylan answered with a grin.

"Well, I'm very impressed. I can tell that you were helpful in working through this dilemma."

A faint smile appeared on Dylan's face. "Can I go now?"

"In a minute." Mr. Peters's face turned very serious. "How are you, Dylan?"

The boy stirred uncomfortably. "Fine."

"Are you sure?"

"Yeah."

"Okay, well if you need to come and talk to me, you know where to find me."

Dylan shrugged and repeated his earlier question. "Can I go now?"

"Yeah. Go." As Dylan walked away, Mr. Peters called out, "Thank-you, Dylan."

Dylan paused for a brief second and then left the room.

Just before lunch, Mrs. Giles took her group of students into the library for creative writing. Dylan and Albert sat at different tables on opposite sides of the room. Everyone was writing quietly when Dylan noticed a pair of scissors. He picked them up.

"Dylan! Put those down." Mrs. Giles demanded. "You don't need them for this exercise."

He rubbed his thumb over the points and smiled at her. Then he pointed at her and pretended to stab himself in the chest.

"You're going to have to work in the office if you don't listen to me."

Dylan ignored her and started spinning the scissors around his index finger. After a couple of rotations they flew off and stuck into the carpet. Just as Dylan reached for them, Mrs. Giles stepped on the scissors and held them beneath her foot, trapping his fingers.

"You old bitch!" he shrieked.

Everyone in the library stopped what they were doing and stared at the shaking, red-faced boy.

"Go to the office! Right now!"

Albert muttered something under his breath and snickered. Dylan walked over to him, messed up his hair, and slammed his face into the table. Then he ran out of the school. Mr. Peters heard the commotion and dashed into the library. The first thing he noticed was Albert's disheveled appearance. He seemed stunned and shaken.

"Did Dylan do this?" Mr. Peters asked angrily.

Mrs. Giles nodded. Mr. Peters tilted Albert's head back to get a better look.

"Are you okay, Albert?"

Albert stuck out his lower lip and dabbed it with his finger. He seemed pleased by the drop of blood on his fingertip.

Mrs. Giles put her arm around Albert. "Let's get you fixed up. Come with me."

Dylan sped across the field and into the neighborhood. A group of older students was walking down the street, so he ducked into an alley. Out of breath, he collapsed beside a tent trailer and leaned up against the wheel.

He opened the envelope and peered in at the stiff, black insect. Then he examined the designs on his palms. The indentations seemed less prominent.

"They're starting to heal," Dylan whispered as he traced the pattern with his thumb.

Then he rolled one palm over the other and adjusted the placement of each impression until they lined up. The two opposing designs locked into place. Dylan closed his eyes and raised his glowing hands toward his face.

32

Family Reunion

DYLAN RECLINED ON THE STRAW MATTRESS that had been tossed into his cell. He stared up at the ceiling for hours, trying to decide what to do.

Nero has to be stopped. With my power, there'll be no limit to what he can do. I have to kill him—but how? He's too powerful. If I go to battle with him and die, he'll gain my power, which will make everything worse. I can't allow him to have even more authority than he already has. Maybe escape is best. If I'm gone, he'll still be king, but he'll not have my part of Aarial. If I leave, he'll spend his energy pursuing me instead of on destruction. But that's only a short-term solution. He'll eventually find me.

Dylan stood up and started pacing the room.

Ravelle told me that I am the only person who has a chance of stopping Nero.

Dylan was startled from his thoughts by the sound of rattling keys outside the door. A faint light entered the room, and the limping guard who had given him the mattress dragged his lame foot into the room.

"Come."

"Where are we going?" Dylan asked.

The guard ignored him and threw shackles between the bars.

"Put these on," he blurted.

Dylan wrapped the irons around his ankles and wrists while the guard studied his movements closely. Once the guard was convinced that the manacles were securely fastened, he opened the cell. As they stepped into the hall, the guard pushed him from behind. Dylan could not stop himself from smashing into the wall; his muscles still ached, and his body felt like rubber.

The two of them travelled down the cold, drafty corridors in silence. Flickering torches guided their path. After many twists and turns, they stopped at two giant oak doors. Dylan's shackles were removed. The doors opened and the guard pushed Dylan into the room with such force that he was knocked off his feet. A familiar cry rang out.

"Oh, Dylan!"

His mother's arms enveloped him. She cried and whispered his name over and over. Then she cupped his face in her hands and stared into his eyes before pulling his head to her chest.

"I've missed you so much, Dylan. How are you? Let me look at you." She rubbed her eyes, then grasped his shoulders and leaned back. "Look at you. You are so much broader."

Dylan could not find the words to express himself. He reveled in the joy of being held by his mother. They sat on the floor in each other's arms and rocked gently. Finally, Dylan looked up at her. His sad, questioning eyes revealed what he was thinking.

Her eyes closed, and she tilted her head forward. "Yes, Daddy is dead."

At that moment, the floodgates opened, and for the first time, he wept for his father. The tears flowed like rain while his mother held his sobbing, shaking body. Slowly, he regained control of his emotions, and his mother loosened her grip. She stood and helped him to his feet. Her fingers traced over one of his many facial scars.

Dylan noticed that she appeared older and worn. Her beautiful, long black hair had been cut short. Her brown eyes were just as intense, but the skin around them had darkened. Her cheeks were sunken, and she looked tired.

Dylan's mother noticed that he did not look healthy either, but they didn't need to tell each other their thoughts. Each knew what the other was thinking.

"I miss our old lives," Dylan whispered in her ear, and out of the corner of his eye, he saw a figure move.

"Taya!" he cried out before running to her.

She stood slowly and braced herself for a hug. As Dylan squeezed her, she winced. Dylan sensed her pain and loosened his grip.

"Are you okay?"

Taya nodded and shot him a weak smile.

"I was so worried about you. When I saw you being carried away by the trog, I wondered if I'd ever see you again."

"So did I," Taya said with pain in her voice.

"You weren't supposed to follow me, you know."

"I couldn't help it. I waited around for a few days, but I couldn't stand not knowing. I decided that I would rather put myself in danger than wonder."

"How did you find me?"

"You were easy to follow. You left a trail of dead trogs and environmental destruction. It was like following the path of a hurricane. I don't know how you got as far as you did without being captured. Any bloodhound would have found you in a minute." She managed a mischievous smile. "I lost you at the ocean."

Dylan's eyes brightened. "You're amazing."

Nima dragged two stools up to Taya's chair, and the three of them sat. No words passed among them for several minutes. They relished the quiet moment.

Nima broke the silence. "Taya has told me everything." She looked down. "I don't know if things can ever go back to the way they once were."

Dylan raised his shoulders and sat up straight. "I can make things better, Mother. I'm going to defeat Nero and take away his power."

"Please," she sighed, "let's not talk of such things at the moment. Tell me about all of the good things that have happened since we last talked."

Dylan spoke at length about the training he and Taya had had with Ravelle and Tiko. Nima wanted to know every detail of how they had been trained and what they had learned. She also enjoyed hearing about Acorn and the connection between them.

"What happened to Acorn?"

Dylan frowned. "I don't know where he is. He just disappeared one day, and I haven't seen him since. You've been here for a long time, Mother. How've you been treated?"

She lifted her shoulders and tried to appear brave and contented. "I've been treated well. Nero has ignored me for the most part, which is good."

Taya spoke up. "What have you been doing while you've been here?"

"Not much," her mother replied. "For the first few months, I was left alone. I was thrown food twice a day. The food servant was the only person I had any interaction with, and *that* was minimal. He would open the door and slide a plate of mush across the floor—that was it. I got so bored that I started to go insane. Being alone with one's thoughts makes you a little crazy after a while."

She raised her eyes and feigned a smile. "For the past two months, I've been doing odd jobs, which is better than being alone in my cold, dark cell. I never thought I could get so much pleasure from scrubbing floors."

She stopped speaking, and her gaze drifted across the room.

Dylan broke the silence. "Is he really...your son? Our brother?"

Tears welled in Nima's eyes. "Yes," she sniffed.

"I don't understand."

"That was a difficult time for your father and me. We were very poor, and your father didn't believe we could care for a child. After much consideration, we decided that allowing the king to raise our son would be in the child's best interests. We thought he would have a better life than we could give. Who could have guessed about the evil lurking in that small child? Was it because of the way he was raised or was there something in his makeup that led to the person he became? Who knows. I've always wondered how things could have been if we had raised him."

Dylan stared into his mother's eyes. "I've missed you so much, and I miss Father and our old lives in Duffle." Dylan put his head down.

Just as he stopped speaking, the doors flew open. The three of them turned, and Nero floated into the room like a ballroom dancer. He walked the circumference of the sparsely decorated room while gazing at them the entire time. Then he paused for several seconds, studying the three of them. Finally, he flew across the room and slapped his hands down on the dining table.

"Isn't this a nice little family reunion?" he mocked. "Carry on your conversation."

No one spoke.

"You are very quiet today, and you know what? I don't like it!" he spat. "Guests at my dinner table, speak. I will not have you moping in silence."

Nero hopped over the table and grabbed Nima by the arm. She winced and let out a faint cry. Dylan stood up, and his mother gave him a look that he could easily read: *sit down.*

Nero tightened his grip on her and grinned at Dylan. "We have a brave one here, but not too bright." He spoke calmly and emphatically. "If you want to see the morning, I recommend that you sit down…little brother."

Dylan wanted to pounce on him. His heart quickened and his jaw clenched. *Calm down,* he repeated in his head. *I must have patience. If I try to do something now, I'll be killed.*

Ravelle's words flashed before him. *If you must sacrifice yourself, do it for the right reasons. Do not give in to your pride or vanity. Your mission is far greater than you and me or even your family.*

Nero's arrogance oozed from every pore. He gently stroked his beard and tilted his head back, revealing a carefree attitude of superiority. Dylan looked into his mother's eyes again. She nodded her head in the direction of a chair. Dylan inhaled deeply and exhaled slowly as he lowered himself.

"*This is not the right time to strike,*" Dylan said to himself.

Nero dragged Nima to the middle of the room. "May I have this dance?"

The king drifted over the floor with the grace of a danseur. Slowly, frustration set in as his stumbling partner resisted in the only way she could—she danced without emotion or enthusiasm.

"Sit down!" he screamed, and he pushed her away from him.

Dylan and Taya tried to get to her before she flew backward across the table, but they were too late. Then she collapsed in a chair. Tears filled her eyes. Nero strode across the room toward the huge window. He put his hands on the distorted glass and looked out over his kingdom, which was bathed in blue moonlight.

Dylan, Taya, and their mother tried to comfort each other without words. They stood and embraced while Nero gazed out at the star-filled sky. Then he turned and walked back toward them.

"Oh, isn't this cute," he sneered. "Just one big happy family."

They loosened their grips on one another and went back to their chairs. Just as they sat down, Nero screamed, "You don't sit until I tell you to sit! Show some respect for your king!"

Slowly, they stood and exchanged fiery glances. Nero gracefully stepped to the head of the table and eased himself into an elegantly ornate chair.

He raised his hands in a welcoming gesture. "You may be seated, my little peasant family."

Dylan looked at his mother, who would not make eye contact with him. Then he looked at Taya. He could tell she was steaming deep inside.

Nero studied each of them for a moment as they pulled up their chairs to the table and sat down. "Isn't this nice—just one big, happy family sitting down to dinner."

Dylan wondered why Nero had asked them to dine with him. Did he enjoy watching their expressions as he tormented them? Was he preparing them for something?

Several servants carried in the food. Within minutes, the empty table was a steaming feast of color and wondrous aromas. The sound of knives and forks hitting the plates made the silence even more noticeable.

After a few minutes of quiet, Nero slammed a fist on the table and cried out, "You are all being very rude. I want you to enjoy your meal and socialize like you did in Duffle. I will not have all of you feeling sorry for yourselves in silence. Your self-pity is infuriating."

All three of them froze while Nero went into a tirade about manners. They glanced at one another and watched Nero slam his fists and raise his voice.

When Nero stopped, Dylan spoke. "Why are we all gathered here? What do you want from us?"

"Can't a man show his guests a little hospitality? You show no appreciation for the feast I have provided."

Dylan sensed he had another reason for getting them together. *Perhaps he just wants to see what it's like to be a part of this family.*

The silence continued while Nero seethed. He slammed his mug down and cut his food forcefully. His breathing and movements were exaggerated. Dylan's hunger was replaced by knots in his stomach. Then Nero sprang to his feet, knocking his chair over. He slammed both of his fists on the table, and plates and glasses shattered as they fell on the floor.

"Take them away!" As he said this, three guards entered the room. "How can a man enjoy his meal with a bunch of antisocial peasants? You sit there and revel in self-pity! Well, I would rather dine alone."

Taya and Nima were taken out of the room first. Dylan's guard stood behind him and waited for Nero's order.

Nero leaned onto the table and stared into Dylan's eyes. "I hope you enjoyed your last meal," he said, and he signaled the guard to take him away.

The guard wrapped the shackles around his hands and feet and then pushed him through the door.

Dylan was not feeling as weak as he had before the meal. His strength was returning. Perhaps it was the meal; perhaps it was seeing his family; perhaps it was the healing power of Aarial. Whatever the reason, his muscles did not ache, and he started to feel Aarial returning—he had noticed that it seemed to need rest.

"Nero wants you to see something," the guard mumbled.

Except for the echo of their footsteps, the halls were silent. Dylan shivered at the putrid scent of rotting flesh that the icy breeze carried through the stone corridor. Then a faint moaning travelled toward them. As they continued, the moaning intensified, and soon, human cries reverberated off the walls. A chill travelled down Dylan's spine.

Dylan turned his head to the guard. He caught a glimmer of a lopsided smile, and then the guard knocked him forward with his club. On his right, Dylan thought he caught sight of a man splayed out on the floor in a dark cell. A torch in the hallway lit up another cell, where two men were chained to the wall in a crucifix position. Dylan paused at the sight. Their chins rested upon their chests. One of the men lifted his head and made eye contact with Dylan for an instant before his neck gave out, and his head drooped again. The guard pushed Dylan forward.

Someone screamed, and few seconds later, they passed a cell where a man was being whipped. He howled in pain. At cell after cell, Dylan observed various forms of torture. Nausea welled up in him. His pace slowed while his thoughts raced.

I have to make my move. It's now or never, Dylan thought.

"I've killed a dozen trogs!" Dylan's words resonated off the walls, making them more powerful. Then he formed a thought: *Drop your keys.*

The guard slammed him in the back. "Shut up!" The guard spoke forcefully, but Dylan sensed a fear rise up in him.

Dylan glanced back and noticed the guard check his pocket for his keys. *Did he hear me?* Dylan thought.

As they rounded a corner, Dylan was suddenly pulled toward a solid metal door. He felt the power of Olam behind it. The guard pushed him again. Dylan's spirits picked up. His sword was vital to getting out of the dungeon.

"I killed Tracker." At this, the guard stumbled and tripped into Dylan. He formed the thought again: *Drop your keys.*

They rounded another corner. "I! Am going to kill Nero." At this, the guard laughed. *Drop your keys.* "You can remain faithful, and die, or you can join me, and live."

As they neared his cell, Dylan heard the guard fumbling with his keys. Dylan held his breath while his muscles tightened and his ears popped. *Drop. Your.* "KEYS!" The last word spewed out of him like a volcanic eruption.

Dylan heard the keys hit the stone floor. He turned around and saw the guard back away fearfully, pressing his palms against his temples.

"You're in my head," he whimpered.

Dylan sat down and unlocked the shackles while the guard continued to whimper, "You're in my head. Get out of my head." When Dylan had freed himself, he unlocked the door to his cell and then the barred door inside.

"Get in."

The guard wanted to resist but could not. Inside, the broken man slid down the stone wall and wept quietly. Dylan locked both doors and fled down the corridor.

Collin Paulson

33

A Cry For Help

"I SPOKE TO DYLAN'S FOSTER MOTHER," MRS. Evans said.

"What did she have to say?" Mr. Peters asked.

"She apologized for his behavior yesterday and said that she would deal with it." Mrs. Evans rubbed her neck.

"What's wrong, Mrs. Evans?"

She began slowly. "Apparently, Dylan came home last night screaming that the world would be a better place if he were dead."

"That's a real cry for help, Mrs. Evans. Is she worried he might hurt himself?"

Mrs. Evans lifted her shoulders. "I don't know. She took it seriously though. They're meeting with his art therapist again."

"That's good. Dylan seems to like her."

"Anyway, I told her not to bring him back for a couple of days."

"What are we going to do?" Mr. Peters asked. "He's shown us that he *is* a danger to the other students. I know Albert isn't innocent, but that's irrelevant. Dylan could have given him a head injury. We cannot tolerate this anymore."

"Did you speak to Albert's parents?" Mrs. Evans inquired.

"Yes, I did. That was very difficult. His mother is very understanding because she knows what Albert can be like, but she wanted to know that this would not happen again. I told her that it wouldn't." Mr. Peters paused. "Can I promise her that?"

Mrs. Evans interjected. "We'll keep those two completely separated. I don't want them going near each other. I've asked Albert to come to my office this morning, and I'll tell him to keep his distance. If he's seen anywhere near Dylan, he'll be the one punished, not Dylan. Albert needs to know that we want to protect him, but he must cooperate with us."

The secretary peered into the office. "Mrs. Jules, the behavioral specialist, is here."

"Send her in, please."

She entered the room in a flurry. "I apologize, but I can't stay long. I have a nine-thirty meeting at Nickle School. I just want to touch base."

Mrs. Evans said, "Thank-you for coming on such short notice. I thought we should let you know what's been going on."

Mrs. Jules faced Mr. Peters. "Mrs. Evans told me about what happened yesterday. Other than that incident, how's he been doing?"

"Little has changed."

"Would you like him removed from the school?"

"Yes," Mrs. Evans said bluntly. She glanced at Mr. Peters before continuing. "I've always supported the decision to keep him here, but I can't anymore. He's too dangerous."

Mrs. Evans got up and opened the filing cabinet. "This is where I hid the knife we confiscated from Dylan." She moved folders out of the way and pulled out an empty envelope tucked in the back. "The knife was in here."

"So where is it now?" Mr. Peters asked.

"I don't know. It was here last week. I'm the only one who knew it was here."

"Did Dylan know where you put it?" Mr. Peters asked.

"There's no way he could have known, but I don't know who else would have taken it. I've left him alone in my office, but only for a few minutes at a time. I don't know how he could have located it and taken it so quickly, but he must have. I forgot to ask Ms. Truss about it. I'll ask her to look for it at home."

"I'll look into another placement for him," said Mrs. Jules. "He's too much to handle in a regular classroom, and all of the behavior classes are full right now. They only accept six to eight of the most troubled kids, and there are no spaces available. Can you keep him here until something comes up?"

Mrs. Evans looked to Mr. Peters, who nodded. "I guess we don't have a choice."

"He is to be watched constantly. He is not to be alone at any time. Follow the rules you set up with him. If there are any aggressive acts or threats of violence, send him home immediately. Do not allow the situation to escalate. How has that behavior contract been working, Mr. Peters?"

"I haven't been consistent with that. It's too hard to keep on top of it with all the things that have been going on."

"Well try," Ms. Jules said. "The main thing I am concerned with is that there is nothing positive in his life. I know it may be difficult to find things to praise him for, but he needs it. He needs to know that he's doing something right." Ms. Jules stood up. "I apologize, but I really need to get going. Phone me anytime. I'd like to be kept informed."

When Mr. Peters entered his classroom, Jake was sitting at his desk.

"What's up, Jake? You never come in before the bell."

Mr. Peters sat down in the desk across from him.

"Yesterday… yesterday, when Ted pulled down my pants, everyone saw my boxer shorts."

Mr. Peters tried to hide his smile. "That must have been embarrassing for you, but everyone has seen boxer shorts before. They'll soon forget about it."

"Yeah, but I was wearing my Bart Simpson shorts."

Mr. Peters let out a snort.

"See, even you think it's funny."

"I'm sorry," Mr. Peters chuckled, "but it is kind of funny. Look, we all have funny shorts in our drawers. I've got a pair with hearts that say 'I Love You' all over them."

Jake smirked at the thought of seeing Mr. Peters in his I Love You shorts. "Yeah, but there's more. On the left butt cheek of my shorts is Bart Simpson's face and on the other butt cheek is the word *Kowabunga!*"

"Oh boy." Mr. Peters grinned. "This gets better and better. Well, how is that any different than a T-shirt? I've seen that same image on a shirt."

"Yeah, I guess, but you know what I overheard some of the kids say today when I got on the bus? They said 'Kowadunga' as I walked by. Kowadunga, as in *cow dung*." He paused. "Some of the little girls were pointing and giggling at me as I walked past them on the playground. You know how quickly things spread. I've lost all of their respect. They used to look up to me; some were even afraid of me. Now they just laugh at me."

"It'll pass, Jake. Don't let it bother you. Just be who you are and they'll forget."

"Oh, I don't think so. My dad has had the same nickname since he was eight. I'm going to be known as Cow Dung for the rest of my life." Jake dropped his head and giggled.

"Well, I'm glad you still have your sense of humor. Now run along. Everything will be okay. One piece of advice—don't show them that it bothers you.

Jake nodded and walked toward the door.

"Hey Jake!" Mr. Peters called. "Rock on, dude."

34
An Impressive Warrior

As Dylan dashed down the hall, the heavy keys jingle-jangled in the darkness. He tightened his grip on them to stop them from banging against each other. Footsteps echoed in another hallway. He froze. It was impossible to tell exactly where they were coming from, so Dylan continued—slowly and quietly. Then the rattle of distant keys stopped him, and he pressed his body against the wall. The sound grew louder. Dylan's heart pounded. He looked down the hall—one way, then the other. There was nowhere to hide. He ran in the opposite direction of the noise.

At the first door, he stopped and started going through his keys. The guard was getting closer, closer, closer. Soon he would be around the corner and would spot Dylan. In a panic, Dylan leaned against door with all his weight and fumbled through the keys. Key after key entered the lock but wouldn't turn. If the next key wasn't the right one, the guard would spot him. *Click!* Dylan fell to the floor as the door swung open.

As softly as he could, he closed the door and pressed his ear against the cold surface. The footsteps grew louder and louder, and then they stopped—at his door. Dylan held his breath at the sound of a key entering the lock. He slid away from the door, pressing his body against the wall. Thoughts of his missing sword entered his mind. Dylan prepared himself to pounce as soon as the sentry stepped over the threshold. With great force, a man in shackles was thrown into the room. The door slammed behind him, and the guard's laughter echoed off the walls.

Dylan remained silent. The prisoner lay on his side with his feet bound by a short chain, and his arms were behind his back in shackles. He did not move for several minutes. Then he lifted his head slightly.

Dylan slid down the wall and sat on the floor. The prisoner's gaze locked on him.

He squinted into the corner. "Who's there? Is someone there?" Then he started screaming, "What do you want? Why are you here? Who are you?" The man was close to tears.

Dylan flew over to the prostrate man and put his hand over his mouth. "Shut up!" The man struggled for several minutes, but Dylan held on to him firmly. "I'm not letting go until you're quiet. We can help each other. I'm not your enemy."

Dylan slowly loosened his grip and removed his hand from the man's mouth. He slid back into the dark corner.

"Who are you?"

"I'm Dylan. Maybe we can help each other. Do you know the layout of this place?"

Dylan sensed that he was in the company of a broken man. He had a deep voice, with great power behind it, but he sounded frail. "What do you want from me? I'm just a farmer. I mean no harm."

"What's your name and where do you come from?" Dylan asked.

"I am Tikva, and I come from Tipple."

Dylan perked up.

"Nero has destroyed my home and killed most of my people." Then he paused to get his breath. "Do you work for Nero?"

"No! I'm Nero's nemesis. I don't work for him." Dylan stood. "I know of Tipple and what happened there. I'm sorry. I spent some time with your people. I come from Duffle, which faced a similar fate."

"How do I know that you're telling the truth? You could be a spy for Nero."

"Your people took me in and fed me. I happened upon them at a ceremony where an old lady was led onto a raft and pushed across a lake. I spent time with Sheil."

Tikva sniffed back a tear. Dylan walked over to him and showed him the keys. Tikva rolled onto his stomach, while Dylan searched for the right key.

"They think you're dead."

"I know," he whimpered. "I have to get back to them."

"How long have you been here, Tikva?" Dylan asked as he unlocked his shackles.

"I don't know. I've lost track of time. I was brought here after the uprising. Many of the prisoners here are from Tipple. We put up a good struggle and killed many trogs. Nero was and still is extremely angry with the people of Tipple. We're tortured daily."

"How well do you know this place?" Dylan asked.

"I can walk to the torture rooms with my eyes closed. I have been up and down these hallways so many times. I can take you anywhere you want to go."

"I want to free my mother and sister. Do you know where they might be?"

"I can't say for sure, but all of the women are kept in the same wing."

"She was brought here just before me."

"If she's in one of the cells, we'll find her. They're all nearby."

Dylan walked to the door and unlocked it.

"What are you doing? We can't go now. I need rest."

Dylan spun around. "We must go now. I just escaped from my cell, and Nero will turn this place upside down when he discovers I'm gone."

Tikva tried to get to his feet, but he couldn't. He grimaced and clenched his teeth. Dylan helped him up.

"I'm sorry, but I cannot delay."

"In exchange for my help, I want the keys," Tikva demanded.

"Help me find my family, and the keys are yours."

Dylan opened the door slowly and peered around the corner. His head snapped back into the room and he pulled it shut.

"Someone is near," he whispered.

The two of them waited as someone passed by their cell. When the hall was silent again, Dylan opened the door and peered both ways.

"Let's go," Dylan commanded. "There's something I need before you take me to my mother."

The two of them sped down the hall as quietly as possible. Dylan felt the allure of Olam. Within seconds, they were outside the door Dylan had passed earlier in the evening. After trying several keys, Dylan opened the door.

"Wow!"

They were taken aback by the store of weapons. Dylan ran to his sword and grasped the handle. All of his concerns vanished for the moment. He felt the power of Aarial with Olam in his hands. He swung it around his head and body with grace and violence. Tikva stared in awe.

Dylan stopped and waved his arm. "Take your pick."

Tikva tested the weight and balance of several weapons. The broken man suddenly became an impressive warrior. Dylan could tell that he was an experienced swordsman. After several minutes, Tikva chose a sword. He tied a sheath around his waist and slid the sword into it. Dylan found his knife and strapped it to his leg. He found another small blade and strapped it to his other leg. Then he grabbed a second sword and sheath.

"I'm following you now. Let's go find my mother."

The two men fled down the hall so quickly and silently that the prisoners they passed did not notice them. They flew up and down several hallways that led to dead ends. At one door, Dylan stopped.

Tikva turned. "What are you doing? We can't stop now. Your mother is just up here."

Dylan paid no attention to him. He raced through the keys and opened the cell. Taya was crouching in the corner, shivering. Dylan rushed over, sat down beside her, and swept her into his arms. She stared up at him blankly.

"You're so cold," Dylan cried.

He rubbed her back, trying to warm her. She was still shivering when he commanded her to stand.

"You're going to freeze to death if you don't start moving."

By this time, Tikva had entered and closed the door. He paced impatiently and watched in silence as Dylan helped his sister move about the room. The shivering stopped after a few minutes.

"Okay, let's go," Tikva said. "We can't waste any more time."

Dylan strapped a sword onto her waist while Tikva opened the door and made sure the hallway was clear.

"This is Tikva," Dylan uttered.

Tikva nodded, and Taya responded with a halfhearted smile. Dylan pulled her to the door, and the three of them continued down the hall. Footsteps rushed toward them, so they ran back to Taya's room and waited for them to pass.

Then they were off again. Every time they came to an intersection of hallways, they slowed and proceeded with caution. Tikva appeared uncertain when they stopped at one of the intersections.

"I've only been in this wing once. I think her cell is this way." He led them down the darkest hall.

Dylan sensed that his mother was near, and he rushed past Tikva. At a massive wooden door, Dylan stopped and pulled out his keys. The sight of them stunned his mother. She ran to Dylan and hugged him as he stepped in. Taya joined in, and Tikva closed the door behind him. Dylan noticed that her room had a large, barred window and a bed.

He looked out at the stars. "We're leaving, Mother. I need to get away from here now. I cannot allow Nero to take Aarial. If he gets my power, he will be unstoppable. I will escape or die trying, and if I die, it must be out of Nero's reach." Dylan turned to Tikva. "How can we get out of here?"

"You can't escape through the hallways. All corridors lead to a central area where the guards gather and sleep. There's no way around them." There was silence for a few moments while he thought. "You may be able to escape onto the roof, but that's dangerous. It's very high."

"Then that's what we'll do. Lead us to the roof and the keys are yours."

Tikva grabbed the bars in Nima's room, but they were solid. He led them out into the hall and proceeded to run to each window. He twisted and pushed on the bars.

"Some of the bars are loose," he said. "We just have to find them."

All three of them went from one window to the next, grasping the bars as they proceeded down the hall. Taya felt a bar turn in one of the windows. "Over here," she called.

Dylan ran to the window and pulled at the metal rods. One of the bars came out easily, and he threw it onto the ground. The next bar was tighter, but he managed to loosen it. Frantically, he threw his weight on

it—pushing, pulling, and twisting. It fell onto the roof, causing all of the others to come loose and fall.

"Thank-you, Tikva, and good luck. I hope we meet again."

Dylan threw Tikva the keys and motioned for his mother and sister to move toward the window. Tikva fled back the way they had come as Dylan boosted Taya up to the window. Then he boosted his mother, and finally, he climbed out onto the steep, damp roof.

35
Friends and Foes

THE NEXT DAY, DYLAN AND HIS foster mother burst into the school in a flurry. Ms. Truss had come to discuss the violent behavior Dylan had displayed a few days earlier. In Mrs. Evans's office, Dylan did not speak. He kept his head down and his body tensed while Ms. Truss ranted and raved about all the bad things he did at home. Mr. Peters could not tell if he was cringing in fear or anger. After fifteen minutes of put-downs and ridicule, Ms. Truss left. Mr. Peters, Mrs. Evans, and Dylan remained.

"We realize that there are a lot of stresses in your life right now, Dylan," Mrs. Evans said soothingly, "but is there any possible way you can leave your problems outside of the school? When you're here, we'd like you to forget about what's going on beyond these walls. It all comes back to the safety of our students. How can we ensure that other students are safe around you?"

Dylan did not say anything for a moment. When he realized that he was not going to be let off the hook, he uttered, "I don't know."

"Well, I'm going to tell you. You're going to be supervised every minute of every day. I'm sorry for that, but I'm afraid that you may harm someone else, and we cannot allow that. If you are aggressive—physically or verbally—you will be asked to leave."

"Who cares? I don't wanna be here anyway."

"You are suspended in school for the time being."

"What does that mean?" Dylan grumbled.

"It means you won't be allowed into the classroom. You'll be doing all of your work here in the office."

Dylan shrugged his shoulders.

"I'll allow you to go to the playground at recess as long as Mrs. Giles is within three paces of you—at all times. Do you agree to these terms?"

267

Dylan shrugged again. "I don't care."

Mrs. Evans exhaled. "Mrs. Giles is waiting to take you outside until the bell rings."

Dylan stood and shuffled out of Mrs. Evans's office.

"Good morning," Mrs. Giles said, feigning cheerfulness.

Dylan shuffled past her and walked down the hall to the back doors. Mrs. Giles followed silently. He walked across the compound and sat down on the wooden perimeter of the playground. While dragging a stick through the dirt, he observed Ted and Sam sitting on the ground tracing out a new project in the pebbles. They were so focused on what they were doing that they didn't notice the ominous shadow until it covered their work. Ted and Sam could tell whom the shadow belonged to by the enormous feet that stood before them. Their gaze travelled up his legs, past his chest, and locked on his bloodshot eyes. Ted clamped his mouth shut and stared up at him fearfully.

"I'm going to get you," Jake scowled. His sausage finger waved like a conductor's wand. "You just wait," he said, seething.

Jake stormed away at the sight of Ms. Steinwood. Ted fell back in the rocks.

"Why didn't I just leave him alone," Ted whined. "Now I have to watch over my shoulder for the rest of my life."

"Keep your friends close and your enemies closer!"

"What?" Ted looked at Sam. Then he noticed Dylan standing over him. "Oh. Hi, Dylan. What...what did you say?"

"Keep your friends close and your enemies closer!"

Ted looked up at him curiously and raised his eyebrows. "What do you mean?"

"Just what I said."

Ted stared at the ground. It came to him slowly. "Do you mean that I should become his friend?"

"That's not what I said."

Ted thought for a while longer. "That's a good idea. If I keep my enemies close, I'll know what they're planning." Ted looked up. "Yes that's..." He searched for Dylan, but he was gone. "That's a good plan... but...but how do I do that?"

At a desk in the office, Dylan found a pile of work with a note from Mr. Peters explaining what he needed to work on for the morning.

"Can I go to the bathroom?" he asked the secretary. She nodded her approval.

As he left the office, he crashed into Jake, who knocked the attendance cards to the ground as he fell back. Jake was about to yell when he noticed who had bumped him. Without a word, he knelt down to pick up the cards. Dylan stepped on one them, and Jake tilted his head and looked up at him.

"Keep your friends close and your enemies closer," Dylan said mysteriously.

Jake pulled the card from under Dylan's foot and stood. "What?"

"Keep your friends close and your enemies closer," Dylan repeated.

"What does that mean?" Jake asked angrily. Dylan glared up at him, and Jake's anger quickly turned to trepidation. "What...what does that mean?" he stuttered.

Dylan breathed in and raised his shoulders. "In life, you'll encounter villains. Learn to deal with them." Then he turned and walked away.

Jake was left staring at the ground in confusion. "Who's the villain? Me? Ted? Or him?" he asked himself out loud.

A short time later, Dylan returned to the office. He read silently until the phone in Mrs. Evans's office broke his concentration.

"Mrs. Evans here." She paused. "Oh, hello, Mrs. Jules." Dylan's ears perked up at the familiar name. "That was quick. I thought the special programs were all full." Mrs. Evans stopped and listened. "Wow. Well that's...that's good news...I guess. The end of next week? Okay, thank-you. I'll let Mr. Peters know."

Mrs. Evans hung up the phone. As she walked out of her office, she noticed Dylan's scattered pile of notebooks. She picked up his novel from the floor. "Where's Dylan, Mrs. Miller?"

The secretary stood up and looked over the counter at the empty desk. "I don't know. He was here a minute ago."

Dylan sprinted down the hall. While glancing over his shoulder, he stumbled over his untied shoelaces and landed on his chest. The envelope slipped out of his pocket and slid under a door—into the

caretaker's broom closet. He stood up quickly and opened the door in a panic. The envelope was floating in a small puddle beneath a dripping mop. Dylan wiped it on his shirt, slid it back into his front pocket, and sat down on an upturned metal can. With the back of his hand, he closed the door, shutting out all light except for the dim glow that emanated from his palms. He adjusted his hands and raised them toward his face.

36

War Cry

THE GUARD FROZE AT THE SIGHT of Tikva rounding the corner. The Tipple leader raised his sword and sped toward his fleeing opponent, who was killed instantly as the sword entered his back. Tikva dragged the bleeding corpse into a dark corner and continued on.

He seized several weapons from the storeroom and then proceeded down the hall to his companions. At the first cell, he found the great warrior Tyr slouched in the corner—his head slumped back and his mouth and eyes wide open.

"I'm too late," Tikva said with a sigh. He turned to leave.

"Tikva!" the man groaned. A slight smile of recognition appeared on his face.

"Oh, good, you're alive," Tikva shot back. "I thought you were dead."

"Me too." He coughed violently.

"I don't have time to go into detail, Tyr, so listen closely. You are to open all of the cells and arm each man. Get Vimy to help you. He's in the next room. Do you understand?" Tyr nodded and caught the flying keys. "Go quietly."

Tyr was on his feet and unlocking Vimy's door before Tikva was speaking into the next cell. The man who had appeared to be dying only a few moments before was rejuvenated by his leader's orders.

"Don't say a word, just listen," Tikva whispered into the next cell. "Your door is going to be unlocked, and you are going to be armed. Don't leave your cell or open your door until I give the signal. When you hear it, come out fighting."

Tikva ran to the next cell and repeated what he had just said. He continued on until he had talked to everyone in the wing. Vimy and Tyr worked out a system and proceeded quickly. Tyr unlocked the doors while Vimy tossed in the weapons. Soon, every door was unlocked, and all of the prisoners were armed.

At the sound of racing footsteps, Vimy, Tyr, and Tikva each found a corner cell with a view of an intersecting corridor. A powerful voice pounded off the walls. Every man's heart thumped violently in his chest.

"Where is that imbecile?"

A weaker, terrified voice whined, "I...I don't know, Sir. I haven't seen him all day."

"This is the second time Shom has missed roll call. I am going to teach that insect a lesson. I give him our prized prisoner, and he continues to disobey."

As Nero passed one of the cells, the old fool of Tipple, Terach, jumped out of his cell, and his sword bounced off Nero's armor. Nero drew his sword and sliced off Terach's arm in one sweep. The man cried out in pain, and Nero smiled as he ran his sword threw the man's belly.

"Why is this man not locked up?"

"I...I don't know, Sir."

Nero grabbed the guard by the arm and dragged him back down the hall in the direction from which they had come. "Go get the guards," he said, seething, "and check every cell!"

Tikva left his cell and tiptoed down the main hall. "Stay in your rooms," he called out to the others. He dragged Terach back into his cell.

While the men of Tipple waited, Nero stormed down the corridors, knocking over anyone who got in his way. Several of his guards were thrown to the ground in his fury. Nero bellowed at the sight of Dylan's unguarded cell. He shook with anger and dropped the keys several times as he tried to fit the right one into the keyhole.

"Bloody Hell! Which bloody key is it?"

He threw his shoulder at the door and pounded on it violently. The noise thundered down the corridor.

A guard slithered up sheepishly. "Can I help you, Sir?" he squeaked.

"Open this door!"

The guard wiped Nero's spit from his face and tried not to breath in his foul air as the key slid into the lock.

"Now. Get out of my way!" he howled as he knocked him to the ground.

A shapeless, chattering figure crouched in the dark corner.

"Where is your prisoner, you simpleton?" His voice rumbled, and his words bounced off all four walls.

The shapeless figure squeaked out an inaudible response.

"What did you say?" Nero wailed.

"He tricked me, Sir," he said shakily, cowering.

"How?"

"I don't know. He put things into my head. He made me give him the keys and then locked me up."

A primitive, guttural sound spewed from Nero's throat. He flew out of the room and slammed the door shut. Then…silence. Shom whimpered quietly in the cell. Then the door suddenly opened again, and Shom saw a guard bounce off the bars. The keys flew from his hands and into the cell.

"Open that door!"

Shom stared at the keys then up at the guard who was now whimpering at the thought of what was going to happen to him. Shom kicked the keys back toward the door and then wet himself as he watched his colleague's shaking hands attempt to unlock the door.

Finally, the door opened, and Nero rushed in. With one hand on Shom's neck, he pressed him up against the wall. Slowly, he raised him off the ground and stared into his eyes. Then he grabbed him with both hands, one on his neck and one on his crotch, and threw him against the opposite wall. His body crumpled to the ground like a sack of potatoes.

A grotesque expression appeared on Nero's face as he studied his moistened hand. "You pissed yourself!"

Nero picked him up again, and with a grunt, tossed him against the other wall.

"You're disgusting!" he screamed at the limp form. "Get up!"

No response. Nero lifted Shom above his head and with all his might threw him at the ceiling.

"Lock this door, and *never* open it!" he yelled at the guard.

Nero stormed out of the room.

A dozen guards returned to the hall where Terach had been cut down, and the group leader yelled, "Check every cell and make sure no one has escaped."

"Now!" Tikva screamed.

At his command, the men rushed out of their cells and knocked several guards over with the weight of the doors. The prisoners surrounded the guards and defeated them easily, but the more talented swordsmen killed some of the prisoners. Each man had an opponent. The inmates were weak, but their fervent anger gave them an edge, and soon the prisoners outnumbered the surviving guards. In the flurry, two guards rushed away.

Within minutes, not one of Nero's men was standing. The prisoners dragged the dead men into one of the cells. At the sound of another army of men echoing through the halls, the prisoners stopped to listen.

"We'll ambush them," Tikva cried. "Come with me."

They followed him to the end of the main corridor, where another hall ran perpendicular to their wing. He traced out a rough map on the dusty floor.

"They're going to come into this hallway," he said, pointing. "We're going to split into four groups. One group will wait here and another one here. The third and fourth group will go down those two passageways and come back up this hall to attack them from behind; they'll be surrounded."

Everyone nodded in agreement.

"Be brave, men! Think of all the terrible things they've done. All of you have lost someone. You've all been tortured. As you fight, think of those things. If we fail, we will fail knowing we've paid them back in the only way we could—by taking their lives."

Tikva quickly organized four groups and sent them to their posts. The army of footsteps grew louder. The men of Tipple waited, silently. A rhythmic, muted war cry pounded in their chests.

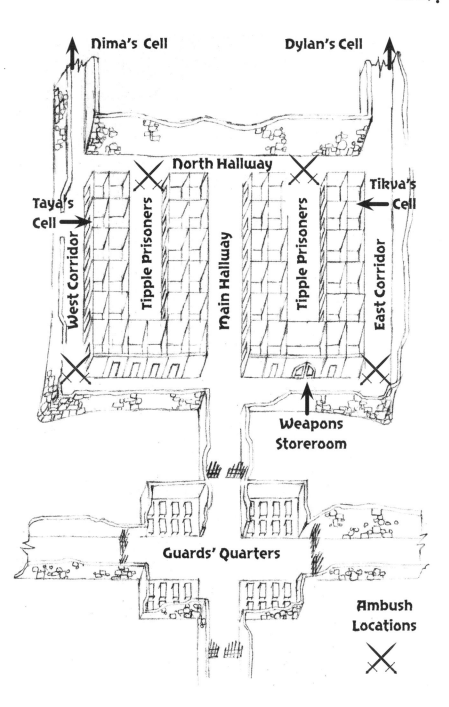

Nima's Cell

Dylan's Cell

North Hallway

Taya's Cell

Tikva's Cell

West Corridor

Tipple prisoners

Main Hallway

Tipple prisoners

East Corridor

Weapons Storeroom

Guards' Quarters

Ambush Locations

Collin Paulson

37

Now or Never

EVENING DEW COVERED THE ANGLED ROOF with a glassy sheen. Dylan, Nima, and Taya travelled slowly across the glazed surface and leapt onto a flat roof. As they peered over the edge, their sudden excitement was quickly replaced with hopelessness. The ground was a great distance—too far to jump.

"We have to find a low point," Dylan whispered despondently.

He ran around the perimeter of the flat roof and examined their surroundings. The massive castle was a mishmash of angled and flat roofs of various heights. Towers and spires sprouted up randomly, seemingly without purpose.

"Over there," Dylan said, pointing to a lower roof near an enormous tree outside the castle. "That looks like the only possibility."

"It's too far," Taya said. "And how are we to get across all these rooftops?"

"Do you see a better spot?"

Taya shook her head.

"We can do this, Taya." He put his arm around her. "Come on," he said gently, "follow me."

Dylan stepped onto an angled roof and placed one foot on each side of the peak.

"Be careful," he shouted over his shoulder. "It's slippery."

● ● ●

NERO SPED AWAY FROM DYLAN'S CELL with his cape flowing parallel to the ground. The guard hurried behind him, trying to keep up. He had to run in order to match Nero's pace.

Aluf, the head of the soldiers, led his men into the prisoners' wing. "Check all cells!" the leader screamed.

One of the guards stopped at a cell and gasped. Several men gathered around him and stared blankly at the pile of dead guards.

Aluf rushed over to them. "Oh my God! What's happened here?"

A few moments later, someone yelled, "They've escaped!"

Fear rose up like a mist at dawn among the guards as the two groups of Tipple prisoners in the north hallway waited patiently. The prisoners in the west and east corridors crept toward the main hallway.

"Get it together, men!" Aluf commanded. "They're still here. There's no way all of them could have escaped. My troupe, follow me back toward the gates. Teo's group, split into two and proceed down the north hallway. Check out the west and east corridors. We WILL find them."

Sweat beaded on the brows of the waiting prisoners. The silent war cry quickened in their chests.

Nero stepped into the north hall, where the prisoners stood. He froze at the sight. Then he stepped back, pressed himself against the wall, and peered around the corner. The men of Tipple were too focused on the sounds of the approaching guards to notice Nero. The king recoiled and slid down the wall.

"What's going on?" he cried through clenched teeth. "I've got a bunch of monkeys working for me."

He sat for a moment. The clash of metal on metal and the cries of fighting and dying men arose like thunder.

"I will not allow these peasants to stop me from taking Aarial."

Nero stepped into the hall of the fighting men. He towered over them, and for a moment, the fighting stopped; the men parted as they stared up in awe. Then the prisoners blocked his path, and he began hacking them down. Several of his own guards got in the way of his blade as he sliced his way through the group easily, without receiving a scratch. As he passed the last pair of dueling men, he turned and watched his men being overtaken by the skilled peasants.

From a distance, Nero spotted Nima's open door.

"Oh my God!"

He flew into the room, picked up the bed, and threw it against the wall. On his way out, he slammed the door shut. It closed with a thunderous *bang!* With his head in his hands, he roared and spun into the wall before collapsing into a sobbing heap.

"Those ungrateful termites!" Tears of despair dropped onto the stone floor. "No…no…no."

The icy floor against his cheek slowed his breathing. Slowly, his eyes cleared, and everything came into focus. A metal bar caught his eye. Instantly, he was on his feet and staring out the barless window at the brightening horizon. He picked up a bar and threw it onto the roof. "AHH!"

Dylan turned to the scream and the sound of metal bouncing off the roof above him.

"We're out of time." Dylan cried. "Go! Quicker. We're almost there."

Dylan waited for Taya and Nima to pass in front of him, and he pointed to where they needed to go. They proceeded across the roof.

"STOP!"

They all froze and looked back in the direction of the command. They could see Nero in the distance. He jumped from one rooftop to another, and then he was out of sight.

"You two go ahead. Jump onto this roof," Dylan said, pointing to the next rooftop, "then jump into the tree and climb down."

"No," Taya protested. "I'll slow him down so you can get away. You're more important than I am."

"You won't slow him down. He'll crush you like a bug. GO!"

Taya glanced up at him desperately.

"GO!" he shouted again.

Dylan ran back and hid under the overhang of the roof above them. He crouched and waited. "This is it. It's now or never."

As Taya and his mother disappeared onto the next roof, Dylan turned inward. Images passed before his eyes. He pictured himself in Stellar Hall, absorbing the things he needed to know. He saw Taya and himself training with Ravelle. The images twisted and swirled into a single water droplet—a suspended teardrop; the last memory of his father at the Gnarled Oak.

Thud! Dylan was shaken out of his reverie. At the edge of the roof, Nero smiled as he watched the two women run away from him, but his heart stopped and the blood left his face when he realized that Dylan was nowhere to be seen. As he spun around, he was knocked off his feet by Dylan's powerful sword. He slid down the roof and landed on a lower, flat roof.

He managed to struggle to his feet while fitfully sucking in needed air. Glancing down at his shoulder, he saw an opening in his mail. Warm blood trickled across his chest.

Dylan watched Taya and Nima slide off the roof and into the tree. Then he proceeded cautiously. He took small steps down the angled roof and stopped at the edge. Nero was on one knee and appeared to be favoring his wounded shoulder.

"You're more skilled than I thought, little brother." Nero tried to speak with his usual force, but Dylan could tell that he was in pain. "Your powers are well developed. I'm impressed by the way you got my guard to lock himself up. I've not had to use that part of Aarial because everyone is afraid of me and will do as I say."

"I am not afraid of you," Dylan cried out in a deeper voice than ever before.

"Oh, is that right?" Nero smiled. "Come on down, little brother; let's have some fun."

Dylan made a move to jump but stopped himself when he saw Nero tighten his grip on his sword and run toward the place where Dylan would have landed. In one smooth movement, Dylan pulled out his knife, and threw it into Nero's hand. The king dropped his sword and cried out. Dylan ran to a spot further away from Nero and jumped onto the lower roof as Nero pulled Dylan's blade out of his hand. Blood trailed down his wrist.

Then he lunged at Dylan with his sword a-blazing. The boy stood still and stared into his opponent's eyes. He blocked Nero's sword with his own, but the power of Nero's sword knocked Dylan's out of his hands. Nero lost his balance and continued on past Dylan, who spun around and picked up his sword.

This time, Dylan approached Nero, who was still trying to get his balance. The two swords clashed, and sparks flew as they stabbed at each other and blocked blows. Dylan had never faced such a tough opponent. Nero had power and arrogance behind his sword, while Dylan had speed and skill. Each of them was fighting for his life, and for Aarial.

Time passed quickly. They were both tiring, but Nero was losing blood, and with that, strength. He knew he had to pour it on or he would be defeated. He started forcing every ounce of Aarial into his blows and pushed Dylan toward the edge of the roof. Dylan fought hard but could not gain control. Then with one terrifying blow, Nero knocked Dylan's sword out of his hands and off the roof. The boy fell back, and his head hung over the edge.

Time slowed as Dylan watched Nero raise his sword high and thrust it down in the direction of his heart. He raised his arm and rolled away as the blade sliced open his forearm. The momentum carried Nero forward, and Dylan returned the blow with an elbow to Nero's ribs, knocking him off the roof.

Dylan clutched his bleeding forearm and lay back on the roof. He was still for a moment and breathed a sigh of disbelief. Slowly, he peered over the edge, hoping to see a lifeless corpse. Instead, he saw Nero dangling from a hideous gargoyle that stared down at him mockingly. He could only hang on with one hand, for his wounded hand had little strength left in it.

Taya and Nima watched silently.

Nero struggled to pull himself up but was unable. He swung his feet wildly, trying to walk up the wall, but the distance between the gargoyle and the side of the castle was too great. His good hand held on while the bloodied hand helped sporadically. He fought for a while and then gave up and hung motionless.

No words passed between them, but Dylan felt an uneasy connection as he stared into the eyes of his father's son. Everything before him slowed as Nero's hand weakened. The king blinked and smiled up his brother.

"Life," he hissed, "is a curse." Nero gasped one last time. "Death...is the cure." Then he threw both of his arms away from the castle.

Nero's final vision was his own reflection in the eyes of a terrified boy. A roar echoed throughout the kingdom as the blade of Dylan's sword tore through Nero's back. Nero stared up at the sky vacantly, and blood trickled out of his mouth.

Then a ball of light with the tail of a comet shot out of Nero's body and circled the ground. Taya and Nima froze at the sight. A deafening *crack* echoed throughout the valley as the light knocked Taya off her feet. Nima was upon her motionless daughter immediately.

Dylan recklessly searched for a way down. He climbed back onto the roof from which he had first struck Nero, and then leapt down to the roof beside the tree. After scrambling down the tree and sprinting around the castle, he came upon a motionless Taya. Nima hovered over her daughter with tears rolling down her cheeks. Dylan's head dropped to his chest. His heart pounded and his hands trembled.

"No...no...no," he whimpered.

Then, without warning, Taya opened her eyes. A crooked smile appeared on one side of her face. Dylan smiled back at her.

"There's something different about you," he said curiously.

Then it struck him. Nero's eyes flashed before him and faded into Taya's. The power of Aarial stared back at him.

38

Unlikely Friendship

"I HATE THIS!"

Ted glanced over at Jake, who was complaining at the teacher's desk.

"What's wrong, Jake?"

"I don't get it. Why do we have to do this anyway?"

"To exercise your brain," Mr. Peters said, pointing at his head.

"Yeah, well, I know kids in other schools, and none of them have to do this kind of work. It's too hard."

"Would you rather get something easy?"

"Yes," Jake blurted, surprised that he would be asked such an obvious question.

"Well, then you wouldn't have to think."

Jake rolled his eyes and stomped back to his desk. Mr. Peters followed him and leaned over his notebook.

"Can I help him?"

Mr. Peters and Jake glanced up at Ted, who was standing near Jake's desk, swaying anxiously.

"Sure, Ted." Mr. Peters was dumbfounded. "That...that would be great."

Ted wondered who was most surprised at his offer—Jake, Mr. Peters, or himself. The teacher walked away and Ted pulled up a chair. Without making eye contact, he studied the page and pointed out where Jake had gone wrong. He drew an arrow from one part of the problem to another. Then he recalculated some of the numbers.

"Oh, I get it!" Jake exclaimed. Suddenly, he remembered that he shouldn't display such enthusiasm. "Thanks," he said bluntly.

Ted walked back to his desk with an air of satisfaction.

"Dylan?"

He looked up at Mrs. Evans, who was standing over his temporary desk.

"Come into my office, please."

Dylan dropped his book and followed the principal.

"You've been working in the office very well over the past two days. I'm impressed by how calm you've been."

Dylan lifted one shoulder.

"Dylan?" Mrs. Evans rubbed her eyes and exhaled heavily. "I have to talk to you about something. I know about the knives." Dylan swallowed hard. His eyes shifted from her to his sweaty palms. "Your foster mother told me she found half a dozen knives hidden in various spots throughout your home."

"I don't need them anymore," Dylan said flatly.

"Well, that's good, but I'm a little concerned that you thought you needed them in the first place."

"Well, it doesn't matter because I don't need them anymore," he repeated.

"I'm also concerned that you went through my filing cabinet."

Dylan glanced at her briefly and returned to studying his hands. "Yeah, well I don't need them anymore, so we can drop it."

"That's not the point, Dylan. You invaded my privacy. You stole from me."

"No!" Dylan cried indignantly. "You stole from me."

"Okay, I can see that we aren't going to get anywhere with this," Mrs. Evans said angrily. "I've already explained why weapons are not allowed in school, so I'm not going to waste any more time talking to you about it. I'll allow you to return to class tomorrow if you promise me that you won't bring any more knives or weapons of any kind. Will you promise me that?

"Yes. I already told you that I don't need them anymore."

"Thank-you, Dylan. Now, continue with the work you've been doing, and at the end of the day, you can take your books back to class in preparation for tomorrow."

Dylan was unusually quiet over the next two days. Mr. Peters enjoyed the change, but he was also concerned. Dylan was deep in thought most of the time, and he was slow to respond when spoken to. He got into small arguments over minor incidents, but for the most part, he was detached and uninvolved.

At the end of the week Mr. Peters stood at the window of his classroom and gazed out at the fine drizzle covering the schoolyard. "I love Fridays," he said to himself.

The darkened skies had opened up that morning and left behind numerous puddles of various sizes and depths. Some of the students were marching through them while others huddled under the overhang. He noticed Ted, Sam, and a third, taller, boy leaning up against the wall, deep in conversation. A hood covered the bigger boy's face.

"Who's that?" Mr. Peters squinted.

Ted grabbed the taller boy by the shoulders and spun him around playfully. The three of them laughed.

"Hey, that's Jake! Ted and Jake are friends now?"

The bell startled Mr. Peters out of his thoughts. Moments later, everyone proceeded noisily into the classroom. Most of them slid into the room in their stocking feet, carrying their indoor shoes. They gathered in the meeting area and talked quietly while tying up their laces. Everyone appeared to be in the room, and Mr. Peters was about to get started when Dylan flew in. He stepped over his classmates, soaking them with his dripping, muddy boots.

The teacher was just about to say something when Alex yelled, "Hey! Take your boots off."

Dylan turned red. He spun around and flicked Lyle in the temple.

"Ow!" Lyle rubbed his head. "I didn't say anything."

"Go to your desk!" ordered Mr. Peters.

Dylan stomped out of the room, and Mr. Peters followed him.

Just as Dylan was about to throw the outside door open, Mr. Peters grabbed his arm. "What's wrong, Dylan?"

Dylan turned and faced Mr. Peters. "I don't need your crap anymore. Everyone is always picking on me."

"I'm worried about you, Dylan."

"Well you don't have to be any longer because I'm leaving this stinking place. I heard the principal talking. She said I'm going to a new school...one that doesn't suck!"

He threw open the door and it smashed against the outside wall. Mr. Peters was about to follow him, but the noise coming out of his classroom pulled him back.

A short time later, when all of the students were reading quietly, Mr. Peters glanced out the window and noticed a mysterious figure crouching in a corner of the compound. A giggle distracted him, and he turned to survey the room. He glared at Albert, who was swimming on the carpet.

"You're not a fish, Albert."

Albert turned red and flopped back into his seat. Mr. Peters turned back to the window. He rubbed the moisture off the glass and squinted through the mist. The figure was gone.

39

Terror Lifted

DYLAN AND NIMA HELPED TAYA TO her feet. She was shaken but uninjured.

"We have to get away from here!" he exclaimed quickly.

Dylan yanked his sword out of Nero's corpse and rinsed Olam in the moat. He sensed that no one was around but wondered why the castle entrance was unguarded. They stole across the drawbridge and sped away from the castle toward a dense forest in the distance.

At the sound of galloping hooves, Dylan stopped and drew his sword.

"You two keep moving. I'll meet you in the forest."

He turned and faced two large men on black horses racing across the open field. They dismounted and stepped cautiously toward the awaiting warrior. Dylan readied himself for battle even though he sensed that he was not in danger. When they were within striking distance, they bowed and rested their hands upon the ground.

"Mighty warrior," one of the men called out in reverence. "We are forever indebted! You have rescued us from evil rule."

Without easing up, Dylan spoke through clenched teeth. "What about the others?"

"We are your loyal servants—all of us. We will do as you command."

"How do you go from wanting to kill me to being my loyal servant?"

Neither one of them spoke.

"Stand up," Dylan commanded.

They stood with their heads bowed.

"The battle was brewing, Sir, within the castle walls—death and destruction." The guard looked down at his bloodied hands. "Then... something happened. We stopped fighting. It happened so suddenly. In the heat of the battle, we dropped our weapons—the cloak of tension and terror lifted. The uninjured started helping the wounded. A man

came running down the halls screaming over and over, 'The king is dead! King Nero is dead!' Everyone cried out with joy as his dark cloud dissipated." He paused for a moment and, for the first time, made eye contact with Dylan. "You have freed us." He bowed again. "We are your humble servants."

"Okay, that's enough. Get up." Dylan frowned. "Help me carry Taya into the castle."

Dylan caught up with his mother and sister and explained the situation. When they turned around to walk toward the castle, the two guards were kneeling on the ground again.

"We are at your command, your Royal Highnesses."

A tear rolled down the cheek of one of the guards.

"Why are your crying?" Taya asked curiously.

"I am crying for joy. I see great compassion in our new leaders. You will be fair and kind."

Taya smiled and limped toward the castle. The two guards made a seat with their hands and lifted her off the ground.

"Let me down," Taya said as they neared the castle.

"You need to rest. We'll let you down onto a comfortable bed."

"Let me down. Now!" she ordered.

Her command was firm, and the guards did not question her. They set her down, and she limped for a few steps and then stopped.

She faced Dylan and whispered, "I don't know what's come over me, but…suddenly I feel…I feel invincible and clearer in thought than I have ever been."

"It's Aarial," Dylan said, and he hugged her. The two of them felt the union of the great power in their embrace.

"Give me your sword."

Dylan handed over Olam, and she felt the power surge into her body. She swung it around her head and body like a bamboo baton. Everyone stared in awe. She weakened quickly, and just before the weight of the sword pulled her to the ground, she handed it to Dylan. Her legs wobbled, and the guards were upon her before she collapsed.

The massive castle doors opened as they reached the drawbridge. The five of them walked over the moat and wondered what awaited them. Two guards separated and allowed them to pass as they entered the compound. Great cries of joy and cheering surrounded them as they stepped toward the palace. People hung out of windows and over railings trying to get a glimpse of them.

A trog circled high above their heads. Dylan grasped the hilt of his sword instinctively. They walked up the steps, and the trog landed upon a palace balcony. The cheering stopped at the sight of the trog perched upon the railing, glaring down at their savior.

"I wonder how the trogs fit into all of this," Dylan whispered into Taya's ear.

She shrugged her shoulders. "I guess we'll find out soon enough."

They entered the palace and were taken aback by the grandeur.

"Whoa!" Dylan said, exhaling heavily. "Look at this place! This is what we've been working for all these years? Our sweat has been turned into king's gold."

Taya was taken to a comfortable room where a small fire burned in the hearth. The guards placed her upon the bed, and before the curtains had been drawn shut, she was asleep. Nima was then shown to her room, where she asked for a bath to be prepared. Dylan requested a tour of the palace, and the two guards who had brought them to the castle led him. Dylan sensed Nero's presence as they entered a cold, darkened room.

"I will *not* sleep in this room," Dylan hissed. "Open the curtains."

Dylan jumped at the sight of a trog staring in at him from the balcony. He drew his sword and walked through the doors. The trog hopped off the railing onto the ground. With his head lowered, he bowed toward Dylan.

The trog cleared his throat and spoke slowly. "Greetings, your Highness. Ettore, at your command, Sir. I am your loyal servant."

"Lay down your arms!" Dylan commanded.

Without hesitation, Ettore placed his sword and knife upon a table. Then he backed away. Dylan walked over to the worn, rusted weapons and examined them.

As he studied them, he spoke. "Where are the other trogs, Ettore?"

"They are returning to serve you."

"How do they know what's happened?"

"Everyone knows, Sir. Your authority is felt throughout the land. Our orders to pillage and destroy are no more. We will do as you command."

Ettore stopped speaking, but Dylan sensed that he had more to say.

"What is it?" Dylan questioned

"You have great power and wisdom. You will be a great leader, but I sense that you are not alone."

Dylan did not respond.

"The girl shares your power?"

"Yes, we rule together."

"I will inform the others that we serve two masters. What are your orders, your Royal Highness?"

"I don't have any yet, but be prepared." Dylan paused. "Go now."

Ettore turned and was about to leave when Dylan spoke. "Stop. Let your men know that they are starting with a clean slate. I've not forgotten all of the terrible things they've done, but I'm willing to give them a second chance. I know your orders came from Nero, so you may argue that you didn't have a choice."

Ettore stirred nervously.

"Well, I disagree with that argument. You did have a choice. The trogs could have chosen to disobey and do the right thing. Your troops did more than follow orders; they enjoyed the orders. I will never forget, but I may forgive, depending on what I see. If one trog crosses me, my memory of what you've done will serve me well, and I'll destroy your species."

"Trogs are loyal to their leader, Sir. We'll do as you command. We'll never cross you. Any trog who disobeys will expire by my hand."

Dylan stepped back and nodded toward Ettore's sword and knife. Ettore picked up his weapons and leapt off the balcony. Dylan returned to Nero's room.

"Lock the doors to this room and *never* open them," he said to the guards. Dylan exited and then turned. "Actually, I want these doors bolted shut and walled over. There should be no sign that this chamber ever existed. Now, show me to another room."

His new room was not as large as Nero's chamber, but it was warmer and more comfortable. From his balcony, he could see the ocean beyond the castle walls. He lay down upon the fine feather bed and, for the first time in ages, fell into a deep, peaceful sleep.

Collin Paulson

40

Another Chapter

THE SIGHT OF TED, SAM, JAKE, and Dylan digging in the playground pebbles immediately caught Mr. Peters's attention. Ted spotted his teacher walking toward them, so he jumped up.

"Mr. Peters! Mr. Peters!" Ted called out excitedly as he ran toward him. "We're-building-a-castle-and-we-need-materials-to-make-a- catapult."

"Whoa! Slow down, Ted." Mr. Peters laughed. "I didn't hear a word you said."

"Can we borrow some materials for a catapult?" Ted repeated between gasps.

The other three boys were now on their feet. Mr. Peters squinted at the approaching group.

"What's going on here?"

"We're building a castle and we want to destroy our enemies with a catapult. Dylan has a great plan for how to build one."

"No, I don't mean 'what are you doing,' I mean 'what's going on?'"

"What do you mean, Mr. P.?" Sam asked.

"Correct me if I'm wrong, but I don't remember all of you getting along so well."

Simultaneously, all three boys glanced at Dylan, who lingered at the back of the group.

"Oh yeah. That." Ted smiled. "We have an understanding now. Right, Jake?"

Jake nodded.

"I'm glad to hear it. You're really not so different once you get to know each other. I've always thought—"

"Yeah, whatever," Ted cut in. "Can we borrow popsicle sticks and elastic bands and stuff?"

"Well, I'm on supervision right now, so I can't get them for you."

"That's okay. We can get them."

Mr. Peters grinned at their beaming faces. "Okay. But be quick. You're not supposed to be in the school yet."

"We will."

Jake, Ted, and Sam ran off in the direction of the school.

"Show me what you've been working on, Dylan." As Dylan led his teacher to their project, Mr. Peters asked, "Why do I get the sense that you had a hand in this budding friendship between Jake and the other boys?"

Dylan shrugged his shoulders and smirked. "I don't know."

"You are such a mystery sometimes, Dylan. I wish I knew what was going on in that head of yours."

"No, you don't," Dylan responded abruptly.

WE'RE STARTING THE DAY WITH READING Buddies," Mr. Peters said to the class after he had taken attendance. "We're going to their classroom this time, so please treat their room with respect. Does anyone *not* know who his or her partner is?" Mr. Peters waited for a response. "Okay, good. When we get to their room, sit behind Miss Kelly's students and wait for your buddy to stand up."

They arrived at Miss Kelly's closed door a moment later. Mr. Peters peered into the room and spoke to the teacher.

"We have to wait a minute," he whispered to his students. "Have a seat on the floor."

After a few moments, Miss Kelly opened the door and tiptoed into the hallway. "My students are waiting for you." Her voice was barely audible. "Come in and find your buddy without making a noise."

The students responded to the challenge. They tiptoed into the room and quickly found their partners. Dylan slid over to his buddy, Jacob, like a baseball player sliding to home plate. The younger boy laughed out loud. They found a quiet corner of the room and opened *Where the Wild Things Are*.

"Look at that," Mr. Peters whispered to Miss Kelly. "Look how good he is with Jacob. He gets along so well with younger kids."

"I know," she agreed. "How many times have we done this? Five times?"

Mr. Peters nodded.

"Jacob's reading hasn't improved all that much, but he's much more interested in it. Dylan has taught him the joy of reading."

"That's nice to hear. It has been very good for Dylan, too. It gives him a real sense of accomplishment. He's so far behind in so many things, but reading is one thing he can do well."

The teachers looked around the room at the other students, and when Jacob laughed again, their focus returned to the two boys. "Jacob seems to really like him, which is unusual. Dylan's usually being frowned upon rather than looked up to."

"He would make a good big brother," Miss Kelly added.

After lunch, Mr. Peters took attendance and waited for everyone to quieten down.

"Okay, how are things coming with the preparation for the student-led conferences?" Mr. Peters waited for a response.

Janna raised her hand. "Mine is coming along okay, but I'm having trouble deciding what to show my parents. I've got so many good things, and I can't narrow down what I want to show them."

Mr. Peters smiled. "Well, you're lucky, Janna. How about everyone else?"

No one responded.

"Before we continue, who can remind us of what a student-led conference is?"

Janna raised her hand. "A student-led conference is when we get to show our parents all the stuff we've been doing."

"That's right, Janna. Instead of doing the regular parent-teacher interview, we're doing this so that you can be more involved."

The students continued to organize their work to be displayed. Some of the students had to finish projects in order to have them ready, while others had to try to make their projects a little more presentable. Mr. Peters walked over to Dylan, who was sitting with his head down.

"What are you doing, Dylan?"

"This is stupid," he complained.

"Why do you say that?"

"Because it is."

"Well, that's not a good enough reason. I'd like you to get some of your things together to show Grandma."

"She's not coming."

"Why not?"

"She doesn't care about what I do in school. She said she doesn't have time."

"So you don't have anyone to show your work to?"

"No. Mrs. Evans said that I could show it to her, but that's stupid; she's the principal. Besides, I don't have anything to show. I haven't done any work."

"Sure you have, Dylan. Look at your artwork. I love what you did with the pastels. For today, why don't you continue working on that drawing you were doing last art class?"

A short time later, Mr. Peters heard a tearing noise from Dylan's corner of the room. He observed Dylan walk across the room and stuff his shredded picture into the garbage can. Mr. Peters followed him out of the room and found him sitting under the coats with his arms wrapped around his knees. He looked up at his teacher and dried his eyes with the sleeve of his shirt.

"What's wrong, Dylan?"

Dylan did not respond. Mr. Peters moved in closer to him.

"What is it, Dylan?"

He lowered his head. "I'm moving."

"Where are you going?"

"A group home. And this time it's for sure."

Mr. Peters patted him on the shoulder. "I'm sorry to hear that, Dylan. Maybe it will be a good group home."

"There's no such thing. I've seen 'em all."

"Just remember, Dylan, this is just another chapter in a great literary work. All of these events make you who you are."

Dylan rolled his eyes.

Bedlam erupted from the room.

"I'll be right back, Dylan." Mr. Peters stood. "I have to check on your classmates. Wait here. I won't be a moment."

A few minutes later, Mr. Peters walked back into the hallway. He peeked under the coats, then left and right, then up and down the hallway. Dylan was gone.

41
Restoring Order

BANG, BANG, BANG!

Dylan jumped up and flew over to his sword. A man stepped into the room.

"Your breakfast is ready, Sir."

"Oh...thank-you," Dylan mumbled, wiping the sleep from his eyes. "How long have I been out?"

"You've been in and out of sleep for almost two days, Sir."

"Really?"

The servant nodded and opened the drapery. A warm glow flooded the room. Dylan's initial shock of being awakened wore off with the rising sun. He stood on the balcony and bathed in the light.

The rags he had been wearing were neatly folded on a bureau. He lifted them to his nose and absorbed the fresh, clean smell. In the closet were a variety of brightly colored outfits that appeared to be his size. He started trying things on and quickly realized that they had been made for him. The robe he chose to wear was deep purple with a gold belt.

Upon exiting the room, a guard announced, "You have a special guest, Sir. He's waiting for you in the breakfast room."

"Who is it?"

"I don't know. He wouldn't reveal his name. He just said that you would be outraged if you found out he had been here and had not been allowed in. We've searched him for weapons, and he has none. Two guards are watching him. If you want him turned away, it will be done."

They proceeded down the hall at a great pace. At each window they passed, Dylan made an effort to look out at the new day. He felt refreshed with each breath of air. At the end of an ornate hallway, two doors opened automatically. For a moment, Dylan was blinded by the sun that radiated into the room through a wall of windows. A large, crackling fire heated the room.

Through the fingers of the hand shielding his eyes, he spotted the special guest. "Aah," Dylan sighed. "I was hoping it would be you."

Ravelle stood slowly and walked toward his student. They embraced in silence.

How fragile you've become, Dylan thought. "Leave us alone," he commanded.

The two guards walked to the door. "We'll be standing guard if you need us, Sir."

Dylan took a step back to get a better look at his mentor. "Yes. I do look old," Ravelle said, answering Dylan's unspoken observation. "One tends to age in their third century. I'm not immortal, and I'm sorry to say that I'm in my final years."

Dylan smiled sadly. "You got here very quickly. How did you find out what happened?"

"It's in the air; far and wide it's known. Most do not know exactly what's happened, but they understand that their lives are better." Ravelle paused and looked deep into his eyes. "You…have excelled."

"Thank-you," Dylan said softly. "And thank-you for coming. You are a father to me. All of this would not have happened without you. You trained me for this day."

"Yes, I played a part, but the major player was Aarial. The very power that caused so much destruction has brought peace to our world. That's why I have come. I'm here to remind you of the devastation that Aarial can cause and to remind you of our agreement. Aarial must be returned to Queen Gaia. Only she can control it."

"But the people want me to rule," Dylan interrupted.

"I can see that Aarial has become very important to you, but you have to transfer the power—both you and Taya. You have some time left, and you can use it to undo some of the wrongs that have taken place, but it is not yours to keep."

"Who is this Queen Gaia? Why has no one heard of her? Even if there is such a woman, how can she be a queen without being known?"

"You will understand when you meet her."

"I don't feel comfortable passing it on." Then without warning, he raised his voice and said, "Besides, it belongs to me!"

"No. It does not belong to you. Think of the world and future generations. Another Nero will emerge. You are noble, and you will use your power appropriately. But...you may have an heir less righteous than yourself, and he or she may use it as Nero did. Does one person—good or bad—deserve to have total control?"

"Yes! I deserve total control!" Dylan snapped.

"Why? What have you done to deserve it? I can see that Aarial is already taking over. Think about the good of the people. The system will work itself out, without you or your heirs being in control."

Dylan paced the room and wrestled with his thoughts. A few minutes later, he sighed and turned to Ravelle. "You're right, Ravelle. Aarial is taking over. I feel like I'm losing control. All of my energy has been so focused on getting Nero, but now that he's gone, Aarial is pushing me in the direction of power."

Ravelle exhaled heavily. "I must rest now."

Dylan called the guards in, and they escorted Ravelle out. He passed Taya in the hall, and they embraced and exchanged a few words.

"It's nice to see that you've joined the living again," Taya said when she entered the room Dylan was in.

Dylan was deep in thought, and Taya could see that he needed to be left alone. She walked over to the window and looked out at the beautiful landscape.

"How have you been feeling since you received Aarial?" Dylan finally asked.

Taya paused for a moment and thought about the question. "It's difficult to explain. In some ways I feel better than I ever have, and in other ways, I'm afraid. Perhaps I need time to adjust to it, but I constantly feel like I'm on the verge of losing control." She paused for another moment. "I feel invincible...and...unbalanced."

"Time doesn't alleviate those feelings. I've felt that way since I received Aarial. It takes over. Ravelle was here to tell me that we have to get rid of it."

"How?"

"Well, I don't really know. I don't think that he even knows. He's told me from the beginning that I am to return the power to Queen Gaia."

"Who's she?"

"That's what I keep asking. No one has given me a clear answer to that question. I don't even know if she's human."

"Well, I don't mind getting rid of it because I don't like the idea of having anything that once belonged to Nero, but I'm concerned about this queen having it, especially if no one knows her. It all sounds very mysterious."

"We have to trust Ravelle, Taya. He is wise, and he wouldn't steer us in the wrong direction."

Nima walked into the room and hugged them. They all sat down at the breakfast table, and after a few moments of small talk, Dylan changed the subject.

"Mother, we have to give up Aarial."

"Yes, I know."

"How do you know?" Taya asked.

"I was married to a man who possessed Aarial for a very long time. He rarely spoke about it, but when he did, he talked about how afraid he was. He mentioned Queen Gaia and wished that she would come for it. Aarial destroyed him. It took control of his thoughts and actions."

"It's comforting to know that both you and father agree with what has to be done." Dylan dragged his fingers through his hair. "Before we transfer it, we need to use it to right the wrongs. We need to come up with a plan to help everyone. I've been told that people are returning to their villages, but most of the towns are in ruins. We need to help rebuild those towns. The trogs have become our allies, so I want to use them. They are strong and can get to the towns quickly."

"But can you trust them?" Nima interrupted.

"Yes. I believe we can. Look out the north window."

"Oh my God! That's a sign of trust?" Nima cried and looked away.

Taya cringed but couldn't turn away from the two massive heads dripping blood over the courtyard. "I don't get it. Why do they kill one another?"

"Those are two dissenters. They are examples to the others."

"Well, I don't like it." Nima said.

"I don't like it either," Dylan agreed, "but that's how they create order. Trogs are very loyal and will obey whoever is in charge. They're like worker bees. We'll get them to help rebuild. I also want caravans of people sent out to help in the restoration."

Over breakfast, they organized what had to be done. Taya agreed to explain the plan to the guards and servants within the castle, while Dylan was to give orders to the trogs. "I'll address them tomorrow at noon in the theater. I'll get the word out now," he said.

THE NEXT DAY, DYLAN PEERED OUT from behind a curtain to observe the trogs gathering in the theatre. They poured into the room in a disorderly fashion, pushing and shoving their way down the aisles. The seats were not large enough for them, so they stood in front of them. A horrible stench filled the room. Dylan stepped onto the stage.

Silence.

"Trogs have caused great destruction. You may blame Nero, but I believe that you added to the horror." Dylan paused for several seconds.

"Things are different now. I'm in charge, and I want to rebuild what you have destroyed. The damage you have inflicted is going to be repaired by you—all of you. You're going to break into groups and help the people of this land. You're going to travel the countryside and offer assistance in any way you can. If you're asked to build a house, you will build a house. If you're asked to transport supplies, that's what you will do. No task is too menial or too great."

The trogs listened intently, without a hint of dissension.

"I will be receiving reports of your activities. You will be rewarded for your work, and severely punished for transgressions. If you do not follow orders, I will come down on you with such a vengeance that you will wish you had never existed. We'll start tomorrow. Ettore and Jadar and I will discuss the plans in greater detail."

Dylan left the stage and observed the trogs exit the room in a much more orderly fashion than they had arrived.

Under Dylan's supervision, Ettore and Jadar grouped the trogs and decided who would lead each group. The two trogs did not smile or partake in any small talk. They wanted to get down to business quickly and get things started.

"The trogs are taking to the sky," Dylan told Taya when they sat down to discuss their meetings. "They will do whatever we ask."

"The guards, and anyone who is able, will be going out in caravans across the countryside," Taya said. "There is a sense of renewal. Everyone is excited and wanting to rebuild."

"Excellent," Dylan said, smiling.

"What about all of the prisoners?" Taya asked.

"They've been set free. Some of them have little to return to, so they're going to remain in the castle and help from here. I spoke to Tikva yesterday, and he agreed to assist in getting people back to their villages."

◆ ◆ ◆

OVER THE NEXT FEW MONTHS, ETTORE and Jadar carried Taya and Dylan to various towns, and the siblings were pleased by the progress. Dylan, Taya, and Nima met regularly to discuss what was happening. Ravelle also attended a few meetings and provided much-needed wisdom. Taya and Dylan did not give a lot of thought to transferring Aarial, for they were so focused on the task at hand. Ravelle said nothing about their power, but his mere presence reminded them of their final task.

Everything was returning to normal, and they were starting to feel that their efforts were coming to an end. At night, Dylan often thought about Queen Gaia and tried to picture her. He wondered why she hadn't made herself available.

◆ ◆ ◆

DYLAN AND NERO STOOD BEFORE THE *cheering crowd—brothers, arm in arm. Dylan had never felt such joy in all his life. They smiled and waved at the thousands assembled before them.*

Nero turned his head and whispered into Dylan's ear, "It is time," and plunged a dagger into his chest.

Dylan gasped and shot up from his mattress. Standing over him was a ghostly figure, shimmering in the dim light.

"Ravelle, is that you?"

Ravelle's eyes widened, and he tilted his head back. "It is time," he said icily.

The door slammed shut, and a cold breeze brushed against Dylan's face.

Collin Paulson

42

Deepening Depression

"MR. PETERS, YOU HAVE A CALL on line two, Mr. Peters, line two."

The teacher jumped up from his desk and walked into the library.

"Mr. Peters here."

"Hello, Mr. Peters. This is Ms. Truss," she said quickly. "I just wanted to make you aware that Dylan is moving to a group home in Edmonton."

"Oh, really? I knew he was going to a group home, but I didn't know he was leaving the city. How is he reacting to the news?"

"He's pretty angry. Dylan doesn't deal well with change."

"Not only is he moving," Mr. Peters interjected, "but he's losing a mother. You are the only mother he's known for quite some time."

"I'm getting older, Mr. Peters, and I can't handle him anymore," Ms. Truss said apologetically. "He's too much for me."

Mr. Peters breathed heavily into the phone. "Do you know anything about the group home, Ms. Truss?"

"Not much. I know it's fairly small—five or six kids. He'll be there until they can find a foster home for him."

"What are the chances of that happening?" Mr. Peters asked.

"Not great. There are so few available, and the ones that have openings don't want to take on such difficult children."

"Thank-you for letting me know. Oh, by the way, when is he moving?"

"On the weekend, but his last day of school is tomorrow."

"What? That's so quick!"

"Yeah, I know, but when a placement comes up, you have to grab it immediately or it will be filled by someone else."

Mr. Peters hung up the phone and stared off into space. *I can't believe he's leaving.*

The sight of Dylan standing beside his desk was not a surprise.

"Good morning, Dylan."

Dylan stared into the forest on the poster in a silent trance.

Mr. Peters placed his hand on Dylan's shoulder. "How are you this morning?"

Dylan shook his head and looked at Mr. Peters, who was now sitting on the corner of his desk between Dylan and the poster.

"I'm moving," he said quietly.

"I know, Dylan. How are you feeling?"

Dylan's head fell back and his shoulders dropped. "I hate group homes," he muttered at the ceiling. "The kids are mean, and there are too many rules. They treat you like a baby, and you never get any privacy."

"Maybe it'll be a nice group home."

"No, that's not possible."

Mr. Peters sighed. "I'm going to miss you, Dylan. You've become an important person in my life."

Dylan collapsed into his teacher like a wounded soldier. His arms hung lifeless by his sides, and his body trembled gently. Mr. Peters wrapped his arms around the boy's shrunken shoulders and held him firmly. Dylan sobbed quietly while Mr. Peters patted his back. As quickly as he had collapsed, he stopped and straightened up. Mr. Peters grasped his shoulders and stooped to his eye level.

"You're going to be okay, Dylan. I know it may not seem like that right now, but you've got what it takes—self-reliance."

Dylan squinted at him questioningly.

"Self-reliance is the ability to depend on yourself, to make decisions for yourself, to rely on your own powers and abilities…to…to be your own person. To be self-reliant is to be free. You are a survivor, Dylan."

Dylan wiped his face and turned away. Mr. Peters watched him walk into the hallway. The outside door opened and closed quietly. Through the classroom window, he observed Dylan shuffle across the playground with his head down. A few objects appeared to catch his eye, but instead of picking them up, he kicked at them with his toe.

When the bell rang, everyone ran toward the school; everyone except for Dylan. He didn't respond to the bell at all. Mrs. Giles walked up and informed him that it was time for class. He looked toward the playground and saw that everyone had gone. Then he turned and walked toward the school.

Dylan's fiery attitude had been replaced by darkening shadows under his eyes. As the day progressed, his square frame became increasingly rounded. He responded lethargically and appeared to be constantly on the verge of tears. Everyone steered clear of the cloud that hung over his desk. He spent most of the day reading or staring off into space.

For the last fifteen minutes of the day, Mr. Peters took his students outside. It was an unusually warm day, and he wanted to see the sun. Ms. Steinwood was already there with her students. They greeted each other on the chain bridge and watched their students interact. Jake, Sam, and Ted had joined three boys from the other class and were testing out their catapult on the opposing group's castle. In the heat of the battle, Ted stood and walked over to Dylan, who was digging a hole.

"Do you want to join us, Dylan?"

Dylan glanced up at him and shook his head. Ted smiled up at Mr. Peters and walked back to his group.

"What's happening with Dylan?" Ms. Steinwood asked. "I heard he's leaving us."

"Yes, he is. They found a group home for him in Edmonton."

"That may be the best place for him," Ms. Steinwood commented.

"I think it's the *only* place for him, but it isn't the *best* place. I worked in group homes for years. They're not good for anyone. I saw so many good kids with minor problems leave the group home as delinquents. Most of them feel unloved and alone, so they connect with other residents. They teach each other things that they would not otherwise be exposed to."

"How long will he be there?"

"He's supposed to be there until they find him a home." Mr. Peters paused and watched Dylan for a moment before he continued. "They won't find a home for him. There are no happy endings for kids like

him. Who's going to want to adopt him? He'll be shipped from group home to institution to group home."

"So what's the solution?"

"There isn't one. The ideal would be adoption into a loving family, but that won't happen. The funny thing is that he thinks he's alone, but there are so many others just like him."

The bell rang, and Mr. Peters watched his students run to their bags and jackets, quickly pick them up, and run off. The creative playground was soon deserted—except for one student. Dylan continued to dig into the pebbles, completely unaware of his surroundings.

"Time to go home, Dylan."

Mr. Peters waited for a response.

"Dylan!" Mr. Peters yelled.

The boy squinted up at him.

"Are you okay?"

Dylan nodded. "I'm going to dig for a while."

"Okay, well don't stay too long. Grandma will be waiting for you."

Dylan went back to his digging. The envelope slipped out of his pocket and onto the pebbles. He spied Mr. Peters walking toward the school, so he picked up the envelope and made his way to the Hidden Forest.

The black fly rolled around freely, unhindered by the faded impressions in his palms. The deep ridges had healed, leaving only a slight discoloration in the shape of Tracker's medallion. He placed the fly back into the envelope and slid it into his pocket. The warmth of his glowing hands sent shivers up his spine.

43

And You Are My Masterpiece

IME SLOWED AS DYLAN WATCHED NERO raise his sword high and thrust it down in the direction of his heart. He raised his arm and rolled away as the blade sliced open his forearm. The momentum carried Nero forward, and Dylan returned the blow with an elbow to Nero's ribs, knocking him off the roof.

Dylan clutched his bleeding forearm and lay back on the roof. He was still for a moment and breathed a sigh of disbelief. Slowly, he peered over the edge, hoping to see a lifeless corpse. Instead, he saw Nero dangling from a hideous gargoyle that stared down at him mockingly. He could only hang on with one hand, for his wounded hand had little strength left in it.

Taya and Nima watched silently.

Nero struggled to pull himself up but was unable. He swung his feet wildly, trying to walk up the wall, but the distance between the gargoyle and the side of the castle was too great. His good hand held on while the bloodied hand helped sporadically. He fought for a while and then gave up and hung motionless.

No words passed between them, but Dylan felt an uneasy connection as he stared into the eyes of his father's son. Everything before him slowed as Nero's hand weakened. The king blinked and smiled up his brother.

"Life," he hissed, "is a curse." Nero gasped one last time. "Death...is the cure." Then he threw both of his arms away from the castle.

"Ahhhhh!"

Two guards flew into the room. "What is it, Sir?"

"Whoa!" Dylan panted, rubbing his forehead. "It was just...just a bad dream."

The two guards searched his chamber.

"It's okay," he reassured. "It was just a nightmare."

Dylan splashed water on his face and pondered the dream as he stared at his rippling reflection in the water basin. A few moments later, he was dressed and heading toward Taya's room. They met in the hall.

"We have to go!" he stated quickly.

She smiled sadly. "I know."

Dylan and Taya set off for the dining hall. On the way, Dylan ordered a guard to invite Ravelle. They entered the hall and sat down at the table set for three.

"You scared me last night, Ravelle," Dylan said as his mentor walked in and sat down.

Ravelle looked up at him curiously.

"You don't remember coming to my room? In the middle of the night?"

Ravelle continued to stare at him. "No. I came to your room? Why would I do that?"

"You said, 'it is time.'"

"Well, isn't that curious? I don't remember."

"Where do we find Queen Gaia, and how do we transfer the power to her?"

"I don't know."

"Oh my God!" Dylan slapped his face with his hands and exploded. "You continually remind me that I am to give up Aarial, and when I finally agree, you tell me that you don't know how I should do so!"

"I'm sorry, Dylan. Some of my knowledge comes from conversations from the past; some of it comes from dreams. I am old, and I have trouble remembering details these days. Ore, one of the first possessors of Aarial, first told me about Queen Gaia—that was over two hundreds years ago. I must have had a dream last night that told me the time had come."

"You're going on a dream?"

"Don't discount my dreams!" Ravelle countered angrily. "My dreams are very real. Have I ever wronged you?"

"No. I'm sorry, Ravelle. I'm just a little anxious." Dylan paused for a moment. "What now? Where should we go from here?"

"My advice is that you return to where it all started."

"To Stellar Hall?"

"No, think back even further. What happened before you came to Stellar Hall?"

"The Gnarled Oak!"

Ravelle nodded, and Dylan continued. "Yes, that makes sense. Perhaps we can learn something there."

"The Gnarled Oak is where it all began. Return, and you will learn of Queen Gaia."

Dylan ordered the guards to tell Ettore and Jadar to meet him and Taya outside. Then he and his sister swallowed a few bites and tossed some bread and cheese into their packs.

"We have to keep this quiet, Taya. I don't want anyone to know. We'll tell those who ask that we're returning to Duffle for an inspection."

Ettore and Jadar met them in the courtyard.

"We're going to Duffle, Ettore. We would like to get there as quickly as possible."

"Yes, Sir."

Once harnesses had been attached to the trogs, they took flight. Ettore carried Dylan, and Jadar, Taya. They flew low over the villages so their passengers could view the reconstruction. Everything appeared to be returning to normal. The towns looked better than they ever had. New, better-constructed buildings had replaced dilapidated structures.

The trogs needed frequent rests and much water, but they did not complain. They stopped in several communities so Dylan and Taya could speak with the residents. The siblings were honored in every village. People thanked them for their freedom and independence— things they had never experienced.

At last, Ettore announced, "Duffle is near. We will be there before the sun sets."

Dylan had been paying attention to the sun. He had watched it rise and continue its arc throughout the day. *The world is so beautiful from up above,* he thought. Meandering rivers divided open valleys and lush forests. Lakes spotted the landscape and sparkled in the sunlight.

Now the sun was on the horizon, creating another kind of beauty. Everything was bathed in an orange and pink glow. Just as the sun dipped beyond the horizon, Dylan saw the lights of Duffle flicker in the distance.

The trogs landed on a deserted path in the middle of town. Dylan thanked Ettore and Jadar. The trogs did not want to leave them there, but Dylan insisted and told them that they would get word to them when they were needed again.

"Where should we spend the night?" Dylan asked his sister.

"I think we should go straight to the Gnarled Oak," Taya responded. "We don't want to have to explain ourselves to anyone. If we leave tonight, no one in Duffle will even know we were here."

The two of them made their way out of town via the back streets. Everyone appeared to be in their homes, preparing meals. They peered into several windows and took in the warmth of family dinners. Just outside of town, they stopped and ate the last of their rations by moonlight.

"I miss Duffle, Dylan. I want to come back here. I don't want to rule. I want to remain in Duffle and live a normal life."

"There's nothing stopping you, Taya. As soon as we transfer Aarial, we will lose the hold we have over people. They may continue to admire us for the work we've done, but their respect will be genuine. Right now, part of their admiration is involuntary. They may not even know it, but they revere Aarial, not us."

"Will you come home with me, Dylan?"

"I don't know, Taya." Dylan lowered his head.

"Well, where else will you go?"

"I can't tell you that because I don't know. If I can, I'll return to Duffle. That's where I belong."

Dylan stood and grabbed Taya by the hand. The two of them walked in silence.

Taya stopped at Gilmore Pond. "Do you remember the fun we had here? That seems like such a long time ago."

Dylan did not speak. He took one last look at the pond, gazed up at the heavens, and continued on. The full moon guided their path to the Gnarled Oak. Dylan placed both of his hands on the tree.

"What now?" Taya asked.

"We climb."

Taya's gaze travelled up the trunk and locked on the platform that surrounded the tree. She squinted and scratched her head.

"What is that? The branches have changed into a platform."

"You'll see."

Within minutes, he was up the tree and resting inside the tree-bark nest. Taya climbed slowly, cautiously. She peered over the rim, and Dylan pulled her in. They sat on the outer edge and bathed in the faint glow that emanated from the center of the tree.

The intensity of light grew gradually. Then a sudden blast of radiance shot up like a geyser and returned to a dull glow. Dylan slid across the slippery surface to the light, and Taya followed. He sat on one side of the beam and invited Taya to sit on the other side so that they were face-to-face. Dylan placed his fingertips on Taya's temples and instructed her to mirror his action.

Another blast of light shot up between them. The powerful beam separated their minds from their electrified, convulsing bodies and transformed them into all-seeing, all-knowing entities. They sensed intense cold and scorching heat, dry air and air so thick with moisture they could taste it. For the first time, Taya viewed what Dylan had been seeing—deserts, rainforests, mountains, oceans passed before them. Every landscape was dependent upon the other, every living creature connected to its environment. The whole world breathed as one.

At great speed, they soared straight up into the heavens and hovered for a moment—mindful of their surroundings, unaware of their bodies. Then down, down, down, back to earth and into familiar tunnels, through Stellar Hall and into the river that flowed underground. They seeped deeper and deeper into the earth and then…nothing, beyond silence, beyond darkness—an absence of matter.

A celestial voice rose up, unlike any sound they had ever heard. With the haunting melody, a glowing ember floated up and down gently. As the melody waned, the light dimmed. Then the voice spoke and the ember returned.

"I am Gaia; I am the earth." The female voice seeped into their pores and touched them deep within. "I am an artist, and you are my masterpiece. There was a time when I was known to the human species, but you have lost touch. I bestowed Aarial upon your ancestors with the hope of bringing humans back to me. How could I have foreseen the corrupt nature of the human spirit? Aarial was not meant for personal gain."

The voice paused and the light dimmed.

"Dylan and Taya, the two of you have proven to be worthy receptacles, but it is time to return the power to me so that I can use it to heal. For centuries, it has been within my grasp, but now I need it in its entirety. I considered retrieving it before your father transferred it to you, but that would have left Nero alone and created a greater imbalance. Without you, Nero would have been unstoppable."

The light dimmed as the voice stopped, and they were in complete darkness again. Moments passed. The light brightened, and Gaia started again.

"I am in need of repair, for mankind has caused great damage to my being. I am an artist, and my creation is being destroyed. Of all my children, only the human child has had the ability to alter my creation. Now that Aarial is returned to me, I will attempt to repair the damage. I...am the earth."

Again, the light dimmed as the voice faded.

"Taya." The ember brightened. "You are to educate. Create a collective consciousness of respect for all that I provide. Parts of me are ailing, and as a result, every living creature is ailing—we breathe as one; we are a single organism. The human species will not survive without me. The lives of all creatures depend on what you do. Spread the word and bring the human animal back to me."

The haunting tune returned with the glowing ember.

"Dylan, you have demonstrated great strength and courage. Where your ancestors failed, you succeeded. Your mission is complete."

And with those words, everything went dark.

A flare surged into Dylan's convulsing body. "No! No! No! It can't be over. I need a mission. I need the journey."

The light brightened. "Your mission is over. Your journey has just begun."

Dylan's head dropped to his chest. "I need a mission. I need the journey," he chanted quietly.

The geyser of light between the brother and sister faded slowly, and as it did, the Gnarled Oak began to crumble. Branches fell off and large strips of bark peeled away from the trunk. Then the light died, and a loud creaking resonated from the base of the tree. Within seconds, it crashed to the ground and shook the very earth that had given it life.

Collin Paulson

44

Life is a Journey

HUMP, THUMP, THUD!

Mr. Peters automatically grabbed the top platform of the stepladder and spun his head in the direction of the noise—the opposite side of the classroom. The artwork slipped out of his hand, and thumbtacks rained down as the ladder wobbled. The teacher shifted his weight to stop the ladder from tipping, but he overcompensated, causing it to rock on the opposing two legs. He lost his balance and crashed into the door in front of him. Quickly, he threw his right arm over the top of it and then hung from the swinging door by his armpit while the ladder crash to the floor.

"Ow, ow, ow," he repeated quickly, wondering about the scrape on the inside of his arm and rib cage. The pain diminished at the sight of one hundred and fifty thumbtacks standing at attention, waiting for him to let go.

"Why didn't I wear my shoes?" he whined, glancing down at his stocking feet.

The thought of calling out for help crossed his mind but quickly subsided with the realization that the pain of a tack in the foot was better than a lifetime of humiliation.

He stretched his left leg, curled his foot around the doorknob, and inched his armpit forward until he was standing upright. A second glance at the floor revealed that the tacks had dispersed themselves in a scatter plot formation. He instinctively looked for the line of best fit and then gave his head a shake at the ridiculous response to his predicament.

I am such a twit.

Slowly, he pushed the door away from the wall—just enough so that he could wrap his other leg around the door and rest it on the handle on the other side. Then ever so gently, he moved around the door so that all of his weight was on the inside doorknob and placed his right foot on top of the left.

"There's a clear spot," he said to himself. "I just have to leap over that cluster of tacks."

Mr. Peters had not thoroughly thought through the physics of such a maneuver, however; pushing off a moving object does not propel a person very far. As he leapt off the doorknob, the door slammed shut, and he dropped straight down into the middle of the scattered tacks. His heels landed on a clear spot, but he was off balance and fell backward in slow motion.

"Owwwww!" he screamed, holding himself up on his feet and hands. He lifted his left hand, leaving his body in a backward three-point stance. With his two upper incisor teeth, he pulled the embedded tack out of his palm and sucked the blood oozing out of the tiny hole.

"Mr. Peters, Mr. Peters!" echoed in the hall. "I heard you scre—"

The door flew open and slammed him in the head, knocking him off balance and adding a fourth support—his bum—to the three-point stance.

"Ahhh!"

Mr. Grant peered in. "I heard you scream. What's going—"

"Get...out!" Mr. Peters growled through clenched teeth.

Now crouching on two feet, he pulled his pants away from his bum and propelled the tacks into the hall. He studied the ground and stepped carefully through the thorny minefield.

"Can I help you?" Mr. Grant asked, covering his smile.

"Get out," Mr. Peters repeated.

"Okay. Sorry." Mr. Grant closed the door and whispered to an approaching Ms. Steinwood, "I think he wants to be alone right now."

Mr. Peters hobbled over to his desk, licked the blood from the palm of his hand, then shoved a tissue down the back of his pants to see the effect of the bum tacks. Five large drops of blood on the tissue revealed the extent of his wounds.

"Great!" he complained. "Now I'm going to need a tetanus shot—just my luck." He closed his eyes and shuddered at the thought of where his last needle had been administered. "How many holes can I put in my body in one day?"

Out of the corner of his eye, he saw something move.

"What are you doing down there, Dylan? How did you get in?" He looked to the closed door.

Dylan raised himself up from his hands and knees and stood. He wavered for a moment and dabbed his forehead with his fingertip.

"What happened to you? You're bleeding."

"That makes two of us." Dylan smiled. "I'm okay."

"What happened to your face and arms? Who scratched you?"

"I fell off the monkey bars last night."

Mr. Peters shot him a sideways, questioning glance. "Yeah, right." He paused and looked at the door again. "I don't get it. How did you get in here without being seen?"

"I snuck in."

"But I was hanging paintings over the door frame. How could you get through the door and under the ladder without me noticing?"

Dylan shrugged his shoulders. "I can be pretty sneaky, and you need glasses."

Something struck Mr. Peters. Dylan had changed—he looked broad, strong, confident. "Except for your bleeding forehead and scratches on your arms, you look pretty good. Your spark has returned. You were such a sad case yesterday."

Dylan looked down at the scrapes across his forearms.

"I'm glad you're here, Dylan. I was worried when you didn't show up this morning. I thought you were going to skip town without saying good-bye."

Dylan looked up at him curiously. "What time is it?"

"It's 12:30—lunchtime."

"Really?" Dylan rubbed the back of his neck. "Can I go outside now?"

"Of course. I don't know why you're in here in the first place."

Dylan turned to the poster and then walked toward the door.

"Dylan?" Mr. Peters glanced down at the floor. "What's this?" He picked up a worn, folded piece of paper.

Dylan flew over to him instantly. "That's mine," he blurted. "It's nothing."

He snatched it from his teacher's hands and proceeded toward the door again. His pace slowed as he raised it to his ear and shook it. Then he opened the envelope over a desk, turned it upside down, and flicked it with his finger. Dylan's expression turned to one of terror.

"What's wrong, Dylan?"

He tore the envelope apart in a panic.

"What was in there?"

Dylan was pale and stricken. "Oh...nothing." He glanced back at the picture one more time and then tiptoed over the tacks and into the hall.

"Get away from me!" Dylan burst through the door.

"What is it now?" Mr. Peters shouted.

Mrs. Giles entered the room. "Dylan had a problem with a group of boys on the compound."

"*They* had the problem, not me!" Dylan snapped.

"He said the f-word and then threw their ball on the roof.

"Why would you do that, Dylan?"

"Because they wouldn't let me play."

"It's true." Ted stepped into the room. "The other kids were being really mean."

"Well, that's no excuse, Dylan. Sometimes, it's better to walk away from a problem than cause a bigger one."

"You always tell me to face my problems," Dylan spat.

"Yes, but that isn't facing your problems—that's being...look...I'm not going to deal with this on your last day."

Ted spun around and faced Dylan. "This is your last day?"

"Yeah," Dylan sighed.

Ted sat down beside him. "Are you going back to Duffle?" He mumbled under his breath.

"No." Dylan stomped away and slid into his desk, where he rested his head upon his folded arms.

Ted glanced up at a downcast Mr. Peters, who was walking over to them. "I think he needs to be alone right now, Ted."

"Okay." Ted joined his gathering classmates at the carpet.

"I'm not going to deal with this, Mrs. Giles. This is his last day, so I'm going to ignore it. I know I shouldn't, but I want him to leave the school on a positive note. Can you please take attendance for me and start News Hawks?"

Mrs. Giles nodded.

Mr. Peters walked over to Dylan's desk and knelt down beside him.

"Let's make your last day a good one. Do you think you can make it through the afternoon without a blowout?"

Dylan did not speak for a moment. Then he turned his head and looked at his teacher. "Yes."

"Good." Mr. Peters smiled at him. "I'm really going to miss that scowl of yours, Dylan."

Dylan cupped his hand over his mouth and whispered, "Don't tell anyone I'm leaving."

"You don't want to say good-bye to everyone?"

"No, and I want to leave before the final bell."

"Okay. If that's what you want. Now, go join the group."

Mr. Peters sat behind his class and watched the students present their news articles. Sam was talking about anthropomorphism and showing an ad with cats dressed up as cowboys.

"What have I done?" Mr. Peters cut in with a pained expression. "I've created a classroom of anthropomorphism researchers who are going to spend the rest of their days searching out and reporting anthropomorphic sightings."

"You taught us that word, Mr. Peters," Janna said, laughing.

"Yeah, I know, but I didn't think you'd all become obsessed with it." He paused for a moment. "I'm just kidding. I'm actually quite impressed with how well all of you understand it. Who says kids can't learn big words?"

"Me!" Jake blurted, louder than intended.

"Okay class, this afternoon, we're going to finish up our reports. I realize that you are all at different stages, but you really need to be wrapping them up. I'm only going to give you a couple more hours of class time to work on them. If you have a lot left, you should start doing some of it at home. Over the next hour, I'll come around to each group and find out where you're at. The last hour of the day is going to be spent finishing off our art projects—or restarting them. Some of you have decided that you'd like to do another one, and that's fine. Are there any questions?"

Dylan busied himself cleaning out his desk. He ignored the curious glances from his classmates and told Albert to get lost when he asked him what he was doing. He spent the rest of his time doodling and reading.

Near the end of the day, he walked up to Mr. Peters. "Can I go now?"

Mr. Peters looked at his watch. "Not yet, Dylan. I'll tell you when."

"I hate waiting around."

"Yeah, I know. It won't be long, though."

Ted stepped between them. "Can I talk to Dylan?"

"Of course," Mr. Peters responded.

Ted walked to the risers and sat down. Dylan followed.

"Here." Ted extended his hand, palm up.

"That's not yours to give," Dylan said, frowning.

"Yes, it is."

"That belongs to Sam."

"I traded Sam a month's worth of snacks for it."

"Why?"

"I don't know. It will give you good luck and protect you from enemies."

"Only this," Dylan said, pointing to his head, "protects you from villains."

"Yeah, I guess you're right. Take it anyway, so you won't forget us."

Dylan closed his fingers over it, and Ted wrapped both of his hands around Dylan's fist. The intensity of Ted's eyes electrified the air and drew Dylan closer.

"Good luck, Dylan…and thank-you."

"Mm. Yeah," Dylan mumbled, shifting his eyes away from Ted's fiery gaze.

As Ted walked away, Dylan studied the grimace on the plastic samurai warrior. "Thank-you," he whispered inaudibly.

Mr. Peters exhaled. "Okay, Dylan," Mr. Peters said, quietly. "Time to go."

The two of them walked into the hall. Dylan was putting on his jacket when Mr. Peters cried out, "Oh, I almost forgot! Wait here." He ran back into the classroom and came out carrying a large plastic bag.

"I'm really going to miss you, Dylan. The chapter you've added to my book of life has challenged me, angered me, and...enlightened me. You've opened my eyes and changed my life. I'll never forget you, Dylan. Thank-you for making me who I am. We may never meet again, but we are connected—forever. I wish you all the best. I truly hope you find happiness in—"

"What's in the bag?" Dylan interrupted impatiently.

Mr. Peters smirked and handed it to him. Dylan peered in and pulled out two badminton racquets. His eyes lit up. One of the racquets had a cover over it, while the other was bare. Dylan dropped the covered racquet and swung the other one over his head.

"Are these both for me?"

Dylan's smile pierced his teacher's heart. Mr. Peters nodded.

"Why two?"

"Well, you can't play alone." Mr. Peters said. Then he swallowed hard. "I thought that you might like to have one for your partner. The one you're swinging is a cheap one. This one," Mr. Peters said, pointing to the racquet on the ground, "the one that you casually threw aside, is the one you should play with. It's a much better racquet."

Mr. Peters reached down and picked it up.

"I present you," Mr. Peters said, bowing, "with the royal golden racquet."

Dylan stroked the vinyl case with his fingertips. He lifted it to his nose and inhaled deeply. Slowly, he unzipped the cover; the golden handle sparkled. He read the shaft.

"Ex...cal...Excalibur?" Dylan's eyebrows narrowed.

"Excalibur was a magical sword in ancient times. Only one man, King Arthur, could remove it from solid rock. Many tried, but only he succeeded."

Dylan glanced up at Mr. Peters and smiled. Then he slid the racquet out of its case and jumped into a fencing position—left arm curved over his head, right arm extended. He stabbed at the air.

"En garde, you Fais du Braire!" he yelled at his imaginary opponent. Dylan lunged forward and stabbed his racquet at the invisible target.

"Fais du Braire?" Mr. Peters chuckled with a puzzled expression. "What does that mean?"

Dylan just smiled and shrugged his shoulders. Then he sheathed the racquet and walked to the end of the hall. He paused and looked back at Mr. Peters, who was watching him.

"Life is a journey, Mr. Peters." Then he bowed to his teacher and said, "And every journey begins with a single step." As the final word left his lips, he leapt at the door and smashed it against the outside wall. Dylan disappeared through the opening.

Mr. Peters stood motionless for a moment. "And sometimes," he said, turning back to the classroom, "sometimes, it begins with a giant leap." Just as he stepped over the threshold and into his room, the outside door clicked shut.

About the Author

COLLIN PAULSON IS A TEACHER WHO wrote this book in response to all of his students who said, "Why don't you write something?" *Aarial* is his first novel and hopefully it is the first of many. Collin was born and raised in Calgary, Alberta, and still lives here today with his beautiful wife and two amazing children.

THANK YOU FOR TAKING THE TIME to read *Aarial*. I hope you enjoyed it, and I would love to hear from you. Please email me <**contact@aarial.ca**>, visit my website <**www.aarial.ca**> or look for my Aarial page on Facebook.